Sunset

Christmas Treasury

By the Editors of Sunset Books
and Sunset Magazine

Lane Publishing Co. ■ **Menlo Park, California**

Season's Greetings!

Christmas comes but once a year—and what better way to get into the Christmas spirit than to create a little of the season's magic for those you love. To help you, we've gathered together a dazzling array of exciting gift ideas, recipes, and projects in this big, comprehensive volume.

Open to the first section and you'll find a wealth of ideas for home-cooked and handcrafted gifts—from the kitchen, the sewing room, and the woodshop.

To help you add holiday sparkle to your house, the second section of our book offers a number of delightful ideas and projects for Christmas decorating. And when you're ready to wrap your gifts, choose from our selection of one-of-a-kind gift wraps and greeting cards.

The last section of our book offers a stunning array of party ideas and menus for all your holiday entertaining. We show you how to stage an open house for 25 to 125 guests or host an intimate dinner party for a few close friends. And, for your Christmas Day feast, we offer tempting menus for five festive dinners, from a traditional roast goose to a succulent tangerine-glazed beef roast.

No matter what your interest and skills, there's something here for you to make, bake, or create. Now's the time to start—Christmas will be here before you know it!

For their valuable assistance in helping to prepare this book, we'd like to thank Scott Atkinson, Phyllis Elving, Myriam Kirkman, Kathy Oetinger, and Elizabeth Overbeck. Special thanks go to Kathy Barone for laying out the individual book pages, and to Joan Griffiths for her expert assistance in compiling the food sections of this book.

Book Editors
Cynthia Overbeck Bix
Helen Sweetland

Coordinating Editor
Suzanne Normand Mathison

Contributing Editor
Rebecca LaBrum

Design
Sandra Popovich

Photography

Glenn Christiansen: 12, 35, 36, 99, 139, 170. **Kris Knutson:** 215, 219, 236, 239, 247. **Michael Lamotte:** 220. **Gregg Mancuso:** 146. **Stephen Marley:** 1, 4, 44, 57, 60, 61, 62, 65, 66, 69, 71, 72, 73, 74, 84, 85, 96, 97, 100, 101, 102, 103, 104, 106, 109, 111, 113, 117, 119, 123, 127, 130, 137, 148, 149, 150, 151, 153, 155, 156, 157, 161, 165, 167, 169, 174, 177, 178, 179, 188, 189, 191, 195, 196, 197, 199, 200, 201, 202, 203, 204, 205, 206, 208, 209, 210, 212, 235, 243. **Don Normark:** 133. **Norman A. Plate:** 134, 173 (top left), 223, 248. **Bill Ross:** 135. **Teri Sandison:** 183. **David Stubbs:** 9, 142, 144, 145 (bottom left; bottom right). **Darrow M. Watt:** 6, 17, 20, 25, 28, 41, 52, 77, 78, 80, 81, 82, 86, 87, 89, 90, 91, 92, 93, 94, 95, 132, 140, 143, 145 (top), 147, 158, 159, 168, 171, 172, 173 (top right; bottom), 181, 185, 192, 193, 194. **Doug Wilson:** 141. **Tom Wyatt:** 31, 49, 160, 162, 163, 227, 231.

Photo Styling

Karen Hazarian: 215, 236, 239, 247. **JoAnn Masaoka:** 1, 4, 44, 57, 62, 65, 66, 69, 71, 72 (bottom), 73, 75, 77, 78, 84, 85, 89, 90, 91, 92, 93, 94, 95, 97, 100, 101, 102, 103, 104, 106, 109, 111, 113, 117, 119, 123, 127, 130, 137, 148, 149, 150, 151, 153, 155, 156, 157, 161, 165, 167, 168, 169, 174, 177, 179, 188, 189, 191, 195, 196, 197, 199, 200, 201, 202, 203, 204, 206, 208, 209, 210, 212, 214, 227, 231, 235, 242. **James McNair:** 219, 220. **Susan Massey-Weil:** 60, 61, 72 (top), 96, 178, 205. **Lynne B. Morrall:** 17, 20, 25, 28, 52.

Illustrations

Edith Allgood: 76, 79. **Bill Oetinger:** 32, 38, 61, 67, 71, 73, 74, 83, 97, 98, 100, 101, 102, 103, 105 (bottom), 107, 108, 110, 111, 112, 114, 115, 116, 117, 118, 121, 122, 125, 128, 129, 135, 136, 137, 141, 143, 149, 150, 151, 155, 156, 160 (bottom), 164, 165, 176, 180, 182, 188, 190, 191, 195, 196, 197, 198, 201, 202, 203 (center, right), 208 (center, right), 209. **Rik Olson:** 3, 5, 131, 211. **Jacqueline Osborn:** 64, 89, 91, 93, 95. **Sally Shimizu:** 62, 63, 65, 175.

Front cover: All dressed up to play Santa, our cuddly bear (page 92) presides over work-of-art Cookie Canvases (page 14) and Gingerbread Boys (page 15), delectable gifts of food, and an assortment of packages wrapped in cheery hand-printed paper (page 196). Cover design: Carol Hatchard Goforth. Photograph by Darrow M. Watt.

Back cover: Our warm and satisfying Christmas Morning Breakfast (page 234) is just one of the many tempting menus we offer. Photograph by Stephen Marley.

Sunset Books
   Editor: David E. Clark
   Managing Editor: Elizabeth L. Hogan

First printing September 1987

Contents

Loving Gifts—
Homecooked
& Handcrafted

■

Christmas is the season for giving—and the spirit of generosity is nowhere better expressed than in the giving of handmade gifts to family and friends. A made-by-hand gift shows you've considered the special interests of your recipient, then used your skills to create something unique, just for that person. If you like to sew, you can stitch up a much-needed lap quilt for your great-aunt, or a tailor-made backpack for the young nature-lover in the family. If woodworking is your forte, you can build a countrified whirligig for your favorite gardener. And for creative cooks, there are almost unlimited possibilities for gift making—from luscious truffles and toffees (for a friend with a sweet tooth) to homemade mustards and chutneys for your fellow gourmets.

From your kitchen cupboard, from your sewing basket, from your basement workbench, all kinds of wonderful things can emerge. Put your special skills and talents—and your imagination—to work to make one of the many projects we show you in this section. You'll find that when the gift's handmade, it really is *a gift straight from the heart.*

Homemade
Sweets & Savories

■

Whether it's a trio of sweet Golden Teddy Bear Breads, a basket of cookies, or a jar of homemade chutney, a gift from your kitchen is an irresistible way to express the spirit of the season. In this chapter, you'll find a whole cupboardful of delectable ideas and recipes for holiday giving—and for enjoying at home.

Hand-molded & Pressed Cookies

Using your hands and a few simple tools, you can create an array of fancy Christmas cookies fit for a pastry shop window. For Spritz—a holiday classic—you'll need a cookie press; just by changing the plates, you can make wreaths, trees, starbursts, and any number of other shapes. But our other cookies—crumbly-rich Almond Crescents, nut-crusted Thumbprint Cookies, and more— are all easily shaped by hand.

Almond Crescents
(Pictured on page 231)

A snowy mantle of powdered sugar cloaks these buttery, brandy-spiked nut cookies. Called *kourabiedes,* they're a Greek specialty—perfect for a yuletide cookie tray, or for teatime in any season.

1/2	cup ground almonds
1	cup (1/2 lb.) unsalted butter or margarine, at room temperature
1	large egg yolk
2	tablespoons powdered sugar
1	tablespoon brandy or 1/2 teaspoon vanilla
2	cups all-purpose flour
1/2	teaspoon baking powder Whole cloves (optional)
1 1/2	to 2 cups powdered sugar

Spread almonds in a shallow baking pan and toast in a 350° oven until lightly browned (6 to 8 minutes), shaking pan occasionally. Let cool completely.

In large bowl of an electric mixer, beat butter until creamy. Add egg yolk and the 2 tablespoons sugar, mixing well. Stir in brandy and almonds. In another bowl, stir together flour and baking powder. Gradually add to butter mixture, blending thoroughly.

Pinch off dough in 1-inch balls and roll each into a 2- to 2 1/2-inch rope. Place ropes about 2 inches apart on ungreased baking sheets; shape into crescents. Insert a whole clove in each crescent, if desired. Bake in a 325° oven until very lightly browned (about 30 minutes). Place baking sheets on racks and let cookies cool for 5 minutes.

Sift about half the 1 1/2 to 2 cups sugar over a sheet of wax paper. Transfer cookies to paper, placing them in a single layer. Sift remaining sugar over cookies to cover. Let stand until cool. Store airtight; remove clove (if used) from each cookie before eating. Makes about 2 1/2 dozen.

Anise Pretzels
(Pictured on page 17)

The attractive shape of these anise-flavored cookies makes them a good choice for gifts, parties, or hanging on the tree. The anise flavor may remind you of *springerle,* an old-fashioned German cookie—and if you wish, you can shape the dough as you would for springerle, using the traditional carved rolling pin to produce little square cookies with embossed patterns.

1	cup (1/2 lb.) butter or margarine, at room temperature
1/2	cup sugar
2	large eggs
1 1/2	teaspoons anise extract
3 1/2	cups all-purpose flour
1	large egg beaten with 1 tablespoon water (omit if shaping dough with a springerle rolling pin)
1	to 2 tablespoons anise seeds

In large bowl of an electric mixer, beat butter and sugar until creamy; beat in the 2 eggs, 1 at a time, beating until well combined after each addition. Beat in anise extract. Gradually add flour, blending thoroughly.

Divide dough in half. For pretzels, roll each half into a log 2 inches in diameter. For picture cookies, shape each half into a rectangular slab. Wrap tightly in plastic wrap and refrigerate until easy to handle (at least 1 hour).

For pretzels: Cut logs of dough into 3/8-inch-thick slices. Roll each slice into a rope about 14 inches long, then twist into a pretzel shape. Place on greased baking sheets, spacing at least 1 inch apart. Brush with egg-water mixture, then sprinkle lightly with anise seeds. Bake in a 325° oven until light golden and firm to the touch (about 20 minutes). Transfer to racks and let cool. Store airtight. Makes about 2 dozen.

For picture cookies: On a lightly floured board, roll out dough, half at a time, to form a 1/4-inch-thick rectangle slightly wider than your springerle rolling pin. Pressing down firmly, roll springerle rolling pin once over dough so that designs are sharply imprinted. With a sharp knife, cut pictures into squares, following lines made by springerle rolling pin.

Sprinkle each of 2 greased baking sheets with about 1 tablespoon anise seeds. Set cookies about 1 inch apart on seeds. Bake in a 325° oven until bottoms are golden and tops are firm to the touch but still white (15 to 18 minutes). Transfer to racks and let cool. Store airtight. Makes about 3 1/2 dozen.

Speculaas

In Dutch homes, cookies are baked in profusion for *Sinterklaas avond* (the eve of St. Nicholas Day). Perhaps the best known of these holiday treats are crisp and spicy *speculaas*, traditionally shaped by pressing the dough into elaborately carved wooden molds. If you have a speculaas mold (they're sometimes sold in cookware shops), you'll be able to make cookies with old-fashioned embossed designs; if you don't, you can just roll out the dough and cut it with your favorite cookie cutters.

2   cups all-purpose flour
2   teaspoons ground cinnamon
½   teaspoon **each** baking powder and ground nutmeg
1   teaspoon ground cloves
⅛   teaspoon salt
¼   cup ground blanched almonds
1   cup firmly packed brown sugar
¾   cup (⅜ lb.) firm butter or margarine, cut into pieces
2   tablespoons milk

In a large bowl, stir together flour, cinnamon, baking powder, nutmeg, cloves, and salt. Blend in almonds and sugar until well combined. With a pastry blender or 2 knives, cut in butter until mixture resembles cornmeal; stir in milk. Work dough with your hands until you can form it into a smooth ball.

For molded cookies: Press dough firmly and evenly into a floured wooden speculaas mold; invert onto an ungreased baking sheet and release cookie by tapping back of mold (ease cookies out with the point of a knife, if necessary). Space cookies about 1 inch apart.

For rolled cookies: On a lightly floured board, roll out dough to a thickness of about ¼ inch. Cut out with 2- to 3-inch cookie cutters. Transfer to ungreased baking sheets, spacing cookies about 1 inch apart.

Bake molded or rolled cookies in a 300° oven until lightly browned (20 to 25 minutes). Let cool briefly on baking sheets; transfer to racks and let cool completely. Store airtight. Makes about 4 dozen.

Crisp Oatmeal Fruit Strips
(Pictured on facing page)

Here's a big batch of cookies you can make in a hurry. You shape the dough into long logs, then cut each log into strips after baking. Use your choice of raisins, prunes, or dates in the dough—or try some of each.

1   cup (½ lb.) butter or margarine, at room temperature
1½   cups sugar
1   large egg
2   cups all-purpose flour
2   teaspoons baking soda
2   cups raisins, finely diced pitted prunes, or finely snipped pitted dates
1¼   cups rolled oats

In large bowl of an electric mixer, beat butter and sugar until fluffy. Beat in egg. In another bowl, stir together flour and baking soda; stir into creamed mixture along with raisins and oats.

Divide dough into 15 equal portions. Place 3 or 4 portions on each ungreased 12- by 15-inch baking sheet; pinch and press each dough portion to make an 8-inch-long rope. Position ropes at least 2 inches apart on baking sheets; flatten each rope to make a 2-inch-wide strip.

Bake in a 350° oven until golden brown (about 10 minutes). Let cool on baking sheets for about 2 minutes, then cut each strip diagonally into 1-inch-wide bars. Let cookies cool on baking sheets. Store airtight. Makes about 12 dozen.

Twice-baked Walnut Cookies
(Pictured on facing page)

Toasted to a golden crunch, these anise-accented nut cookies are delightful with coffee or tea. They mail well, too.

4   eggs
1½   cups sugar
¾   cup (⅜ lb.) butter or margarine, melted
2   teaspoons vanilla
1   teaspoon **each** anise extract and black walnut flavoring
½   teaspoon almond extract
1   cup chopped walnuts
5   cups all-purpose flour
4½   teaspoons baking powder

In a large bowl, beat together eggs and sugar with a heavy spoon until well blended. Stir in butter, vanilla, anise extract, black walnut flavoring, almond extract, and walnuts.

In another bowl, stir together flour and baking powder. Gradually stir into creamed mixture, blending well.

On a floured board, divide dough into 8 equal portions. Roll each into a 14-inch rope. Place ropes about 2 inches apart on greased 12- by 15-inch baking sheets.

Bake in a 325° oven until bottoms of ropes are pale gold (about 20 minutes). Let cool for about 2 minutes on baking sheets, then cut each rope diagonally into ½- to ¾-inch-thick slices.

Tip slices onto cut sides; lay close together on baking sheets. Bake in a 375° oven until lightly toasted (about 15 more minutes). Let cool on sheets. Store airtight. Makes about 12 dozen.

Bake up big batches *of delectable Twice-baked Walnut Cookies and Crisp Oatmeal Fruit Strips (facing page) and Almond Ravioli Cookies (page 19) in no time, using quick "assembly-line" techniques.*

Brandy Balls

The flavor of brandy enlivens these rich holiday nuggets. They're much like Almond Crescents (page 7), but filled with pecans instead of almonds —and rolled into balls, not curved into crescents.

> 1¼ cups (⅝ lb.) butter or margarine, at room temperature
>
> ½ cup granulated sugar
>
> 1 large egg yolk
>
> 2 teaspoons brandy flavoring
>
> 3 cups all-purpose flour
>
> ¼ teaspoon salt
>
> 1 cup finely chopped pecans or walnuts
>
> Powdered sugar

In large bowl of an electric mixer, beat butter and granulated sugar until creamy; beat in egg yolk and brandy flavoring. In another bowl, stir together flour and salt; gradually add to butter mixture, blending thoroughly. Stir in pecans until well combined.

Roll dough into 1-inch balls and place about 1 inch apart on lightly greased baking sheets. Bake in a 350° oven until firm to the touch and very light golden (about 25 minutes). Transfer to racks and let cool slightly; while still warm, roll in powdered sugar to coat. Let cool completely. Store airtight. Makes about 4 dozen.

Spritz

(Pictured on page 231)

Buttery, almond-flavored Swedish spritz are always a favorite at holiday time. You can make them in a variety of fancy shapes (depending on which design plate you insert in your cookie press) and dress them up with candied fruit, colored sugar, silver dragées, or other decorations.

> 1   cup (½ lb.) butter, at
>   room temperature
> ¾ cup sugar
> 2   large egg yolks
> 1   teaspoon vanilla
> ½ teaspoon almond extract
> 2½ cups all-purpose flour
> ½ teaspoon baking powder
> ⅛ teaspoon salt
>   Decorations
>   (suggestions follow)

In large bowl of an electric mixer, beat butter until creamy. Gradually add sugar, beating until fluffy. Add egg yolks, 1 at a time, and beat until smooth. Beat in vanilla and almond extract. In another bowl, stir together flour, baking powder, and salt; gradually add to butter mixture, blending thoroughly.

Place dough in a cookie press fitted with a design plate, packing it in firmly and evenly. Force out onto ungreased baking sheets, spacing cookies about 1 inch apart. If kitchen is very warm and dough is soft and

sticky, refrigerate until firm enough to press easily. Decorate as desired.

Bake in a 350° oven until edges are lightly browned (12 to 15 minutes). Transfer to racks and let cool. Store airtight. Makes about 4 dozen.

Decorations. Before baking, top cookies with halved **candied cherries**; or sprinkle with finely chopped **nuts**, **colored decorating sugar**, **nonpareils**, **silver dragées**, or **chocolate sprinkles**. Or brush baked cookies with this chocolate glaze: in top of a double boiler over simmering water, melt together 4 ounces **semisweet chocolate** and ½ teaspoon **solid vegetable shortening**. Apply with a pastry brush. Refrigerate glazed cookies for 10 minutes to harden glaze.

Thumbprint Cookies

A sweet "jewel" of jelly sparkles in the center of each of these nutty drop cookies. It rests in a small indentation made by your thumb—or the tip of a spoon, if you prefer.

> 1   cup (½ lb.) butter or
>   margarine, at room
>   temperature
> ½ cup firmly packed
>   brown sugar
> 2   large eggs, separated
> ½ teaspoon vanilla
> 2½ cups all-purpose flour
> ¼ teaspoon salt
> 1½ cups finely chopped
>   walnuts
> 3   to 4 tablespoons red
>   currant jelly or
>   raspberry jam

In large bowl of an electric mixer, beat butter and sugar until creamy. Beat in egg yolks and vanilla. In another bowl, stir together flour and salt. Gradually add to butter mixture, blending thoroughly.

In a small bowl, lightly beat egg whites. With your hands, roll dough into balls about 1 inch in diameter. Dip each ball in egg whites, then roll in walnuts to coat. Place 1 inch apart on greased baking sheets.

With your thumb or the tip of a spoon, make an indentation in center of each ball. Neatly fill each indentation with about ¼ teaspoon jelly.

Bake in a 375° oven until lightly browned (12 to 15 minutes). Let cool on baking sheets for about a minute, then transfer to racks and let cool completely. Store airtight. Makes about 3½ dozen.

Candy Cane Crisps

The month of December is punctuated with occasions calling for cookies, and these crisp morsels suit the season perfectly.

> 1   cup (½ lb.) butter or
>   margarine, at room
>   temperature
>   About 1¼ cups
>   powdered sugar
> 1½ teaspoons vanilla
> 1⅓ cups all-purpose flour
> 1   cup rolled oats
> ½ teaspoon salt
>   About ¾ cup coarsely
>   crushed candy canes or
>   hard peppermint candy

In large bowl of an electric mixer, beat butter and 1 cup of the sugar until creamy; beat in vanilla. In another bowl, stir together flour, oats, and salt; gradually add to butter mixture, blending thoroughly. Add ¼ cup of the crushed candy canes and mix until well combined.

Roll dough into ¾-inch balls, then roll in remaining sugar (about ¼ cup) to coat. Place balls about 2 inches apart on greased and flour-dusted baking sheets. Flatten cookies with a fork, making a crisscross pattern with fork tines. Sprinkle each with about ½ teaspoon crushed candy canes.

Bake in a 325° oven until edges are lightly browned (18 to 20 minutes). Let cool on baking sheets for 2 to 3 minutes, then transfer to racks and let cool completely. Store airtight. Makes about 4 dozen.

Packaging & Sending Cookies

■

Sending homemade cookies to friends and loved ones in faraway places is a Christmas tradition in many families. Here's how to insure a safe arrival for your gifts.

Which cookies to send

Make sure you select cookies that are good travelers. They must be sturdy enough to make the journey, and must keep well enough to stay fresh until they arrive at their destination. Don't choose anything fragile (Almond Crescents, for example). Also avoid sticky cookies and those with moist icings or frostings. Crisp cookies are fine if they're not too delicate or crumbly, but the most reliable travelers are firm but not brittle cookies.

The cookies listed below, taken from our selection, are especially good candidates for mailing.

Addendum Cookies (page 23)
English Toffee Squares (page 26)
Twice-baked Walnut Cookies (page 8)
Fruit Bars (page 18)
Poppy Seed Nut Slices (page 27)
Fruitcake Cookie Cups (page 22)
Holiday Date-Nut Drops (page 23)
Nürnberger Lebkuchen (page 19)
Brown Sugar Shortbreads (page 15)
Tutti Frutti Oat Bars (page 24)

Wrapping & mailing

Cookies can be wrapped for travel in several ways. You can wrap them in foil—either individually, in pairs (flat sides together), or in small stacks. Or layer the cookies in containers, such as pretty tins, rigid plastic containers, or attractively wrapped foil loaf or pie pans. Separate layers with wax paper, and pack the cookies securely so they won't jostle about and damage each other in transit. If the container you've chosen isn't airtight, seal it in a plastic bag. Be sure to pack soft and crisp ones separately to preserve their textures.

To pack the cookies for mailing, you'll need a stout box lined with foil or wax paper, and plenty of filler for insulation. For filler, use tightly crumpled newspaper or other paper, or styrofoam packing material. Pad the bottom of the box with several inches of filler; then add foil-wrapped cookies or a cookie-filled tin or container. Make sure to insulate well with filler between packages or around the sides of the container. Add several inches of filler on top of the cookies before closing the box.

The post office requires that all packages be sealed securely with reinforced packing tape; don't use masking tape or transparent tape or tie your package with string. If you like, write "Fragile" and "Perishable" on the box; it may not make any difference in how your cookies are handled, but it can't hurt. Send your package first-class, so your cookies will arrive quickly.

Finnish Ribbon Cakes
(Pictured on page 231)

For holiday entertaining, offer a platter of assorted Scandinavian cookies, such as Spritz (page 10), Finnish Rye Cookies (page 13), Swedish Pinwheel Cookies (page 14), and these fancy morsels.

1 cup (½ lb.) butter or margarine, at room temperature
½ cup granulated sugar
1 large egg yolk
1 teaspoon vanilla
½ teaspoon grated lemon peel
2½ cups all-purpose flour
¼ teaspoon salt

About 6 tablespoons raspberry or apricot jam
½ cup powdered sugar mixed with 1 tablespoon water

In large bowl of an electric mixer, beat butter and granulated sugar until creamy; beat in egg yolk, vanilla, and lemon peel. In another bowl, stir together flour and salt. Gradually add to butter mixture, blending thoroughly.

Shape dough into ropes about ¾ inch in diameter and as long as your baking sheets; place them about 2 inches apart on ungreased baking sheets. With the side of your little finger, press a long groove down center of each rope (don't press all the way down to baking sheets).

Bake cookies in a 375° oven for 10 minutes.

Remove cookies from oven and spoon jam into grooves. Return to oven until cookies are firm to touch and light golden brown (5 to 10 minutes). While cookies are hot, drizzle them with powdered sugar mixture (or spread mixture along sides of cookies). Then cut at a 45° angle into 1-inch lengths. Let cool briefly on baking sheets; transfer to racks and let cool completely. Store airtight. Makes about 4 dozen.

Almond Sculpture Cookies

The cookie collection shown on this page requires a special and versatile dough: one that's malleable in the sculptor's hands, stays tender through shaping and reshaping, holds form and detail in the oven—and finally, when baked, produces a cookie that tastes good.

Substituting almond paste for part of the butter in a shortbread-type dough produces just the right qualities. The almond paste not only adds flavor but also makes the dough pliable, so you can push, poke, and pinch it as you would modeling clay. In addition, it makes the dough firm enough to hold embossed and impressed details.

These cookies are especially fun for children to make. Mistakes in shaping sometimes contribute to a cookie's charm, but if you shape one you don't like, start again; handling won't toughen the dough. Let the illustrated shapes get you started, then go on to create your own figures.

To make shapes like those shown here, you use techniques basic to ceramics—forming slabs, rolling ropes of varying thicknesses, and making impressions with a fork's tines or other objects. To get fine strands, force bits of dough through a well-washed garlic press. For contrasting color, you can use both the golden and cocoa doughs in your creations if you wish.

Let your imagination go in creating whimsical cookies from an almond-flavored dough that handles like modeling clay; for special effects, combine golden and cocoa doughs. Design: Dora de Larios.

1   cup (½ lb.) butter or
    margarine, at room
    temperature
1   can (8 oz.) almond paste
¾   cup sugar
1   large egg
3   cups all-purpose flour
    Cocoa-Almond
    Sculpture Dough
    (recipe follows), optional

In large bowl of an electric mixer, beat together butter, almond paste, and sugar until creamy. Beat in egg. Gradually mix in flour until blended. If necessary, cover dough and refrigerate until easy to handle or for up to 3 days.

Form cookies a few at a time, following the general directions above. Shape dough directly on baking sheets, allowing 1 to 2 inches between cookies. For best results, each cookie's maximum thickness should not exceed ¾ inch. Bake in a 300° oven until lightly browned on bottoms (about 20 minutes for ¼-inch-thick cookies, up to 40 minutes for ¾-inch-thick cookies). Let cool briefly on baking sheets, then transfer to racks and let cool completely. Store airtight. Makes about 3⅔ cups dough, enough to make 8 round cookies, each 4 inches in diameter and ½ inch thick.

Cocoa-Almond Sculpture Dough. Follow directions for **Golden Almond Sculpture Cookies**, but decrease flour to 2½ cups and add ½ cup **unsweetened cocoa** with the sugar. Makes about 3¾ cups.

Cutout Cookies

Nothing says "Christmas" like cutout cookies in all the shapes of the season. And few gifts bring more delight than a selection of home-baked, lovingly decorated stars and bells, angels and reindeer—and perhaps a few jaunty gingerbread men with raisin buttons.

We've chosen a variety of rolled and cutout cookies for you here. Some are light and mild-flavored, others dark and spicy; some are crisp, some soft. There are even cookie ornaments with glowing "stained glass" centers—and for the ambitious, a Christmas cabin built of gingerbread logs.

Sugar Cookies

With their pale golden color and delicate vanilla flavor, sugar cookies offer a perfect background for decorating. You can simply sprinkle them with colored sugar, if you like, but it's fun to get a little fancier with icing and other decorations: try a blue-frosted star studded with sparkling silver dragées, or a tree hung with red cinnamon candy "Christmas balls."

Our Easy-to-Cut Cookies let the youngsters join in the fun; they can create their own cookie shapes and choose from a variety of toppings.

- ¾ cup (⅜ lb.) butter or margarine, at room temperature
- 1 cup granulated sugar
- 2 large eggs
- 1 teaspoon vanilla
- 2¾ cups all-purpose flour
- 1 teaspoon **each** baking powder and salt

  Red or green decorating sugar; or granulated sugar

In large bowl of an electric mixer, beat butter and the 1 cup granulated sugar until creamy; beat in eggs and vanilla. In another bowl, stir together flour, baking powder, and salt; gradually add to butter mixture, blending thoroughly, to form a soft dough. Cover tightly with plastic wrap and refrigerate until firm (at least 1 hour) or for up to 3 days.

On a floured board, roll out dough, a portion at a time, to a thickness of ⅛ inch (keep remaining portions refrigerated). Cut out with cookie cutters (about 2½ inches in diameter) and place slightly apart on ungreased baking sheets. Sprinkle with red or green sugar.

Bake in a 400° oven until edges are lightly browned (8 to 10 minutes). Transfer to racks and let cool completely before handling. Store airtight. Makes about 4 dozen.

Easy-to-Cut Cookies

Let children choose one or more fairly simple cookie shapes—block letters, numbers, or shapes such as triangles, squares, and circles. Then trace or draw shapes on sturdy cardboard (about 1/16 inch thick), making each one about 3 by 5 inches. Cut out patterns with scissors, making sure edges are smooth.

Prepare dough as directed for **Sugar Cookies**; divide into 12 equal portions. On a floured board or directly on a lightly floured baking sheet, roll out each portion to a thickness of ⅛ inch. Let children cut around patterns with a dull knife; then lift off excess dough and set aside to reroll for additional cookies. Offer toppings such as **raisins**, **chocolate chips**, whole or chopped **nuts**, **sunflower seeds**, and **flaked coconut** for embellishing cookies. Bake as directed for **Sugar Cookies**. Makes about 2 dozen.

Finnish Rye Cookies

Rye flour gives these cookies their unusual nutty flavor. The shape is a bit unusual, too—each thin round has a small, off-center hole cut in it. In Finland, where they're a Christmas tradition, the cookies are known as *ruiskakut*.

- 1 cup rye flour
- ½ cup all-purpose flour
- ¼ teaspoon salt
- ½ cup sugar
- ½ cup (¼ lb.) firm butter or margarine, cut into pieces
- ¼ cup milk

In a bowl, stir together rye flour, all-purpose flour, salt, and sugar. Add butter and rub in with your fingers until mixture forms fine, even crumbs. Add milk, 1 tablespoon at a time, stirring with a fork until a stiff dough forms. Gather dough into a ball, wrap tightly in plastic wrap, and refrigerate for 1 hour.

On a floured board, roll out dough, a portion at a time, to a thickness of about ⅛ inch. Cut out with a round cookie cutter (about 2½ inches in diameter). Then cut a hole slightly off center in each cookie, using a tiny round cutter about ½ inch in diameter (you can use the cap from a vanilla or other extract bottle). Place slightly apart on lightly greased baking sheets; prick each cookie several times with a fork. (You can bake the little cut-out holes, too—or reroll them to make more cookies.)

Bake in a 375° oven until cookies are lightly browned and firm to the touch (8 to 10 minutes). Transfer baked cookies to racks and let cool. Store airtight. Makes about 2½ dozen.

Swedish Pinwheel Cookies

Rich cookies like these fancy but easily formed pinwheels are favorites in Sweden at Christmas. They have a tender, flaky texture that's achieved by cutting butter into flour as you would for pastry, then rolling and folding the dough several times to make buttery layers.

1   *cup (½ lb.) firm butter or margarine, cut into small pieces*
2   *cups all-purpose flour*
3   *tablespoons cold water*
    About ½ cup thick preserves or jam
1   *large egg, beaten*
    About ½ cup crushed sugar cubes

With a pastry blender or 2 knives, cut butter into flour until fat particles are about the size of peas. Sprinkle in water, stirring with a fork until dough pulls away from bowl; gather into a ball. Wrap tightly in plastic wrap and refrigerate for at least 1 hour.

On a lightly floured board, roll dough into a 14-inch square. Fold square in half and roll into a 7- by 21-inch rectangle; fold in thirds, overlapping layers to make a 7-inch square. Repeat this rolling and folding procedure 2 more times, ending with a 7-inch square. Wrap and refrigerate for at least 30 minutes.

Roll dough into a 14-inch square on a lightly floured board. Using a pastry wheel, trim off any uneven edges; then cut large square into 25 small squares, each about 2¾ inches on a side. Cut in diagonally from all 4 corners of each square almost to center. Place 1 teaspoon preserves in center of each square. At center, overlap alternate corners to form pinwheels; pinch together firmly.

Brush pinwheels all over with egg, then sprinkle with sugar. Place several inches apart on greased baking sheets and bake in a 400° oven until lightly browned (about 12 minutes). Let cookies cool on baking sheets for 3 minutes; transfer to racks and let cool completely. Store airtight. Makes 25.

Cookie Canvases
(Pictured on front cover)

These sturdy cookies make perfect canvases for food-coloring artists of all ages. They're a diverting, delicious project for a casual Christmas party—and when it's time to go home, guests can take their "edible masterpieces" with them.

You'll need to bake the cookies ahead of time, since they're coated with a glaze that must dry for 8 to 24 hours. When it's time to paint, provide several sizes of watercolor brushes, clear water for rinsing them, and small cups of food color—undiluted for bright colors, slightly diluted with water for lighter colors. To prevent colors from bleeding together, let each color dry briefly before painting another over it.

2   *cups (1 lb.) butter or margarine, at room temperature*
2   *cups granulated sugar*
2   *teaspoons vanilla*
5   *cups all-purpose flour*
1   *to 1½ pounds powdered sugar*
6   *to 9 tablespoons warm water*
    Assorted food colors

In large bowl of an electric mixer, beat butter, granulated sugar, and vanilla until creamy. Beat in flour until thoroughly combined. With a floured, stockinet-covered rolling pin, roll out enough dough on an ungreased unrimmed baking sheet to cover sheet in a ¼- to ⅜-inch-thick layer.

For rectangular or square cookies, use a sharp knife and a ruler to cut away a 1-inch strip of dough on all sides of baking sheet; make no other cuts. For round or decorative shapes, use large floured cookie cutters (or use a coffee or tuna can with both ends removed). Cut shapes, leaving at least 1 inch between cookies and lifting away excess dough.

Combine trimmings with remaining dough; then repeat rolling and cutting until all dough is used. Bake in a 300° oven until cookies are pale gold and centers are firm to the touch (25 to 30 minutes).

Meanwhile, place powdered sugar in a large bowl. Gradually add water (about 6 tablespoons per pound), beating constantly, until glaze is smooth and thick; mixture should flow smoothly but set quickly.

Remove cookies from oven. If making rectangles or squares, cut while still hot, using a sharp knife and a ruler; trim to straighten edges. Let cookies of all shapes cool on baking sheets until just warm to the touch (about 7 minutes).

With a wide spatula, transfer cookies to a flat foil-covered surface. Quickly spread each cookie with enough glaze to make a very smooth surface. Do not cover or move cookies until glaze is dry to the touch (8 to 24 hours).

Paint with food colors. Or stack unpainted cookies between pieces of foil and wrap airtight; store at room temperature for up to 4 days, or freeze for longer storage. (If frozen, unwrap and let thaw at room temperature before painting.) Makes about 1 dozen 6-inch cookies or 2 dozen 3- to 4-inch cookies.

Gingerbread Boys

(Pictured on page 17 and front cover)

Before baking these spicy gingerbread boys, you move the arms and legs to give the figures a lively air—and a lot of personality. If you like, punch a hole for hanging in each one; the baked cookies make charming ornaments for your Christmas tree.

  ½ *cup (¼ lb.) butter or*
      margarine, at room
      temperature
  1 *cup firmly packed brown*
      sugar
1½ *cups light molasses*
 ⅔ *cup water or apple juice*
6½ *cups all-purpose flour*
  2 *teaspoons **each** baking*
      soda and salt
  1 *teaspoon **each** ground*
      cinnamon, ginger,
      cloves, and allspice
      Raisins
  1 *large egg white, lightly*
      beaten
      Purchased decorating
      icing in a tube or
      aerosol can

In large bowl of an electric mixer, beat butter and sugar until creamy. Add molasses and beat until blended, then mix in water. In another bowl, stir together flour, baking soda, salt, cinnamon, ginger, cloves, and allspice. Gradually add to butter mixture, blending to form a stiff dough. Cover tightly with plastic wrap and refrigerate for several hours or until next day.

On a floured board, roll out dough, a portion at a time, to a thickness of ³⁄₁₆ inch. Cut out with a 4- to 6-inch gingerbread boy cutter and, with cutter still in place, transfer cookie and cutter with a wide spatula to a lightly greased baking sheet. Lift off cutter and repeat. If desired, insert a short length of plastic drinking straw into each cookie near the top to make a hole for hanging; press straw all the way through to baking sheet. Leave straws in place while baking.

Dip raisins in egg white and press them firmly into dough to make but-tons (use about 3 per cookie). Move arms and legs to animate the figures.

Bake in a 350° oven until lightly browned (10 to 15 minutes). Transfer cookies to racks, remove straws (if used), and let cool completely. Draw faces on cooled cookies with icing. Tie ribbon or thread through holes for hanging, if desired. Store airtight. Makes about 4 dozen.

Sour Cream Spice Cookies

Ground coriander lends a warm, sweet spiciness to these tender sour cream cookies. For variety, you can top the cutouts with pine nuts and a sprinkling of sugar.

  ½ *cup (¼ lb.) butter or*
      margarine, at room
      temperature
  1 *cup sugar*
  1 *large egg*
  ½ *teaspoon **each** vanilla*
      and almond extract
  ½ *teaspoon baking soda*
  ½ *cup sour cream*
  3 *cups all-purpose flour*
1½ *teaspoons baking powder*
  ½ *teaspoon **each** salt and*
      ground coriander

In large bowl of an electric mixer, beat butter and sugar until creamy; beat in egg, vanilla, and almond extract. Stir baking soda into sour cream, then beat into butter mixture. In another bowl, stir together flour, baking powder, salt, and coriander; gradually add to butter mixture, blending thoroughly. Cover tightly with plastic wrap and refrigerate until firm (about 1 hour) or for up to 3 days.

On a lightly floured board, roll out half the dough to a thickness of about ⅛ inch. Cut out with cookie cutters (about 2½ inches in diameter) and place slightly apart on ungreased baking sheets. Repeat with remaining dough. Bake in a 400° oven until golden (8 to 10 minutes). Transfer to racks and let cool. Store airtight. Makes about 5 dozen.

Pine Nut Sugar Cookies

Prepare dough and cut out cookies as directed for **Sour Cream Spice Cookies**, but place on greased baking sheets. Beat 1 large **egg** with 1 teaspoon **water** and brush over cookies; then press **pine nuts** into surface of cookies (you'll need about ½ cup). Sprinkle cookies lightly with **sugar** and bake in a 375° oven until edges are golden (about 10 minutes).

Brown Sugar Shortbreads

You need just four ingredients to make these buttery brown sugar cookies. To give them a festive air, you might top each with a dot of buttercream frosting and half a candied cherry.

  1 *cup (½ lb.) butter or*
      margarine, at room
      temperature
1¼ *cups firmly packed*
      brown sugar
  1 *teaspoon vanilla*
2½ *cups all-purpose flour*

In large bowl of an electric mixer, beat butter and sugar until creamy. Add vanilla; then gradually beat in flour, blending thoroughly. Gather dough into a ball, wrap tightly in plastic wrap, and refrigerate until firm (about 1 hour) or for up to 3 days.

On a lightly floured board, roll out dough to a thickness of ¼ inch. Cut out with cookie cutters (about 2½ inches in diameter) and place slightly apart on lightly greased baking sheets. Bake in a 300° oven until firm to the touch (35 to 40 minutes; press very lightly to test). Transfer to racks and let cool. Store airtight. Makes about 3 dozen.

Stained-glass Cookies
(Pictured on facing page)

Shimmering red or green candy centers accent these crisp cutout cookies. Each one has a loop of ribbon attached, so you can hang them on your Christmas tree or tie them to gifts as edible decorations. The cookies are made from a sour cream dough flavored with nutmeg—but if you prefer, you can substitute the dough used for our Gingerbread Log Cabin (page 20).

For shaping, you'll need a 4-inch round cookie cutter (or a tuna can with ends removed) and some smaller cutters for making the center cutouts. Also have ready about 7½ yards of ¼-inch ribbon for hanging.

Though these ornaments are quite durable, their candy centers may run if you hang them near a hot light or where humidity is high. To prevent this, we recommend heat-sealing the cookies in plastic wrap (directions follow).

- ½ cup (¼ lb.) butter or margarine, at room temperature
- ½ cup solid vegetable shortening
- 1½ cups sugar
- ½ cup sour cream
- 1 teaspoon vanilla
- 1 large egg
- 3¾ cups all-purpose flour
- 1 teaspoon ground nutmeg
- ½ teaspoon **each** baking soda and salt
- 2 cups sugar
- 1 cup light corn syrup
- ½ cup water
  Red or green food color
- ½ to 1 teaspoon flavoring, such as raspberry, peppermint, or pineapple

In large bowl of an electric mixer, beat butter, shortening, and the 1½ cups sugar until creamy; beat in sour cream, vanilla, and egg. In another bowl, stir together flour, nutmeg, baking soda, and salt; gradually add to butter mixture, blending thoroughly. Cover dough tightly with plastic wrap and refrigerate until next day.

Divide dough into quarters. Work with 1 portion at a time; keep remaining dough refrigerated until ready to roll. Roll out on a floured board to a thickness of ⅛ inch. Cut out with a 4-inch round cookie cutter and transfer to greased baking sheets, spacing cookies about 1 inch apart. Refrigerate sheets. When cookies are cold, cut out centers with a smaller cutter. Refrigerate scraps to reroll with remaining dough.

Bake cookies in a 375° oven just until firm but not yet browned around edges (6 to 7 minutes). Let cool on baking sheets for 5 minutes; transfer to a flat surface and let cool completely.

Cut ¼-inch ribbon into 8-inch lengths. Loop a piece of ribbon through center of each cooled cookie; tie securely at top. Arrange cookies, right side up, on greased baking sheets.

For candy centers, place two 1-cup glass measuring cups in a 375° oven to preheat. Combine the 2 cups sugar, corn syrup, and water in a 2-quart pan. Cook over medium-high heat, stirring, until sugar is dissolved. Then cook without stirring until syrup reaches 280°F (hard crack stage) on a candy thermometer. Remove from heat; stir in your choice of food color and flavoring.

Remove 1 measuring cup from oven; fill with half the syrup (keep remaining syrup over low heat). As soon as syrup in cup stops bubbling, hold cup with a potholder and pour syrup in a thin stream to fill cookie centers. Repeat, using second cup and remaining syrup. Let cookies cool completely; twist gently to loosen, then slide off sheets. Store airtight in a single layer in a cool, dry place, or heat-seal in plastic wrap (see below). Makes about 2½ dozen.

To heat-seal, lay a piece of brown paper (or a piece of paper bag) on a baking sheet. Set sheet in oven and heat to 300°. Tear plastic wrap into 8-inch lengths. Wrap each cookie; secure with cellophane tape. Place about 4 cookies at a time, right sides up, on paper; close oven door for 20 seconds. Remove and let cool.

Nutmeg Crisps

Made from a buttermilk dough and flavored with ground nutmeg, these simple cookies go well with tea, coffee, or holiday eggnog. For extra-fresh nutmeg flavor, try buying whole nutmeg and grating it yourself.

- 1 cup (½ lb.) butter or margarine, at room temperature
- 1 cup sugar
- 1 large egg
- 3½ cups all-purpose flour
- ⅛ teaspoon salt
- 1 teaspoon **each** ground nutmeg and baking soda
- ½ cup buttermilk

In large bowl of an electric mixer, beat butter and sugar until creamy; beat in egg until well combined. In another bowl, stir together flour, salt, nutmeg, and baking soda; add to butter mixture alternately with buttermilk, beating thoroughly after each addition. Gather dough into a ball, wrap tightly in plastic wrap, and refrigerate until firm (2 to 3 hours) or for up to 3 days.

On a well-floured board, roll out dough, a portion at a time, to a thickness of about ⅛ inch (keep remaining portions refrigerated). Cut out with cookie cutters (about 2½ inches in diameter) and place slightly apart on ungreased baking sheets.

Bake in a 350° oven until lightly browned (about 10 minutes). Transfer to racks and let cool. Store airtight. Makes about 7 dozen.

Santa is sure to feel welcome when he sees the tree decorated with Anise Pretzels (page 7), Gingerbread Boys (page 15), and Stained-glass Cookies (facing page). Nürnberger Lebkuchen (page 19) and Fruitcake Cookie Cups (page 22) make tempting accompaniments for steaming hot cocoa.

Fruit Bars

When you're choosing cookies to mail to faraway friends, don't forget these tender, fruit-filled bars. They become softer and more flavorful a day or two after baking—so they'll arrive at their destination tasting perfectly delicious.

   ½ cup (¼ lb.) butter or
       margarine, at room
       temperature
   ½ cup **each** granulated
       sugar and firmly packed
       brown sugar
   2 large eggs
   ½ teaspoon vanilla
   1 cup whole wheat flour
   1¼ cups all-purpose flour
   ¼ cup toasted unsweetened
       wheat germ
   ¼ teaspoon **each** salt and
       baking soda
       Fruit Filling
       (recipes follow)

In large bowl of an electric mixer, beat butter, granulated sugar, and brown sugar until creamy. Beat in eggs and vanilla. In another bowl, stir together whole wheat flour, all-purpose flour, wheat germ, salt, and baking soda; gradually add to butter mixture, blending thoroughly.

Cover dough tightly with plastic wrap and refrigerate until easy to handle (at least 1 hour) or until next day.

Divide dough into 2 equal portions. Return 1 portion to refrigerator. On a floured board, roll out other portion to a straight-edged 9- by 15-inch rectangle; cut lengthwise into 3 strips.

Divide cooled Fruit Filling of your choice into 6 equal portions and evenly distribute 1 portion down center of each strip, bringing it out to ends. Use a long spatula to lift sides of each dough strip over filling, overlapping edges slightly on top. Press together lightly. Cut strips in half crosswise; lift and invert onto greased baking sheets (seam side should be down). Brush off excess flour. Refrigerate for about 15 minutes. Meanwhile, repeat rolling and filling with remaining dough.

Bake in a 375° oven until browned (15 to 20 minutes). Let cool on baking sheets on a rack for about 10 minutes; then cut each strip crosswise into 4 pieces. Transfer cookies to racks and let cool completely. Store covered. Makes 4 dozen.

Fig Filling. Using a food processor or a food chopper fitted with a medium blade, grind together 1 pound **dried figs** (about 2 cups lightly packed) and ½ cup **walnuts** or almonds. Turn into a medium-size pan and add ⅓ cup **sugar**, ½ cup **water**, 1 teaspoon grated **lemon peel**, and 2 tablespoons **lemon juice**. Place over medium heat and cook, stirring, until mixture boils and becomes very thick (5 to 8 minutes). Let cool completely.

Prune Filling. Follow directions for **Fig Filling**, but substitute 2 cups lightly packed **moist-pack pitted prunes** for figs and add ¾ teaspoon **ground cinnamon** with sugar.

Apricot Filling. Follow directions for **Fig Filling**, but substitute 3 cups lightly packed **dried apricots** for figs and use 1 teaspoon grated **orange peel** in place of lemon peel.

Date Filling. Follow directions for **Fig Filling**, but substitute 1 pound **pitted dates** for figs and increase lemon peel to 2 teaspoons.

Anise Cookies

If you enjoy the flavor of anise, you'll want to add these crisp cutouts to your holiday baking. They're made with anise sugar: plain granulated sugar that has been mixed with anise seeds, then allowed to stand for a day. When you make the cookies, you can add the seeds to the dough along with the sugar, or sift them out first for a subtler flavor.

   ¾ cup sugar
   2 teaspoons anise seeds
   1 cup (½ lb.) butter or
       margarine, at room
       temperature
   1 large egg
   2 tablespoons brandy or
       1 tablespoon **each** lemon
       juice and water
   3 cups all-purpose flour
   1 teaspoon baking powder
   ½ teaspoon **each** salt and
       ground cinnamon

Combine sugar and anise seeds; cover tightly and let stand for about 24 hours. Sift out and discard seeds, if desired.

In large bowl of an electric mixer, beat butter and ½ cup of the anise sugar until creamy. Beat in egg and brandy. In another bowl, stir together flour, baking powder, salt, and cinnamon; gradually add to butter mixture, blending thoroughly. Gather dough into a ball, wrap tightly in plastic wrap, and refrigerate until firm (about 1 hour) or for up to 3 days.

Roll out dough on a lightly floured board to a thickness of ⅛ inch. Cut out with cookie cutters (about 2½ inches in diameter) and place 1 inch apart on lightly greased baking sheets. Sift and discard seeds from remaining ¼ cup anise sugar (if you haven't already done so) and sprinkle sugar evenly over cookies.

Bake in a 350° oven until golden brown (about 12 minutes). Transfer to racks and let cool. Store airtight. Makes about 5 dozen.

Almond Ravioli Cookies
(Pictured on page 9)

Do you need a big batch of cookies for a big party? Try these little almond-filled bites. To make them, you use a ravioli-making technique familiar from Italian cooking: roll out one sheet of dough, top with dots of filling, and press on a second sheet of dough. Then just cut the cookies—about 150 of them!—apart.

    1   cup (½ lb.) butter or
        margarine, at room
        temperature
    1½ cups powdered sugar
    1   large egg
    1   teaspoon vanilla
    2½ cups all-purpose flour
    1   teaspoon **each** baking
        soda and cream of tartar
        About ⅔ cup almond
        paste
        About ⅓ cup sliced
        almonds

In large bowl of an electric mixer, beat butter and sugar until creamy; beat in egg and vanilla. In another bowl, stir together flour, baking soda, and cream of tartar; gradually add to butter mixture, blending thoroughly. Divide dough in half. Wrap each half tightly in plastic wrap and refrigerate until firm (2 to 3 hours) or for up to 3 days.

Place 1 portion of dough between 2 pieces of wax paper and roll out to a 10- by 15-inch rectangle. Peel off and discard top paper.

With a pastry wheel or a long-bladed knife, lightly mark dough into 1-inch squares. Place a small ball of almond paste (use a scant ¼ teaspoon for each) in the center of each square; refrigerate while rolling top layer.

Repeat rolling procedure for second portion of dough. Peel off and discard top paper. Invert sheet of dough onto almond-paste-topped dough. Peel off and discard paper.

Gently press top layer of dough around mounds of filling.

Flour a pastry wheel or sharp knife and cut filled dough into 1-inch squares, then run pastry wheel around outer edges to seal (or press with fingers). Place cookies about 1 inch apart on ungreased baking sheets. Push a sliced almond diagonally into center of each cookie.

Bake in a 350° oven until golden (10 to 12 minutes). Transfer to racks and let cool. Store airtight. Makes about 12½ dozen.

Nürnberger Lebkuchen
(Pictured on page 17)

In Nürnberg, Germany, Christmas baking begins in November with the preparation of *lebkuchen*—spicy, cakelike honey cookies that need to age for several weeks to become soft and chewy.

    1   cup honey
    ¾   cup firmly packed dark
        brown sugar
    1   large egg, lightly beaten
    1   tablespoon lemon juice
    1   teaspoon grated
        lemon peel
    2⅓ cups all-purpose flour
    1   teaspoon ground
        cinnamon
    ½   teaspoon **each** ground
        allspice, cloves, and
        nutmeg
    ½   teaspoon **each** salt and
        baking soda
    ⅓   cup **each** finely chopped
        candied citron and finely
        chopped almonds
        About 24 candied
        cherries, cut in half
    6   to 8 ounces whole
        blanched almonds
        Rum Glaze
        (recipe follows)

Heat honey in a small pan over medium-high heat just until it begins to bubble. Remove from heat and let cool slightly. Stir in sugar, egg, lemon juice, and lemon peel; let cool to lukewarm.

In a large bowl, stir together flour, cinnamon, allspice, cloves, nutmeg, salt, and baking soda. Add honey mixture, citron, and chopped almonds; stir until well blended (dough will be soft). Cover tightly with plastic wrap and refrigerate for at least 8 hours or for up to 2 days.

Work with ¼ of the dough at a time, keeping remaining dough refrigerated. On a heavily floured board, roll out dough with a floured rolling pin to a thickness of ⅜ inch. Cut dough with a 2½-inch round cookie cutter; place cookies 2 inches apart on baking sheets lined with lightly greased parchment paper.

Press a cherry half into center of each cookie; surround with 3 almonds arranged like flower petals. Bake in a 375° oven until golden brown (12 to 15 minutes). Remove cookies from oven and immediately brush Rum Glaze over tops with a pastry brush; transfer to racks and let cool. As soon as top glaze dries, turn cookies over and brush glaze over bottoms.

When cookies are completely cooled and dry, pack into airtight containers and store at room temperature for at least 2 weeks or for up to 3 months. If cookies get slightly hard, add a thin slice of apple to each container; cover tightly and store until cookies are moist again (about 1 day), then discard apple. Makes about 4 dozen.

Rum Glaze. Stir together 1 cup **powdered sugar** and 5 tablespoons **rum** or water until very smooth.

Gingerbread Log Cabin
(Pictured below)

Surrounded with soft powdered-sugar snowdrifts, this little cabin makes an enchanting centerpiece for a children's Christmas party. It's easily assembled from gingerbread "logs" cut out with homemade cardboard patterns; you'll also need a 12-inch square of stiff cardboard for a foundation. Complete the edible winter wonderland with decorative details cut from leftover dough. Or use your favorite holiday decorations—tiny Christmas trees, figurines, toy reindeer, and the like.

- ³⁄₄ cup solid vegetable shortening
- ³⁄₄ cup granulated sugar
- ³⁄₄ cup molasses
- 2 tablespoons water
- 3¹⁄₄ cups all-purpose flour
- 1 teaspoon **each** salt, baking soda, and ground ginger
- ¹⁄₄ teaspoon **each** ground nutmeg and allspice
  White Icing (recipe follows)
  About 4 cups powdered sugar

In large bowl of an electric mixer, beat shortening and granulated sugar until creamy; beat in molasses and water. In another bowl, stir together

Set in a drift of powdered-sugar "snow," our charming Gingerbread Log Cabin is certain to delight grownups and children alike.

flour, salt, baking soda, ginger, nutmeg, and allspice; gradually add to shortening mixture, blending thoroughly. Cover tightly with plastic wrap and refrigerate until firm (about 2 hours).

Meanwhile, prepare foundation for cabin by covering a 12-inch square of stiff cardboard with foil. Also prepare patterns for cutting logs: cut lightweight cardboard into a 4- by 6-inch rectangle (for the roof); ½-inch-wide strips that are 2, 3½, and 6 inches long (for logs); and a ½-inch square (for spacers).

With a floured rolling pin, roll out ⅓ of the dough on a floured board to a thickness of ⅛ inch (keep remaining dough refrigerated). Make 2 roof sections by cutting around roof pattern with a sharp knife; transfer carefully to a lightly greased baking sheet.

Roll out scraps and all remaining dough to a thickness of ⅜ inch. Then cut out eight 2-inch-long logs, two 3½-inch-long logs, seventeen 6-inch-long logs, and 30 spacers (½-inch squares). Transfer cookies to lightly greased baking sheets (bake separately from roof sections), arranging about 1 inch apart. From remaining dough, cut out trees or other decorative details. Extra spacers can be used for chimney and stepping stones.

Bake in a 350° oven until just firm to the touch (12 to 15 minutes; cookies will harden as they cool). As soon as roof section is baked, lay pattern on each section and evenly trim 1 long edge (where the 2 sections will meet). Let cookies cool briefly on baking sheets, then transfer to racks and let cool completely. If not assembling cabin at once, package airtight; freeze if desired.

With a pastry brush, paint foil-covered foundation with White Icing, then sift some of the powdered sugar over icing to cover lightly.

To assemble cabin, start with a 6-inch log in back, two 2-inch logs in front. Top with 6-inch logs on sides, letting ends extend; use icing as glue where logs join. Continue building in this way for 2 more layers, using spacers at inner edges of 2-inch logs and gluing with icing as needed.

For the fourth layer, use 6-inch logs all around. Add 3 spacers across the doorway; then top with 6-inch logs across front and back.

Using spacers and 3½- and 2½-inch logs, build up gables on front and back of cabin. Place a spacer atop each gable.

Ice roof pieces and sift sugar over them. Ice top logs and spacers; set roof in place, trimmed edges together.

Decorate cabin and its grounds as desired with extra shapes. In most dry climates, cabin will keep for about 1 week. In humid areas, cookies may absorb moisture and start to sag, so plan to keep cabin for only 2 or 3 days before eating.

White Icing. In a bowl, beat together 2 cups **powdered sugar** and ¼ cup **water** until smooth.

Swedish Ginger Thins
(Pictured on page 231)

Very spicy, very dark, very thin, and very crisp—these are the words to describe *pepparkakor*, Sweden's version of gingersnaps. For the holidays, cut them into fancy shapes; then dress them up further with decorative icing, if you like.

- ⅔ cup (⅓ lb.) *butter or margarine*
- ⅓ cup **each** *granulated sugar and firmly packed brown sugar*
- 2 *tablespoons dark corn syrup*
- 2 *teaspoons **each** ground ginger and cloves*
- 1 *tablespoon ground cinnamon*
- 2 *teaspoons baking soda*
- ¼ *cup water*
- 2½ *cups all-purpose flour*
  Royal Icing (recipe follows) or purchased decorating icing in a tube or aerosol can (optional)
  Multicolored candy sprinkles (optional)

In a medium-size pan, combine butter, granulated sugar, brown sugar, and corn syrup; place over medium heat and stir until butter is melted. Remove from heat, stir in ginger, cloves, and cinnamon, and let cool slightly. Stir baking soda into water and add to butter mixture, blending thoroughly. Then stir in flour until well combined (dough will be quite soft). Cover tightly with plastic wrap and refrigerate until firm (2 to 3 hours) or for up to 3 days.

On a floured board, roll out dough, a portion at a time, to a thickness of about 1/16 inch. Cut out with cookie cutters (about 2½ inches in diameter). If necessary, dip cutters in flour to prevent dough from sticking to them. Place cookies slightly apart on ungreased baking sheets. Bake in a 325° oven until slightly darker brown and firm to the touch (10 to 12 minutes). Transfer to racks and let cool completely.

If desired, press Royal Icing through a decorating tube, making swirls or other designs on cookies. Decorate icing with candy sprinkles, if desired. Let icing dry before storing cookies. Store airtight. Makes about 5 dozen.

Royal Icing. In small bowl of an electric mixer, beat 1 large **egg white** with ⅛ teaspoon **cream of tartar** and a dash of **salt** for 1 minute on high speed. Add 2 cups **powdered sugar** and beat slowly until blended; then beat on high speed until very stiff (3 to 5 minutes).

Drop Cookies

If your children like to help with the holiday baking, be sure to mix up a batch or two of drop cookies. Shaping couldn't be easier; you just drop the dough from a spoon onto baking sheets or, in the case of our Fruitcake Cookie Cups, into small paper bonbon cups. Most of the choices here are chunky with fruit, nuts, and other goodies, but you'll find some plainer cookies, too—like golden Bourbon Chews.

Bourbon Chews

These cookies are spirited in more ways than one. Molasses and ginger provide part of their spicy character; bourbon whiskey does the rest.

       1   cup all-purpose flour
     ½   cup sugar
       1   teaspoon ground ginger
     ¼   teaspoon salt
     ⅓   cup light molasses
     ½   cup (¼ lb.) butter or
            margarine
       3   tablespoons bourbon
            whiskey
     ¼   cup chopped almonds
            or walnuts

In a small bowl, stir together flour, sugar, ginger, and salt; set aside. In a 1-quart pan, bring molasses to a boil over high heat; add butter and stir until melted. Remove from heat and stir in flour mixture, bourbon, and almonds until batter is smooth and well combined.

Drop batter by level tablespoonfuls onto greased baking sheets, spacing cookies about 3 inches apart; then spread each into a 2-inch circle with the back of a spoon. Bake in a 300° oven until cookies look dry and are no longer sticky to the touch (8 to 10 minutes). Let cool on baking sheets for about 3 minutes, then transfer to racks and let cool completely. Store airtight. Makes about 2 dozen.

Fruitcake Cookie Cups
(Pictured on page 17)

Like miniature Christmas fruitcakes, these moist cookies age well. You bake them in little paper bonbon cups, available in cookware shops.

     ¼   cup (⅛ lb.) butter or
            margarine, at room
            temperature
     ½   cup firmly packed
            brown sugar
     ¼   cup apple jelly or red
            currant jelly
       2   large eggs
       1   teaspoon vanilla
    1½   cups all-purpose flour
       2   teaspoons baking soda
     ½   teaspoon **each** ground
            allspice, cloves,
            cinnamon, and nutmeg
       1   cup chopped walnuts
            or pecans
       1   cup currants or raisins
       1   cup chopped candied
            cherries or mixed
            candied fruit

In large bowl of an electric mixer, beat butter and sugar until creamy; beat in jelly, eggs, and vanilla. In another bowl, stir together flour, baking soda, allspice, cloves, cinnamon, and nutmeg. Blend half the flour mixture into butter mixture. Add walnuts, currants, and cherries to remaining flour mixture; then stir into butter mixture, blending thoroughly.

Spoon 1½ to 2 teaspoons batter into each paper bonbon cup and place about 1 inch apart on baking sheets; or drop batter by rounded teaspoonfuls directly onto lightly greased baking sheets, spacing cookies about 2 inches apart. Bake in a 300° oven until centers spring back when lightly touched (17 to 20 minutes). Let cool on racks. Store airtight. Makes about 6 dozen.

Glazed Mincemeat Drops

Old-fashioned mincemeat recipes usually call for beef and suet. These cookies are made with purchased mincemeat, which contains mainly fruit and sweeteners with little or no meat—but they still boast traditional spicy flavor and festive seasonal appeal.

       1   cup (½ lb.) butter or
            margarine, at room
            temperature
    1½   cups firmly packed
            brown sugar
       3   large eggs
       3   cups all-purpose flour
     ½   teaspoon **each** baking
            powder and salt
       1   teaspoon **each** baking
            soda and ground
            cinnamon
       1   cup rolled oats
       2   cups prepared
            mincemeat
       1   cup chopped walnuts
            Spicy Glaze
            (recipe follows)

In large bowl of an electric mixer, beat butter and sugar until creamy; beat in eggs. In another bowl, stir together flour, baking powder, salt, baking soda, cinnamon, and oats. Gradually add to butter mixture, blending thoroughly. Stir in mincemeat and walnuts.

Drop dough by level tablespoon-fuls onto greased baking sheets, spacing cookies 3 inches apart. Bake in a 400° oven until golden brown (8 to 10 minutes).

Transfer cookies to racks. Prepare Spicy Glaze and spread over tops of cookies while they're still warm; let cool completely. Store airtight. Makes 6 to 7 dozen.

Spicy Glaze. In a bowl, stir together 3 cups **powdered sugar**, ¾ teaspoon **ground cinnamon**, and 3 tablespoons *each* **brandy** and **water** (or 6 tablespoons **water**) until smooth.

Addendum Cookies

Holiday time calls for cookies—often lots of different cookies, in not much time. If you need to turn out a variety of cookies quickly, you've found the right recipe. You make one basic dough and divide it up, then stir your choice of additions into each portion of dough—and presto, several different kinds of cookies from one batch!

    1   cup (½ lb.) butter or
        margarine, at room
        temperature
    1   cup each granulated
        sugar and firmly packed
        brown sugar
    2   large eggs
    2   teaspoons vanilla
    2½ cups all-purpose flour
    1   teaspoon baking soda
    ½   teaspoon salt
        Addenda
        (suggestions follow)

In large bowl of an electric mixer, beat butter, granulated sugar, and brown sugar until creamy; then beat in eggs and vanilla. In another bowl, stir together flour, baking soda, and salt; gradually add to butter mixture, blending thoroughly. Divide dough in half and mix 1 addendum into each portion. (You may also divide dough into quarters, then mix half an addendum into each quarter; or double an addendum and mix it into the entire batch of dough.)

Drop dough by rounded tea-spoonfuls onto ungreased baking sheets, spacing cookies 2 inches apart. Bake in a 350° oven until just set in center when lightly touched (12 to 15 minutes). Transfer to racks and let cool. Store airtight. Makes 8 to 10 dozen.

Addenda. Stir one of the following into each half of the dough:

- 2 ounces **unsweetened chocolate**, melted and cooled, and ½ cup finely crushed **hard peppermint candy**.

- 2 ounces **unsweetened chocolate**, melted and cooled, 1½ teaspoons **rum flavoring**, and ½ cup crushed **peanut brittle** or chopped salted peanuts.

- ¼ cup **sour cream**, 1 teaspoon **ground nutmeg**, and ½ cup dry-roasted **sunflower seeds**.

- 1 cup **rolled oats**, 1 teaspoon grated **orange peel**, ¼ cup **orange juice**, and ½ cup **raisins** or snipped pitted dates.

- ½ cup **applesauce**, ½ cup **wheat germ** or crushed ready-to-eat cereal flakes, ½ cup chopped **nuts**, and 1 teaspoon **pumpkin pie spice** or ground cinnamon.

- 1 cup **granola-style cereal** (break up any large lumps before measuring), 1 cup snipped **pitted dates** or dried apricots, 1 teaspoon **ground cinnamon**, and ¼ cup **milk**.

Holiday Date-Nut Drops

Much like Fruitcake Cookie Cups (see facing page), these tender drops are studded with nuts and fruit. For a party-pretty finish, top each cookie with a walnut half or candied cherry before baking.

    ½   cup (¼ lb.) butter or
        margarine, at room
        temperature
    1   cup firmly packed
        brown sugar
    1   large egg
    1   teaspoon vanilla
    1⅔ cups all-purpose flour
    ½   teaspoon baking soda
    ¼   teaspoon salt
    ¼   cup buttermilk
    ½   cup chopped walnuts
    1   cup quartered red or
        green candied cherries
        (or some of each)
    1   cup snipped pitted dates
    1   cup raisins
        Walnut halves or red or
        green candied cherry
        halves

In large bowl of an electric mixer, beat butter and sugar until fluffy. Beat in egg and vanilla. In another bowl, stir together flour, baking soda, and salt; add to creamed mixture alternately with buttermilk. Stir in chopped walnuts, quartered cherries, dates, and raisins.

Drop dough by generous tea-spoonfuls onto greased baking sheets, spacing cookies about 2 inches apart. Top each cookie with a walnut or cherry half. Bake in a 375° oven until centers spring back when lightly pressed (8 to 10 minutes). Transfer to racks and let cool. Store airtight. Makes about 5 dozen.

Bar Cookies

Baked in a pan, then cut into strips, squares, or triangles, bar cookies are both simple to make and ideal for carrying to parties. Here's a handful of choices, from crisp English Toffee Squares to rich Triple-layered Mint Brownies, spread with creamy icing and glazed with chocolate. You can cut the bars to the size we suggest, or make them smaller, for daintier bites at a dessert buffet or tea party.

Tutti Frutti Oat Bars

Apple juice and three kinds of dried fruit—raisins, apricots, and dates—go into the filling for these oat-topped treats. Chewy and not too sweet, they're a nice addition to a cookie tray.

- ½ cup (¼ lb.) butter or margarine, at room temperature
- 1 cup firmly packed brown sugar
- 1½ cups all-purpose flour
- ½ teaspoon **each** baking soda and salt
- 1½ cups rolled oats
- 2 tablespoons water
  Fruit Filling (recipe follows)

In large bowl of an electric mixer, beat butter and sugar until creamy. In another bowl, stir together flour, baking soda, and salt; gradually add to butter mixture, blending thoroughly. Add oats and water and mix until well combined and crumbly.

Pat half the crumb mixture firmly into a greased 9- by 13-inch baking pan. Spread with cooled filling. Spoon remaining crumb mixture evenly over filling; pat down firmly. Bake in a 350° oven until lightly browned (about 35 minutes). Let cool in pan on a rack, then cut into 1½- by 2½-inch bars. Store covered. Makes about 2½ dozen.

Fruit Filling. In a small pan, combine ¼ cup **sugar** and 1 tablespoon **cornstarch**. Stir in 1 cup **unsweetened apple juice**, 1 teaspoon grated **lemon peel**, 1 tablespoon **lemon juice**, 1 cup **raisins**, and ½ cup *each* finely chopped, lightly packed **dried apricots** and lightly packed snipped **pitted dates**. Cook over medium heat, stirring, until mixture boils and thickens; let cool.

Scottish Shortbread
(Pictured on facing page)

If you're asked to take cookies along to a small holiday gathering, you're certain to please with Scottish Shortbread, a butter-rich cookie of delightful simplicity. Or try our ginger variation, enlivened with crystallized ginger as well as the ground spice.

- 1¼ cups all-purpose flour
- 3 tablespoons cornstarch
- ¼ cup sugar
- ½ cup (¼ lb.) firm butter, cut into pieces
  Sugar

In a bowl, stir together flour, cornstarch, and the ¼ cup sugar. Rub in butter with your fingers until mixture is very crumbly and no large particles remain. With your hands, gather mixture into a ball; place in an ungreased 8- or 9-inch round baking pan with a removable bottom, or in a 9-inch springform pan. Firmly press out dough into an even layer.

With the tines of a fork, make impressions around edge of dough; then prick surface evenly. Bake in a 325° oven until pale golden brown (about 40 minutes). Remove from oven and, while hot, cut with a sharp knife into 8 to 12 wedges. Sprinkle with about 1 tablespoon sugar. Let cool completely; then remove sides of pan and lift out cookies. Store airtight. Makes 8 to 12.

Ginger Shortbread

Follow directions for **Scottish Shortbread**, but substitute ½ teaspoon **ground ginger** for cornstarch. After rubbing in butter, stir in 2 tablespoons minced **crystallized ginger**.

Persimmon Bars

These soft, spicy bars, spread with a tangy glaze, are just about perfect for any festive holiday occasion. When preparing the persimmon purée, be sure to use Hachiya-type persimmons—the kind that turn very soft as they ripen. You'll recognize Hachiya persimmons by their pointed tips.

- 1 cup persimmon purée (directions follow)
- 1 teaspoon baking soda
- 1 large egg
- 1 cup sugar
- ½ cup salad oil
- 1 package (8 oz.) pitted dates, finely snipped
- 1¾ cups all-purpose flour
- 1 teaspoon **each** salt, ground cinnamon, and ground nutmeg
- ¼ teaspoon ground cloves
- 1 cup chopped walnuts or pecans
  Lemon Glaze (recipe follows)

Prepare persimmon purée; measure out 1 cup and stir in baking soda. Set aside. In a large bowl, lightly beat egg; then stir in sugar, oil, and dates.

An enduring tradition in Scotland, rich, buttery Scottish Shortbread (facing page) is an irresistible Christmas treat.

In another bowl, stir together flour, salt, cinnamon, nutmeg, and cloves; add to date mixture alternately with persimmon mixture, stirring just until blended. Stir in walnuts. Spread batter evenly in a lightly greased, flour-dusted rimmed 10- by 15-inch baking pan. Bake in a 350° oven until top is lightly browned and a wooden pick inserted in center comes out clean (about 25 minutes).

Let cool in pan on a rack for 5 minutes, then spread with Lemon Glaze. Let cool completely; cut into 2- by 2½-inch bars. Store covered. Makes 2½ dozen.

Persimmon purée. You'll need fully ripe **Hachiya-type persimmons**—pulp should be soft and jellylike. Cut fruits in half and scoop out pulp with a spoon. Discard skin, seeds, and stem. In a blender or food processor, whirl pulp, a portion at a time, until smooth (you'll need 2 or 3 medium-

size persimmons for 1 cup purée). For each cup purée, thoroughly stir in 1½ teaspoons **lemon juice**. To store, freeze in 1-cup batches in rigid containers; thaw, covered, at room temperature.

Lemon Glaze. In a small bowl, stir together 1 cup **powdered sugar** and 2 tablespoons **lemon juice** until smooth.

Triple-layered Mint Brownies

Extravagance is allowed at Christmas time—and that's all the excuse you need to make these devastatingly rich treats. A thin, nut-laden brownie is topped with creamy mint frosting, then covered with dark chocolate.

- 2 ounces unsweetened chocolate
- 3/4 cup (3/8 lb.) butter or margarine
- 1 large egg
- 1/2 cup granulated sugar
- 1/4 cup all-purpose flour
- 1 cup chopped almonds or pecans
- 2 cups powdered sugar
- 1/2 teaspoon vanilla
- 1 teaspoon mint extract
- 2 to 3 tablespoons whipping cream
- Red or green food color (optional)

For the first layer, place 1 ounce of the chocolate and 1/4 cup of the butter in the top of a double boiler over simmering water (or in a small pan over lowest possible heat). Stir until melted.

In a small bowl, beat egg and granulated sugar, then gradually beat in chocolate mixture. Stir in flour and almonds. Spread batter evenly in a lightly greased 9-inch square baking pan; bake in a 350° oven until brownie feels dry on top (20 to 25 minutes). Let cool completely in pan on a rack.

For the second layer, place 1/4 cup of the butter, powdered sugar, vanilla, and mint extract in small bowl of an electric mixer. Beat together; then beat in enough cream to make frosting spreadable. Tint with food color, if desired. Spread evenly over cooled brownie.

For the third layer, combine remaining 1 ounce chocolate and remaining 1/4 cup butter in the top of a double boiler over simmering water (or in a small pan over lowest possible heat). Stir until melted. Drizzle over frosting layer; tilt pan so chocolate covers surface evenly. Refrigerate until chocolate is hardened (about 15 minutes). Cut into 2 1/4-inch squares. Store, covered, in refrigerator. Makes 16.

Buttery Cookie Brittle

This delectable confection—part cookie, part candy—is studded with bits of almond brickle. You bake it in a single sheet, then break it into irregular chunks to serve.

- 1/2 cup (1/4 lb.) butter or margarine, at room temperature
- 3/4 teaspoon vanilla
- 1 cup all-purpose flour
- 1/2 cup sugar
- 1 package (6 oz.) almond brickle bits

In large bowl of an electric mixer, beat butter and vanilla until creamy. Blend in flour and sugar, then stir in brickle bits (mixture will be quite crumbly).

Spread mixture evenly over bottom of an ungreased 9- by 13-inch baking pan. Lay a piece of wax paper on top and press firmly to pack crumbs evenly. Discard paper.

Bake in a 375° oven until golden around edges (15 to 20 minutes). Let brittle cool in pan on a rack for 10 minutes; then loosen with a wide spatula, turn out onto rack, and let cool completely. Break into pieces. Store airtight for up to 2 days; freeze for longer storage. Makes about 3 dozen 1 1/2- by 2-inch chunks.

English Toffee Squares

When you need a dessert for a large gathering, you'll appreciate this recipe. With little effort, you can produce five to six dozen delicious and easily portable toffee-flavored bar cookies.

- 1 cup (1/2 lb.) butter or margarine, at room temperature
- 1 cup sugar
- 1 large egg
- 2 cups all-purpose flour
- 1 teaspoon ground cinnamon
- 1 cup chopped pecans or walnuts

In large bowl of an electric mixer, beat butter and sugar until creamy. Separate egg. Beat yolk into butter mixture; cover and reserve white.

In another bowl, stir together flour and cinnamon; add to butter mixture, using your hands if necessary to blend thoroughly.

With your hands, spread dough evenly over bottom of a greased rimmed 10- by 15-inch baking pan. Beat egg white lightly, then brush over dough to cover evenly. Sprinkle pecans over top; press in lightly.

Bake in a 275° oven until firm when lightly touched (about 1 hour). While still hot, cut into about 1 1/2-inch squares. Let cool in pan on a rack. Store airtight. Makes 5 to 6 dozen.

Icebox Cookies

If you want to produce fresh-baked cookies any time, at a moment's notice, icebox cookies are for you. Make the dough in advance and store it in refrigerator or freezer; when unexpected holiday guests arrive, you can bake up teatime accompaniments or take-home treats in no time. For next-door neighbors and nearby friends, you might even consider giving rolls of the unbaked dough, plus the recipe and baking instructions.

Poppy Seed Nut Slices

Hazelnuts and poppy seeds team up to give these crunchy little cookies their distinctive flavor.

> 1   cup (½ lb.) butter or margarine, at room temperature
> 1   cup sugar
> 1   large egg
> 1   teaspoon vanilla
> 2½   cups all-purpose flour
> ⅓   cup poppy seeds
> ½   teaspoon ground cinnamon
> ¼   teaspoon **each** salt and ground ginger
> 1½   cups coarsely chopped hazelnuts

In large bowl of an electric mixer, beat butter and sugar until creamy; beat in egg and vanilla. In another bowl, stir together flour, poppy seeds, cinnamon, salt, and ginger; gradually add to butter mixture, blending thoroughly. Add hazelnuts, mixing with your hands if necessary to distribute nuts evenly. Shape dough into 2 or 3 rolls, each 1½ inches in diameter; wrap in wax paper and refrigerate until firm (at least 2 hours) or for up to 3 days (freeze for longer storage).

Unwrap dough. Using a sharp knife, cut into ¼-inch-thick slices; place slices about 1 inch apart on un- greased baking sheets. Bake in a 350° oven until edges are golden (12 to 15 minutes). Transfer to racks and let cool. Store airtight. Makes about 7 dozen.

Spiced Almond Thins

Sour cream, brown sugar, cinnamon, and nutmeg combine in a wafer with a spicy, old-fashioned flavor that's just right for the season. Crisp bits of almond give the cookies a pebbly appearance.

> 1   cup (½ lb.) butter or margarine, at room temperature
> 1   cup firmly packed brown sugar
> 2   cups all-purpose flour
> 2   teaspoons ground cinnamon
> ½   teaspoon ground nutmeg
> ¼   teaspoon baking soda
> ¼   cup sour cream
> ½   cup slivered almonds

In large bowl of an electric mixer, beat butter and sugar until creamy. In another bowl, stir together flour, cinnamon, and nutmeg. Stir baking soda into sour cream; add to butter mixture alternately with flour mixture, blending thoroughly. Stir in al- monds until well combined. Shape dough into a 2½-inch-thick rectan- gular log; wrap in wax paper and re- frigerate until firm (at least 2 hours) or for up to 3 days (freeze for longer storage).

Unwrap dough. Using a sharp knife, cut into ⅛-inch-thick slices; place slices about 1 inch apart on un- greased baking sheets. Bake in a 350° oven until golden brown (about 10 minutes). Let cool for about a min- ute on baking sheets, then transfer to racks and let cool completely. Store airtight. Makes about 5 dozen.

French Butter Wafers

Fragile butter wafers, accented only with vanilla, provide an elegant, sim- ple counterpoint to extra-rich holi- day fare. (Since butter is responsible for much of the cookies' delicate flavor, it's best not to substitute margarine in this recipe.)

> 1   cup (½ lb.) butter, at room temperature
> 1¼   cups powdered sugar
> 1   large egg
> 1   teaspoon vanilla
> 2   cups all-purpose flour
> 1   teaspoon **each** baking soda and cream of tartar
> ⅛   teaspoon salt

In large bowl of an electric mixer, beat butter until creamy. Beat in sugar; add egg and vanilla and beat well. In another bowl, stir together flour, baking soda, cream of tartar, and salt; gradually add to butter mix- ture, blending thoroughly. Shape dough into a roll 1½ inches in diame- ter; wrap in wax paper and refriger- ate until firm (at least 2 hours) or for up to 3 days (freeze for longer storage).

Unwrap dough. Using a sharp knife, cut into ⅜-inch-thick slices; place slices 2 inches apart on un- greased baking sheets. Bake in a 350° oven until golden (10 to 12 minutes). Let cool on baking sheets for about a minute, then transfer to racks and let cool completely. Store airtight. Makes about 4 dozen.

Black & White Squares
(Pictured below)

Jaunty stripes of vanilla- and chocolate-flavored dough give these little squares a festive appearance.

- ½ cup (¼ lb.) butter or margarine, at room temperature
- ½ cup sugar
- 1 large egg yolk
- 1½ cups all-purpose flour
- 1½ teaspoons baking powder
- ⅛ teaspoon salt
- 3 tablespoons milk
- ½ teaspoon vanilla
- 1 ounce unsweetened chocolate

In large bowl of an electric mixer, beat butter and sugar until creamy; beat in egg yolk. In another bowl, stir together flour, baking powder, and salt. In a small cup, combine milk and vanilla. Add dry ingredients to butter mixture alternately with milk mixture, blending thoroughly after each addition.

In the top of a double boiler over simmering water or in a small pan over lowest possible heat, melt chocolate, stirring constantly; let cool slightly. Divide dough in half; take 1 tablespoon dough from one half and add it to the other half. Stir chocolate into smaller portion of dough, blending until well combined.

Shape each portion of dough into a roll 1½ inches in diameter. Wrap each in wax paper; flatten sides to make square logs. Refrigerate until firm (at least 2 hours) or for up to 3 days (freeze for longer storage).

Unwrap dough. Using a sharp knife, slice each log lengthwise into fourths. Then reassemble logs, using 2 dark slices and 2 light slices for each, alternating colors to make stripes. Gently press layers together.

Cut logs crosswise into ⅛-inch-thick slices (if layers start to separate, refrigerate until dough is firmer). Place slices about 1 inch apart on greased baking sheets. Bake in a 350° oven until light golden (about 10 minutes). Transfer to racks and let cool. Store airtight. Makes about 4 dozen.

Boldly striped Black & White Squares are fun and easy to make; you form dark and light-colored logs, then cut and stack to create a pattern.

Quick Breads

Top choice for snacking throughout the year, quick breads are always popular Christmas gifts from your kitchen—and it's no wonder. They're easy to make, delicious to eat, and supremely simple to package. Just bake the loaves in foil pans; cool them right in the pans, wrap in plastic wrap, and decorate as you like. Most supermarkets sell foil loaf pans in various sizes; during the holidays, you'll sometimes find them in gold, red, or green as well as the usual silver.

Eggnog Almond Tea Loaf

When the Christmas spirit moves you, try this rich quick bread made with eggnog. Enjoy it at home, or give it as a gift—either way, it spreads holiday cheer.

  1   cup chopped blanched almonds
2½   cups all-purpose flour
  ¾   cup sugar
3½   teaspoons baking powder
  1   teaspoon salt
  ½   teaspoon **each** ground nutmeg and grated lemon peel
  1   large egg
  3   tablespoons salad oil
1¼   cups commercial eggnog

Spread almonds in a shallow baking pan and toast in a 350° oven until golden (about 8 minutes), stirring frequently. In a large bowl, stir together flour, sugar, baking powder, salt, nutmeg, lemon peel, and toasted almonds. In a small bowl, lightly beat egg, then beat in oil and eggnog. Add liquid mixture to flour mixture and stir just until well blended. Pour batter into a greased, flour-dusted 5- by 9-inch loaf pan (or three 3½- by 5-inch pans).

Bake in a 350° oven until a wooden pick inserted in center of bread comes out clean (about 1 hour for large loaf, 40 minutes for small loaves). Let cool in pan on a rack for 10 minutes, then turn out onto rack and let cool completely. Makes 1 large loaf or 3 small loaves.

Glazed Lemon Bread

Here's an old-fashioned favorite to enjoy in any season. While it's hot from the oven, you poke it with a skewer until it's full of holes, then drizzle it with a sweet, lemony glaze. The cooled bread is easy to slice and has a fine, even texture, much like pound cake.

1½   cups all-purpose flour
  1   cup sugar
  1   teaspoon baking powder
  ½   teaspoon salt
  2   large eggs
  ½   cup **each** milk and salad oil
1½   teaspoons grated lemon peel
      Lemon Glaze (recipe follows)

In a large bowl, stir together flour, sugar, baking powder, and salt. In a small bowl, lightly beat eggs, then beat in milk, oil, and lemon peel. Add liquid mixture to flour mixture and stir just until blended.

Pour batter into a greased, flour-dusted 5- by 9-inch loaf pan. Bake in a 350° oven until a wooden pick inserted in center comes out clean (40 to 45 minutes).

When bread is done, use a long wooden skewer to poke numerous holes all the way to bottom of loaf. Drizzle hot Lemon Glaze over top so that it slowly soaks into bread. Let bread cool in pan on a rack for about 15 minutes; then turn out onto rack and let cool completely. Makes 1 loaf.

Lemon Glaze. In a small pan, combine 4½ tablespoons **lemon juice** and ⅓ cup **sugar**. Stir over medium heat until sugar is dissolved.

Date-Nut Loaf

Like fruitcake, this loaf is rich-tasting, satisfying, and loaded with fruit—dates, golden raisins, and walnuts. If you like, spread each dark, sweet slice with cream cheese.

1¼   cups all-purpose flour
  1   teaspoon **each** baking powder and baking soda
  ½   cup sugar
  ¼   teaspoon salt
  ½   teaspoon ground cinnamon
  1   package (8 oz.) pitted dates, snipped
  ½   cup **each** golden raisins and chopped walnuts
  2   tablespoons butter or margarine
  ½   teaspoon vanilla
  1   cup hot water
  1   large egg, lightly beaten

In a large bowl, stir together flour, baking powder, baking soda, sugar, salt, cinnamon, dates, raisins, and walnuts until thoroughly blended. In another bowl, stir together butter, vanilla, and hot water until butter is melted; then stir in egg. Pour butter mixture into dry ingredients and stir just until well blended. Pour batter into a greased 4½- by 8½-inch loaf pan.

Bake in a 325° oven until bread begins to pull away from sides of pan and a wooden pick inserted in center comes out clean—about 1 hour and 25 minutes. (Or bake for 1 hour in a 5- by 9-inch pan, or 45 minutes in two 3⅜- by 7⅜-inch pans.) Let cool in pan on a rack for 10 minutes; then turn out onto rack and let cool completely. Makes 1 large loaf or 2 small loaves.

Panettone

Traditional Milanese *panettone* is a yeast bread, but this quick version is every bit as delicious. We suggest baking it in a brown paper bag, but you can certainly use a panettone mold if you have one.

1	large egg
2	large egg yolks
¾	cup sugar
½	cup (¼ lb.) butter or margarine, melted and cooled
1	teaspoon grated lemon peel
1	teaspoon **each** anise seeds and anise extract
¼	cup **each** pine nuts, raisins, and coarsely chopped mixed candied fruit
2⅔	cups all-purpose flour
2	teaspoons baking powder
½	teaspoon salt
1	cup milk

In large bowl of an electric mixer, beat egg, egg yolks, and sugar until thick and lemon-colored. Beat in butter; then add lemon peel, anise seeds, anise extract, pine nuts, raisins, and candied fruit. In another bowl, stir together flour, baking powder, and salt. Blend half the dry ingredients into egg mixture. Stir in half the milk; add remaining dry ingredients and mix well. Blend in remaining milk.

Fold down top of a paper bag (one that measures 3½ by 6 inches on the bottom) to form a cuff so bag stands about 4 inches high. Butter inside of bag generously, set on a baking sheet, and pour in batter. (Or use a greased, flour-dusted panettone mold approximately 6 inches in diameter and 4 inches deep.)

Bake in a 325° oven until bread is well browned on top and a wooden skewer inserted in center comes out clean. To serve hot, tear off paper bag and cut bread into wedges. To serve cold, wrap bread (still in bag) in a cloth, then in foil, and let cool completely to mellow the flavors. Makes 1 loaf.

Mincemeat Bread
(Pictured on facing page)

Baked in a fluted tube pan, this spicy, pretty bread is delightful any time of day. Try it sliced thin and buttered, with tea or a hot fruit punch; or toast thicker slices for a holiday breakfast.

½	cup (¼ lb.) butter or margarine, at room temperature
1	cup sugar
3	large eggs
2	cups all-purpose flour
1	tablespoon baking powder
½	teaspoon **each** salt and ground cinnamon
1½	cups prepared mincemeat
¾	cup chopped nuts

In large bowl of an electric mixer, beat butter and sugar until creamy. Add eggs, 1 at a time, beating well after each addition; continue to beat until mixture is fluffy and pale yellow. In another bowl, stir together flour, baking powder, salt, and cinnamon. Add dry ingredients to creamed mixture alternately with mincemeat, mixing until thoroughly blended. Stir in nuts.

Spread batter in a generously greased, flour-dusted 8-cup fluted tube pan (or in a lightly greased, flour-dusted 5- by 9-inch loaf pan). Bake in a 350° oven until bread is lightly browned on top and a wooden pick inserted in center comes out clean (50 to 55 minutes for tube pan, about 1 hour for loaf pan). Loosen bread from pan and let cool on a rack for 10 minutes; then turn out onto rack and let cool completely. Makes 1 loaf.

Quick Orange Loaves
(Pictured on facing page)

Flecks of fresh orange add color and tangy flavor to a cinnamon-spiced nut bread. The recipe makes two plump loaves—one to enjoy right away, one to freeze or give to friends.

	About 4 large oranges
3	cups all-purpose flour
1	teaspoon **each** salt and baking soda
½	teaspoon baking powder
2	teaspoons ground cinnamon
1	cup chopped nuts
3	large eggs
1½	cups sugar
1	cup salad oil
1	teaspoon vanilla

Grate 1 tablespoon orange peel. Then cut off and discard remaining peel and all white membrane from oranges. Pick out seeds; finely chop enough of the pulp to make 2 cups. In a small bowl, combine the 2 cups pulp and grated peel; set aside. In another bowl, stir together flour, salt, baking soda, baking powder, cinnamon, and nuts; set aside.

In a medium-size bowl, lightly beat eggs. Add sugar and oil and stir until blended. Stir in vanilla and orange mixture. Add flour mixture all at once and stir just until evenly moistened. Then divide batter evenly between 2 greased, flour-dusted 4½- by 8½-inch loaf pans.

Bake in a 350° oven until a wooden pick inserted in center of bread comes out clean (50 to 60 minutes). Let cool in pans on a rack for 10 minutes, then turn out onto rack and let cool completely. Wrap airtight and let stand for a day before slicing; or refrigerate for up to a week (freeze for longer storage). Makes 2 loaves.

Poppy Seed Loaf

Crunchy poppy seeds give an exciting burst of flavor to this mellow, moist tea bread. It's especially tasty when paired with our lemon-accented apricot spread; for gift giving, you might package the spread in a pretty crock or small plastic tub.

¼ cup (⅛ lb.) butter or margarine, at room temperature

1 cup sugar

2 large eggs

1 teaspoon grated orange peel

2 cups all-purpose flour

2½ teaspoons baking powder

½ teaspoon salt

¼ teaspoon ground nutmeg

1 cup milk

⅓ cup poppy seeds

½ cup chopped nuts

½ cup golden raisins (optional)

Tangy Apricot Spread (recipe follows)

Beat together butter and sugar until creamy; add eggs, 1 at a time, beating well after each addition. Mix in orange peel. In another bowl, stir together flour, baking powder, salt, and nutmeg until thoroughly blended. Add flour mixture to creamed mixture alternately with milk, stirring until well blended; then stir in poppy seeds, nuts, and raisins, if desired. Turn batter into a well-greased, flour-dusted 5- by 9-inch loaf pan.

Bake in a 350° oven until bread begins to pull away from sides of pan and a wooden pick inserted in center comes out clean (about 1 hour and 10 minutes). Let cool in pan on a rack for 10 minutes, then turn out onto rack and let cool completely. Offer Tangy Apricot Spread with bread. Makes 1 loaf.

Tangy Apricot Spread. Beat together ½ cup (¼ lb.) **butter** or margarine (at room temperature), ¼ cup **apricot jam**, 1 teaspoon grated **lemon peel**, and 1 tablespoon **lemon juice**.

*A **tempting array** of holiday sweet breads includes (clockwise from top) Quick Orange Loaf (facing page), Dresden-style Stollen (page 40), Anise Bread (page 37), and Mincemeat Bread (facing page).*

Cranberry Tea Bread

A bit different from many cranberry-nut quick breads, this loaf is richly spiced and made with canned cranberry sauce rather than chopped fresh or frozen berries.

¾ cup (⅜ lb.) butter or margarine, at room temperature

1½ cups firmly packed brown sugar

4 large eggs

3 cups all-purpose flour

2 teaspoons **each** baking powder and baking soda

2 teaspoons ground cinnamon

½ teaspoon ground cloves

1 can (1 lb.) whole-berry cranberry sauce

⅔ cup **each** chopped walnuts and golden raisins

In large bowl of an electric mixer, beat butter and sugar until creamy. Beat in eggs, 1 at a time, beating well after each addition. In another bowl, stir together flour, baking powder, baking soda, cinnamon, and cloves; add to creamed mixture and stir until well blended. Mix in cranberry sauce, walnuts, and raisins.

Divide batter evenly between 2 greased, flour-dusted 5- by 9-inch loaf pans. Bake in a 350° oven until a wooden pick inserted in center of bread comes out clean (about 1 hour). Let cool in pans on a rack for 10 minutes, then turn out onto rack and let cool completely. Makes 2 loaves.

Yeast Breads

In almost every country, special sweet yeast breads are a holiday tradition. We present some of these favorites here—fruited German *stollen*, lemon-glazed Swedish *kardemummakrans*, and more. Our collection includes newer recipes, too, like plump Golden Teddy Bear Breads and little "surprise packages" filled with sweet or savory cheese. Any one would be a wonderful centerpiece for brunch or breakfast, or a warm and thoughtful gift for friends.

Part of what makes all these breads so special is imaginative shaping: some are braided, others formed into wreaths or pretzels or snowflakes. There's even an elegant Christmas tree, with curling branches to decorate with glowing candied cherries.

Golden Teddy Bear Breads
(Pictured on page 6)

Golden, charming, and sweetly scented, these teddy bear breads will entice even a Grinch on Christmas morning. The rich egg breads can be frozen, so you can bake the bears ahead if you like.

> 1   *package active dry yeast*
> ¼   *cup warm water (about 110°F)*
> ½   *cup (¼ lb.) butter or margarine, at room temperature*
> ½   *cup sugar*
> 2   *tablespoons vanilla*
> ⅓   *cup warm milk (about 110°F)*
> ½   *teaspoon salt*
> 5   *large eggs*
>   *About 4¾ cups all-purpose flour*
> 1   *large egg beaten with 1 tablespoon milk*

In large bowl of an electric mixer, sprinkle yeast over warm water and let stand for about 5 minutes to soften. Stir in butter, sugar, vanilla, milk, salt, and the 5 eggs; beat until combined. Stir in 3 cups of the flour; beat on high speed until smooth and stretchy (about 6 minutes). Add 1¾ cups more flour. *If using a dough hook, beat on high speed until dough pulls cleanly from bowl sides. To mix by hand, stir with a heavy spoon until flour is incorporated.*

Cover dough and let rise in a warm place until doubled—about 1 hour. (Or refrigerate until doubled —18 to 24 hours.)

Scrape dough out onto a lightly floured board and knead briefly to release air, adding more flour as needed to prevent sticking. Cut dough into 4 equal pieces; cover until ready to shape.

For each bear, divide 1 dough quarter into these portions: 3 tablespoons for arms, 3 tablespoons for legs, ½ cup for body, about ¼ cup for head, and 1 to 1½ tablespoons for ears, face features, and belly button.

Follow picture below as you shape bear; each shaped piece should be about ½ inch thick. Roll arm and leg portions into 8-inch-long ropes. Shape into arcs as shown on a greased 12- by 15-inch baking sheet, spacing arcs 1 inch apart at their centers. Press center 3 inches of arcs, then brush flattened portions with egg-milk mixture.

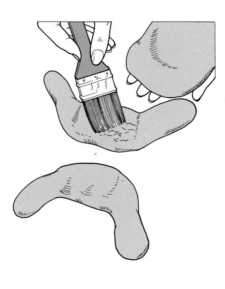

Shape body dough into an oval 5 inches long, gently pulling top surface toward underside to make smooth. Place body on flattened part of arcs. Press and tuck bottom of trunk underneath arc to secure. If necessary, pull arms and legs to make each 2½ inches long.

Shape head into a ball, pulling top surface toward underside to make smooth. Press into a 2½-inch-diameter circle. Press top ½ inch of body to flatten; brush with egg-milk mixture. Place head on baking sheet so it overlaps flat part of body; press to seal.

Shape ⅔ of remaining dough into 2 ears. Flatten 2 spots on top sides of head, about ¼ inch in; brush with egg-milk mixture. Press ears in place.

Roll remaining dough into 4 or 5 balls: 2 for eyes, 1 for belly button, 1 for nose, and 1 for snout, if desired. (Make nose and snout pieces slightly bigger.) With a finger, poke small holes in bear for dough pieces. Brush holes with egg-milk mixture. Place dough in holes.

Loosely cover shaped bears with plastic wrap and let rise in a warm place until puffy (25 to 30 minutes). Gently brush with egg-milk mixture. Bake in a 350° oven until golden (16 to 18 minutes). If baking 2 bears at a time in 1 oven, switch position of baking sheets halfway through baking.

Let bears cool on baking sheets for 10 minutes, then transfer to a rack. Serve warm or cool. If made ahead, wrap airtight and freeze for up to 1 month. Makes 4 bear breads (¾ lb. each); each makes 2 or 3 servings.

Miniature Breads

Tiny braided loaves and rings made from an egg-rich yeast dough are pleasing gifts—and a pretty offering for a Christmas or New Year's breakfast.

- 1   package active dry yeast
- 1¼ cups warm water (about 110°F)
- 1   teaspoon salt
- ¼   cup **each** sugar and salad oil
- 2   large eggs, lightly beaten
- 2   or 3 drops yellow food color (optional)
    About 5 cups all-purpose flour
- 1   large egg yolk beaten with 1 tablespoon water
    About 1 tablespoon sesame or poppy seeds (optional)

In a large bowl, sprinkle yeast over warm water and let stand for about 5 minutes to soften. Stir in salt, sugar, oil, eggs, and food color (if used). Add 2½ cups of the flour and beat until batter is smooth.

If using a dough hook, gradually beat in 2 cups more flour, beating between additions until dough pulls away from bowl in stretchy strands. *If mixing by hand,* slowly add 2 cups more flour, beating constantly with a heavy spoon until dough is smooth and stretchy.

Scrape dough out onto a board sprinkled with about ¼ cup more flour; knead until smooth and satiny (about 15 minutes), adding more flour as needed to prevent sticking. Place dough in a greased bowl, turn over to grease top, cover, and let rise in a warm place until doubled (1¼ hours).

Punch dough down and knead briefly on floured board to release air, then divide in half. Roll each half into a 24-inch log, then cut each log into 15 equal pieces. Working with 3 pieces at a time (keep remaining dough covered with plastic wrap),

roll each into a 24-inch rope. Pinch ropes together at one end and braid to a 21-inch length.

To make loaves, cut braid into 3-inch lengths, pinching both ends. For rings, cut braid into 7-inch lengths, pinching ends together to form a circle. Place breads 2 inches apart on greased baking sheets. Cover and let rise in a warm place until dough is smooth and puffy (about 15 minutes).

When breads are ready to bake, lightly brush with egg yolk mixture. Sprinkle with sesame or poppy seeds, if desired. Bake in a 400° oven until light golden brown (about 12 minutes). Makes 70 loaves or 30 rings.

Swedish Kardemummakrans

(Pictured on page 41)

Flavored with aromatic cardamom, our braided Swedish wreaths can be made ahead, then reheated for a special breakfast treat. Since cutting tends to squash this tender bread, it's best to pull it apart to serve.

- 1   package active dry yeast
- ¼   cup warm water (about 110°F)
- 2½ cups warm milk (about 110°F)
- ¾   cup (⅜ lb.) butter or margarine, melted and cooled
- 1   large egg
- ½   teaspoon salt
- 1   cup sugar
- 1½ teaspoons ground cardamom
    About 8 cups all-purpose flour
    Lemon Icing (recipe follows)
    Red or green candied cherries, halved (optional)

In a large bowl, sprinkle yeast over warm water and let stand for about 5 minutes to soften. Stir in milk, butter, egg, salt, sugar, and cardamom until blended.

With a heavy spoon, stir in 7 cups of the flour or enough to form a stiff dough. Scrape dough out onto a lightly floured board and knead until smooth and elastic (about 10 minutes), adding more flour as needed to prevent sticking. Place dough in a greased bowl, turn over to grease top, cover, and let rise in a warm place until almost doubled (1½ to 2 hours).

Punch dough down and knead briefly on a floured board to release air. Then divide into 6 equal portions; roll each into a rope about 24 inches long. Place 3 ropes on a greased baking sheet, pinch tops together, and braid loosely. Form braid into a ring, pinching ends together. Repeat to make a second braided wreath. Cover and let rise in a warm place until almost doubled (about 40 minutes).

Bake in a 350° oven until loaves are medium brown (35 to 40 minutes). Transfer loaves to a rack and let cool for 10 minutes, then serve warm. Or, if made ahead, let cool completely, then wrap airtight and freeze. Thaw unwrapped. To reheat, wrap in foil and heat in a 350° oven for about 20 minutes.

To serve, spoon half the Lemon Icing around top of each warm wreath, letting it drizzle down sides. Decorate with cherries, if desired. Makes 2 loaves.

Lemon Icing. Combine 2 cups **powdered sugar**, ¼ cup **milk**, and 1 teaspoon **lemon extract**. Stir until smooth.

Cut-and-Slash Loaves
(Pictured on facing page)

Two easy techniques—cut and slash—bring holiday designs to a simple sweet bread. Knife cuts form a simple round or triangle into a snowflake, wreath, or tree; slashes made with a razor blade add decorative touches.

   1   package active dry yeast
  ¼   cup warm water (about 110°F)
  ¾   cup warm milk (about 110°F)
  ½   cup (¼ lb.) butter or margarine, melted and cooled
  ½   cup sugar
  ½   teaspoon salt
  1   teaspoon grated lemon peel
  3   large eggs
 4¼ to 4½ cups all-purpose flour

In a large bowl, sprinkle yeast over warm water and let stand for about 5 minutes to soften. Mix in milk, butter, sugar, salt, lemon peel, 2 of the eggs, and 2 cups of the flour; stir to blend, then beat until smooth.

If using a dough hook, add 2¼ cups more flour and beat until dough pulls from bowl sides and feels only slightly sticky; add more flour if needed.

If mixing by hand, stir in 2¼ cups more flour with a heavy spoon. Then scrape dough onto a floured board and knead until smooth and satiny (10 to 15 minutes). Add more flour as needed to prevent sticking.

Place dough in a greased bowl; turn over to grease top. Cover dough mixed by either method; let rise in a warm place until doubled (1 to 1½ hours).

Punch dough down; knead briefly on a floured board to release air, then divide in half. Shape each portion, following directions below. Lightly cover with plastic wrap and let rise in a warm place until almost doubled (30 to 45 minutes). Beat remaining egg. Brush dough with egg; slash as directed below.

Bake in 350° oven until browned (25 to 30 minutes). Transfer to racks; let cool for about 10 minutes, then serve warm. Or, if made ahead, wrap airtight and freeze; thaw unwrapped. To reheat, cover loaves lightly with foil and heat in a 350° oven until warm (7 to 10 minutes). Makes 2 loaves.

Snowflake. Form 1 portion of dough into a ball. Place in center of a greased 10- by 15-inch baking sheet. Press dough into a flat 8-inch round. Make 4 equidistant 3-inch cuts toward center.

After shaped dough has risen, brush with egg. Using a razor blade, make a 3-inch slash down center of each quarter, then cut three 1½- to 2-inch slashes down each side of each center slash.

Wreath. Press 1 portion of dough into an 8-inch round as described for snowflake. Poke a hole in center and pull equally from each side of hole to make a 2-inch opening in center; keep dough an even ¾-inch thickness as you work. Cut 2- to 2½-inch slanting cuts in from edge, spacing them about 3 inches apart (see photo on facing page).

After shaped dough has risen, brush with egg. Using a razor blade, cut a 3-inch slash down center of each leaf.

Tree. On a greased 10- by 15-inch baking sheet, form 1 portion of dough into a flat triangle with a 6-inch base and 9-inch sides. Make 2½- to 3½-inch slanting cuts along the sides, spacing them about 3 inches apart (see photo on facing page).

After shaped dough has risen, brush with egg. Using a razor blade, slash down triangle's center and cut a 2- to 3-inch-long slash down each branch.

Christmas Surprise Bread Bundles
(Pictured on page 36)

Tie bright bows around golden bread bundles, and the butter-rich dough becomes gift wrapping for the sweet or tangy cheese filling inside. You need to chill the dough for easy handling, so start a day ahead—or even weeks ahead, since the bread bundles freeze well.

   1   package active dry yeast
  ¼   cup warm water (about 110°F)
  ½   cup (¼ lb.) butter or margarine, melted
  ½   cup half-and-half, light cream, or milk
  3   tablespoons sugar (omit if using savory filling)
  3   large eggs
  4 to 4½ cups all-purpose flour
  1   teaspoon ground nutmeg
  ½   teaspoon salt
      Sweet Cheese Filling or Savory Cheese Filling (recipes follow)
  1   large egg beaten with 1 tablespoon water

In large bowl of an electric mixer, sprinkle yeast over warm water and let stand for about 5 minutes to soften. Mix butter, half-and-half, and sugar (if used); add to yeast mixture with the 3 eggs, 2 cups of the flour, nutmeg, and salt. Stir to blend. Beat on medium speed for 2 minutes.

If using a dough hook, gradually mix in 2 cups more flour; beat on medium speed until dough pulls from bowl sides. Add 2 to 4 more tablespoons flour, if needed. Remove hook; scrape down bowl.

To mix by hand, beat in 1¾ cups more flour with a heavy spoon. Scrape dough out onto a board coated with about ¼ cup flour; knead until smooth and elastic (about 10 minutes).

Place dough in a greased bowl; turn over to grease top. Cover dough

(Continued on page 36)

Handsome golden Cut-and-Slash Loaves (*facing page*), *shaped as fanciful wreath, tree, and snowflake, are delightful, easy-to-make gifts.*

mixed by either method and let rise in a warm place until doubled (about 1½ hours). Punch down; knead briefly, then wrap airtight and refrigerate for at least 2 hours or until next day.

Knead dough briefly on a floured board to release air, then divide into 16 equal portions. Shape each portion into a 6- to 6½-inch circle. Place equal portions (2 to 2½ tablespoons) of filling in center of each circle. Draw dough up around filling and pleat; then pinch firmly just above filling, letting top of dough flare loosely. As you finish bundles, place them 2 inches apart on greased 10- by 15-inch baking sheets; cover loosely with plastic wrap and keep cold until all dough is shaped.

Place baking sheets with covered bundles in a warm place and let rise until puffy (about 30 minutes); then uncover. To seal firmly, lightly pinch pleats together again. Brush surfaces with egg-water mixture. Bake in a 350° oven until golden brown (about 25 minutes). Serve warm or at room temperature. If made ahead, let cool completely; wrap airtight and freeze for up to 6 months. Thaw unwrapped. To reheat, set slightly apart on baking sheets and heat in a 325° oven for about 20 minutes. Makes 16 buns.

Sweet Cheese Filling. Beat together 2 large packages (8 oz. *each*)

Sweet little Christmas Surprise Bread Bundles, *gaily beribboned, make special presents from your kitchen. (Recipe begins on page 34.)*

cream cheese, at room temperature; ½ cup **powdered sugar**; 1 large **egg**; 2 teaspoons grated **orange peel**; and ¼ teaspoon **almond extract**. Stir in 1 cup **raisins** and ½ cup chopped **candied orange peel**. Use, or cover and refrigerate until next day.

Savory Cheese Filling. Beat together 1 large package (8 oz.) **cream cheese**, at room temperature; 8 ounces **feta cheese**, crumbled; 1 large **egg**; and 1 cup finely chopped **green onions** (including tops). Use, or cover and refrigerate until next day.

Vanocka

For many families, a holiday morning means a special breakfast bread. In Czechoslovakia, this might be *vanocka*—a plump and glossy braided loaf, filled with chopped candied fruit and nuts and flavored with lemon.

- 2   packages active dry yeast
- 1   cup warm water (about 110°F)
    About 5 cups all-purpose flour
- ½   cup **each** raisins and water
- 2   tablespoons rum or brandy (optional)
- 1   cup (½ lb.) butter or margarine, at room temperature
- ½   cup sugar
- 2   large eggs
- 1   teaspoon **each** salt and grated lemon peel
- ½   cup **each** chopped blanched almonds and chopped mixed candied fruit
- 1   large egg beaten with 1 tablespoon water

In a large bowl, sprinkle yeast over the 1 cup warm water and let stand for about 5 minutes to soften. Stir in 1 cup of the flour and beat until well blended. Cover and let stand in a warm place until bubbly (about 1 hour).

Meanwhile, in a small bowl, soak raisins in the ½ cup water for 1 hour. Pour off and discard water; add rum, if desired, and set aside.

In a large bowl, beat butter until creamy. Gradually add sugar, beating until light and fluffy. Add the 2 eggs, 1 at a time, beating well after each addition. Stir in salt and lemon peel. Add butter mixture to yeast mixture, stirring until blended.

Gradually beat in 2 cups more flour. Stir in raisins, almonds, and candied fruit. Gradually beat in about 1½ cups more flour or enough to make a stiff dough.

Scrape dough out onto a floured board and knead until smooth and satiny (about 10 minutes), adding more flour as needed to prevent sticking. Place dough in a greased bowl; turn over to grease top. Cover and let rise in a warm place until doubled (about 1½ hours).

Punch dough down; knead briefly on a floured board to release air. Divide into 6 equal portions and roll each into a 10-inch-long rope. For each loaf, arrange 3 ropes side by side on a greased 12- by 15-inch baking sheet. Pinch together at top and braid loosely; pinch ends together and tuck underneath. Cover and let rise in a warm place until almost doubled (30 to 40 minutes).

Brush loaves with egg mixture and bake in a 350° oven until browned (about 30 minutes). Transfer to racks to cool. Makes 2 loaves.

Anise Bread
(Pictured on page 31)

For festive occasions in northeastern New Mexico, it's a tradition to bake a sweet yeast bread with the flavor of anise. Serve this tender treat warm or toasted to enhance its spicy fragrance.

- 1   package active dry yeast
- ½   cup warm water (about 110°F)
- ½   cup warm milk (about 110°F)
- 2   tablespoons granulated sugar
- 1½ tablespoons anise seeds
- ½   cup (¼ lb.) butter or margarine, melted and cooled
- 2   large eggs
- ½   teaspoon salt
- 4½ to 5 cups all-purpose flour
- ⅔   cup firmly packed brown sugar mixed with ½ teaspoon ground cinnamon
    Sugar Glaze (recipe follows)

In a large bowl, sprinkle yeast over warm water and let stand for about 5 minutes to soften. Add milk, granulated sugar, anise seeds, 3 tablespoons of the butter, eggs, salt, and 1½ cups of the flour. Beat for about 5 minutes, then gradually beat in about 2½ cups more flour to make a soft dough.

Scrape dough out onto a floured board; knead until smooth and satiny (15 to 20 minutes), adding more flour as needed to prevent sticking. Place dough in a greased bowl; turn over to grease top. Cover and let rise in a warm place until doubled (about 1½ hours). Punch dough down, knead briefly on a lightly floured board to release air, and roll out into a 12- by 22-inch rectangle. Brush remaining 5 tablespoons butter over dough to within ½ inch of edges. Sprinkle brown sugar–cinnamon mixture evenly over butter. Starting with a long side, roll up dough tightly jelly roll style; pinch edge to seal.

Being careful not to stretch roll, place it seam side down in a greased 10-inch tube pan; pinch ends together to close circle. With a razor blade or floured sharp knife, make 7 evenly spaced slashes, ½ inch deep, on top. Cover and let rise in a warm place until almost doubled (about 45 minutes).

Bake in a 350° oven until loaf is lightly browned (50 to 60 minutes). Let cool in pan for 5 minutes; then turn out onto a rack. While bread is still warm, spoon on Sugar Glaze, letting it drizzle down sides. Makes 1 loaf.

Sugar Glaze. Blend ½ cup **powdered sugar** with 1 tablespoon **water** until smooth.

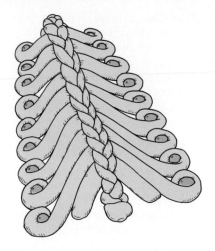

Christmas Tree Bread

With its braided trunk and glossy, elegantly curled branches, this Christmas tree is a lovely choice for brunch any time during the Yuletide season. The recipe makes three trees; you might heat-seal one or two in plastic wrap (see page 57) to give to friends.

2	*packages active dry yeast*
½	*cup warm water (about 110°F)*
4	*large eggs, lightly beaten*
1⅔	*cups evaporated milk, at room temperature*
	Pinch of ground saffron
1	*teaspoon salt*
1½	*cups sugar*
	About 9 cups all-purpose flour
1	*cup (½ lb.) butter or margarine, melted and cooled*
	Red or green candied cherries, halved
1	*large egg, beaten*

In a very large bowl, sprinkle yeast over warm water and let stand for about 5 minutes to soften. Mix in the 4 eggs, evaporated milk, saffron, salt, and sugar. Beat until saffron is evenly distributed.

Gradually add 4½ cups of the flour, beating until dough is smooth and elastic. Stir in butter until well blended.

If using a dough hook, beat in 4 cups more flour or enough to form a stiff dough. *If mixing by hand,* beat in 4 cups more flour with a heavy spoon, mixing to make a stiff dough.

Sprinkle a board with about ½ cup more flour. Scrape dough out onto board, cover lightly, and let stand for 15 minutes. Then knead until smooth and elastic, adding more flour as needed to prevent sticking. Place dough in a greased bowl; turn over to grease top. Cover tightly with plastic wrap and refrigerate until next day.

Cut dough into 3 equal parts. To shape each tree, divide 1 part into 16 equal portions; roll each into a 12-inch strand.

Shape each tree on a greased large baking sheet as shown below. First, cut two 5-inch pieces from one 12-inch strand to form top pair of branches; curl 1 end of each of these branches and bring cut ends together at center top of tree. Reserve excess dough to use later. Use another 12-inch strand to make second pair of branches, cutting strand into two 6-inch pieces. To make succeeding pairs of branches, use 1 rope for each branch; curl 1 end and arrange branches so each curled end extends about ½ inch farther out from center of tree than the curl just above it (curls should just touch each other). Cut off excess dough at center as you form each branch.

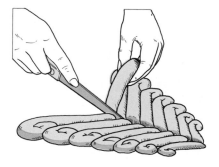

Continue making branches until you have placed 9 pairs. Then combine all excess dough scraps; use some of this dough to roll an 8-inch-long strand to fit below last pair of branches (leave ends uncurled as shown above right). Roll remaining dough to make 3 thin strands, each about 20 inches long. Braid these for trunk of tree. Press trunk in place; then press a cherry half into curl at end of each branch.

Cover bread and let rise in a warm place for 25 minutes. Brush with beaten egg; bake in a 400° oven for 10 minutes. Brush again with egg and continue to bake until bread is golden brown (15 to 20 more minutes). Makes 3 loaves.

Bohemian Christmas Braid

Much like Vanocka (page 37), this braided loaf is flavored with lemon peel and studded with almonds and fruit. The shaping is a bit different, though—this is a double braid (a smaller braid atop a larger one). Almond-flavored icing, pecan halves, and cherries provide a fancy Christmas finish.

1	*package active dry yeast*
¼	*cup warm water (about 110°F)*
1	*cup warm milk (about 110°F)*
⅓	*cup sugar*
1½	*teaspoons **each** salt and grated lemon peel*
1	*teaspoon ground mace*
2	*tablespoons butter or margarine, at room temperature*
1	*large egg*
	About 4 cups all-purpose flour
½	*cup **each** raisins and chopped unblanched almonds*

*Almond Icing
(recipe follows)
Pecan halves
Red candied cherries,
halved*

In large bowl of an electric mixer, sprinkle yeast over warm water and let stand for about 5 minutes to soften. Add milk, sugar, salt, lemon peel, mace, butter, egg, and 1½ cups of the flour. Beat on medium speed until smooth (about 5 minutes).

If using a dough hook, beat in about 2½ cups more flour or enough to form a soft, elastic dough. *To mix by hand,* beat in about 2½ cups more flour with a heavy spoon.

Scrape dough out of bowl and shape into a ball, then place in a greased bowl and turn over to grease top. Cover and let rise in a warm place until doubled (about 1 hour).

Stir down dough, blending in raisins and almonds. Then scrape dough out onto a board coated with about 2 tablespoons flour and knead lightly until smooth.

Divide dough into 4 equal pieces. Shape 3 pieces into smooth ropes about 16 inches long. Place ropes side by side on a greased baking sheet and braid tightly; pinch ends to seal, then tuck underneath.

Divide remaining dough into 3 pieces. Shape each into a smooth 10-inch-long rope. Braid tightly; pinch ends to seal, then tuck underneath. Lightly moisten top of large braid with water and place smaller braid on top. Cover lightly and let rise in a warm place until almost doubled (about 30 minutes).

Bake in a 350° oven until well browned (25 to 30 minutes). Transfer to a rack and let cool for about 10 minutes, then serve warm. Or, if made ahead, let cool completely, then wrap airtight and freeze; thaw unwrapped. To reheat, wrap loaf in foil and place in a 350° oven for about 20 minutes.

To serve, drizzle warm bread with icing and decorate with pecan halves and cherries. Makes 1 loaf.

Almond Icing. Stir together ¾ cup **powdered sugar**, 2 to 3 teaspoons **milk**, and ⅛ teaspoon **almond extract**.

Belgian Cramique
(Pictured on page 41)

This beautiful, golden-crusted raisin bread is made up of topknotted brioche-type rolls, arranged and baked in a wreath.

1	cup milk
¼	cup (⅛ lb.) butter or margarine, cut into pieces
⅓	cup sugar
1	teaspoon salt
2	packages active dry yeast
½	cup warm water (about 110°F)
3	large eggs
5½	to 6 cups all-purpose flour
1	cup raisins
1	large egg yolk beaten with 1 tablespoon water

In a pan, combine milk, butter, sugar, and salt. Heat, stirring, to about 110°F (butter need not melt completely). In a large bowl, sprinkle yeast over warm water and let stand for about 5 minutes to soften. Stir softened yeast and eggs into milk mixture. Gradually beat in 5 cups of the flour to make a soft dough.

Add raisins and scrape dough out onto a floured board; knead until smooth and satiny (5 to 20 minutes), adding more flour as needed to prevent sticking. Place dough in a greased bowl; turn over to grease top. Cover and let rise in a warm place until doubled (about 45 minutes).

Punch dough down and knead briefly on a floured board to release air; then divide into 12 equal parts. Pinch off about ⅕ of each part and set aside to shape topknots. Shape each larger piece into a smooth ball; place, smooth side up, around edges of 2 greased 9-inch round cake pans (each pan will hold 6 balls). Shape each smaller piece into a teardrop that is smooth on top. With your finger, poke a hole in center of each large ball and insert pointed end of teardrop in hole—settle it securely or it may pop off at an angle while baking. Cover and let rise in a

warm place until almost doubled (about 45 minutes).

Brush loaves with egg yolk mixture, being careful not to let it accumulate in joints of topknots. Bake in a 350° oven until richly browned (about 45 minutes). Let cool in pans for 5 minutes, then turn out onto racks to cool completely. Makes 2 wreaths.

Swedish Letter Buns (Lussekätter)

In Sweden during the holiday season, sweet little S-shaped rolls are typically served with the hot wine punch called *glögg.* They're made from a light, buttery dough flavored with cardamom or saffron, then adorned with raisins.

½	cup (¼ lb.) butter or margarine
¾	cup whipping cream or milk
⅓	cup sugar
½	teaspoon salt
1	teaspoon ground cardamom or ¹⁄₁₆ teaspoon ground saffron
1	package active dry yeast
¼	cup warm water (about 110°F)
1	large egg
	About 4 cups all-purpose flour
	About ⅓ cup raisins
1	large egg yolk beaten with 1 tablespoon water

In a small pan, melt butter; remove from heat and stir in cream, sugar, salt, and cardamom. Let cool to lukewarm.

In large bowl of an electric mixer, sprinkle yeast over warm water and let stand for about 5 minutes to soften. Add cooled cream mixture, egg, and 2 cups of the flour. Mix until well blended, then beat on medium speed for 2 more minutes.

If using a dough hook, gradually beat in about 1½ cups more flour to

(Continued on next page)

make a stiff dough. *To mix by hand,* stir in about 1½ cups more flour with a heavy spoon; beat to make a stiff dough.

Scrape dough out onto a floured board and knead until smooth and satiny (about 10 minutes), adding more flour as needed to prevent sticking. Place dough in a greased bowl; turn over to grease top. Cover and let rise in a warm place until doubled (about 1½ hours).

Punch dough down; knead briefly on a floured board to release air. To shape rolls, divide dough into 24 equal pieces; roll each piece on a flat surface with your palm to make a rope about 9 inches long, and coil ends of each in opposite directions to form an S shape. Push a raisin deep into center of each coil.

Place rolls about 2 inches apart on 2 greased 14- by 17-inch baking sheets. Cover and let rise in a warm place until puffy and almost doubled (about 45 minutes). Brush rolls with egg yolk mixture. With racks placed in the upper and lower middle of a 375° oven, bake buns until golden brown on bottoms and lightly browned around edges (about 15 minutes; switch positions of baking sheets halfway through baking, if necessary for even browning). Makes 2 dozen rolls.

Dresden-style Stollen
(Pictured on page 31)

There are many versions of Germany's famous *stollen;* one of the most popular is this one from Dresden. Its rich, buttery dough, studded with candied orange peel, almonds, raisins, and currants, is folded a special way to form an ellipse-shaped loaf, then dusted with powdered sugar after baking.

½ cup milk
1 cup (½ lb.) butter or margarine
½ cup granulated sugar
2 packages active dry yeast
½ cup warm water (about 110°F)
½ teaspoon salt
1 teaspoon **each** grated lemon peel and almond extract
About 5¼ cups all-purpose flour
2 large eggs
⅓ cup finely chopped candied orange peel
½ cup **each** dark raisins, golden raisins, currants, and slivered almonds
1 large egg white beaten with 1 teaspoon water
¼ cup (⅛ lb). butter or margarine, melted
⅓ cup powdered sugar

In a small pan, combine milk, the 1 cup butter, and granulated sugar. Set over medium-low heat and heat to scalding (120°F), stirring to dissolve sugar and melt butter. Set aside; let cool to lukewarm.

In a large bowl, sprinkle yeast over warm water and let stand for about 5 minutes to soften. Add cooled milk mixture, salt, lemon peel, almond extract, and 3 cups of the flour; beat until well blended. Add eggs, 1 at a time, beating well after each addition. Gradually stir in orange peel, raisins, currants, almonds, and 2 cups more flour.

Scrape dough out onto a floured board and knead until smooth and satiny (about 10 minutes), adding more flour as needed to prevent sticking. Place dough in a greased bowl; turn over to grease top. Cover and let rise in a warm place until doubled (about 1½ hours).

Punch dough down. Knead briefly on a floured board to release air, then divide in half. Place each portion on a lightly greased 12- by 15-inch baking sheet and shape into a 7- by 9-inch oval about ¾ inch thick. Brush surface with some of the egg white mixture. Crease each oval lengthwise, slightly off center, and fold so top edge lies about an inch back from bottom edge. Brush

evenly with remaining egg white mixture. Cover and let rise in a warm place until puffy and almost doubled (35 to 45 minutes).

Bake in a 375° oven until richly browned (about 25 minutes). Brush loaves evenly with the ¼ cup melted butter and sift powdered sugar over tops. Return to oven and bake for 3 more minutes. Transfer to racks and let cool. Makes 2 loaves.

Russian Krendl'
(Pictured on facing page)

Krendl' is a traditional birthday treat in Russia—at Christmastime, it celebrates the birth of Jesus.

2 packages active dry yeast
½ cup warm water (about 110°F)
1¼ teaspoons salt
3 tablespoons sugar
2 teaspoons vanilla
1 cup warm milk (about 110°F)
About 6 cups all-purpose flour
6 large egg yolks, lightly beaten
½ cup (¼ lb.) plus 1 tablespoon butter or margarine, melted and cooled
½ teaspoon ground cinnamon
¼ cup sugar
⅔ cup chopped seeded canned kumquats
1 cup **each** chopped moist-pack pitted prunes and chopped dried apples
1 large egg yolk beaten with 1 tablespoon water
Sugar Glaze (recipe follows)
¼ cup sliced almonds

In a large bowl, sprinkle yeast over warm water and let stand for about 5 minutes to soften. Add salt, the 3 tablespoons sugar, vanilla, and milk. Beat in 2 cups of the flour to make a smooth batter.

Blend in the 6 egg yolks and ½ cup of the butter, then stir in about

A selection of festive sweet breads brings Old World tradition to your holidays. From top: *Russian Krendl'* (facing page), *Swedish Kardemummakrans* (page 33), and *Belgian Cramique* (page 39).

3½ cups more flour or enough to make a soft dough. Scrape out onto a lightly floured board and knead until smooth (about 5 minutes), adding more flour as needed to prevent sticking. Place dough in a greased bowl; turn over to grease top. Cover and let rise in a warm place until doubled (about 45 minutes).

Punch dough down and knead briefly on a floured board to release air. Divide dough in half; roll each half into a 9- by 30-inch rectangle. Spread rectangles with remaining 1 tablespoon butter, dividing evenly.

Combine cinnamon and the ¼ cup sugar; sprinkle half the mixture over each rectangle. Then scatter half of the kumquats, prunes, and apples evenly over each rectangle.

To shape loaves, tightly roll up each rectangle jelly roll style, starting from a long side. Moisten edge with water and pinch seam to seal along side of roll.

Place each roll, seam side down, on a greased baking sheet; form into a modified pretzel shape by crossing 1 end over the other and tucking ends under center of roll. Flatten loaf slightly.

Cover loaves and let rise in a warm place until almost doubled (about 40 minutes). Brush with egg yolk mix-

ture and bake in a 350° oven until browned (40 to 45 minutes). Transfer to a rack; let cool for 20 minutes, then serve warm. Or, if made ahead, let cool completely; wrap airtight and freeze. To reheat, wrap frozen loaves in foil; heat in a 350° oven for 50 minutes.

To serve, brush half the glaze on each warm loaf. Immediately sprinkle with almonds. Makes 2 loaves.

Sugar Glaze. Beat together 1 tablespoon **butter** or margarine (melted), 2 tablespoons **hot water**, 1½ cups **powdered sugar**, and ¼ teaspoon grated **lemon peel** until smooth.

Cakes

To many of us, Christmas cake means only fruitcake—rich, dense loaves of wall-to-wall fruit and nuts, cut into thin slices that gleam with the gold of apricots and pineapple, the red and green of candied cherries. But other cakes shouldn't be forgotten. Dainty cheesecake miniatures, buttery pound cakes soaked with liqueur, even old-fashioned carrot cake are all worthy of a place on the holiday table. In these pages, we've selected some of our favorite Christmas cakes—some with fruit, some without, and all exceptionally good.

Liqueur Pound Cake

Rich cakes soaked in liqueur are a delightful surprise for friends during the holiday season. Because they store well unrefrigerated, they make perfect gifts to leave under the tree or to send to loved ones in distant places. The recipe makes four cakes.

> 1½ cups (¾ lb.) butter or margarine, at room temperature
> 1 pound powdered sugar
> 6 large eggs
> 1 teaspoon vanilla
> 2¾ cups cake flour
> Liqueur Syrup (recipe follows)

In large bowl of an electric mixer, beat butter until creamy. Sift powdered sugar; gradually add to butter, beating until mixture is light and fluffy. Add eggs, 1 at a time, beating well after each addition. Beat in vanilla. Gradually mix flour into creamed mixture.

Scrape batter evenly into four greased, flour-dusted 3½- by 7-inch loaf pans. Smooth top of batter.

Bake in a 300° oven until a wooden pick inserted in center of cake comes out clean (about 50 minutes). Let cool in pans on a rack for 5 minutes. Run a knife around edges of each pan and turn cake out; immediately return cake to pan. With a slender wooden skewer or a fork, poke 1-inch-deep holes, about ½ inch apart, all over top of cake. Immediately pour an equal amount of Liqueur Syrup over each cake. Let cool on a rack for about 30 minutes.

Remove from pans and serve; or wrap securely and store in a cool area for up to 2 weeks, in the refrigerator for up to 1 month, or in the freezer for up to 6 months. Bring to room temperature before serving. Makes 4 cakes, 4 to 6 servings each.

Liqueur Syrup. In a 2- to 3-quart pan, combine 2 cups **sugar**, ½ cup **light corn syrup**, and ¾ cup **water**. Set over medium-high heat and stir slowly until mixture comes to a simmer. Continue heating, without stirring, until mixture boils. Cover and continue to boil until sugar is dissolved and liquid is clear—about 1 minute. (If you don't cover pan and if you stir while syrup boils, crunchy sugar crystals will form in the finished cake.)

Remove from heat, uncover, and let stand until slightly cooled (about 5 minutes). Stir in 1¼ cups **rum** or almond-, hazelnut-, or orange-flavored liqueur. Use; or let cool, then cover and let stand at room temperature until next day. Makes 3½ cups.

Chocolate Liqueur Pound Cake

Follow directions for **Liqueur Pound Cake**, but decrease powdered sugar to 3 cups (12 oz.). Combine butter and sugar, then add 5 ounces **semisweet chocolate**, melted. Cakes develop a thin, crisp top crust as they bake.

Prepare **Liqueur Syrup** as directed, but decrease water to ½ cup and increase rum or liqueur to 1½ cups. Options include almond-, hazelnut-, orange-, coffee-, and chocolate-flavored liqueur. As syrup soaks through cake, top crust softens.

Carrot Cake

The best cakes are good any time—so there's no reason your friends shouldn't enjoy carrot cake during the Christmas season. Topped with a smooth cream cheese frosting and studded with nuts and pineapple, this all-year favorite is just about irresistible.

> 4 large eggs
> 1½ cups salad oil
> 2 cups sugar
> 2 cups all-purpose flour
> 1½ teaspoons baking soda
> 2 teaspoons **each** baking powder and ground cinnamon
> ½ teaspoon ground nutmeg
> 1 teaspoon salt
> 2 cups shredded carrots
> ½ cup coarsely chopped walnuts or pecans
> 1 can (8 oz.) crushed pineapple, drained
> Cream Cheese Frosting (recipe follows)

In a large bowl, beat eggs just until blended; add oil and sugar and beat until thoroughly mixed. In another bowl, stir together flour, baking soda, baking powder, cinnamon, nutmeg, and salt. Add to egg mixture, stirring just until blended; then mix in carrots, walnuts, and pineapple.

Pour batter into a greased, flour-dusted 9- by 13-inch baking pan or a 12-cup fluted tube or Bundt pan. Bake in a 350° oven until a wooden pick inserted in center comes out clean (45 minutes for a 9- by 13-inch pan, 55 minutes for a tube or Bundt pan).

Let cool. If you used a tube or Bundt pan, let cake cool in pan on a rack for 15 minutes; then invert onto rack and let cool completely.

Spread Cream Cheese Frosting over cooled cake. Makes 12 to 15 servings.

Cream Cheese Frosting. In small bowl of an electric mixer, combine 2 small packages (3 oz. *each*) **cream cheese**, at room temperature; 6 tablespoons **butter** or margarine, at room temperature; and 1 teaspoon grated **orange peel**. Beat until smooth. Add 1 teaspoon **vanilla** and 2 cups **powdered sugar**; beat until creamy. (Or combine all ingredients in a food processor and whirl until blended.)

Golden Apricot-Almond Fruitcake

Here's an exceptionally pretty light fruitcake, made with dried apricots, slivered almonds, and lots of golden raisins. Bake it in two large or four smaller loaves; spoon rum over the hot cakes for extra flavor, if you like.

1½	cups dried apricots
⅔	cup water
¾	cup (⅜ lb.) butter or margarine, at room temperature
¾	cup sugar
4	large eggs
½	teaspoon **each** salt and baking soda
2	cups all-purpose flour
1	cup **each** red candied cherries and slivered almonds
1½	cups golden raisins
½	teaspoon grated lemon peel
¼	cup rum (optional)

Cut apricots into quarters. In a 1-quart pan, combine apricots and water; bring to a boil, then reduce heat and simmer, uncovered, until tender (about 2 minutes). Let cool.

In large bowl of an electric mixer, beat butter and sugar until creamy. Add eggs, 1 at a time, beating well after each addition. Stir together salt, baking soda, and 1½ cups of the flour; stir into creamed mixture. Combine cooled apricots with cherries, almonds, raisins, lemon peel, and remaining ½ cup flour; add to batter and blend well.

Spoon batter into 2 greased, flour-dusted 4½- by 8½-inch loaf pans or 4 greased, flour-dusted 3⅜- by 7⅜-inch loaf pans. Bake in a 275° oven until a wooden pick inserted in center of cake comes out clean (about 1½ hours; 1¼ hours for smaller cakes).

Let cool in pans on racks. If desired, spoon 2 tablespoons rum over each cake (1 tablespoon over each small cake) while cakes are still warm. To store, turn out of pans; wrap airtight and refrigerate or freeze. Makes 2 large or 4 smaller loaves.

Spiced Apple Fruitcake

Unlike most fruitcakes, this spicy version is made entirely with dried fruits—in particular, plenty of dried apples—rather than the usual candied cherries, pineapple, and peels. Applesauce makes the cake deliciously moist.

1	package (8 oz.) mixed dried fruit, chopped
1	package (6 oz.) dried apples, chopped
¼	cup brandy
½	cup water
2¼	cups sugar
¾	cup **each** golden and dark raisins
¾	cup (⅜ lb.) butter or margarine, at room temperature
3	large eggs
1	teaspoon grated lemon peel
1	jar (14 oz.) applesauce
3	cups all-purpose flour
¼	teaspoon salt
¾	teaspoon **each** baking soda and ground cloves
1½	teaspoons **each** baking powder and ground cinnamon
1½	cups coarsely chopped walnuts, almonds, or hazelnuts
	Brandy (optional)

In a pan, combine mixed dried fruit, apples, the ¼ cup brandy, water, and ¼ cup of the sugar. Bring to a boil; then reduce heat, cover, and simmer until liquid is absorbed (about 10 minutes). Add raisins; set aside.

In large bowl of an electric mixer, beat butter and remaining 2 cups sugar until creamy. Add eggs, 1 at a time, beating well after each addition. Blend in lemon peel and applesauce. In another bowl, stir together 2½ cups of the flour, salt, baking soda, cloves, baking powder, and cinnamon; stir into creamed mixture. Combine dried fruit mixture, walnuts, and remaining ½ cup flour. Add to batter and stir to blend.

Spoon batter into 2 greased, flour-dusted (or paper-lined) 5- by 9-inch loaf pans or 4 greased, flour-dusted 3⅜- by 7⅜-inch loaf pans. Bake in a 325° oven until a wooden pick inserted in center of cakes comes out clean (about 1¾ hours for large loaves, 1 hour for small loaves).

Let cool in pans on racks. If desired, spoon 2 tablespoons brandy over each cake (1 tablespoon over each small cake) while cakes are still warm. To store, turn out of pans; wrap airtight and refrigerate or freeze. Makes 2 large or 4 small loaves.

Colorful Fruitcake Rounds

(Pictured at right)

Miniature home-baked fruitcakes make especially attractive gifts. These are baked in small juice cans; when they're sliced, big chunks of fruit and nuts show in a colorful pattern.

- 1 package (6 oz.) dried apricots, quartered
- 2 packages (8 oz. **each**) pitted dates, snipped into thirds
- 1 pound candied pineapple, cut into ½-inch pieces
- 1 package (8 oz.) **each** red and green candied cherries, halved
- 1 cup **each** walnut halves and whole almonds
- 1 cup Brazil nuts, cut into thirds
- 2 cups all-purpose flour
- 2 teaspoons baking powder
- ½ teaspoon salt
- 4 large eggs
- 1 cup sugar
- ½ teaspoon **each** vanilla and lemon extract

In a large bowl, combine apricots, dates, pineapple, cherries, and all nuts. Mix well; set aside. In another bowl, stir together flour, baking powder, and salt. Set aside. In large bowl of an electric mixer, beat eggs; gradually beat in sugar, vanilla, and lemon extract, beating until thick and lemon-colored. Beat in flour mixture until smooth (about 2 minutes). Pour batter over fruit and nuts, blending thoroughly to separate pieces of fruit.

Thoroughly grease 16 small (6-oz.) metal juice cans with a pastry brush. Pack fruitcake mixture into

A tempting selection of festive cakes to bake for friends includes rich Eggnog Pound Cake and Cheesecake Petits Fours (facing page) and Colorful Fruitcake Rounds (this page).

cans a few tablespoons at a time, filling all spaces; fill cans ¾ full. Arrange cans upright on baking sheets, 1 inch apart, and bake in a 300° oven until a wooden pick inserted in center of cake comes out clean (35 to 40 minutes). Let stand in cans on racks until cool enough to handle. Then remove bottoms of juice cans and gently push out cakes; let cool completely on racks. Wrap well and refrigerate for at least 1 week before slicing.

For individual rounds, cut fruit-cakes crosswise into ½-inch slices with a serrated knife. For gift giving, heat-seal rounds in plastic wrap, if you like, following directions on page 57. Seal 12 individually wrapped rounds at a time, allowing 20 to 30 seconds per batch. Makes about 7½ dozen rounds.

Colorful Fruitcake Loaves

Prepare fruitcake mixture as directed for **Colorful Fruitcake Rounds**;

pack batter evenly into 2 greased 4- by 7-inch loaf pans. Bake in a 300° oven until a wooden pick inserted in center of cakes comes out clean (about 1 hour and 10 minutes). Let cool in pans on racks. Remove from pans, wrap well, and store for at least 1 week before slicing. Makes 2 loaves.

Cheesecake Petits Fours
(Pictured on facing page)

These dainty cheesecake squares are just two-bite size. Served plain or glazed with apricot jam and topped with sliced almonds, they make delicious pick-up-to-eat sweets for a tea or open house.

- 2¼ cups graham cracker crumbs
- ¾ cup sugar
- 5 tablespoons butter or margarine, melted
- 3 large packages (8 oz. **each**) cream cheese
- 1 tablespoon lemon juice
- 1½ teaspoons grated lemon peel
- 4 large eggs
- 1½ cups sour cream
- 1 cup apricot jam (optional)
- ½ cup sliced almonds (optional)

Combine graham cracker crumbs, 3 tablespoons of the sugar, and butter; mix well. Pat crumb mixture over the bottom of a rimmed 10- by 15-inch baking pan. Bake in a 350° oven for 5 minutes. Let cool on a rack.

In large bowl of an electric mixer, beat together cream cheese, remaining sugar, lemon juice, and lemon peel. Add eggs, 1 at a time, beating well after each addition. Blend in sour cream. Pour cheesecake mixture over crust and spread evenly.

Bake in a 350° oven until cheesecake looks set in center when pan is gently shaken (about 20 minutes). Let cool on a rack. Cover and refrigerate until cold (at least 3 hours) or for up to 2 days.

Using a sharp knife, cut into about 1½-inch squares. Draw knife smoothly across cheesecake; wipe blade after each cut. With a spatula, lift squares from pan onto a serving plate.

If you want to glaze the squares, heat jam in a 1-quart or smaller pan until melted, stirring. Spoon evenly onto top of each cheesecake petit four. Top each with 2 or 3 amond slices, if desired. Serve petits fours, or let stand for up to 2 hours; or refrigerate, uncovered, for up to 4 hours. Makes 5½ dozen; allow 3 or 4 pieces per person.

Eggnog Pound Cake
(Pictured on facing page)

Luscious-tasting pound cake is easy to make in a hurry when you start with cake mix and purchased eggnog. To enhance the festive eggnog flavor, we added a little extra nutmeg and rum.

- About 2 tablespoons butter or margarine, at room temperature
- ½ cup sliced almonds
- 1 package (about 18¼ oz.) yellow cake mix
- ⅛ teaspoon ground nutmeg
- 2 large eggs
- 1½ cups commercial eggnog
- ¼ cup (⅛ lb.) butter or margarine, melted
- 2 tablespoons rum or ¼ teaspoon rum flavoring

Generously butter a 10-inch fluted tube or Bundt pan, using about 2 tablespoons butter. Press almonds on sides and bottom of pan; set pan aside.

In large bowl of an electric mixer, combine cake mix, nutmeg, eggs, eggnog, the ¼ cup melted butter, and rum. Beat on medium speed until smooth and creamy—about 4 minutes.

Pour batter into prepared pan. Bake in a 350° oven until a wooden pick inserted in center comes out clean (45 to 55 minutes). Let cool in

pan on a rack for 10 minutes; then invert cake onto rack and let cool completely. Makes 10 to 12 servings.

Raisin-Nut Loaves

Baked in shiny foil pans, these moist, spicy little loaves are ready to give as gifts almost as soon as you take them from the oven. You might wrap the unfrosted cakes—pans and all—in plastic wrap, then decorate with bright ribbon bows. Or ice the loaves with Cream Cheese Frosting and present them, unwrapped, to favorite neighbors.

- 2 cups **each** sugar, water, and raisins
- ½ cup (¼ lb.) butter or margarine
- 3 cups all-purpose flour
- 1 teaspoon **each** baking soda, ground allspice, ground nutmeg, and ground cinnamon
- 1 tablespoon bourbon whiskey or water
- ½ cup chopped walnuts
  Cream Cheese Frosting (page 43), optional

In a 3-quart pan, combine sugar, water, raisins, and butter. Bring to a boil, stirring until butter is melted; then reduce heat, cover, and simmer for 10 minutes. Let cool to room temperature, but do not refrigerate.

Stir together flour, baking soda, allspice, nutmeg, and cinnamon; gradually add to cooled sugar mixture, mixing until well blended. Stir in bourbon and walnuts. Pour batter into 4 greased, flour-dusted small foil loaf pans, each about 3½ by 6 inches. Bake in a 350° oven until a wooden pick inserted in center of cake comes out clean (about 45 minutes). Let cool in pans on a rack. Spread with Cream Cheese Frosting, if desired. Or, to store, wrap unfrosted loaves tightly in plastic wrap and hold at room temperature for up to 2 weeks. Frost just before serving, if desired. Makes 4 loaves.

Candies

Visions of sugarplums belong to just about everybody's view of Christmas. And in these pages, we've gathered a collection of candies worth dreaming about: creamy fudge, tangy fruit bonbons, toffee topped with milk chocolate and hazelnuts. They're all perfect for holiday giving.

Creamy Vanilla Caramels

Creamy-rich, individually wrapped homemade caramels take time to prepare, but they're a marvelous gift for the candy lovers on your list.

    2   cups sugar
    1   cup light corn syrup
    2   cups half-and-half or
        light cream, at room
        temperature
    ½   cup (¼ lb.) butter or
        margarine, at room
        temperature
    1   teaspoon vanilla
    ½   teaspoon salt

In a heavy 3-quart pan, combine sugar, corn syrup, and 1 cup of the half-and-half. Bring to a full boil over medium heat, stirring constantly; then boil for 10 minutes, stirring.

Still stirring constantly, add remaining 1 cup half-and-half very slowly; mixture should continue to boil as you add half-and-half. Continue to boil for 5 more minutes, stirring constantly. Then add butter, about 1 tablespoon at a time, stirring; mixture should continue to boil.

Position a candy thermometer in caramel mixture; when temperature reaches 230°F, reduce heat to medium-low. Continue to cook and stir until temperature reaches 248°F. Immediately remove from heat and let cool for 10 minutes; then stir in vanilla and salt. Pour into a well-buttered 8-inch square baking pan. Let cool until firm.

With a knife, loosen candy around pan edges; then turn out of pan (if it doesn't come out easily, set pan over low heat for a few seconds). With a paper towel, wipe any extra butter off surface. Using a sharp, heavy knife and a sawing motion, cut candy into 1- by 2-inch pieces. Wrap individually in wax paper or plastic wrap. Makes 32 pieces (about 1½ pounds).

Chocolate Creme Fudge

A simplified method using marshmallow creme makes this creamy fudge just about foolproof. In very little time, you can make several batches for entertaining or gift giving.

For variety, you might want to change the basic fudge's flavor. We include easy directions for peppermint, chocolate-peanut, and butterscotch fudges—and even a "blond" fudge made with white candy coating and lightly accented with lemon peel.

We suggest cutting the fudge into squares for serving; you can also pat the squares into balls and roll them in finely chopped nuts or coconut.

    1   can (5 oz.) evaporated
          milk
    1⅓   cups sugar
    ¼   teaspoon salt
    ¼   cup (⅛ lb.) butter or
          margarine
    1   package (6 oz.)
          semisweet chocolate chips
    ¾   cup or ½ jar (7-oz. size)
          marshmallow creme
    1   teaspoon vanilla
    ½   cup chopped walnuts
          or pecans

In a 2½- to 3-quart pan, combine evaporated milk, sugar, salt, and butter. Bring to a rolling boil over medium-low heat, stirring; boil for 5 minutes, stirring constantly. (If heat is too high, mixture will scorch.)

Remove from heat; add chocolate chips and stir until melted. Quickly stir in marshmallow creme, vanilla, and walnuts until blended. Pour into a buttered 8-inch square or round baking pan; spread to make an even layer. Let cool, then cover and refrigerate. Cut into 1-inch squares to serve. If made ahead, wrap airtight and refrigerate for up to 2 weeks. Makes 2 pounds (about 5 dozen pieces).

Peppermint Creme Fudge

Follow directions for **Chocolate Creme Fudge**, but omit walnuts. Instead, stir in ⅔ cup crushed **hard peppermint candy**.

Choco-Peanut Creme Fudge

Follow directions for **Chocolate Creme Fudge**, but omit salt and butter; instead, combine 1 cup **crunchy peanut butter** with milk and sugar. Omit walnuts; add ¼ cup coarsely chopped **unsalted peanuts**.

Butterscotch Fudge

Follow directions for **Chocolate Creme Fudge**, but substitute 1 package (6 oz.) **butterscotch-flavored chips** for chocolate chips.

Blond Creme Fudge

Follow directions for **Chocolate Creme Fudge**, but omit chocolate chips. Instead, add 6 ounces **white candy coating** (for buying information, see Almond Bark, page 50), coarsely chopped, and ½ teaspoon grated **lemon peel**.

Peanut Butter–Brown Sugar Fudge

The world is full of peanut butter lovers—and any one of them would love a panful of this creamy fudge at holiday time.

- 1 cup firmly packed brown sugar
- 2 tablespoons butter or margarine
- 1 cup granulated sugar
- ½ cup evaporated milk
- ¼ cup creamy peanut butter
- 1 cup miniature marshmallows
- 1 teaspoon vanilla
- ¼ cup chopped dry-roasted peanuts

In a 3- to 4-quart pan, combine brown sugar, butter, granulated sugar, and evaporated milk. Bring to a boil over high heat, then boil until syrup registers 234°F (soft ball stage) on a candy thermometer (about 5 minutes).

Add peanut butter and sprinkle in marshmallows; *do not stir.* Remove from heat and let cool to about 150°F. Add vanilla. With a wooden spoon, beat vigorously until mixture is creamy and loses its shiny appearance (about 5 minutes).

Quickly spread in a well-buttered 8- or 9-inch square pan. Sprinkle peanuts over top and press in lightly. Let stand, uncovered, until firm; cut into 1- to 1½-inch squares to serve. If made ahead, cover and refrigerate for up to 1 week. Makes 3 to 7 dozen pieces.

Hazelnut Chocolate Truffles

Think about making these enticing truffles for a friend who likes European-style milk chocolate—the kind that's flavored with hazelnuts. Made from hazelnut "butter" mixed with melted chocolate and egg yolks, they're very rich and very special.

(For the chocolate, you can use either bar chocolate or chips.)

- 1 cup hazelnuts
- ¾ cup (⅜ lb.) butter or margarine, melted
- 3 ounces **each** semisweet chocolate and milk chocolate
- 5 large egg yolks
- 1 cup unsifted powdered sugar
- 1 teaspoon vanilla
  About 1 cup chocolate sprinkles or finely chopped nuts

Spread hazelnuts in a shallow baking pan and toast in a 350° oven until pale golden beneath skins (10 to 15 minutes), shaking pan occasionally. Let nuts cool slightly, then pour into a dishcloth and fold cloth to enclose. Rub briskly between your palms to remove as much of skins as possible. Chop nuts.

Pour 6 tablespoons of the butter into a blender or food processor. Add chopped nuts and whirl until very smooth and creamy, stopping motor periodically to stir nut mixture. Set mixture aside.

In a small pan, heat remaining 6 tablespoons butter until it bubbles and foams. Remove from heat, add semisweet and milk chocolates; stir until melted and smooth; set aside.

In large bowl of an electric mixer, beat egg yolks until foamy. Gradually add sugar, beating until mixture is thick; add vanilla. With mixer on medium speed, add nut-butter mixture, 1 tablespoon at a time, beating well after each addition. Then begin adding warm chocolate mixture, 1 teaspoon at a time, beating briskly after each addition. After 6 teaspoons have been added, increase additions to 1 tablespoon; when all chocolate has been added, continue to beat until mixture is well blended and smooth. Cover and refrigerate for 30 minutes.

Put chocolate sprinkles in a small bowl. Scoop out rounded teaspoonfuls of the truffle mixture and form into balls, then roll in sprinkles to coat. If made ahead, cover and refrigerate for up to 10 days or freeze for up to 1 month. Makes about 7 dozen truffles.

Apricot Slims
(Pictured on page 49)

Dried apricots, coconut, a spoonful of orange juice, and some chopped nuts are all you need to make these tangy delights.

- 1 package (6 oz.) dried apricots
- ⅓ cup unsweetened grated or flaked coconut
- 1 tablespoon orange juice
  About ¼ cup finely chopped almonds

If apricots are not moist, place them in a wire strainer and steam over simmering water for 5 minutes.

Put apricots through a food chopper fitted with a fine blade. Add coconut and put through food chopper again. Stir in orange juice and mix well. (Or combine apricots, coconut, and orange juice in a food processor and whirl until mixture begins to hold together in a ball—about 1 minute.) Divide mixture into 4 equal parts and wrap each in wax paper or plastic wrap. Refrigerate until cold and easy to handle.

To shape each part, sprinkle about 1 tablespoon almonds on a board; roll dough back and forth with your palms over nuts, forming a 16-inch rope. To serve, slice diagonally into 2-inch pieces. Makes 32 pieces.

Pear Slims

Follow directions for **Apricot Slims**, but substitute 6 ounces **moist-pack dried pears** for apricots; remove any bits of stem or core from pears. Instead of orange juice, use 1 tablespoon **lemon juice**; instead of almonds, roll each rope in about 1 tablespoon **unsweetened grated or flaked coconut**.

Fruit & Nut Slices
(Pictured on facing page)

A little less rich than many Christmas candies, these chewy treats will still satisfy a sweet tooth. To make them, you just grind together dried fruit, nuts, and coconut, then blend the mixture with peanut butter. (Use either creamy or crunchy peanut butter, as you prefer.)

8	ounces dried figs (about 1 cup lightly packed)
1	package (8 oz.) pitted dates
1	cup **each** raisins and unsweetened grated or flaked coconut
1½	cups chopped almonds or walnuts
1	teaspoon grated lemon peel
¼	cup lemon juice
1	cup peanut butter

Combine figs, dates, raisins, coconut, and 1 cup of the almonds. Put mixture twice through a food chopper fitted with a medium blade. Or combine ingredients in a bowl, then whirl in a food processor, a portion at a time, until mixture begins to hold together in a ball (about 1 minute); start and stop motor 4 or 5 times and push mixture down from sides of work bowl as necessary.

Add lemon peel, lemon juice, and peanut butter; mix well with a wooden spoon. Divide mixture in half and shape each half into a log about 12 inches long.

For each log, sprinkle ¼ cup of remaining almonds on a piece of wax paper and roll log in almonds to coat. Wrap tightly and refrigerate for at least 3 hours or until ready to serve; then cut into ⅜-inch slices. Makes about 5 dozen pieces.

Fruit & Granola Slices

Follow directions for **Fruit & Nut Slices**, but omit almonds. Instead, stir 1 cup **granola-style cereal** (break up any large lumps before measuring) into fruits after grinding. Coat each log with about ⅓ cup **granola-style cereal**.

Coconut-Date Logs
(Pictured on facing page)

Anybody who likes granola cereal will enjoy these goodies. Plenty of dates, granola, and nuts combine in crunchy little logs coated with coconut.

1	package (8 oz.) pitted dates, snipped
½	cup (¼ lb.) butter or margarine
1	teaspoon vanilla
¾	cup finely chopped walnuts, almonds, or pecans
¾	cup granola-style cereal (break up any large lumps before measuring)
	About ⅔ cup unsweetened grated or flaked coconut

In a pan, combine dates, butter, and vanilla. Place over low heat and stir until butter is melted and blended with dates (about 4 minutes). Refrigerate just until mixture is firm enough to mold and shape. Mix in walnuts and granola.

Sprinkle coconut on a plate or a sheet of wax paper. To shape each candy, press about 1 tablespoon of the mixture into a log about 1½ inches long; then roll in coconut to cover completely. Makes about 3 dozen.

Walnut Nuggets
(Pictured on facing page)

A tray of tempting dried fruits—plump prunes, apricots, dates, and more—is traditional Christmas fare in many households. Here, those classic fruits are combined with candied cherries and lots of nuts in an appealing candy. For an extra-pretty finish, each piece is topped with a perfect walnut half.

10	ounces walnut halves or pieces
5½	ounces whole blanched or unblanched almonds
1	package (8 oz.) pitted dates
½	cup moist-pack pitted prunes
4	ounces (about ¾ cup) dried apricots
2	tablespoons lemon juice
5	ounces (about ¾ cup) red candied cherries, finely chopped

Pick out about 36 of the most perfect walnut halves or large pieces; set aside. Combine remaining walnuts and almonds; you should have 2½ to 3 cups. Then combine nuts with dates, prunes, and apricots. Put mixture twice through a food chopper fitted with a medium blade. Or combine ingredients in a bowl, then whirl in a food processor, a portion at a time, until mixture begins to hold together in a ball (about 1 minute); start and stop motor 4 or 5 times and push mixture down from sides of work bowl as necessary.

With a fork or your fingers, mix in lemon juice and cherries until well blended. Divide into 3 equal parts and roll each into a 12-inch log (refrigerate briefly if too soft to roll). Wrap each roll tightly in wax paper or plastic wrap and refrigerate for at least 3 hours or until ready to serve. Then cut into 1-inch sections, turn cut side down, and press a walnut half into top of each. Makes about 3 dozen pieces.

Make up a pretty trayful *of sweets with refreshingly light fruit flavors this holiday season.*
From left to right on platter, here are Apricot Slims (page 47) and Walnut Nuggets, Coconut-
Date Logs, and Fruit & Nut Slices (facing page).

Sugared Walnuts & Pecans

Sweet and crunchy sugared nuts are always a welcome treat. These are lightly spiced with cinnamon and nutmeg and sparked with a touch of orange peel.

- 4 cups walnut or pecan halves; or 2 cups of each
- 3/4 cup firmly packed brown sugar
- 1/3 cup evaporated milk
- 1/2 teaspoon **each** ground cinnamon and grated orange peel
- 1/4 teaspoon ground nutmeg

Spread nuts evenly in a large, shallow baking pan. Toast in a 350° oven for about 5 minutes; let cool.

In a pan, stir together sugar, evaporated milk, cinnamon, orange peel, and nutmeg. Bring to a boil over medium heat; boil for 2 minutes without stirring. Remove from heat; let cool for 3 to 5 minutes, then pour evenly over nuts in baking pan. Mix quickly until nuts are well coated. Spread nuts out again in pan and let dry for several hours; then lift with a spatula and break apart. Store airtight. Makes 4 cups.

Homemade Marzipan

As easily as you form dough into breads and rolls, you can turn lumps of marzipan into simple shapes—fruits, vegetables, conical trees, even piglets or chicks. The smooth nut paste, made from finely ground almonds, sugar, and egg whites, handles much like children's play-dough.

When you make your own marzipan from fresh almonds, it has a delicious natural nut flavor, remarkably different from the typical brightly colored, heavily flavored candy store confections. (It's less expensive than purchased marzipan, too.) Lightly browning the marzipan shapes in the oven brings out the flavor.

- 1 pound (about 3 cups) whole blanched almonds
- 3 cups sugar
- 3 large egg whites
- 1 teaspoon orange flower water
- 1/4 teaspoon almond extract
- 2 to 3 tablespoons light corn syrup
- 1 large egg yolk mixed with 1 tablespoon water

In a food processor or blender, whirl 1/3 of the almonds until powdery (there should not be any discernible pieces of nuts). Add 1 cup of the sugar and process until blended. Empty into a large bowl; repeat with remaining almonds and remaining 2 cups sugar.

Beat egg whites with a fork until frothy. Mix in orange flower water, almond extract, and 2 tablespoons of the corn syrup. Drizzle egg white mixture over almond mixture; mix thoroughly with a heavy-duty mixer on low speed or work mixture with your hands as if you were kneading dough.

Form marzipan into a ball; if it doesn't hold together easily, work in a little more corn syrup. Place in an airtight plastic container; refrigerate for at least 2 days or up to 2 weeks before shaping.

To shape marzipan, use about 1½ tablespoons for each piece, keeping in mind that very thick or very thin candies will not brown evenly. Place your creations on ungreased baking sheets. (At this point, you may cover lightly with plastic wrap and let stand at room temperature for up to 24 hours.)

To bake, brush *very lightly* with egg yolk mixture. Bake in a 400° oven just until bottoms are lightly browned (5 to 6 minutes). Then broil 3 to 4 inches below heat just until tops are browned to your liking; watch constantly so candies won't burn.

With a wide spatula, transfer marzipan to wire racks to cool. Serve; or package airtight and store for up to 1 week. Makes 2½ to 2¾ pounds (about 3¾ cups), enough for 40 to 48 pieces.

Almond Bark

Here's a confection that couldn't be much simpler to make: you just melt semisweet chocolate or white candy coating, then stir in whole toasted almonds.

White candy coating is sometimes called white chocolate; it's sold in most candy stores, at the candy counters of some department stores, and in some well-stocked supermarkets.

- 1 cup whole unblanched almonds
- 3 packages (6 oz. **each**) semisweet chocolate chips or 1 pound white candy coating
- 2 tablespoons solid vegetable shortening (do not substitute butter or other shortening)

Spread almonds in a baking pan and toast in a 350° oven for about 8 minutes, shaking pan occasionally. Let cool.

Line a rimmed 10- by 15-inch baking pan with wax paper, covering bottom and sides of pan.

Place chocolate chips or candy coating in the top of a double boiler. Add shortening; stir over barely simmering water just until mixture begins to melt. Remove from heat; stir until completely melted. Stir in toasted almonds.

Turn mixture into pan and spread to distribute nuts evenly; to spread more smoothly, drop pan onto counter several times from a height of about 8 inches. Refrigerate candy just until firm. Break into pieces before serving. To store, cover airtight and refrigerate for up to 3 weeks. Makes about 1¼ pounds.

Rocky Road

Like the popular ice cream, this quick-to-fix chocolate candy is studded with marshmallows and nuts. The recipe makes a lot, so you can give some away as gifts and still have a supply on hand for the family.

- 1 large package (12 oz.) semisweet chocolate chips or 12 ounces white candy coating
- 2 tablespoons solid vegetable shortening (do not substitute butter or other shortening)
- 1 bag (10½ oz.) miniature marshmallows
- 2 cups coarsely chopped nuts

Line two 8-inch square pans with wax paper, covering bottoms and sides of pans. (Or arrange 8 to 10 dozen paper bonbon cases on rimmed baking sheets.)

Place chocolate chips or candy coating in the top of a double boiler. Add shortening; stir over barely simmering water just until mixture begins to melt. Remove from heat; stir until completely melted. Stir in marshmallows and nuts.

Divide mixture between pans, spreading it evenly over pan bottoms; or drop by rounded teaspoonfuls into bonbon cases. Refrigerate just until firm. Before serving, cut candy in pans into 1-inch squares. To store, cover airtight and refrigerate for up to 3 weeks. Makes 8 to 10 dozen pieces.

Hazelnut-topped Toffee

Chocolate candy bars make a quick coating for this caramel-flavored toffee. You need to lay the chocolate atop the toffee as soon as it's poured into the pan—so have the bars unwrapped and ready to use before you start to cook.

- 1 cup (½ lb.) butter (do not substitute margarine)
- 1 cup firmly packed brown sugar
- 6 bars (1⅜ oz. **each**) milk chocolate
- ½ cup finely chopped hazelnuts

In a deep pan, combine butter and sugar. Cook over medium-high heat, stirring constantly, until mixture registers 300°F (hard crack stage) on a candy thermometer. Pour immediately into a buttered 9-inch square baking pan. Lay chocolate bars evenly over hot candy and let stand until softened, then spread into a smooth layer. Sprinkle with hazelnuts, pressing them in lightly with your fingers.

Refrigerate until chocolate is firm. Invert candy onto a flat surface and break apart into small pieces. Makes about 3 dozen pieces.

Chocolate Toffee

Ground sweet chocolate, plenty of walnuts, and a full pint of cream go into a luscious candy that's sure to please even the sweetest sweet tooth.

- 3 cups sugar
- 1 cup dark corn syrup
- ½ cup (¼ lb.) butter or margarine
- ¼ cup ground sweet chocolate
- 2 cups whipping cream
- 1½ cups chopped walnuts
- 2 teaspoons vanilla

Combine sugar, corn syrup, butter, ground chocolate, and cream in a wide, deep, heavy frying pan. Bring to a boil; boil, stirring occasionally, until candy registers 280°F (hard ball stage) on a candy thermometer (about 1 hour). Sprinkle ¾ cup of the walnuts over bottom of a buttered, shallow 11- by 15-inch baking pan or over a buttered marble slab. Remove candy from heat and stir in vanilla. Pour at once into prepared pan (or onto marble) and sprinkle remaining ¾ cup walnuts evenly over top.

Let cool for about 10 minutes, then score in 1-inch squares with sharp knife. Let cool in pan for several hours. Then invert pan and tap lightly to remove candy. Finish cutting; set pieces in small paper cups or pack between layers of wax paper in an airtight container. Makes 2 pounds.

Almond Toffee

Slivered almonds and almond extract flavor this rich toffee. Set each square in a little paper bonbon cup, if you like; or just arrange the squares in a pretty tin or other airtight container.

- 1 cup **each** sugar and dark corn syrup
- ¼ cup (⅛ lb.) butter or margarine
- 1 cup whipping cream
- 1 teaspoon vanilla
- ½ teaspoon almond extract
- ½ cup slivered almonds

Combine sugar, corn syrup, butter, and cream in a heavy 3-quart pan. Bring to a boil, stirring. Then simmer slowly over low heat, stirring occasionally, until candy registers 280°F (hard ball stage) on a candy thermometer (about 45 minutes). Remove from heat; stir in vanilla and almond extract. Pour into a well-buttered, shallow 7- by 11-inch baking pan or onto a buttered marble slab. Sprinkle almonds over top. Let cool for about 10 minutes, then score in 1-inch squares with a sharp knife. Let cool for several hours in pan. Then invert pan and tap lightly to remove candy. Finish cutting along original scoring lines; set pieces of candy in small paper cups or pack them between layers of wax paper in an airtight container. Makes about 1 pound.

Preserves & Relishes

A jar or two of your own bright homemade jam or relish is a gift that's sure to be appreciated. If you like, dress up the jars as suggested on page 57; for the relishes and chutneys, you might also attach a tag offering ideas for use. And if you're giving a preserve that must be refrigerated, be sure to note that on the label, too.

If you want to make a bigger batch of jam, jelly, or marmalade, don't double the recipe; if you do, you may end up with liquid. Instead, just prepare the recipe two times.

Pear Jam

This fresh-tasting jam is marvelous on toast, English muffins, bagels, even warm gingerbread.

 3 *pounds pears*
 ¼ *cup lemon juice*
 1 *box (2 oz.) dry pectin*
 5½ *cups sugar*

Spicy Pepper Jellies *(facing page), sparkling with Christmas red and green, make a delicious accompaniment to fresh cream cheese and crackers.*

Peel, core, and cube pears, then mash with a potato masher (or whirl in a food processor, but do not purée). You should have 4 cups mashed fruit.

In an 8- to 10-quart pan, combine fruit, lemon juice, and pectin. Place over high heat; stirring constantly, bring to a rolling boil that cannot be stirred down. Still stirring, add sugar. Return to a boil that cannot be stirred down, then boil for exactly 2 minutes. Remove from heat and skim off foam.

Ladle jam into hot, sterilized ½- or 1-pint canning jars, filling to within ¼ inch of rims. Wipe rims clean; top with hot, sterilized lids and firmly screw on bands.

Place jars, sides not touching, on a rack in a canning or other deep kettle; add boiling water to cover jars by 1 to 2 inches. Hold at simmering (180°F) for 10 minutes. Lift out jars and let cool on a towel away from drafts.

Test seal of each jar by pressing center of lid. If it stays down, seal is good. If it pops up, there's no seal; refrigerate unsealed jam and use within 1 month. Makes 6½ cups.

Spicy Pepper Jelly
(Pictured on facing page)

Bright red or green bell peppers give a delightfully assertive flavor to this jelly. Serve as a festive accompaniment to meat or as a topping for crackers spread with cream cheese.

- 4   *large green or red bell peppers, seeded and cut into pieces*
- 2½   *cups vinegar*
- 6   *cups sugar*
- 2   *pouches (3 oz. **each**) liquid pectin*

Place cut-up bell peppers in a blender or food processor and whirl until finely chopped. Pour into a 5-quart pan and stir in vinegar and sugar until well blended. Bring to a rolling boil over high heat, stirring constantly. Pour in pectin all at once and return to a boil; cook, uncovered, stirring frequently, until thickened

(about 3 minutes). Remove from heat and skim off foam.

Pour jelly into hot, sterilized ½-pint canning jars, filling to within about ⅛ inch of rims. Wipe rims clean; top with hot, sterilized lids and firmly screw on bands. Let cool on a towel away from drafts. Test seal of each jar by pressing center of lid. If it stays down, seal is good. If it pops up, there's no seal; store unsealed jelly in the refrigerator and use within 1 month. Makes 3 pints.

Cranberry-Orange Jam

This recipe offers you a choice of textures. It cooks down into a tangy, thick jam—or, for a smooth and glistening jelly, it can be poured through a jelly bag or small sterilized wire strainer when you fill the jars.

- 1   *pound fresh cranberries*
- 3   *cups water*
- ¾   *cup orange juice*
- ¼   *cup lemon juice*
- 4   *cups sugar*
- 2   *pouches (3 oz. **each**) liquid pectin*

Rinse cranberries well and place in a 5-quart pan. Add water and bring to a boil; reduce heat and simmer, uncovered, for 10 minutes. Drain well, reserving liquid. Place berries in a blender or food processor and whirl until puréed, then add enough of the reserved liquid to make 4 cups.

Return berry purée to pan and stir in orange juice, lemon juice, and sugar until well blended. Bring mixture to a boil over high heat, stirring constantly; boil, uncovered, for 1 minute. Remove from heat and stir in pectin all at once. Skim off foam.

Ladle jam into hot, sterilized ½-pint canning jars, filling to within ⅛ inch of rims. Skim off any foam. Wipe rims clean; top with hot, sterilized lids and firmly screw on bands. Let cool on a towel away from drafts. Test seal of each jar by pressing center of lid. If it stays down, seal is good. If it pops up, there's no seal; store unsealed jam in the refrigerator and use within 1 month. Makes 3 pints.

Lemon Marmalade

For this exquisitely tart marmalade, you use only the juice and the thin yellow surface peel of the lemons.

- About 11 *medium-size lemons, rinsed*
- ½   *cup water*
- 6   *cups sugar*
- 1   *pouch (3 oz.) liquid pectin*

Use a sharp knife to slice off all the thin outer yellow peel from lemons; cut peel into slivers. Then squeeze juice from lemons. You should have 1¾ cups peel and 2 cups juice.

Place lemon peel, water, and ½ cup of the lemon juice in a 3-quart pan. Bring to a boil; reduce heat, cover, and simmer, stirring occasionally, until peel is tender and translucent (about 25 minutes).

Stir in sugar and remaining lemon juice until well blended. Bring to a rolling boil over high heat, stirring constantly. Remove from heat, cover, and let stand at room temperature for 18 to 24 hours.

Rapidly return marmalade to a boil, stirring to prevent sticking. Stir in pectin all at once and boil, stirring constantly, for exactly 1 minute. Remove from heat and quickly skim off any foam.

Ladle marmalade into hot, sterilized ½-pint canning jars, filling to within ⅛ inch of rims. Wipe rims clean; top with hot, sterilized lids and firmly screw on bands. Let cool on a towel away from drafts. Test seal of each jar by pressing center of lid. If it stays down, seal is good. If it pops up, there's no seal; store unsealed marmalade in the refrigerator and use within 1 month. Makes 2 pints.

Sweet Red Bell Pepper Relish

Mellow, full-flavored red bell peppers are perfect for a bright relish to serve with barbecued or roasted meat.

> 3 pounds onions (about 6 large onions), cut into 1-inch chunks
>
> 6 pounds red bell peppers (about 12 large peppers), seeded and cut into 1-inch squares
>
> 4 cups distilled white vinegar
>
> 3 cups sugar
>
> 2 tablespoons salt
>
> 1 tablespoon mustard seeds

In a food processor, whirl onions and bell peppers, a portion at a time, until coarsely chopped. (Or put through a food chopper fitted with a medium blade.)

Put vegetables in a 6- to 8-quart pan and stir in vinegar, sugar, salt, and mustard seeds. Bring to a boil over high heat, stirring constantly. Then reduce heat to medium and boil gently, uncovered, until reduced by about a third; stir often to prevent sticking.

Ladle hot relish into 7 or 8 hot, sterilized 1-pint canning jars, filling to within ¼ inch of rims. Run a narrow spatula down between relish and jar to release any air. Wipe rims clean; top with hot, sterilized lids and firmly screw on bands.

Place jars, sides not touching, on a rack in a canning or other deep kettle; add boiling water to cover jars by 1 to 2 inches. Hold at simmering (180°F) for 15 minutes. Lift out jars and let cool on a towel away from drafts. Test seal of each jar by pressing center of lid. If it stays down, seal is good. If it pops up, there's no seal; store unsealed relish in the refrigerator and use within 1 month. Makes 3½ to 4 quarts.

Tomato Lemon Chutney

A sauce for sausages, a spicy chutney, or a sophisticated catsup—pick the definition that appeals to you most. By any description, this condiment adds just the right flourish to a platter of bratwurst or kielbasa.

> 1 or 2 lemons
>
> 1 can (about 1 lb.) tomatoes
>
> 1 tablespoon salad oil or olive oil
>
> 1 small dried hot red chile
>
> 1 tablespoon mustard seeds
>
> ½ teaspoon cumin seeds
>
> ¼ teaspoon ground nutmeg
>
> ½ cup **each** raisins and sugar

Grate enough lemon peel to make 2 teaspoons; set aside.

Using a sharp knife, cut peel and all white membrane from 1 lemon. In a blender, whirl lemon with tomatoes and their liquid just until blended.

In a 1½- to 2-quart pan, combine oil, chile, lemon peel, mustard seeds, cumin seeds, and nutmeg. Cook over medium-high heat, stirring, until seeds begin to pop. Add tomato mixture, raisins, and sugar.

Boil gently, uncovered, until mixture thickens to a jamlike consistency (about 20 minutes), stirring often. Let cool, then cover and refrigerate for up to 3 days; reheat before serving. Makes 1¾ cups.

Mango-Apricot-Date Chutney

Mangoes are the primary ingredient in many chutneys, including the popular Major Grey type. This one's made with dried mangoes from an Asian market—where you'll also find the preserved or pickled ginger. Serve with curries, as a relish alongside meats or poultry, or, spooned over a block of cream cheese, as an appetizer spread with crackers.

> 3½ cups water
>
> ½ pound **each** dried mangoes and dried apricots; or 1 pound dried apricots
>
> ¾ cup **each** golden raisins and currants
>
> 1¼ cups pitted dates, coarsely snipped or chopped
>
> 1½ cups white wine vinegar
>
> 1¼ cups firmly packed brown sugar
>
> 1 cup preserved ginger in syrup or pickled ginger, drained and coarsely chopped
>
> 1 tablespoon mustard seeds
>
> 1½ teaspoons chili powder
> Salt

In a 5- to 6-quart pan, combine water and mangoes. Bring to a simmer, cover, and cook for 5 minutes. Add apricots and continue to simmer, covered, for 5 more minutes. (If using all apricots, simmer for only 5 minutes *total*.) Add raisins, currants, dates, vinegar, sugar, ginger, mustard seeds, and chili powder. Simmer, uncovered, stirring more frequently as mixture thickens, until almost all liquid has evaporated and chutney is thick (45 minutes to 1 hour). Season to taste with salt. Let cool, then spoon into jars; seal jars tightly and refrigerate for up to 2 months. Makes 6 to 7 cups.

Mustards

Spicy or sweet, smooth or coarse—mustards vary widely in texture and flavor. Why not cook up a selection of homemade mustards as a unique holiday gift for the mustard lovers among your friends? Packed in hand-labeled glass jars or stoneware crocks, this savory condiment is one food item almost anyone is sure to appreciate.

When you make your own mustard, you can use whole seeds for a coarse-textured product; if you want a smooth mustard, you'll have to rely on dry mustard (also called mustard flour). If you plan to make several batches, look for bulk seeds or dry mustard in spice shops.

Mustard is hottest when freshly made, mellower as it ages. If you want to give a really hot version, don't make it too far in advance; if you prefer milder mustard, let it age. Most commercial mustards are aged for at least a month before they reach the market.

Below, we offer recipes for a smooth Dijon-style mustard (with two flavor variations) and two coarse mustards: an old-fashioned French type and a spicy German mustard. The French mustard is piquant, medium-hot, and subtly spiced. The German one can be made quite coarse, or puréed more for a smoother texture; it's sweet and warmly spiced.

In making both our smooth and coarse mustards, the first step is to combine dry mustard, or a mixture of mustard seeds and dry mustard, with cold water, then let the mixture stand for 10 to 20 minutes. This soaking is required to release the mustard's full potency and avoid a bitter "off" flavor.

An infusion of vinegar, wine, and spices adds flavor and dilutes the mustard-water paste. The concentration of this mixture also affects the mustard's pungency. When the infusion is reduced by half, as suggested here, the resulting mustard is medium-hot. But cooking heat and time temper mustard's hotness: if you want a very hot mustard, use a more reduced infusion so the mustard will need less cooking to thicken.

French Old-fashioned Mustard

Soak ½ cup **white mustard seeds** and 1 tablespoon **dry mustard** in ½ cup **cold water** for at least 3 hours.

In a 1- to 2-quart noncorrosive pan, combine ½ cup *each* **white wine vinegar** and **dry white wine**; 1 small **onion**, chopped, or ½ cup chopped shallots; 2 cloves **garlic**, minced or pressed; 1 teaspoon *each* **salt** and **sugar**; ½ teaspoon **dry tarragon**; 1 **bay leaf**; and ⅛ teaspoon *each* **ground allspice** and **turmeric**. Simmer, uncovered, over medium heat until reduced by half (10 to 15 minutes). Pour liquid through a wire strainer into mustard seed mixture; whirl in a blender until coarsely ground. Cook in the top of a double boiler over simmering water, stirring occasionally, until thickened (8 to 12 minutes). Let cool, then pack in a covered jar or crock and refrigerate for at least 3 days or up to 2 years. Makes about 1 cup.

Dijon-style Mustard

Smoothly stir ½ cup **cold water** into 1 cup **dry mustard**; let stand for at least 10 minutes.

Meanwhile, in a 2- to 3-quart noncorrosive pan, combine 1⅓ cups *each* **dry white wine** and **white wine vinegar**; 1 small **onion**, chopped, or ½ cup chopped shallots; 3 large cloves **garlic**, pressed or minced; 2 **bay leaves**; 8 **whole allspice**; 2 teaspoons *each* **salt** and **sugar**; and 1 teaspoon **dry tarragon**. Bring to a boil; boil, uncovered, until reduced by half (or slightly more for a hotter mustard)—15 to 20 minutes.

Pour mixture through a wire strainer into mustard paste, pressing all juices out. Blend and cook, stirring occasionally, in the top of a double boiler over simmering water until as thick as very heavy cream (10 to 15 minutes; mixture thickens slightly more as it cools). Let cool, pack into small covered jars or crocks, and refrigerate for up to 2 years. Makes about 2 cups.

Tarragon Dijon Mustard

Follow directions for **Dijon-style Mustard**, stirring 2 teaspoons **dry tarragon** into mustard after cooking.

Green Peppercorn Dijon Mustard

Follow directions for **Dijon-style Mustard**, stirring 2 tablespoons finely chopped **green peppercorns** into mustard after cooking.

Spiced German Mustard

Soak ⅓ cup **white mustard seeds** and ¼ cup **dry mustard** in ½ cup **cold water** for at least 3 hours.

In a 1- to 2-quart noncorrosive pan, combine 1 cup **cider vinegar**; 1 small **onion**, chopped; 2 tablespoons firmly packed **brown sugar**; 1 teaspoon **salt**; 2 cloves **garlic**, pressed or minced; ½ teaspoon **ground cinnamon**; ¼ teaspoon *each* **ground allspice**, **dill seeds**, and **dry tarragon**; and ⅛ teaspoon **turmeric**. Simmer, uncovered, over medium heat until reduced by about half (10 to 15 minutes). Pour liquid through a wire strainer into mustard seed mixture; whirl in a blender or food processor until puréed to the texture you like. Cook in the top of a double boiler over simmering water, stirring occasionally, until thickened (10 to 15 minutes; mustard thickens slightly more as it cools). Stir in 1 to 2 tablespoons **honey**. Let cool, pack in a covered jar or crock, and refrigerate for at least 3 days or up to 2 years. Makes about 1 cup.

Flavored Vinegars

You start with inexpensive jug vinegar and some empty bottles. Then add flavorings, a professional-looking seal, a personalized label, and voilà! It's estate-bottled vinegar, a delicious and practical gift for almost anyone on your Christmas list. Sealed in a handsome decorative bottle, it's even more special.

Flavoring wine vinegars

Fresh herbs, chiles, and whole spices are all ideal flavorings for vinegars. We suggest four seasonings and combinations below; you might also try others, such as rosemary or sweet basil. Whatever your choices, you'll find it surprisingly simple to produce a whole array of different vinegars in very little time.

Be sure to begin the process well in advance, though, since you'll need to let the vinegar stand for several weeks to absorb the flavors of the herbs and spices. In that time, the vinegar's sharp flavor will soften and mellow, resulting in a delightful blend.

To prepare flavored vinegars, simply put herbs and spices of your choice into a decorative bottle or clean jar and fill it with plain wine vinegar. Leave an inch free at the top of the bottle if you plan to insert a cork. Add caps or corks (see "Sealing & dressing up the bottles," below) and let the bottles stand undisturbed in a cool, dark place for at least 3 weeks so flavors can develop. The vinegars keep well for about 4 months.

Each of our suggested flavoring combinations is enough for a ⅘-quart bottle or two ⅖-quart bottles; double the amount for half-gallons.

Sealing & dressing up the bottles

To cap bottles, you'll need screw caps or plastic-topped, push-in corks. Or use fresh corks—but you'll need a corking device to insert them. Corking and capping supplies are sold in winemaking stores.

To seal the bottle tops, use sealing wax or candle ends. Place either type of wax in a tall, thin, juice-type can; set can in a pan with a small amount of water over low heat until wax is melted. If you use candle wax, you may need to dip bottle tops several times for a good coating.

If you'd like to decorate the bottles with ribbon, cut a short length of ribbon; then run it up the neck, over the mouth, and down the other side of the bottle and glue in place before dipping in wax. The ribbon can be pulled up to lift up the wax for unsealing.

You can also glue or tie on additional ribbons and add a label or tag identifying the vinegar. (For labeling ideas, see the facing page.) Be sure to indicate the bottling date on the label; also note that once the bottle has been opened, the vinegar should all be used within 3 or 4 months.

Spicy Chile Vinegar

Poke into a bottle 4 **bay leaves**, 6 **small dried hot red chiles**, and 4 large cloves **garlic** (peeled). Fill with **red or white wine vinegar**.

Garlic-Lemon-Mint Vinegar

Put into a jar 4 large cloves **garlic** (peeled) and 4 long sprigs **fresh mint** (washed and dried). Add a ¼-inch-wide strip **lemon peel** (cut in a continuous spiral); break strip in half for small bottles. Fill with **white wine vinegar**.

Garlic Vinegar

Peel 6 large cloves **garlic** and impale them on a thin bamboo skewer (or put 3 garlic cloves on each of 2 skewers). Insert in bottle and fill with **red wine vinegar**.

Tarragon or Dill Vinegar

Wash and dry 4 sprigs (*each* about 5 inches long) **fresh tarragon** or dill; poke into bottle. Fill with **red or white wine vinegar**.

Dressing Up Gifts From the Kitchen

■

A gift of food lovingly made in your kitchen deserves extra-special wrapping and presentation. Here are just a few simple ideas for ways to wrap and decorate the cookies, cakes, breads, candies, and home-canned goodies you want to give this season.

To show off breads, cakes, or cookie assortments and to help keep them fresh, heat-seal them in plastic wrap. You can seal food as is, in a foil pan, or on a heavy cardboard base. First cover food with a piece of heavy plastic wrap just large enough to overlap the edges at the bottom; pull the plastic gently across the top and fold the ends neatly underneath. Preheat oven to 300° and set a protective piece of brown wrapping paper on the oven rack or a baking sheet. Set the wrapped food on the paper; heat for 5 to 10 seconds to seal. Let cool briefly; then decorate with a colorful ribbon as shown at right.

Present cookies, as well as nuts or dried fruits, stacked in a custom-made transparent tube like that shown at right. Make the tube from .005- to .010-weight acetate or polyester film, available in art supply stores. To make a tube, simply wrap the acetate around a cylinder form the same diameter as or slightly larger than the cookies; seal the seam with clear tape. Close one end with an acetate round cut to fit inside; tape edge. Fill tube with cookies, then close the other end. Tie with a ribbon to conceal the tape.

Select a good-looking basket for presenting breads or cakes. If you wish, line the basket with a holiday napkin or paper doilies. (The basket makes a nice present in itself.)

Fill an unusual glass container with candies or cookies; add a paper doily frill under the lid and finish with a label and ribbon.

Select special decorative jars for sauces, jellies, and relishes, or use plain canning jars and dress them up with doilies or fabric rounds on the lids. You can also pack sauces and mustards in stoneware crocks; ours (shown below) is topped with rustic burlap, hand-printed with a greeting. (If you give preserves or other bottled food that hasn't been sealed by processing in a hot water bath, be sure to label it for refrigeration.)

Create a "theme" package for related foods such as homemade marinades, vinegars, and herb blends by covering an ordinary drink carton with adhesive-backed paper or fabric as shown below.

Make your own labels and tags using any paper that strikes your fancy; even lacy doilies will work well. Or start with plain gummed labels from office supply or stationery stores and decorate them, using a set of rubber stamp letters and/or individual decorative stamps. You can also make potato-printed or stenciled labels or tags, following the directions on pages 196 and 197.

Gifts from your kitchen *look extra-special when you package them imaginatively. Ideas include crocks and pretty jars or bottles, rustic baskets, a paper-wrapped carton of related food items, and a see-through cookie tube.*

Herb & Spice Blends

Fragrant spice and herb mixtures, personally styled, are helpful and flavorful shortcuts when cooking. And because they're quick to prepare and keep well, they also make thoughtful little gifts. If you decide to make them in quantity, shop for the ingredients in spice shops, health food markets, or other stores selling herbs and spices in bulk.

For attractive presentation, pack the blends in handsome plastic canisters or pretty jars that can double as gift packages and storage containers. With each mixture, include a few ideas for use (we've listed some suggestions after each recipe).

Cajun Spice

In a blender, combine 1 tablespoon *each* **ground red pepper** (cayenne) and **garlic salt**; 2 teaspoons **dry basil**; 1½ teaspoons *each* **crushed bay leaves** and **coarsely ground black pepper**; 1 teaspoon *each* **white pepper**, **dry rubbed sage**, and **ground thyme**; and ½ teaspoon **ground allspice**. Whirl until bay leaves are finely ground. Store airtight. Makes about 5 tablespoons.

Suggestions for use. Sprinkle generously over fish, poultry, or beef before sautéing, broiling, or baking.

Sweet Curry

In a bowl, mix 2 tablespoons *each* **ground coriander** and **ground cumin**; 1 tablespoon **ground mace**; 2 teaspoons *each* **ground cardamom** and **ground cinnamon**; 1 teaspoon *each* **ground cloves**, **ground nutmeg**, **ground turmeric**, and **coarsely ground black pepper** (optional); and ½ teaspoon **ground red pepper** (cayenne). Store airtight. Makes about 7 tablespoons.

Suggestions for use. Mix to taste with braised lamb or cooked rice; or dust on eggplant slices and sauté.

Herbs from Provence

In a blender, combine 2 tablespoons **dry basil**; 4 teaspoons **dry oregano leaves**; 2 teaspoons *each* **dry marjoram leaves**, **dry tarragon**, **dry thyme leaves**, and **dry savory leaves**; 1½ teaspoons **crushed bay leaves**; and 1 teaspoon *each* **fennel seeds**, **dry mint leaves**, **ground sage**, **dry rosemary**, and **dry lavender** (optional). Whirl until mixture is a fine powder. Store airtight. Makes about 7 tablespoons.

Suggestions for use. Sprinkle lightly on meat or poultry before barbecuing, broiling, or baking; or mix to taste with sautéed or steamed vegetables.

Salad Seasoning

Mix 1 tablespoon *each* **pepper** and **garlic powder**, 2 tablespoons **salt**, 4 tablespoons **onion powder**, and 6 tablespoons **parsley flakes**. Makes about 1 cup.

Suggestions for use. Add to sour cream or yogurt to make a zesty dip for raw vegetables; or use in salad dressings (see below).

Creamy salad dressing. Mix 2 teaspoons **Salad Seasoning**, 1 cup **mayonnaise**, and ⅔ cup **buttermilk**; refrigerate. Use on lettuce or cabbage salads.

Herb oil & vinegar dressing. Mix 1¼ teaspoons **Salad Seasoning** with ½ cup **salad oil** and ¼ cup **red or white wine vinegar**. Shake just before using. Serve with tossed green salads.

Chinese Five-Spice

In a blender, combine 2 tablespoons *each* **fennel seeds** and **Szechwan peppercorns** (available in Asian markets); 4 **star anise** (or 1 teaspoon *each* anise seeds and ground cinnamon); 1¼ teaspoons **whole cloves** or 1 teaspoon ground cloves; and 1 **cinnamon stick** (2 inches long), broken into several pieces, or 1 teaspoon ground cinnamon. Whirl until a coarse powder forms. Store airtight. Makes about 5 tablespoons.

Suggestions for use. Sprinkle lightly on chicken or fish before broiling or baking; or mix to taste with stir-fried vegetables.

Herb Seasoning Salt

In a jar, stir together 1 teaspoon *each* **garlic powder**, **onion powder**, and **pepper**; 1 tablespoon *each* **dry thyme leaves** and **salt**; 2 tablespoons *each* **dry rosemary**, **dry marjoram leaves**, **dry oregano leaves**, **dry basil**, and **parsley flakes**; and 3 tablespoons **sesame seeds**. Secure lid and shake until well blended. Makes 1 cup.

Suggestions for use. Sprinkle lightly on chicken, white fish, omelets, or vegetables before cooking; or use in the quick recipe below.

Herb garlic bread. Stir 2 teaspoons **Herb Seasoning Salt** into 1 cup (½ lb.) **butter** or margarine (at room temperature). Spread on slices of **French bread**, reassemble as a loaf, wrap in foil, and bake in a 400° oven until hot (15 to 20 minutes).

Sauces & Marinades

"I can't think of a thing to make for dinner!" When it comes to family meals, that's a common complaint during the holiday season. We're often so busy planning and cooking for parties that there's no energy left for preparing everyday suppers.

For good friends—and for yourself!—here's a little bottled inspiration. These sauces and marinades make it easy to produce a simple yet flavorful meal, and all are uncomplicated recipes that use readily accessible ingredients. If you plan to give them away, you might pack them in 1- or 2-cup quantities and offer several kinds together. With each one, include directions for use, a copy of the recipe, and a reminder to keep each refrigerated.

Sherry Herb Marinade

Use this herb-scented marinade on chicken or fish. You'll need about 1 cup marinade for a cut-up 3½- to 4-pound chicken, ½ cup for 1 pound of fish fillets. Marinate in the refrigerator, turning occasionally, for 4 hours to overnight for chicken, 1 to 2 hours for fish. Then barbecue or broil.

- 2 cups dry sherry
- ¾ cup salad oil
- ⅓ cup **each** instant minced onion and Dijon mustard
- 6 tablespoons white wine vinegar
- 6 cloves garlic, pressed or minced
- 1 tablespoon **each** dry thyme leaves and crushed dry rosemary
- ¼ teaspoon pepper

Mix sherry, oil, onion, mustard, vinegar, garlic, thyme, rosemary, and pepper. Cover and refrigerate for up to 3 weeks. Shake before using. Makes 4 cups.

Cumin-Cinnamon Marinade

This sweet-spiced wine marinade is delicious with lamb chops. Use about ¾ cup for 1 pound of chops; marinate for 2 to 4 hours, then barbecue or broil.

- 3 cups dry red wine
- 1 cup olive oil or salad oil
- ¼ cup instant minced onion
- 8 cloves garlic, pressed or minced
- 2 teaspoons **each** ground cinnamon and cumin seeds
- 1½ teaspoons ground cumin

Mix wine, oil, onion, garlic, cinnamon, cumin seeds, and ground cumin. Cover and refrigerate for up to 3 weeks. Shake well before using. Makes about 4 cups.

Fennel-Chili Marinade

Try this marinade on pork chops. Use about ½ cup on 1 pound of chops; marinate for 4 hours or overnight, then broil or barbecue.

- 3 cups dry white wine
- ½ cup olive oil or salad oil
- 8 cloves garlic, pressed or minced
- 1½ tablespoons **each** crushed fennel seeds and dry basil
- 1½ to 2 teaspoons crushed dried hot red chiles
- ½ cup white wine vinegar

Mix wine, oil, garlic, fennel seeds, basil, chiles, and vinegar. Cover and refrigerate for up to 3 weeks. Shake well before using. Makes 4 cups.

Savory Barbecue Sauce

Full-flavored barbecue sauce is a wonderful baste for a thick roast or any barbecued beef or poultry. The recipe makes more than enough for a 5-pound chuck roast; for a cut-up chicken or spareribs, allow ¾ to 1 cup (use during last 15 to 30 minutes of cooking).

- ¼ cup olive oil or salad oil
- 1 medium-size onion, thinly sliced and separated into rings
- 1 clove garlic, minced or pressed
- ½ cup thinly sliced celery
- ¾ cup **each** catsup and tomato-based chili sauce
- ½ cup water
- 2 tablespoons **each** Worcestershire, wine vinegar, and lemon juice
- 1 teaspoon **each** prepared horseradish and prepared mustard
- ½ teaspoon hickory-smoked salt
  Few drops liquid hot pepper seasoning
- ½ teaspoon pepper
- 3 tablespoons firmly packed brown sugar
- ½ cup dry sherry

Heat oil in a wide frying pan over medium heat. Add onion and cook, stirring often, until soft (about 10 minutes). Add garlic, celery, catsup, chili sauce, water, Worcestershire, vinegar, lemon juice, horseradish, mustard, smoked salt, hot pepper seasoning, pepper, sugar, and sherry. Bring to a boil; then reduce heat and simmer, uncovered, for 30 minutes. Remove from heat and let cool, then pour into jars. Seal jars tightly and refrigerate for up to 1 week (freeze for longer storage). Makes about 3½ cups.

Hand-stitched Treasures

■

*From your sewing basket come special handmade gifts
that are sure to become someone's cherished favorites.
Charming country aprons and hand-stenciled rugs
are just two of the treasures you can create with a little
imagination and lots of loving care.*

Chef's Aprons

(Also pictured on facing page)

An apron sewn and imaginatively embellished by hand is a bright and welcome gift for adult and junior cooks alike. Each of our jaunty aprons starts with a basic chef's apron design, but color and decoration are up to you. We made a Western denim version complete with rivets and bandanna, a country charmer trimmed with a stenciled motif, and a bright child's apron featuring capacious pockets to hold art or school supplies as well as cooking utensils.

Materials

For each adult's apron, you'll need 1 yard of 45-inch-wide cotton or denim fabric; for a child's apron, buy only ¾ yard. If you want to line the apron, also purchase an equivalent amount of contrasting fabric. For ties, you can use 2½ yards of ribbon or cotton twill tape (or use ½ yard contrasting fabric for ties and pockets).

Making the aprons

1. To cut out apron, use a purchased pattern, trace an apron you own and add ½-inch seam allowances, or follow the dimensions in the drawing at right. If your apron fabric is lightweight, cut a contrasting lining the same size. For ties, cut four 3- by 22-inch pieces from contrasting fabric or four 22-inch lengths of twill tape (cut child's apron ties shorter, to fit). If you like, cut a pocket—one piece from a sturdy fabric such as denim, two pieces if fabric is lightweight.

2. Turn all edges under ¼ inch, then turn again and topstitch. If you are lining apron, pin lining to fabric with raw edges aligned and right sides together; stitch, using a ½-inch seam allowance. Leave a bottom opening; turn apron right side out, then press. Slipstitch opening closed.

3. To make fabric ties, fold each strip in half lengthwise; turn each raw edge in ½ inch. Press. Topstitch on all edges to form a 1- by 21-inch tie. Stitch ties firmly to apron at bib and sides.

4. For a pocket made of a sturdy fabric like denim, turn edges under ¼ inch all around; press. If using lightweight fabric, stitch the two pieces with right sides together, leaving an opening in bottom; turn right side out and press. Slipstitch opening closed.

Topstitch ribbon, fabric strip, or other trim to pocket. If using a stencil motif, apply directly to a solid fabric or stencil onto a strip of muslin and topstitch onto pocket. (For instructions on stenciling fabric, see pages 66 and 67.) Pin pocket to apron where desired; topstitch in place.

5. For other trim, topstitch ribbon, a fabric strip, or a stenciled muslin strip to bib or hemline of apron as desired. If using a stenciled motif on a solid fabric apron, stencil directly onto the apron as for the pocket. Tuck an oven mitt, scissors, or other little gift accessories into pocket.

Design: Kathy Perry.

Stenciled with hearts, stitched up in denim, or trimmed with strips of bright geometric fabric, these easy-to-make aprons are sure to please cooks of all ages.

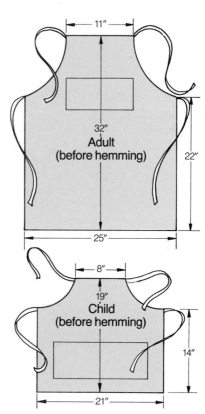

Dimensions of adult apron (top) and child's apron (bottom) include a ½-inch seam allowance all around.

Castle Wall Placemats

Here's a set of placemats almost too pretty to cover up with plates! One of the more complex patchwork patterns, Castle Wall lends itself beautifully to a mixture of solid, striped, and printed fabrics. We've used different shades of green in the placemats shown at right, but you can of course use any color you choose.

Materials

For set of four placemats:

1   *yard dark green solid fabric*
³⁄₄   *yard dark green print fabric (allow more if fabric has stripes or motifs that must be matched)*
⁷⁄₈   *yard light green solid fabric*
¹⁄₄   *yard light green print fabric*
1   *yard solid fabric for backing*
1   *yard polyester quilt batting*
    Thread to match backing
1   *sheet acetate*
    Craft knife
    Metal ruler

Piecing the placemats

Note: Preshrink and press fabrics.

1. Measure pattern pieces (shown at right) and *double* all measurements to make full-size patterns (or enlarge by photocopying as described on page 64). Trace onto acetate, using a ruler to ensure straight lines. In making your acetate templates, be sure to include a ¼-inch seam allowance on all edges. Number all templates and cut them out neatly with a craft knife.

These intricate-looking placemats are pieced from a pleasing combination of solid and printed fabric; machine quilting lends an extra decorative touch and adds to durability.

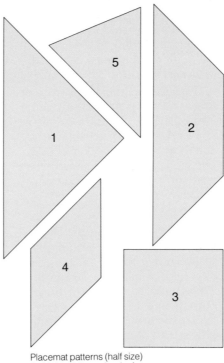

Placemat patterns (half size)
(add ¼ inch to each edge)

2. Measure, mark, and cut the following pieces in the fabrics specified. *Template 1*—from light green solid, 16 pieces; *template 2*—from dark green print, 32 pieces; *template 3*—from light green print, 32 pieces; *template 4*—from dark green solid, 32 pieces; *template 5*—from dark green print, 32 pieces.

From dark green solid, also measure and mark 16 crosswise strips, each 3 by 22 inches, for borders; from light green solid, measure and mark 16 strips, each 2 by 22 inches, for binding. Cut strips.

3. *The following instructions—steps 3 through 8, and steps 1 through 4 in "Assembling the placemats"—are for one placemat. Complete the placemats one at a time, or repeat each step four times before beginning the next step.*

With right sides facing and raw edges aligned, machine-stitch pairs of piece 5 together, using ¼-inch seam allowance. Press seams open and trim extending points. Join two pairs to make half of center octagon. Repeat with remaining two pairs; join halves to form center unit A.

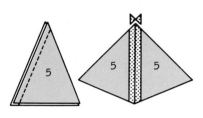

4. Join pieces 1, 2, and 3 to form unit B; press seams toward corner triangle. Repeat to make a total of four units.

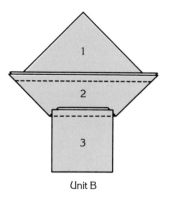

Unit B

5. Form unit C by joining pieces 2 and 3 as shown; repeat to make a total of four units.

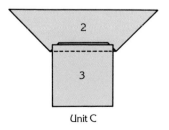

Unit C

6. Starting ¼ inch in from edge, stitch piece 4 to one edge of piece 2 as shown below; stop stitching ¼ inch from other edge. With needle in fabric, raise presser foot, pivot work, and continue stitching to join second edge of piece 4 to edge of piece 3. Stop ¼ inch from edge. Press seams away from piece 4. Trim extending points. Stitch another piece 4 to other side of unit C, forming unit D. Repeat to make a total of four units.

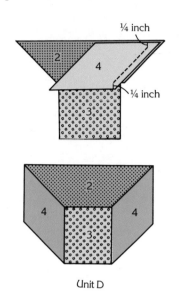

¼ inch

¼ inch

Unit D

7. Attach unit B to unit D, stitching with piece 4 on top and pivoting at corner as before. Stop ¼ inch from edge. Press seam away from piece 4. Join remaining units B and D until you have formed entire outside ring.

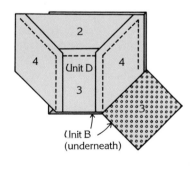

Unit D

Unit B
(underneath)

8. Set center unit A into outside piece, sewing each edge of octagon to a square in outside ring. Start and stop seams ¼ inch from each edge. Press seams toward center. Square should measure 12 inches; trim edges, if necessary.

Assembling the placemats

1. With right sides facing and raw edges aligned, pin dark green border strips to patchwork square, matching midpoints on edges. Stitch, starting and stopping ¼ inch from edges; miter corners. *Do not* trim excess off border strips—as cut, they're the proper length to allow for mitering.

2. Press placemat top carefully. Measure, mark, and cut batting and backing pieces to equal dimensions of placemat top.

3. Baste all three layers together and machine-quilt along lines shown in quilting pattern below.

4. To finish edges with light green binding strips, pin together the placemat top, batting, and backing at the edges; machine-baste through all layers ⅛ inch from the edge. Fold binding strips in half lengthwise, right sides out; press. Place a binding strip along one edge of the placemat top, with raw edges of binding strip and placemat aligned. Machine-stitch ¼ inch from the edge. Repeat on the opposite edge. Fold the strips to the back, fold edge under, and hand-stitch to conceal the machine stitching. Repeat on the other two edges so the binding strips overlap the ends of the first two strips at the corners.

Design: Victoria Sears.

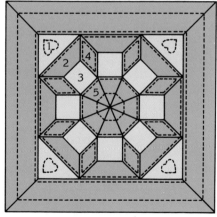

Quilting pattern

How to Enlarge & Transfer a Pattern

Many of our stitched gifts feature a pattern on a grid. Since these patterns are usually a smaller size than the actual items will be, you'll have to enlarge them to the size you need and, in some cases, transfer them to your fabric.

Enlarging a pattern

You can use one of several techniques to "blow up" a pattern accurately. The same methods can be used to reduce a pattern to a smaller size.

Photocopying. For fast, accurate results, take your pattern to a photocopy service. For a small fee, you can have the pattern enlarged on paper or transparent vellum. Better-quality reproductions are available at a higher cost, and some photocopy services can reproduce in color.

Overhead projector. Overhead projectors, available for rent at audio-visual equipment stores, are a very effective tool for resizing patterns. A projector is the best solution when you want to make a substantial enlargement.

Making a grid. You can use a grid to size a pattern without mechanical aids. To do so, you'll need a supply of vellum graph paper.

Place the graph paper over the pattern and trace the design. Identify each vertical and horizontal row with numbers and letters.

Our patterns tell you how big the actual pieces should be by specifying the grid size—"1 square = 2 inches," for example. To enlarge your traced pattern, you'll need graph paper with grids of the size noted on the pattern. If you can't find the proper graph paper, make your own grid on plain paper.

Mark the new grid with the same numbering system you used for the original grid. Transfer the pattern lines carefully from grid box to equivalent grid box (see below).

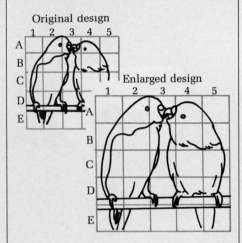

Original design

Enlarged design

Transferring a pattern

Once you've enlarged your pattern, you can simply pin the pieces to the fabric and cut them out. Be sure to read the project directions carefully to see if seam allowances are included in the pattern pieces; if they aren't, add the specified seam allowance when you cut.

For some projects, you may want to transfer a design directly to the fabric rather than pin pattern pieces to it. In these cases, use one of the methods below.

Whether you're pinning pieces on the fabric or transferring a design directly, preshrink and press the fabric before you begin.

Light table. Most of us don't have access to an electric light table, but on a sunny day, it's easy to create your own. Light- to medium-weight fabrics that are light in color are easiest to work with.

Trace your pattern onto tracing paper. Tape the paper, *right* side up, onto a window. Center your fabric, *right* side up, over the paper and tape it in place. Trace the pattern outlines onto the fabric (see "Other marking tools," below).

Dressmaker's carbon. Washable dressmaker's carbon paper is ideal for use on most fabrics, except those with a nap.

Tape your fabric, *right* side up, to a hard, flat surface. Center and pin the pattern to the fabric, leaving the bottom edge free. Slip the carbon paper, shiny side down, between the fabric and the pattern.

With an empty ballpoint pen or blunt pencil, trace the pattern outlines. Press firmly but carefully to avoid tearing the pattern paper.

Heat-transfer pencil. Use this method for smooth-textured fabrics, both lightweight and heavy. You'll find transfer pencils in fabric stores.

Trace your pattern on tracing paper with a felt-tipped pen. Flip the tracing paper to the *wrong* side and retrace the design lines with the transfer pencil.

Center and pin the paper, *right* side up, to the *right* side of the fabric so the transfer pencil marks are against the fabric. Press the paper-and-fabric sandwich according to the pencil manufacturer's instructions.

Other marking tools. Use sewing chalk or a pencil to mark pattern symbols and placement lines on your fabric.

Flying Geese Lap Quilt

Give a gift of cozy comfort when you stitch up this lovely lap quilt in the traditional Flying Geese design. Reversing the colors and direction of blocks from row to row gives the quilt its flowing, optical quality.

Materials

For quilt 33 by 49 inches:

1¼ yards **each** navy and burgundy small-print fabric, 45 inches wide

½ yard **each** navy and burgundy lengthwise floral stripe fabric (if you use print without direction, buy only ¼ yard **each** navy and burgundy and cut crosswise strips)

1½ yards navy medium-print fabric, 45 inches wide, for backing

¾ yard burgundy medium-print fabric for binding

1½ yards polyester quilt batting, 36 inches wide

Thread to match fabrics

1 sheet acetate

Craft knife

Metal ruler

Piecing the quilt top

Note: Preshrink and press fabrics.

1. To make paper pattern, carefully draw block design 2 by 4 inches, as shown below. Trace onto acetate to make one large and one small triangle template, using a ruler to ensure straight lines. Be sure to add a ¼-inch seam allowance to each edge; cut templates out neatly with a craft knife.

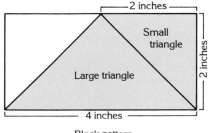

Block pattern
(add ¼ inch to each edge)

2. Measure and mark 96 large triangles and 144 small triangles on small burgundy print, and 72 large triangles and 192 small triangles on small navy print. To save fabric and speed your cutting, place triangles so long edges are on the lengthwise grain and there is no space between pieces. Cut pieces.

3. With right sides facing and raw edges aligned, machine-stitch long edge of a small navy triangle to one short edge of a large burgundy triangle, using ¼-inch seam allowance. Fold out small piece and finger-press seam toward edge; stitch another small navy triangle to other edge of burgundy triangle. Repeat for 24 blocks.

Stitch blocks together to form first vertical row; press carefully. Continue making blocks and rows until you have a total of four rows. Using opposite color scheme, make blocks and stitch together to form three vertical rows.

4. From floral stripe fabrics, measure, mark, and cut enough 1-inch-wide strips (piecing, if necessary) to make four navy and four burgundy divider strips, each 49 inches long.

5. With right sides facing and raw edges aligned, stitch alternating navy and burgundy divider strips between rows and to long outside edges. Press quilt top carefully.

Finishing the quilt

1. Measure and mark backing and batting equal to dimensions of quilt top. Cut pieces.

2. To assemble the quilt, pin together quilt top, batting, and backing at the edges and hand-baste through all three layers in a grid pattern.

3. Quilt the top by hand, outlining each triangle just inside the seam line.

4. Cut a continuous bias strip 1½ inches wide for the binding from medium-print burgundy fabric. Fold the binding strips in half lengthwise, with right sides out; press the folds.

5. To attach the strips, machine-baste the quilt through all three layers ⅛ inch from the edges. Place a binding strip along one edge of the quilt top, with raw edges of strip and quilt aligned. Machine-stitch ¼ inch from edge; repeat on opposite quilt edge. Fold strips to the back and turn edges under, concealing machine stitching; hand-stitch. Repeat for other two edges so binding strips overlap the ends of the first two strips at the corners.

Design: Christine Barnes.

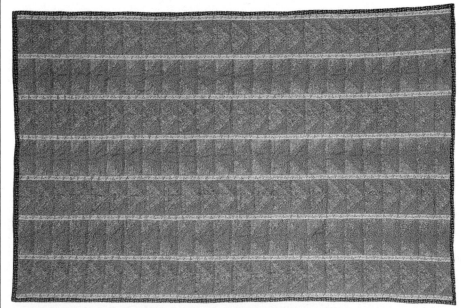

You can create *this lovely, soft lap quilt using basic sewing and quilt-making techniques and just two simple triangle shapes.*

Stenciled Rugs

(Also pictured on page 60)

To give a truly special gift this Christmas, make one of these charming stenciled rugs. Use our patterns for country geese, checkerboards, and flowers, or create your own designs.

You can use a purchased cotton rug as your canvas, then paint on the designs with special fabric paint.

Materials

For one rug:

.005 clear or frosted polyester film: 3 6- by 8-inch pieces

Glass backed with white paper

2- by 3-foot white or solid-color cotton rug (exact size will vary), preshrunk for 20 minutes in a hot dryer

Styrofoam meat trays or egg cartons

Craft knife with #11 blade

Stencil brushes (one for each color of paint)

Masking tape (1 inch wide)

Ultra-fine-line permanent pen

Clear plastic ruler

Fabric paint in the following colors:

For the goose:

Navy blue

Gray-brown (white plus brown, plus a touch of black)

Rust (golden yellow plus red, plus brown)

For the flower:

Navy blue

Light aqua (white plus aqua or turquoise)

Golden yellow

Rust (see above)

Cutting the stencils

To make the stencil patterns, enlarge the patterns shown on the facing page as described on page 64 and transfer onto film, using an ultra-fine-line permanent pen. You'll need to make three separate stencils for each design. First trace all segments marked "1" onto one sheet of film.

A gaggle of geese or a colorful garden of flowers—take your pick and stencil a rug that's sure to become a treasured heirloom.

Then trace all segments marked "2" onto a second piece of film; add dotted lines to indicate where the "1" segments fall (these dotted lines will be used as register marks for lining up the stencils when you paint). Finally, trace all segments marked "3" on the third piece of film; add dotted lines to indicate "1" and "2."

Place film #1 on a piece of glass backed with white paper (this will help you see the lines clearly). Using a craft knife with a #11 blade, cut carefully along the solid lines only. To cut out small circles (as on the goose's scarf), use a paper hole punch. Repeat for films #2 and #3.

Laying out & stenciling the design

Using the photograph above as a guide, paint the rugs according to

the instructions following. *For best results, plan the entire layout of the stenciled design before you begin to paint.*

General stenciling techniques. Secure the first stencil (see instructions for specific rugs) to the rug with masking tape. Place a supply of paint (either straight from the jar or mixed as described above) in a styrofoam meat tray, egg carton, or some similar "palette," one color to a tray. Dip your stencil brush lightly in the paint so that only the flat ends of the bristles pick up paint. Remove excess paint by tapping the brush lightly on a clean area of the tray (the brush should be fairly dry). To apply paint, dab the brush all over the area to be painted, using a straight up-and-down motion. Be sure to cover the area (and edges) completely.

Paint one stencil (and one color) at a time; allow to dry thoroughly (you can use a blow dryer to hasten the process), then tape on the next stencil. Use the dotted registration lines to align each stencil with the design already stenciled. Once you've completed painting your rug, you'll need to set the paint according to manufacturer's directions. Rugs may be treated with stain-resistant spray.

Stenciling the goose rug. To make the goose design, you apply the goose stencils, then create stripes and checkerboards using masking tape.

1. For geese, tape down goose stencil #1 (the head-neck and breast outlines) at one end of the rug, making sure to leave enough room for the feet at the bottom. Fill in stencil with gray-brown paint. Then tape on stencil #2; paint goose back gray-brown, feet and beak rust. Tape on stencil #3 and paint scarf blue, tail feathers gray-brown. A dot of dark paint applied freehand makes an eye.

2. Stencil two more geese, one on each side of the first; space geese about 7 inches apart.

3. Repeat the entire procedure at the opposite end of the rug.

4. To make a checkerboard pattern between two geese, place a strip of 1-inch-wide masking tape along one end of the rug between geese. Measure 1 inch up from the upper edge of the tape and add an identical strip of tape; measure up another inch and tape again. Next to the end goose, place a piece of tape running vertically across the first three strips. Measure over 1 inch and tape down another strip; measure 1 inch and tape down a third strip, then measure 1 more inch and add a fourth strip. Now you have a grid; stencil in the open spaces with gray-brown paint. Remove tape and let paint dry.

5. To fill in the center row of the checkerboard, cover the two horizontal rows of gray-brown squares (and the spaces between) with pieces of tape; place three more pieces of tape vertically from top to bottom, so you have two squares uncovered. Paint these squares rust; remove tape and let paint dry.

6. Repeat the entire procedure to make checkerboards between the other geese at both ends of the rug.

7. Paint checkerboards on the long side in the same way, using masking tape to create 23 inches of checkerboard, beginning and ending with the gray-brown paint.

8. To make the ¼-inch stripes around the center, first tape just inside your checkerboards on all sides, then tape again ¼ inch away, making sure that adjoining tapes form neat and square corners. Where the resulting stripe will cross the geese's heads, mask off the heads with tape. Paint the ¼-inch stripe blue, remove tape, and allow paint to dry.

9. To make the second stripe, tape over the first stripe all around (tape will project ¾ inch beyond the painted stripe). Measure in ½ inch toward center all around and tape. Paint ½-inch stripe blue, remove tape, and allow paint to dry.

10. To create the third stripe, measure in ¼ inch all around and place tape so that the inner edge is at the ¼ inch mark. (The tape will cover the previous stripe.) Measure in another ¼ inch and tape. Paint the ¼-inch stripe rust; remove tape and let paint dry.

Stenciling the flowered rug. To make the flowered design, you first paint the border stripe, then the inner stripes, and finally the flowers.

1. To make the border, place 1-inch-wide masking tape along all four edges of the rug. Using a clear plastic ruler, measure in ½ inch all around and tape again, making sure all tapes meet neatly and squarely at the corners. Paint the resulting ½-inch stripe blue; remove tape and let paint dry.

2. To make the center stripes, measure in 3½ inches from the blue stripe all around and tape. Measure in another ½ inch and tape, again making sure corners are neat and square. Paint the resulting ½-inch stripe rust. Remove tape and let paint dry.

3. To make the innermost stripes, measure in ¼ inch all around from the outer edge of the rust stripe and tape. (The tape will cover half of the rust stripe.) Measure in a final ¼ inch all around and tape. Paint the ¼-inch stripe blue, remove tape, and let paint dry.

4. Stencil the flower design in the 4½-inch open area around the edges, alternating light aqua, rust, and golden yellow randomly as you go. Paint each flower and immediately shade lightly around the center with one of the other colors. Make the center dots blue. Begin by placing a flower cluster in the center of each end and long side. Then place a cluster in each corner; center remaining clusters on the sides between the corner clusters and the center. Be sure to clean your stencils when you change colors.

Design: Gayle Bryan.

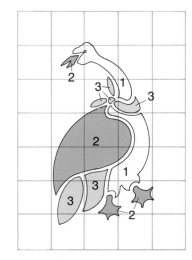

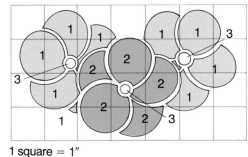

1 square = 1″

Personalized Director's Chairs

Transform a standard director's chair with a hand-stitched, personalized seat and back, and presto—you have a unique and practical gift for that hard-to-shop-for person on your Christmas list. Shown on the facing page are just a few ideas for dressing up a director's chair. You can either decorate a purchased back and seat or sew new ones, as we did.

In embellishing and accessorizing your chair, let your imagination go! On these pages, we show you three options: a chair with coordinating cushions, one with its own magazine holder, and a basic seat and back personalized with the recipient's name.

Materials

Though separate canvas back and seat sets are available for reasonable prices, you'll have a wider selection of colors and patterns if you make your own. Be sure to choose sturdy cotton canvas—or, if you use a lighter-weight fabric, stitch it to a canvas backing.

Chair dimensions do vary, but as a rule of thumb, one chair requires a yard of 36-inch-wide fabric, ¾ yard of 45-inch-wide fabric, or ½ yard of 60-inch-wide fabric. If you're using a patterned designer print like that shown on the chair with the appliquéd letters, buy extra fabric so you can adjust where the pattern will fall on the chair. The exact amount you'll need depends on the fabric pattern.

You'll also need extra fabric for the accessories we show here. To make the cushions, buy a yard of 45-inch-wide fabric (plus an additional ¼ yard if you want to make loops, self-ties, or welting). If you want to use purchased piping, you'll need a total of 4½ yards for both pillows. You may also want to buy a small amount of ribbon to use as ties or loops in lieu of self-ties. In addition, for each pillow purchase an 18-inch nylon zipper and an 18-inch-square polyester pillow form.

For the magazine holder, buy 1 yard of 45-inch-wide fabric, an equal amount of contrasting fabric for lining, and, if you wish, coordinating ribbon for tying the holder to the chair.

The appliquéd letters on the chair back can be made from fabric scraps.

Making the basic panels

On most director's chairs, each end of the back has a channel that slips over the chair back posts. The seat is also anchored to the wooden frame by means of channels in the fabric at both sides. A dowel or length of rope fits through each channel and slips into a groove in the wood between the arm assembly and seat. Examine the chair and cover you purchase to see how it's put together.

Making the seat. To cut out the seat, measure the original panel and add ¾ inch on each long side (front and back) for hems; allow about 1½ inches extra on each end. Turn under the long edges, turn again, and topstitch. On the ends, finish raw edges with a zigzag stitch, then fold over about 1¼ inches on each end and baste; insert the dowel and try the seat in the chair. Once you have a

good fit, topstitch a 1-inch channel in each end, using two rows of stitching spaced ⅛ inch apart for extra strength.

Making the back. For the back panel, measure the original and cut a piece *double* its length from post to post plus about an inch extra all around—for seam allowance on the end and for hems on long edges. Turn long edges under ¼ inch, turn again, topstitch, and press. Match the ends, right sides together; stitch together to form a tube, using a ½-inch seam allowance. Iron the seam allowances flat in one direction, turn tube right side out, and slip over the chair back posts to see where the channels should be. Then stitch channels about 2 inches from each end; for reinforcement, use two rows of stitching spaced ⅛ inch apart. (For a really tidy-looking chair back, position the seam so you'll stitch over it to make one of the channels.)

Making panels with backing. If you're using a lightweight fabric, cut a heavy canvas backing for the seat, making it the finished size of the seat. Cut the lighter-weight fabric to the same length, but make it an inch wider from front to back. Center the canvas on the wrong side of the fabric, pin, and turn the fabric under ¼ inch. Turn again to conceal the canvas's raw edge; topstitch. Finish the short edges with a zigzag stitch and/or pinking shears, then treat the canvas and fabric as one piece to form the channels at the ends. Proceed in the same way for the chair back.

Creating the accessories

Seat cushions, lettering, and/or a magazine holder are just a few ideas for decorating your chair.

Making cushions. To make cushions, measure your chair panels to determine the best size. Make standard knife-edge pillows with welts,

Have a seat! *Dressed up with bright printed fabric, lettering, pillows, even a magazine holder, ordinary director's chairs become unique and special gifts to suit any personality or style.*

using welting made from the same fabric, contrasting fabric, or purchased piping. Add a zipper (cut down to length as necessary) on each pillow so you can remove the covers for washing. Turn and press. Stitch on loops or ties to hold the back cushion to the chair posts; add self-gripping nylon fabric fastener tape or ties to secure the seat cushion.

To make ties or loops, cut 2-inch-wide strips of fabric; fold in half lengthwise and press, then fold in the raw edges to make ½-inch-wide ties and topstitch. (Or use ribbon for ties.) Finally, cut down an 18-inch-square pillow form into two pieces to fit both cushion covers; insert pillows into covers.

Making a magazine holder. To make a magazine holder, measure the distance between the arm posts on one side of the chair; that measurement, plus the height of the chair from the floor, will determine the size of your bag. The bag is made like a mock box pillow with one end open. If you wish, you can line the bag with contrasting fabric. Add ties as for the cushions and tie to the chair arm supports.

Adding lettering. To personalize a chair back with the recipient's name, you have several options. You can stencil directly onto solid color canvas, embroider a name (or have one done professionally by an embroidery shop), or appliqué fabric letters

as shown in the photograph. To appliqué, simply cut out letters in a contrasting fabric, using stencil patterns. Apply them to the chair back fabric before putting the back together, using a machine zigzag stitch around all edges.

Design: Françoise Kirkman and Kathy Perry.

Stadium Cushions

Sports or music fans on your gift list will find these portable cushions welcome gifts. Covered with sturdy cotton in bright, bold colors, they're handy for outdoor plays or concerts, picnics, auto races, New Year's Day football games or parades, or any event where hard, rough bleachers need to be tolerated for long periods. A built-in "pocket" and carrying strap add to the cushion's practicality.

Our bold designs come from the international code-flag alphabet used in naval and air maneuvers. (The entire alphabet is shown on facing page.) You can add a special touch to your gift by combining letters to spell out family names, the recipient's initials, school slogans, team names, or any other "message" you want to send.

The smaller dimensions on our pattern make a cushion small enough to fit most stadium seats (about 12 inches square); you can add a few inches to each side if more room is a must, or make the cushions as big as 16 inches square to use where space isn't cramped.

Materials

For the 12-inch-square pillow, buy ½ yard of 45-inch-wide cotton duck or canvas; for a larger pillow, buy ¾ yard. For either, buy enough cotton duck in contrasting colors to make the design on the cushion front. Also buy ½ yard of cotton webbing (or an extra ⅛ yard of the cushion fabric) to make a strap; purchase thread to match.

Finally, you'll need a 2-inch-thick piece of foam that's ¼ inch larger all around than the cover's outside dimensions. Look in the Yellow Pages under Foam Rubber & Sponge, or buy precut foam pillow forms at a fabric store.

Making the cushion

To cut either the large or small pillow covers, follow the dimensions given on the pattern below. Cut two bottom pieces, one side band, and one top band.

For simple designs like the "O" and "K," you can piece the top together as you would a quilt square; more complicated designs (like the "N" and "M") should be appliquéd onto a single piece of fabric.

If you plan to appliqué the top design, cut one top piece. Then draw and cut out a paper pattern for the design; pin the pattern to contrasting fabric(s) and cut it out. Machine-appliqué it to the pillow top, using a zigzag stitch.

If you plan to piece the top, cut as many separate pieces as you need, remembering to include ½-inch seam allowances and making sure the pieced top will have the proper dimensions. Machine-stitch pieces together with ½-inch seams.

With right sides together, pin side band to top piece of cover along sides B, C, and D. Starting and ending ½ inch from ends, machine-stitch, allowing a ½-inch seam.

On each bottom piece, turn under ¾ inch along one long side; turn raw edges under, press, and machine-stitch.

With right sides together, lay bottom pieces over top piece, matching outer corners and putting finished edge of lower piece over upper one to make a carrying pocket (see lower photograph on facing page). Pin at several places in center to keep pieces from slipping out of alignment (make sure side band is free of pins).

Pin and stitch bottom pieces to raw edges of side band; trim seams and clip corners.

Adding the strap & top band

To make the strap, you can use either webbing or a 3- by 18-inch strip of fabric. For a fabric strap, fold the strip lengthwise, turn raw edges in ½ inch, and topstitch all sides.

Pin one end of the strap or webbing to each end of top band. With right sides together, pin band to top and bottom pieces along free side A; machine-stitch, allowing ½-inch seam. Stitch ends closed. Trim corners; turn cover right side out through back opening. Insert the foam pad.

Design: Françoise Kirkman and Kathy Perry.

First measurements are *for small pillow covers; second measurements are for large ones.*

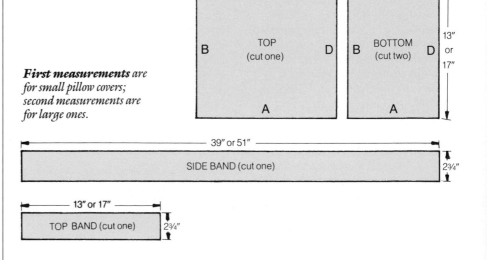

Spell out *a friend's name, school acronym, or any message you like with a row of cheerful cushions designed to soften stadium bleachers. The designs, taken from Navy code flags, give you as many choices as there are letters of the alphabet!*

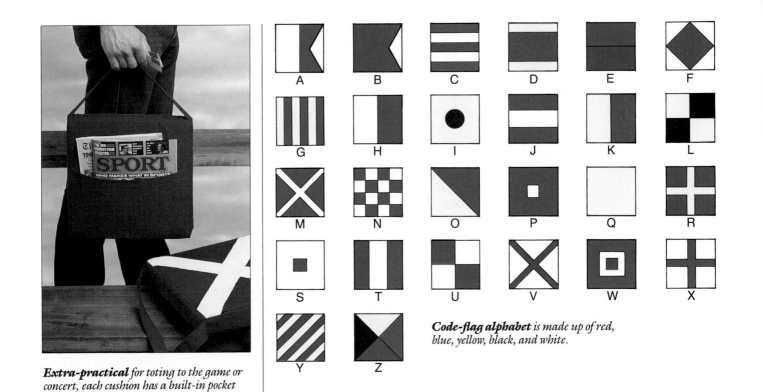

Extra-practical *for toting to the game or concert, each cushion has a built-in pocket and its own carrying strap.*

Code-flag alphabet *is made up of red, blue, yellow, black, and white.*

Exercise Pad

Ensure a soft, safe landing for your favorite fitness enthusiast with this thick, velvety exercise pad. It can be used indoors on wood, tile, or linoleum, and outdoors on brick, cement, or grass. The towel cover pulls off the foam lining for easy laundering. Self-ties attached to the pad cover let you roll it up for carrying or storage.

Materials

For a 66-inch-long mat like the one shown here, choose three terry bath towels, each about 26 by 46 inches. Try to select terry with tight loops, to avoid snagging while sewing. If there's a pattern, check to make sure you can continue it at the seam lines. You'll also need a 1-inch-thick foam pad big enough to fit between the towels—about 24 by 65 inches. For resilience and durability, buy a pad with a density value of 3 to 3.5. If you can't find a foam outlet, buy a plastic-covered pool mat of the appropriate size that's soft enough to roll.

Finally, purchase some nylon self-gripping fabric fastener tape to hold the towel cover closed at the ends.

Reward *the efforts of a health-conscious friend with a bright and cheerful exercise pad you make yourself.*

Making the pad

Cut one towel in half crosswise. Remove the binding on one end of each of the remaining whole towels to stitch together for ties. Sew the raw middle of each half towel to the raw end of one of the other two towels.

With right sides together, pin the lengthwise edges of the towels so they'll fit over the foam. Remove foam, then stitch the side seams. To make the towel cover easy to slip on and off, stitch strips of fastener tape at both ends. To find the best position for the tape, insert the foam. At each end, pull the top down over the foam's edge for a snug fit; then pull the bottom up over that. Mark where you want the tape, remove the cover, and stitch tape firmly to the towels. Sew the reserved strips of binding together and attach at the center to one end of the cover for use as ties when the pad is rolled up.

When the exercising's over, *the pad rolls up into a neat bundle held with self-ties.*

Tote Bag

Everybody can use a sturdy tote bag—for travel, for carrying sports clothing and equipment, for anything and everything. Our attractive canvas bag fits under an airline seat and also travels neatly in a car or bus. At home, it can be folded compactly and stored out of the way.

Materials

You'll need 1¼ yards of 31-inch-wide canvas or ¾ yard of 45-inch-wide heavy denim, and a 22-inch heavy-duty metal separating zipper. If you want straps in matching fabric, increase the amount to 1½ yards of the 31-inch-wide fabric or 1¼ yards of the 45-inch-wide fabric. Or use cotton webbing, as we did; you'll need 2⅜ yards of 1½-inch-wide webbing.

To stitch the tote, use a #16 or #18 needle.

Assembling the bag

Cut one bag piece 23 inches long and 32 inches wide, two 10¼-inch-diameter circles, and two 7-inch-square pockets. For matching fabric straps, cut two straps, each 4 inches wide and 43 inches long; or cut webbing into two equal lengths.

Using sewing chalk, mark a center line across the width of the bag (see diagram at right). Because some fabrics pucker when steam-pressed, test a fabric scrap before pressing bag pieces.

Pockets. Overcast top edge of each pocket, fold under ½ inch, and stitch. (If you like, use a contrasting thread color, or decorate pockets with stitching or iron-on fabric cutouts.) Fold under ½ inch on remaining three sides. On right side of bag, center each pocket with top edge 2½

inches down from 23-inch edge of bag; pin and stitch.

Straps. *If using webbing,* fold under 1½ inches at each end of straps and pin folded ends on center line, with straps extending along each side of pockets. Stitch each strap, starting at bottom line and stopping even with pocket top; stitch across strip, pivot, and continue to starting point. Backstitch to reinforce at the four points shown in the drawing.

If using matching fabric straps, fold strap pieces in half lengthwise with wrong sides together. Turn under ½-inch seam allowance on both long edges. Crease and pin; topstitch both sides of straps. Stitch straps to bag as for webbing.

Bag. Turn under ⅝-inch seam allowance on both 23-inch edges. Lay closed zipper face up. Center one edge of bag along side of zipper; pin and stitch. Pin second folded edge to other side of closed zipper. Separate zipper and stitch. Close zipper, then stitch across bottom edge above zipper stop. If needed, stitch folded edges of bag together at both ends to prevent gapping.

Open zipper part way and turn bag inside out. With right sides together, pin one circle to each end of bag, allowing a ½-inch seam. Baste, easing where necessary; stitch with matching thread. (It's easier to use a zipper foot when stitching circles close to zipper ends.) Reinforce by stitching ⅛ inch into seam allowance. Trim seam to ¼ inch and overcast. Turn bag right side out.

Design: Carol Aiken.

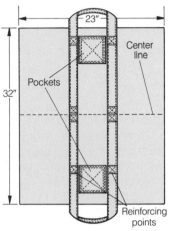

Here's how the bag goes together; note the placement of pockets, straps, and stitched reinforcing points.

Sports enthusiasts and travelers alike will put this handsome, long-wearing canvas tote bag to good use all year round.

Padded Ski Bag

What better gift could you give an avid skier during the snowy winter season than this custom-made padded ski bag? Specially designed for transporting one or two pairs of skis and poles, the handsome bag is sturdy enough to check through as airline baggage; there's extra room inside for hats, goggles, and gloves. Built-in shoulder straps make the bag easy to carry.

Materials

To make the bag shown here, buy 2⅓ yards of 60-inch-wide pack cloth (available at backpacking equipment stores), denim, or ripstop nylon. You'll also need a ½-inch-thick foam pad measuring 26½ by 82 inches. A foam store may be willing to custom-cut a piece for you; otherwise, cut down a larger piece using a ruler, felt-tip marker, and scissors.

Other materials include 2¾ yards of ¾-inch-wide nylon self-gripping fabric fastener tape; 6½ yards of 1-inch-wide nylon webbing; two 1¼-inch-wide snap-together plastic buckles; and two 1-inch metal buckles (buckles are available at sport shops).

To stitch the bag, use an industrial sewing machine if possible. If you're using a regular machine, use a #16 or #18 needle, or a leather needle.

Note: If you want to make a bag to hold two pairs of skis, buy 4⅔ yards of 45-inch fabric, a 45- by 82-inch foam pad, 3 yards of nylon self-gripping fabric fastener tape, and 9½ yards of nylon webbing. Cut fabric in half crosswise and sew two long sides together with a ½-inch seam, making one 84- by 90-inch piece. Cut fastener tape into 83- and 20-inch pieces; pull apart the shorter piece and cut the scratchy (grip) side into 9- and 11-inch pieces. Cut webbing into three pieces: 30 inches, 50 inches, and 12 feet. Then follow the steps below.

Making the bag

1. Turn raw edges of each end (AB and CD on patterns) under ½ inch and pin. Fold the fabric in half lengthwise and machine-stitch ends together.

2. Cut an 83-inch piece of fastener tape and separate it. Pin the scratchy side so it runs lengthwise from point A to point D, 1 inch from the fold, as shown in the "Inside view" pattern below. Machine-stitch along each edge of the fastener tape, reinforcing the ends with a zigzag stitch. Then insert the foam pad between the fabric layers along the open side (BC). Turn the fabric over to pin and stitch the other 83-inch strip of fastener tape (the soft side) along the selvage edge from point B to point C as shown in the "Outside view" pattern, reinforcing each end.

3. Flip the bag back to the inside view. Cut a 14-inch piece of fastener tape and separate the halves. Cut the scratchy side into 6½-inch and 7½-inch pieces and pin all three pieces to

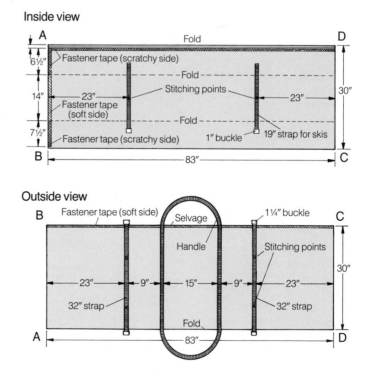

Getting to and from the slopes *is a breeze with this rugged and roomy ski bag. Make it this Christmas for your favorite skier to use all winter long.*

the fabric as indicated on the pattern. Machine-stitch along each edge of the fastener tape and reinforce the ends with a zigzag stitch.

4. Cut the webbing into two 19-inch inside straps, two 32-inch outside straps, and an 11-foot handle. Pin the inside straps to the fabric as shown in the "Inside view" pattern, then attach them at stitching points, stitching through all layers of fabric and foam. If necessary, lessen pressure on machine presser foot. Turn the bag over; center, pin, and machine-stitch the outside straps and handles to the bag at the stitching points indicated on the "Outside view" pattern. (Overlap the handle webbing at one of the stitching points.)

5. Fold the bag in thirds lengthwise, pressing the fastener tape closures. Double-stitch the bottom end (CD) closed.

6. Fasten the larger buckles to the outer straps by looping the webbing over the buckles' attachment bars and zigzag-stitching two parallel lines. Use the same technique to attach the small metal buckles to the inside straps.

Design: Françoise Kirkman.

Animal Slippers

Transform the pitter-patter of little feet into the pad of small, furry paws with our animal slippers. Warm enough for freezing January, soft enough to pamper young toes, these quilted slippers are surprisingly simple to make. We offer three pairs of creatures—romping rabbits, dashing dachshunds, and beguiling bears. To stock your gift list with other species, just alter ears and tails.

Materials

For one pair of slippers:

⅝   yard sturdy cotton or cotton blend fabric, 45 inches wide (you may substitute wool for luxury, but if you do, you must dry-clean the slippers)

⅝   yard coordinating lining fabric

8   6-inch-square cotton scraps (for padded legs)

   Solid-color fabric scraps or felt (for noses and eyes)

   Thread to match fabric

4   buttons (for pupils of eyes)

8   white pompons from curtain fringe (for rabbits' tails)

1   bag polyester batting

Making the slippers

1. The patterns for all three pairs of slippers—dog, rabbit, and bear—are on page 79.

Before transferring your pattern, measure sole length of a shoe that fits well. Divide this figure by 5 to get size of grid square on which to transfer pattern. If measurement comes out to a fraction, round off to nearest ⅛ inch.

2. Rule correct grid on paper (or use printed graph paper of correct size). Enlarge and transfer pattern (see page 64). Cut four body pieces, four ear pieces, and two sole pieces *each* from body and lining fabrics. For bear, trace a nose pattern from body pattern, following the curve of bear snout and the dotted appliqué line on the pattern. Cut four nose

(Continued on page 78)

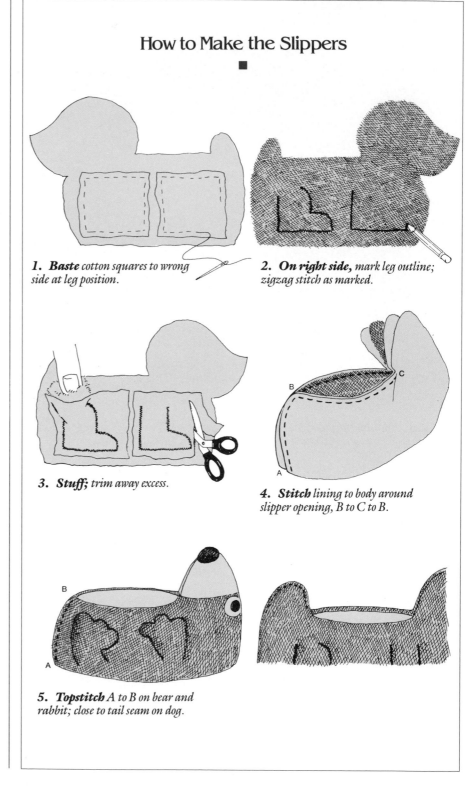

How to Make the Slippers

1. Baste cotton squares to wrong side at leg position.

2. On right side, mark leg outline; zigzag stitch as marked.

3. Stuff; trim away excess.

4. Stitch lining to body around slipper opening, B to C to B.

5. Topstitch A to B on bear and rabbit; close to tail seam on dog.

Children will love to snuggle *their toes inside a pair of our winsome animal slippers.*
The wide-eyed bears grin up at you (or down, if your feet happen to be in the air).

pieces from lining or other contrasting fabric scraps. Cut dog's nose tip and collar from contrasting scraps.

3. Sketches 1, 2, and 3 (see page 76) show how to make padded legs. Baste a 6-inch cotton square to wrong side of each body piece, one for each leg. On right side, lightly mark outlines of front and back legs, keeping marks at least ⅛ inch inside basting. Using contrasting thread, machine-stitch with a zigzag stitch over outlines. Turn to wrong side again; remove basting. Using a narrow dowel or a crochet hook, stuff each leg evenly with polyester batting to make it bulge. Trim away excess cotton scrap close to stitched outline.

4. *For each bear*, press under ¼ inch along straight edges of nose pieces. Topstitch close to pressed edge to attach to each body piece where indicated on pattern. Baste along curved edges.

5. To join all slippers, stitch body pieces, right sides together, from A to B (all seams in slipper body are ½ inch). Repeat for lining pieces. Press seams open. With right sides together, stitch lining to each body

It's an animal parade—*goofy bears lead the way, rabbits hop between, dachshunds bring up the rear.*

around slipper opening (B to C and back to B as in sketch 4, page 76). Stitch again to reinforce corner at C; clip corner. Turn right side out and press.

6. Topstitch from A to B close to seam of rabbit and bear, close to top of dog's tail (see sketch 5, page 76). Topstitching stabilizes the heel and holds the body and lining together during stuffing.

7. With right sides together, baste and stitch each body around head from C to D, joining all four thicknesses. Trim seam; clip curves and corners. Turn to right side; reinforce point C with a few hand stitches.

8. To make each sole, place a layer of batting between wrong sides of sole and lining pieces. Baste all three layers together. With right sides together, matching A and D, stitch sole

to body, leaving seam open between notches on *both* sides. Trim seam; turn right side out. Using a narrow dowel or crochet hook, stuff each slipper with polyester batting. Blindstitch openings closed.

9. Pair and stitch together ears and bear's tail (we used lining fabric for inside of each ear, body fabric for outside; our bear's tail is entirely body fabric). Turn pieces right side out and stuff. Tuck raw edges to inside; blindstitch openings closed. Securely stitch ears and bear's tail in place. Appliqué bear's and dog's nose tips and dog's collar. Sew on clusters of four pompons for each rabbit's tail. Appliqué felt eyes; sew on button pupils.

Design: Françoise Kirkman.

Slipper Patterns

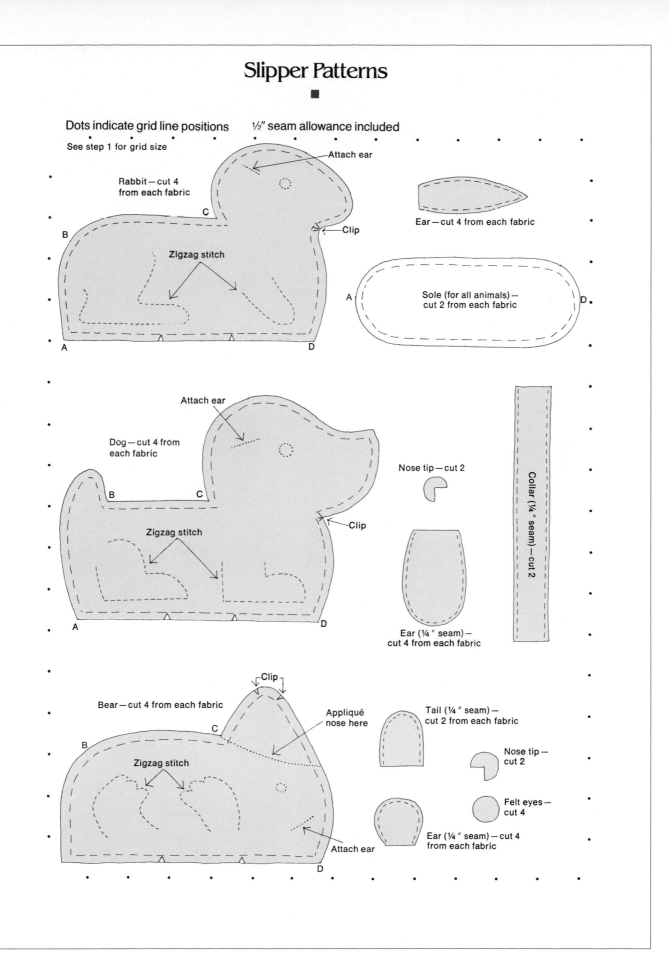

Dots indicate grid line positions
See step 1 for grid size

½″ seam allowance included

Attach ear

Rabbit—cut 4 from each fabric

Clip

Zigzag stitch

Ear—cut 4 from each fabric

Sole (for all animals)—cut 2 from each fabric

Attach ear

Dog—cut 4 from each fabric

Clip

Zigzag stitch

Nose tip—cut 2

Ear (¼″ seam)—cut 4 from each fabric

Collar (¼″ seam)—cut 2

Clip

Bear—cut 4 from each fabric

Appliqué nose here

Zigzag stitch

Attach ear

Tail (¼″ seam)—cut 2 from each fabric

Nose tip—cut 2

Felt eyes—cut 4

Ear (¼″ seam)—cut 4 from each fabric

Dream Bags

Sweet dreams get a head start with these child-size sleeping bags. They make squealing around a hairpin turn, blasting off for the moon, or gently flitting from flower to flower seem possible almost without closing tired eyes.

Big enough for children up to eight years old, the racing car, rocket, or butterfly can be spread out on a living room floor or taken outside on balmy evenings. (The bags aren't designed for cold or wet nights.) Each has a built-in pillow and a generous surface near the head for spreading out small toys, a book, or a favorite stuffed animal.

Wheels, fins, and wings give each bag a special character, but all start with the same basic shell: a 24-inch-wide, 48-inch-long sleeve with a nylon outer layer, an inner layer of polyester batting, and a cotton liner.

In the list at right, we give you only the quantity and type of fabric; you can follow our color scheme or create one that's tailored to the recipient's tastes.

In addition to a sewing machine and scissors, you'll need a yardstick, sewing chalk, and butcher paper for patterns.

Materials

For each bag's basic shell:

2¾ yards medium-weight nylon, 45 inches wide (for the outside shell)

2¼ yards polyester quilt batting, 48 inches wide

2¾ yards cotton (for liner)

Matching thread

For the racing car:

2 yards black cotton (for tires)

½ yard cotton (for exhaust pipe)

⅓ yard cotton (for semicircular pillow front)

½ yard cotton (for axle and number plate)

1 package *each* of two colors of double-fold bias tape

Thread to match fabric and bias tape

For the rocket ship:

1 yard cotton (for pillow)

2 yards cotton (for fins)

1 package *each* of 3 colors of single-fold bias tape

2 packages of double-fold bias tape

Thread to match fabric and bias tape

Note: Our rocket ship has a flame-shaped orange pillow that contrasts with the blue fins. Numbers and striping are bias tape; you can add any flag or ornamental insignia you like.

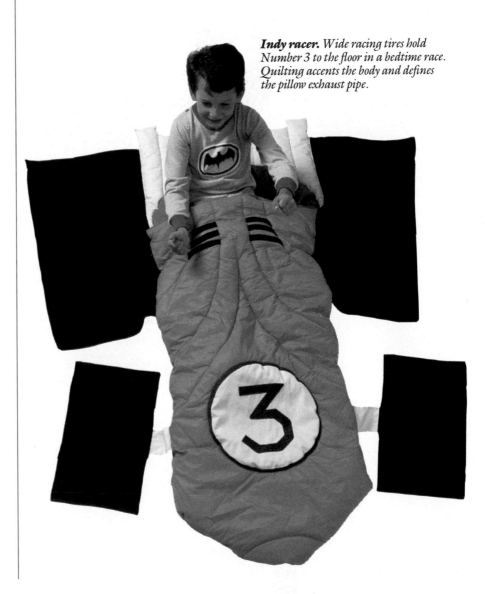

Indy racer. Wide racing tires hold Number 3 to the floor in a bedtime race. Quilting accents the body and defines the pillow exhaust pipe.

For the butterfly:

1 yard cotton (for pillow)

1 yard cotton (for lower wing section)

4 yards cotton (for upper wing section); use 5¼ yards if you choose a one-way design that must be cut on straight grain

½ yard contrasting cotton (for antennae)

1 package single-fold bias tape

Thread to match fabric and bias tape

Note: This bag requires the most fabric because of its big, two-sided wings. We used a striped fabric for the upper wings and a dotted one for the lower sections (see photo on next page), but you could use one patterned fabric for the whole area. To duplicate ours, you'll need the amounts listed above.

Cutting out the pieces

Enlarge the patterns below onto butcher paper, then transfer to fabric (see page 64). Cut two of each piece except for the butterfly antennae and the racer's pillow semicircle, front wheels, and axles.

To make the bag, you'll assemble the various elements (side panels, pillows, and body) separately and join them together before adding the bag liner.

Making the decorative elements

The racer's tires are unadorned, but the rocket and butterfly have other shapes and bias tape appliquéd to

Rocket ship. Letters and striping are bias tape topstitched to the top layer of the blue cotton fins. Quilted details on the pillow repeat its flame shape.

them. Before joining the upper sides together, you must add these elements.

The rocket fins can have lettering and stripes made with single-fold bias tape. Add them and any flags or insignia to the top layer of fabric. Stitch the double-fold tape around the fins' outside edges. Leave open the edge of the fin facing the body.

(Continued on next page)

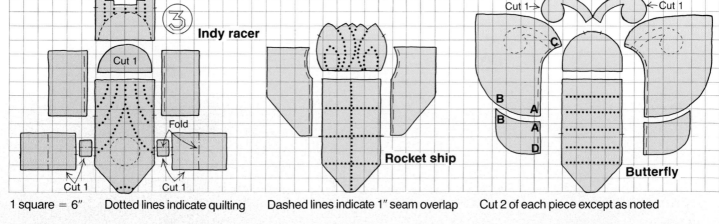

Indy racer · Cut 1 · Fold · Cut 1 · Cut 1

Rocket ship

Butterfly · Cut 1 · Cut 1 · C · B · A · B · A · D

1 square = 6"   Dotted lines indicate quilting   Dashed lines indicate 1" seam overlap   Cut 2 of each piece except as noted

The racing car has front tires with axles that extend to the body and rear tires that join the body directly. Cut out two axle shapes and fold each in half, right sides together; stitch a ½-inch seam along the side opposite the fold. Turn right side out and press. Fold each front tire piece, right sides together, along fold line in diagram (page 81). Stitch a ½-inch seam around raw edges, leaving an opening midway along long side; turn right side out and press. Position axle in opening, then stitch around all sides of tire.

Butterfly wings. Each wing has upper and lower sections made of separate pieces of fabric (four for each wing). After cutting out the antennae, press under the raw edges ¼ inch, then clip curves.

Pin each antenna to an upper wing section as shown by the dotted lines on the pattern; then baste and machine-stitch.

Pin and baste each pair of upper and lower wing sections together between A and B, right sides together; clip curve on lower section to make a smooth stitching line, then machine-stitch pieces together. Press seam.

With right sides together, pin and baste each pair of wings together around their outer edges, leaving opening along CAD; machine-stitch, turn right side out, and press. If desired, trim outer edges of lower wing sections with bias tape, as pictured.

Making the pillows

All three bags have pillows attached to the top of the body section. Cut two pillow pieces (a front and a back) of fabric and one of batting. Clip curves, fold under a ½-inch seam allowance on fabric, and press.

The front piece of the racing car pillow has two parts: an exhaust pipe section overlaid along its base by a semicircle of cotton. After cutting the semicircle, clip along arc, turn under ½ inch, and press. Cut a piece of batting the same size as pressed semicircle, position it on the exhaust pipe piece, and cover with the semicircle. Baste and stitch along arc.

Bright-winged butterfly. Its broad wings carry teddy and friend to Dreamland. Including wings, the bag measures 6 feet wide and long.

Putting the Pieces Together

■

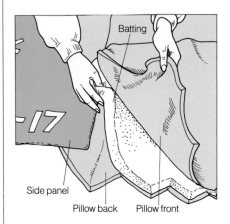

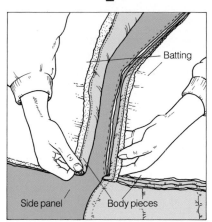

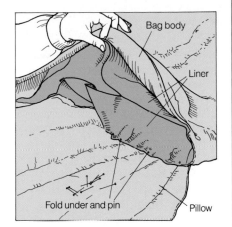

Insert *completed side panel over pillow back, beneath batting and pillow front. Stitch together. Add any quilting details to pillow after assembly.*

Before stitching long sides *of bag together, sandwich side panel between body pieces with batting faces up. After stitching, turn bag right side out.*

Slip the liner *inside bag, then fold and pin the raw edges together along top edge and against the pillow on bottom. Machine-stitch to complete.*

On a flat work surface, place back pillow piece right side down. Next, lay right and left side panels (rear tires, fins, or wings) so they lap 1 inch over the pillow piece. The side panels should be parallel and about 23 inches apart, with the pillow piece bridging the top. Pin in place.

Place batting over back pillow piece and set front pillow piece in place, right side up. Baste all pieces together and topstitch completely around the pillow.

Add quilting details on the pillow for car and rocket, or topstitch a piece of bias tape around the arc of the butterfly pillow.

Making the bag body

For all designs, cut out two identical body pieces *each* from the nylon, batting, and lining materials. Pin batting to wrong side of each nylon body piece, and stitch along dotted lines (nylon side up) to produce quilting as in the photographs on pages 80, 81, and 82. Trim batting even with body edges. For the racer, add the big number plate; for the rocket, add lines of bias tape.

To join the body to the assembled pillow and side sections, hold pillow with base side up. To this edge, pin top edge of back body piece with a ¾-inch seam—right side of body to back side of pillow. Baste and stitch.

Turn over body/pillow section with batting side down and fold one side panel on top of the nylon, with raw edges even. Baste raw edges and repeat for other panel. Lay front body piece, nylon side down, on top with raw edges even. Making sure side panels stay inside body shape, pin, baste, and stitch around bag. Then clip corners, trim off excess batting, and turn right side out.

Adding the cotton liner

Allowing a ½-inch seam, pin the two lining pieces with right sides together; baste and stitch, leaving top end open. Insert lining in bag and turn raw top edges under ½ inch; lay back lining on top of the pillow edge and baste in place, then machine-stitch. Turn under the raw edge of the front body piece, align the folded edges of bag and lining fronts, pin, and topstitch. To keep lining in place, reach inside and tack lining to body along seam lines.

Design: Florence Goguely.

Child's Nature Pack

This simple but very special gift will provide a budding naturalist with inspiration for outdoor activities all year round. No ordinary satchel, our child-size backpack or shoulder bag is stuffed with equipment that can turn a casual stroll through a forest or along a beach into an exciting expedition of discovery.

In stocking the pack, let your imagination (and the natural interests of your young explorer) be your guide. You might include a small net, clear plastic jar, outdoor thermometer, magnifying glass, bug box, and small notebook and pencil. If you want to get a little fancier, add a pair of binoculars.

Materials

To make a pack like the ones shown here, you'll need a 14- by 28-inch piece of pack cloth (available at backpacking equipment stores), 6 inches of nylon self-gripping fabric fastener tape, a yard of 1-inch-wide nylon webbing, and—for the shoulder bag only—a 1-inch-wide snap-together plastic buckle.

To stitch the pack and bag, use a #16 or #18 needle, or a leather needle.

Making the pack

On a piece of paper at least 14 by 28 inches, draw a grid of 2-inch squares; enlarge the pattern at right (see page 64). Pin pattern to fabric, marking letters and location of straps and fastener tape with sewing chalk or pencil. Cut out. Turn the bottom edge (AA) under ½ inch; machine-stitch.

To make hemming the curve of the flap easier, first machine-stitch CDC ½ inch from the edge, then clip the ½-inch seam allowances at both C's, fold along the stitching, pin, and stitch again.

Next, cut the fastener tape into one 4-inch and two 1-inch pieces. Separate each piece. Machine-stitch the soft sides of the fastener tape to the underside of the flap as indicated by the dotted lines on the pattern. Fold AA to CC, wrong sides together; then fold flap down over bag. Pin the scratchy sides of the fastener tape to the outside of the bag, lining them up with the soft sides already sewn in place on the flap. Stitch in place.

For the backpack: Cut the webbing into two equal pieces; turn ends under. Pin the webbing to the fabric as indicated on the pattern. Adjust the straps to the right length for the child. Machine-stitch each end in place by sewing a ¾-inch square crossed by an X.

For the shoulder bag: Cut the webbing into two equal pieces and seal all ends with a small flame. Stitch one end around plastic buckle loop, stitching an X-reinforced square as described above. Using the same method, attach two ends to the out-side of the pack as indicated on the pattern (the free ends should extend toward the flap). Slip the remaining loose end through the ridged piece of the buckle and adjust the length to the child.

Finally, for both pack and shoulder bag, fold AA to CC, right sides together, and stitch both sides (BC). Turn right side out.

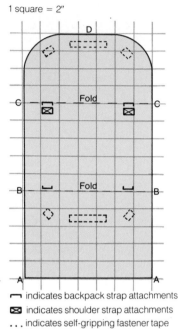

1 square = 2"

⌐ indicates backpack strap attachments
⊠ indicates shoulder strap attachments
... indicates self-gripping fastener tape placement

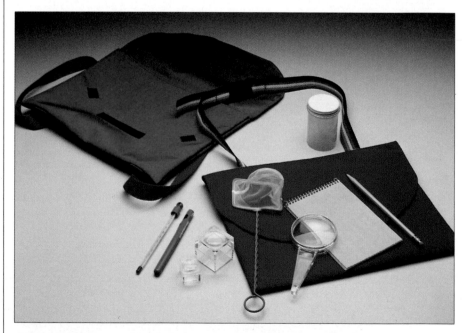

Basic gear *might include a note pad and pencil, magnifying glass, fishnet, bug boxes, outdoor thermometer in a case, and a collecting jar.*

Child-size pack *can be made to sling over the shoulder or carry on the back; it holds all the equipment your young naturalist will need for an afternoon trek.*

Creature Carryalls

Surprise your youngster on Christmas morning with a big, friendly frog, a grinning crocodile, or a cuddly canine. Our appealing menagerie of soft critters is fun to play with, but there's more. Each is a tote bag that's sturdy enough to carry books to school or to stuff with towels and clothes for trips to the beach or gym.

The crocodile, dog, and frog are made with similar construction techniques. Each starts with a body made of two large sides, an underbody, and a zippered opening. To this shell, you add four legs, eyes, carrying straps, and—for the dog—a tail.

Fabric

There's no telling what might end up in these bags, so they should be made with a durable fabric. Choose a heavy cotton, or cotton-polyester blend, denim, or canvas. Line the bags with the same fabric or select a lighter-weight contrasting one.

Use 45-inch-wide fabric for all three carryalls. The dog and crocodile each require 1½ yards for the outside and 1½ yards for the lining; to make the frog, you'll need 2 yards for the outside and 1½ yards for the lining.

Stuffing

For each animal, buy 3 yards of 36-inch-wide polyester quilt batting (or 1¼ yards of 60-inch-wide batting). You'll also need a 1½-pound bag of polyester stuffing for the legs and tail.

Crocodile's smile is the oversize zipper running around his snout. *The stubby legs and ping-pong-ball eyes go on last.*

Additional materials

Heavy-duty zippers are the pearly white teeth of each animal. Use a 20-inch zipper for the dog, a 24-inch zipper for the frog or crocodile.

The whimsically detailed eyes are easy to make. The frog's eyes are foam tennis balls from a toy store, while the other critters' are ping-pong balls. All the pupils are black ⅞-inch-diameter buttons with steel shanks. You'll also need 1⅛-inch shanked buttons that can be covered: one button for mounting each leg and, if you're making the dog, two for securing the tail. The dog's nose is a black 1⅛-inch shanked button. To prevent the fabric from tearing, each button is reinforced with a ¾-inch metal washer (sold in fabric stores as weights for curtains; you can also use a small button). To sew

the buttons in place, you'll need unwaxed dental floss and a long darning needle.

Finally, you'll need about 3 yards of 1¼- or 1½-inch-wide cotton webbing for the handles. (You may want to shorten the straps to suit a child's height.)

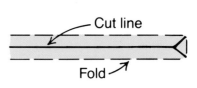

*Detail of **mouth corner** shows solid lines for cutting, dotted lines for turning under.*

Start with the pattern

The sketches on page 88 show the patterns for the animals. Make a grid of 4-inch squares on sturdy paper; enlarge all the pattern pieces for the animal you are making (see page 64). Pin the pattern pieces in place (note that underbody is on the fold), then cut. Remember that you'll need eight leg pieces (four pairs), plus ears and tail for the dog, so lay out pattern pieces carefully to make the most efficient use of your fabric. Repeat for the lining fabric.

First make a cut for the zipper, cutting both outside and lining fabric from snout to letter D. On both lining and outside fabric, turn raw edge along mouth under ¼ inch; clip corners at D and turn under ¼ inch. (See detail sketch on facing page.) Press.

Unless noted otherwise, all seam allowances are ½ inch. Join the two outside parts of the body along AC. Press seam open. Repeat for the lining. Sandwich zipper in between lining and outside layers; baste and machine-stitch.

Next, cut the batting to the size of the pattern. You'll have to cut away some batting to fit around the zipper and inside line AC. Position the batting between the outside fabric and the lining, adding a little extra to the top of the dog's and crocodile's heads. To hold the three parts together, baste around edges and zigzag-stitch through all three layers.

To make the underbody, sandwich the batting between the outside fabric and lining, baste, and use a zigzag stitch to finish the edges. Trim any excess batting from body and underbody. Make a dart in dog's underbody where indicated on pattern.

Completing the body

At this point, each animal has three flat parts—two upper body pieces connected at the nose and an underbody. Before joining the two body pieces and the underbody, add the webbed handles with a carrying loop on the sides of each body piece; for placement, see dotted lines on diagram (page 88). Cut the length of webbing into two pieces, each about 1½ yards long; pin in place, then stitch close to edge, reinforcing the stitching across webbing where it leaves body.

Place the upper body pieces with right sides together; have zipper partially open so you can turn body right side out. Baste and stitch together from C to B. Then baste and stitch underbody to body, right sides together. Clip where indicated at curves and angles; baste around the edges to hold all layers together, and use a zigzag stitch through all layers. Turn animal right side out through zipper.

(Continued on next page)

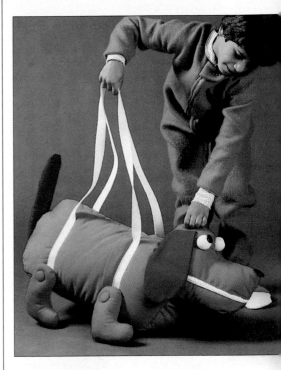

Walking the dog *is easy when you use the sturdy straps as a leash. Each strap loops from front to back on the same side.*

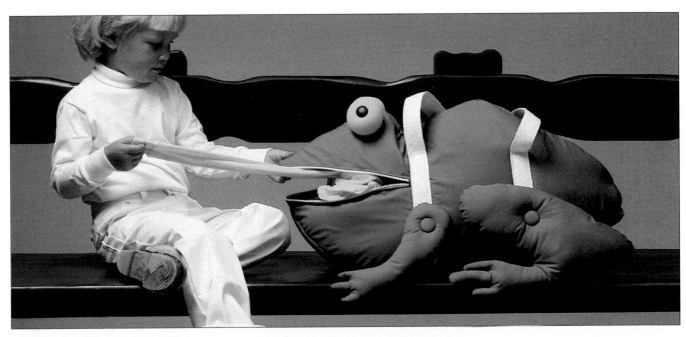

This bug-eyed frog *has foam tennis balls and buttons for eyes. You'll need a knitting needle or slender dowel to push stuffing into the long toes at the tips of its legs.*

Eyes, ears, other appendages

The legs (and dog's tail) come next. Place right sides together and stitch, using a ¼-inch seam allowance and leaving room to turn pieces right side out. Turn, press, and fill with polyester stuffing. Stuff firmly, hand-stitch legs (and tail) closed, and cover the 1⅛-inch buttons with fabric.

To attach each leg (and the dog's tail) to the body, you'll need four thicknesses of dental floss. Position the legs on the webbing, as shown by the X's in the drawing, and run the needle from the inside out. Run it through the washer, lining, batting, outside, webbing, leg, and shank of button, and back again; repeat. Firmly secure the floss inside. The dog's tail needs two buttons to keep it upright.

Use the same technique to secure the eyes to the heads. (For the frog, cut a thin slice from the foam ball to make it rest flat against the head.) Starting from the inside, push the needle through the head, ping-pong (or foam tennis) balls, through shanks on the smaller buttons, and back through the balls. Use the needle to make a hole in the ping-pong ball large enough for the shank. (You could also use large white buttons for eyes with smaller buttons for pupils.) Firmly secure the thread inside.

To complete the dog, add the button nose and ears. For each ear, place fabric right sides together and stitch; turn and press. Place raw edge of ear on dotted line indicated on pattern, with ear facing up toward top of head. Hand-stitch along edge and ½ inch above, stitching through ears, fabric, and stuffing. Let ears flop down to cover stitching.

To protect the critters, spray with a stain-resisting fabric spray.

Design: Françoise Kirkman.

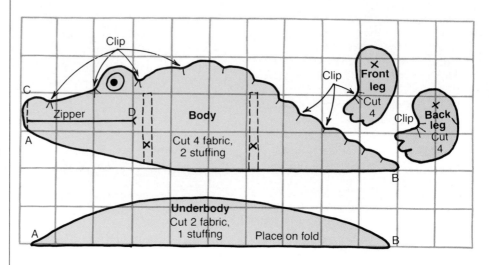

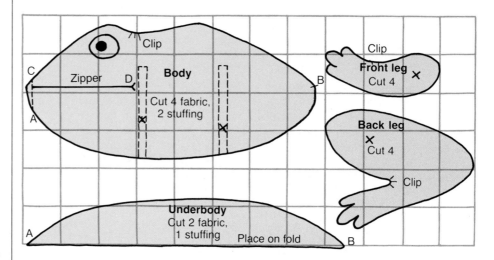

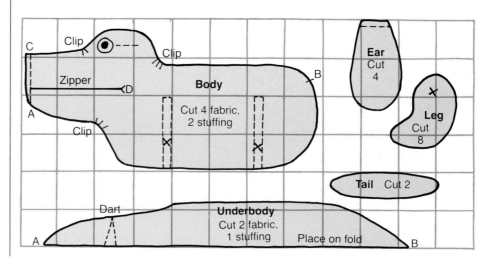

Hobby Horses

Our one-of-a-kind hobby horses—a perky pony and an enchanted unicorn—will provide hours of make-believe fun for imaginative young children.

Materials

For one horse:

⅓ yard low- to medium-pile fake fur
   20- by 4-inch strip high-pile fake fur
½ pound polyester stuffing
2 large and 2 small dome-shaped buttons
   Heavy-duty thread
   White glue
3 feet of ⅜-inch or ½-inch dowel
   Scrap of corduroy (for horse ears)
⅛ yard gold lamé (for unicorn horn)

Assembling the horse

Note: When stitching fake fur, push pile away from seams.

1. Enlarge and transfer pattern pieces (see page 64). Cut head, gusset, and ears from low-pile fabric. (*For horse,* cut two of the four ear pieces from corduroy.) Cut mane from high-pile fabric. (*For unicorn,* cut horn from gold lamé.)

2. Stitch head pieces, right sides together, from A down to neck edge. Pin and stitch mane to gusset at B. Pin gusset/mane to one head piece; stitch from A to C. Repeat for other head piece. Turn right side out and stuff head above neck.

3. Slipstitch one seam joining mane to head below C. Stuff neck except for bottom 2 inches. Insert dowel in neck; spread glue inside neck. Bring remaining seam edges together. Wrap heavy-duty thread around neck to secure it to dowel; let dry. Slipstitch remaining seam closed.

4. Stitch each pair of ears, right sides together, leaving lower edge open. (*For horse,* use 1 fur and 1 corduroy piece for each ear.) Turn right side out; slipstitch to head.

For unicorn, stitch horn pieces, right sides together; turn and stuff. Slipstitch horn to head.

5. Sew large buttons in place for eyes; use small buttons for nostrils. If desired, add bridle of ½-inch-wide ribbon, neck scarf, or fake flowers.

Design: Philippa K. Mars and Babs Kavanaugh.

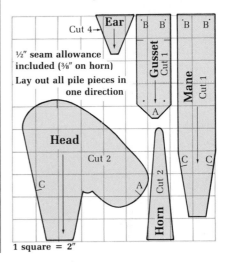

Watch delighted children *gallop around the Christmas tree on these cuddly hobby horses. Both the unicorn and the horse go together quickly; decorative options—bridles, scarves, flowers—are limited only by your imagination.*

Puppet Menagerie

Stitch up this winsome quartet of furred and feathered characters, then watch them come alive on Christmas morning, in the hands of delighted young puppeteers.

Materials

For one skunk or beaver:

³/₈ yard medium-pile fake fur (for skunk, black; for beaver, brown)

   Polyester stuffing

3 black dome-shaped buttons, ½ inch in diameter

   5- by 36-inch strip of white high-pile fake fur (for skunk's gusset, tail, and stripe)

   Scrap of red print fabric (for skunk's scarf)

   Scrap of brown synthetic suede (for beaver tail)

   Scrap of polyester quilt batting (for beaver tail)

³/₈ yard orange ribknit fabric (for beaver's cap)

1 white yarn pompon (for beaver's cap)

   Scrap of white felt (for beaver teeth)

   Scrap of corduroy (for beaver ears)

For one chicken or parrot:

½ yard felt (for chicken, yellow; for parrot, red)

   Polyester stuffing

2 black dome-shaped buttons, ³/₈ inch in diameter

   Fusible web

2 squares **each** of lavender, blue, turquoise, orange, and hot pink felt (for parrot)

1 square **each** of orange and rust felt (for chicken head)

   Scrap of green calico fabric (for chicken's collar)

¾ yard green ribbon, ¼ inch wide (for chicken's collar)

Skunk or beaver

Note: When stitching fake fur, push pile away from seams.

1. Enlarge and transfer pattern pieces (see page 64) and cut fabric pieces following instructions on grid. *For beaver,* cut body, head, gusset, and two of the four ear pieces from medium-pile fur; cut other two ear pieces from corduroy. Cut tail pieces from synthetic suede; cut cap from ribknit fabric. *For skunk,* cut body, head, and ear pieces from medium-pile fur; cut gusset, tail, and stripe pieces from high-pile fur; cut scarf from red fabric.

2. Stitch body pieces, right sides together, leaving bottom open. Clip curves; turn right side out. Turn hem under ¾ inch; topstitch. (*For skunk,* first sew stripe to body back with zigzag stitch along edges.)

3. Pin one head piece to gusset, right sides together, matching symbols; stitch from A to B. Repeat for other head piece; stitch front head seam from A down to neck opening. Clip curves; turn and stuff.

4. Stitch ears, right sides together, leaving bottom open. (*For beaver,* use one fur and one corduroy piece for each ear.) Clip curves and turn. Turn edges under ¼ inch; slipstitch to head.

5. Pin tail pieces, right sides together; stitch, leaving end open. Clip curves; turn. (*For beaver tail,* cut an additional tail piece from batting. Pin synthetic suede tail pieces, right sides together; then pin batting piece against one suede piece and stitch through all three layers. Trim, clip, and turn. Make bar tacks, as marked.) Stitch tail to back body at lower edge.

6. Turn lower edges of head under ¼ inch and slipstitch to body with heavy-duty thread. Sew buttons in place for eyes and nose with heavy-duty thread. (*For beaver teeth,* transfer pattern to white felt; don't cut. Stitch on lines through two pieces of felt; cut teeth out close to stitching, cutting halfway up between teeth at center. Slipstitch teeth to head.)

7. *For skunk's scarf,* turn edges under ¼ inch, turn again ¼ inch, and topstitch. *For beaver's cap,* cut ear slits; fold cap right sides together and zigzag-stitch close to side edge. Fold bottom under ⅛ inch; zigzag-stitch hem. Sew pompon to tip of cap.

Fuzzy fake fur and rainbow-bright felt, *together with simple stitching and a dash of whimsy, make these perky puppet pals.*

Parrot

1. Enlarge and transfer pattern pieces (see page 64) and cut fabric pieces following instructions on grid. Cut body and head from red felt; cut wing, chest, and tail pieces from blue, orange, turquoise, lavender, and pink felt. Also cut corresponding wing and chest pieces from fusible web (cut web for wing pieces A and B along dotted lines).

2. Arrange chest pieces in order of descending size. Bond pieces to each other with fusible web; then bond chest to body front along placement lines.

3. Pin body pieces, right sides together, and stitch, leaving bottom open. Clip curves and turn. Stitch through both layers on wings following marked lines.

4. Arrange the three large wing pieces in order of descending size, matching edges at F; bond to each other and to wing backs on body with fusible web. Center smallest wing piece D over edge F. Pin tail pieces together in order of descending size, adding small tail pieces E; machine-stitch tail to bottom edge of body back through all layers.

5. Outline beak pieces on orange felt; don't cut. Leaving straight sides open, stitch just inside lines through two layers of felt; cut out just outside stitching. Stuff beak loosely.

6. Pin beak to one head piece at B-C. Pin head pieces, right sides together, and stitch, leaving bottom open. Clip, turn, and stuff. With heavy-duty thread, slipstitch head to body, then sew on buttons for eyes.

Chicken

1. Enlarge and transfer pattern pieces (see page 64) and cut fabric pieces following instructions on grid. Cut body and head from yellow felt; cut face pieces from rust felt. Also cut two face pieces from fusible web.

2. Follow Parrot Step 3.

3. Follow Parrot Step 5, but do not stuff beak. Repeat process for comb and wattle pieces, outlining wattle twice on felt.

Buck-toothed beaver, *flamboyant parrot, jaunty chicken, and cuddly skunk make up a foursome that's sure to provide children with ample material for hours of barnyard dramatics.*

4. Bond face pieces onto head pieces as marked, using fusible web. Fold beak pieces lengthwise, with upper beak overlapping lower beak, and folded edges facing away from each other. Pin folded beak, plus comb and wattle, at marked locations on one head piece, as shown at right. Then follow Parrot Step 6.

5. To make collar, cut a 14- by 5-inch rectangle of green calico. Turn short ends under ¼ inch, turn again ¼ inch, and topstitch. Fold fabric in half lengthwise, right sides together; stitch ¼ inch from raw edges. Turn

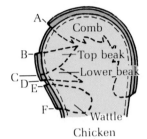

Chicken

and press; stitch ½ inch from seamed edge to form casing. Thread ribbon through casing; gather collar around chicken's neck and tie ribbon in a bow.

Design: Philippa K. Mars & Babs Kavanaugh.

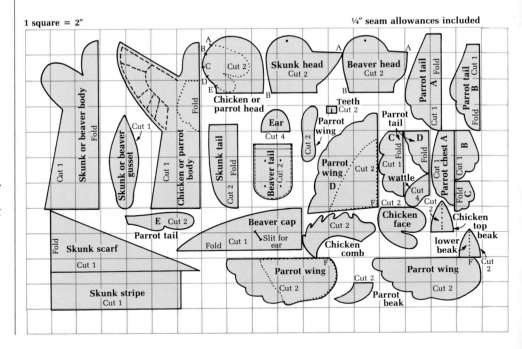

1 square = 2"   ¼" seam allowances included

Toy Bear & Raccoon

(Bear also pictured on front cover)

Sturdy enough to be slept on, hugged, and dragged around by the ears for years to come, our lovable stuffed bear and raccoon will capture any child's heart.

Materials

For one bear or raccoon:

- ½ yard fake fur (for raccoon, gray; for bear, brown)
- 1½ pounds polyester stuffing
- 2 round ½-inch-diameter buttons for eyes

  Scraps of synthetic suede (beige for bear snout, inner ears, paw pads, and soles; brown for bear nose; gray for raccoon inner ears; black for raccoon nose and mouth)

  10-inch-square piece of black fake fur (for raccoon tail and mask)
- ¼ yard firmly woven black fabric (for raccoon hands and feet)

Making the bear

Note: When stitching fake fur, push pile away from seams.

1. Enlarge and transfer bear pattern (solid-line pieces) according to grid scale (see page 64). Cut fabric pieces as directed on grid, adding ½-inch seam allowances. Reverse pattern pieces for body side, head side, and snout side to make left and right sides. Cut snout top, snout sides, chin, paw pads, soles, and two of the four ear pieces from beige suede. Cut a 2-inch circle for nose from brown suede. Cut all other pieces from brown fake fur.

2. Stitch curved darts in body front; press toward center. Appliqué paw pads to arms on body front.

3. Pin and stitch body side pieces to body front, right sides together, leaving feet open at bottom edge. Stitch again to reinforce curves; clip curves. Stitch soles to bottoms of feet, right sides together; clip curves.

Give the classic Christmas gift *of a cuddly stuffed bear to a very special child; your individual touch makes it one of a kind.*

4. Stitch body side pieces, right sides together, along back seam.

5. To make head, stitch snout side pieces to corresponding head side pieces and snout top to head top, right sides together, matching symbols. Stitch chin and neck together, then stitch curved dart in combined piece. With right sides facing, pin one snout/head side piece to chin/neck piece, matching symbols; stitch. Repeat for other side. Then pin and stitch top snout/head piece in place. Clip curves and point; turn head right side out. Stitch darts in nose; glue in place at tip of snout.

6. With body wrong side out and head right side out, pin head upside down in body, snout facing forward. Stitch, leaving back of neck open.

7. Turn bear right side out. Stuff body and head; slipstitch neck opening closed. Hand-stitch button eyes in place.

8. Stitch inner and outer ear pieces, right sides together, leaving bottom edge open. Clip curves and turn right side out. Turn raw edges under ½ inch; slipstitch ears to head.

9. Fold tail piece, right sides together; stitch curved side, leaving end open. Clip curves and trim seam. Turn right side out and stuff. Turn raw edges under ½ inch; slipstitch tail to body at F.

Making the raccoon

Note: When stitching fake fur, push pile away from seams.

1. Enlarge and transfer raccoon pattern (dotted-line pieces) according to grid scale (see page 64). Cut all fabric pieces *except tail* as directed on grid, adding ½-inch seam allowances. Reverse pattern pieces for body side and head side to make left and right sides; reverse hand and foot patterns for two of the four pieces. Cut hand and foot pieces from black woven fabric; cut mask from black fake fur. Cut two of the four ear pieces from gray synthetic suede; cut nose from black synthetic suede. All other pieces are cut from gray fake fur.

2. Stitch darts in body front; press toward center. With right sides together, stitch one hand or foot piece to each arm and leg on body front; repeat for limbs on body side pieces.

3. Pin and stitch body side pieces to body front, right sides together, leaving feet open between points K and L. Stitch again to reinforce curves; clip curves. To close each foot, bring raw edges together, matching seams in center; stitch across end.

4. Stitch body side pieces, right sides together, along back seam.

5. To assemble head, stitch head top to one head side piece, right sides together, matching symbols. Repeat for other head side. Stitch head sides together from B to C. Stitch curved dart in neck, and then stitch to head side pieces, matching symbols. Clip curves and points; turn head right side out.

6. Follow Bear Step 6.

7. Turn raccoon right side out and stuff. Fill hands and feet first, then stitch fingers and toes along markings. Continue stuffing body and head; slipstitch neck opening closed.

8. Trim fur on snout close to backing; also trim mask pieces. Machine zigzag along edge of mask pieces; hand-stitch them in place on face. Cut a 2- by ¼-inch mouth from black synthetic suede. Hand-stitch nose, mouth, and button eyes to face.

9. Follow Bear Step 8.

10. To make tail, cut five 9- by 2½-inch strips *each* of gray and black fur. Alternating colors, stitch them together with ¼-inch seams to make a 10- by 9-inch rectangle. Cut tail pieces from rectangle. Stitch pieces, right sides together, matching fabric stripes. Clip point; turn tail right side out and stuff. Turn raw edges under ½ inch; slipstitch tail to body at F.

Design: Françoise Kirkman.

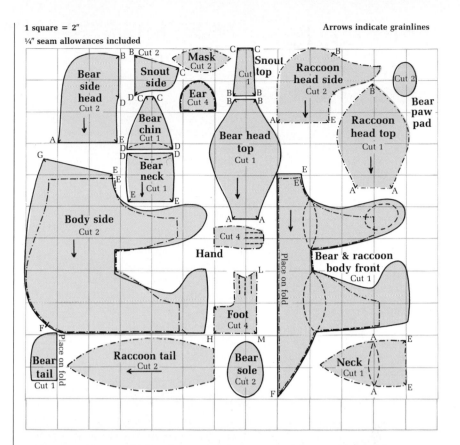

1 square = 2″
¼″ seam allowances included

Arrows indicate grainlines

This bright-eyed raccoon *makes an especially appealing playmate for almost any child on your Christmas list.*

Beanbag Hen & Duck

Comfy to curl up in, tough enough for a rollicking ride, our ring-necked mallard and bright red hen will quickly become favorite friends.

Materials

Note: Use firmly woven cottons or cotton blends, 45 inches wide.

For one beanbag hen:

- 4½ yards red and white print fabric
- ¼ yard red fabric
  - Scraps of white fabric
- 5 pounds polyester stuffing
- 7 cubic feet (2½ bags) styrene foam pellets
  - Heavy-duty thread

For one beanbag duck:

- 1 yard dark green fabric
- ¾ yard white fabric
- ½ yard **each** yellow and black fabric
- 1¾ yards red and white print fabric
- 1½ yards red fabric
  - Scraps of white fabric
- 6 pounds polyester stuffing
- 7 cubic feet (2½ bags) styrene foam pellets

Making the hen

1. Enlarge and transfer appropriate pattern pieces (see page 64) and markings (ignore dashed lines on body top, body side, and underbody). Cut head, beak gusset, neck circle, and body pieces from print fabric; comb and eye pupils from red fabric; and eyes from white scrap.

2. Machine-appliqué eye and pupil in place on each head piece. With right sides together, stitch three comb pieces in place on each head piece; press seams open.

3. Folding right sides together, stitch curved dart F in beak gusset. Matching E, F, and G, stitch one edge of gusset to each head piece, right sides together. Clip curve. Matching comb pieces, right sides together, stitch two head pieces along top curved edge, leaving straight edge (neck) open. Clip curve and corners; turn right side out.

4. Firmly stuff head with polyester stuffing, poking in small amounts at a time. When head is packed full, place neck circle over neck opening, wrong sides together, matching edges. Use zipper foot to stitch neckline seam, enclosing stuffing.

5. Stitch body top to each body side, right sides together, matching B and C; clip curve. With right sides together, matching E, A, and B, stitch underbody to remaining edges of body sides, leaving 10 inches open in one straight side. Clip curves. Insert head (upside down, beak forward) into neck opening. Match D and E; use zipper foot to stitch over neck circle. Turn hen right side out.

6. Have someone hold hen open. Fill with pellets, using funnel of heavy paper to fill completely. Carefully pin closed. Hand-stitch closed with heavy-duty thread.

Making the duck

1. Enlarge and transfer appropriate pattern pieces (see page 64). Separate body pieces as indicated by dashed lines, adding ½ inch to these edges for seam allowances. Cut tail portions of body from black fabric; center body from print; front body from red; head, neck circle, neck gusset, and eye pupils from green; ring from white; and beak, underbeak, and eyes from yellow.

2. Stitch underbeak to neck gusset, right sides together, making curved

***This mother hen** makes a cozy seat for a young reader; you can stitch her together easily on your sewing machine in spite of her portly proportions.*

Our big, bold beanbag duck is loads of fun to ride; styrene foam pellets make its body light and flexible, yet sturdy enough to take a lot of bouncing.

seam F as marked. Stitch remaining long gusset edge to matching edge of neck ring piece, as positioned on grid. Press seam open. Stitch beak and ring pieces to head pieces, as positioned on pattern. Clip seam allowance of head at F. Press seams open. Appliqué eyes and pupils as in Hen Step 2.

3. Stitch head/beak pieces, right sides together, along curved edge of head and out across top of beak. Stitch underbeak/gusset to head/beak, right sides together, easing beak to fit. Clip curves and corners; turn right side out. Finish head as in Hen Step 4. With right sides together, making ½-inch seams, piece patchwork sections of body top, sides, and underbody. Press seams open. Finish duck as in Hen Steps 5 and 6.

Design: Françoise Kirkman.

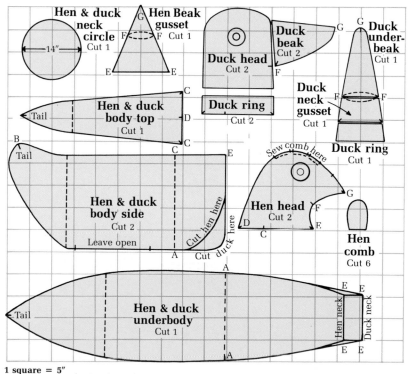

Hen & duck neck circle Cut 1 — 14″

Hen Beak gusset Cut 1 — G F F E E

Duck head Cut 2

Duck beak Cut 2 — G F

Duck under-beak Cut 1 — G

Hen & duck body top Cut 1 — Tail C C D

Duck ring Cut 2

Duck neck gusset Cut 1 — F F

Hen & duck body side Cut 2 — Tail B C Leave open A

Duck ring Cut 1

Hen head Cut 2 — Sew comb here G F E D C

Hen comb Cut 6

Hen & duck underbody Cut 1 — Tail A A E E E E

Cut hen here / Cut duck here / Hen neck / Duck neck

1 square = 5″
½″ seam allowances included

Woodshop
Heirlooms

■

*Practical or fanciful, gifts you make from wood have
value that endures. You can create a toy airplane or
xylophone for a child to treasure, sturdy workout weights,
or even a whimsical whirligig to grace someone's summer garden. From this chapter come these projects and
more, ready for you to make and to give.*

Wine Racks

For the wine connoisseur on your Christmas list, build one of these easy-to-make wine racks. The stacking rack requires some woodworking skill; the smaller, geometric-style rack is a good beginner's project.

Stacking rack

This versatile wine rack is easy to stack in multiple layers and easy to store in a small space when not in use. Three layers of racks hold a case of wine; you can add or subtract layers depending on your current inventory.

The semicircular cutouts cradle the bottles at a slight angle, the proper storage position for wine.

You'll need 1 by 4s for this project; use clear softwood such as redwood, pine, or fir, or hardwood such as mahogany or oak.

From the 1 by 4s, cut six 22½-inch-long pieces for the front and back, and four 10-inch-long pieces for the connectors. Cut four half-circles, each with a 3½-inch diameter, in each front and back piece; space the cutouts 2¾ inches in from each edge and 1 inch apart.

Clean and simple in design, *this geometric wine rack goes together quickly. It neatly stores up to a dozen bottles of wine.*

Then cut ¾-inch-wide, ⅜-inch-deep dadoes, 1 inch in from the ends, on the lower edges of the two top-level boards, on the upper and lower edges of the middle boards, and on the upper edges of the bottom boards. Also cut dadoes of the same size on both edges of the connectors, 1 inch in from the ends. Be sure to cut all dadoes tight. Put the pieces together and sand, if necessary, until they fit snugly.

Sand the remaining surfaces and finish as desired.

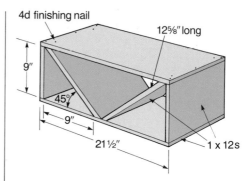

Geometric rack

A triangular shelving system inside a rectangular frame makes a good-looking wine rack for a dozen bottles of wine.

You'll need about 8 feet of 1 by 12 pine (or any clear wood) and twenty 4d finishing nails. Cut the wood according to the dimensions in the drawing above, cutting both ends of each of the dividers at a 45° angle. Sand all surfaces. Assemble the rack with finishing nails and wood glue. After the glue is dry, apply the finish of your choice.

Design: Rick Morrall.

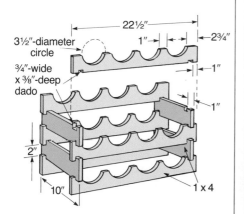

Stack it high or low—*you can adjust this stacking wine rack to fit any number of wine bottles, from just a few to a whole case.*

Bread & Cheese Boards

(Also pictured on front cover)

If you can drill a hole or make a straight saw cut, you can create a custom inlaid cutting-serving board of your own design. We used scraps of hardwood, water-resistant glue, and a variety of dowels to make the three boards pictured on the facing page. Since the boards are quick to complete, you can easily make several to give as gifts. Cost of materials depends on your choice of wood and dowels (check with hardwood dealers to find maple, walnut, and oak dowels).

Make round motifs with different-size dowels in drilled holes; for stripes, set ripped hardwood strips into sawn grooves. Or combine both techniques. After sanding, rub the boards with mineral oil.

Doweled board

To make a dowel-studded board, first drill holes for the dowels. To ensure straight, true holes, use a drill guide (shown at right) or drill press, or rely on a steady hand. A brad point bit or Forstner bit will drill the cleanest holes; but you can use a common twist or spade bit. After drilling, coat the dowel pegs and holes with glue and tap the pegs into the holes, positioning the end grain as desired. The dowels should be flush with the board bottom. Quickly wipe off excess glue.

When the glue is dry, saw off the dowel pegs with a fine-toothed saw (an offset backsaw is shown above right). While sawing, take care not to mar the board or splinter the dowels below the board top. Fill any voids with glue and sawdust.

Sand the board with a portable sander to make everything level and reveal the grain pattern of the dowel ends. To prevent the ends from scorching, keep the sander moving and don't press too hard.

Striped board

To make a striped board, first shape the board roughly. Then, for each stripe, cut a shallow kerf in the surface of the board, using a table saw (shown below) or a radial-arm or hand-held circular saw. If you want wider grooves, use dado blades.

Rip strips of contrasting wood to the width of the kerfs. Generously line the kerfs with glue; lay in the strips. Quickly wipe off excess glue.

When the glue is dry, use a sander to sand the strips flush with the board's surface. Cut the board to shape with a jig, band, or saber saw; then hand-sand for a smooth finish.

Design: Rick Morrall.

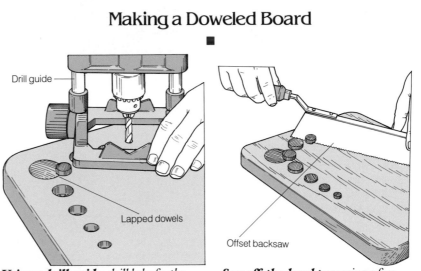

Making a Doweled Board

Using a drill guide, drill holes for the dowels. (Note the pair of lapped dowels already inserted.) Tap glue-coated dowels into place.

Saw off the dowel pegs using a fine-toothed saw (shown is an offset backsaw). Be careful not to mar the board's surface. Sand to level.

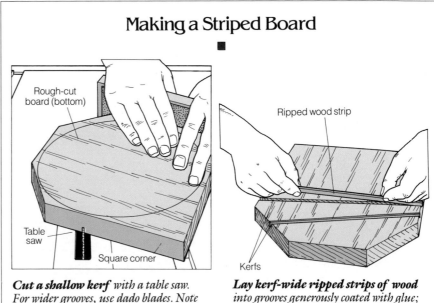

Making a Striped Board

Cut a shallow kerf with a table saw. For wider grooves, use dado blades. Note that one corner of the wood is left square so a miter gauge can be used for the stripe angles.

Lay kerf-wide ripped strips of wood into grooves generously coated with glue; tap strips into place. Sand the strips flush; cut the board to shape, then sand to finish.

Dowel dots *punctuate a maple cutting board (top). The largest dowel, 1-inch maple, is lapped by ¾-inch walnut and flanked by ½-inch oak, then ¼-inch walnut. The round teak board (center) sports stripes of maple and purpleheart; the richly toned purpleheart board (bottom) is distinguished by a ribbon of mahogany and a 1¾-inch oak round.*

Book Rack

This handsome book rack makes a perfect gift for almost anybody. Build it to hold an avid chef's favorite cook books or to keep a student's desk-top reference books in order.

The dowels form tracks that allow you to adjust the rack as desired. We provide a specific dowel length, but you can select any length that fits the recipient's needs.

Materials. Here's what you'll need to complete the project.

2′ of 1 by 3 maple
2′ of 1″ hardwood dowel
2 8″ squares of ³⁄₁₆″ clear acrylic
2 roundhead woodscrews, ¹⁄₂″ by #3

Note: If you plan to cut the acrylic yourself, use a fine plywood blade on your power saw.

Cut two 8-inch end pieces from the maple 1 by 3; cut the dowel into two 12-inch lengths.

Leave the protective paper on the acrylic sheets until you've completed all the cuts and bores. To ensure that the holes are aligned, clamp all the acrylic and maple end pieces together

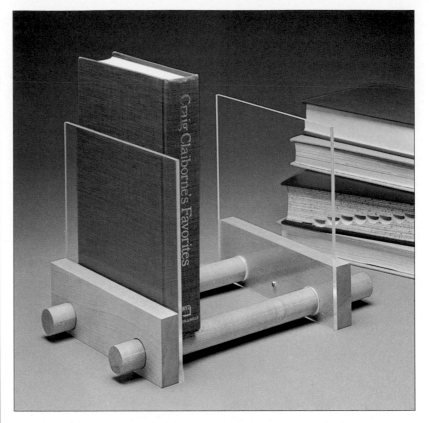

Maple and clear acrylic *combine to make a handsome holder for books; the ends move along dowel tracks for easy width adjustment.*

with a scrap piece of wood on the bottom. Drill a 1-inch hole ¾ inch up and 1½ inches in from each end of the end pieces. Drilling is a critical part of this project; if the holes aren't cut perpendicular or don't line up, the supports won't slide smoothly along the dowels. Drill ¹⁄₁₆-inch pilot holes for the screws through the acrylic and ³⁄₈ inch into the maple.

On the acrylic pieces only, drill through the ¹⁄₁₆-inch holes with a ⁷⁄₆₄-inch bit. Smooth the cut edges of the acrylic with 400-grit wet and dry sandpaper. Attach the acrylic pieces to the maple pieces with woodscrews.

Insert the dowels through both end pieces. Sand the inside of the dowel holes and the dowels if there's any unnecessary binding.

Design: William Crosby.

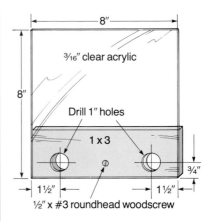

Record Rack

A friend with a well-loved record collection will welcome the gift of an adjustable record rack. The end plates are immobile, providing support for the records. The middle panel slides along the dowel tracks to hold records upright and prevent warping.

Materials. Here's what you'll need to complete the project.

4' of 1 by 12 hardwood
8' of 1" hardwood dowel: 4 @ 2'
1' of ⅜" hardwood dowel
    Glue

Cut the hardwood into three 12½-inch-long pieces for the end plates and the sliding center plate. Mark 1-inch dowel hole locations on one plate as shown in the drawing at right. Clamp the three pieces together and drill the four 1-inch diameter holes through all thicknesses. Drilling is a critical part of this project; if the holes aren't cut perpendicular or don't line up, the center plate won't slide smoothly along the dowels.

Finish the wood, if desired; then slide the center plate onto the 1-inch dowels. If there's any binding, sand the dowels and the inside of the dowel holes in the center plate. Glue and dowel the two end plates: using a ⅜-inch bit, drill in from the edges of the plates into the 1-inch dowels. Glue ⅜-inch dowels in the holes; saw off the excess.

Design: William Crosby.

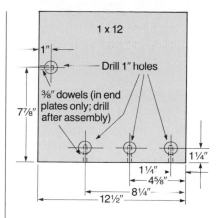

As practical as it is good-looking, this hardwood record rack has a special sliding center panel that holds records firmly upright.

Workout Weights

(Also pictured on page 96)

For a gift of good health, make a set of beautiful hardwood workout weights. You simply cut a pair of blocks and drill a hole in each, then fill the holes with lead shot and glue the weighted blocks to a dowel.

At a lumberyard, select 1¼-inch hardwood dowel (a good size for gripping). Check in the lumberyard scrap bins for the small pieces of hardwood you'll need to make the end blocks; we used cocobolo.

For the added weight, lead shotgun shot works well (we used #9 shot). It's typically sold in 25-pound bags; to find it in smaller quantities, check the Yellow Pages under Ammunition Reloading—Equipment and Suppliers. Or buy a few pounds from someone who reloads his own shells, or use lead wool from a plumbing supply shop.

Cutting & drilling the blocks

To make our hand weights, cut two matching end blocks, each 1⅞ by 2⅝ by 3 inches. Drill a 1¼-inch-diameter, 2¼-inch-deep hole in each. With a steady hand and a drill guide, you can make the holes with a portable drill, but a drill press will give you a straighter, truer hole.

To connect the weights, you'll need two 6¼-inch lengths of dowel. If you want to add a little extra shot to the weights, you can drill holes in the ends of the dowels.

After drilling the holes, bevel all edges of the blocks with a table saw blade set at 45°. Then sand the blocks and the connecting dowels smooth.

Filling & finishing the weights

Fill the holes in the blocks with shot to within ¾ inch of the top; also fill holes in the dowels (if you drilled them) and tape ends of dowels to keep shot in place.

Spread a thin coat of 5-minute epoxy around inside of holes and on matching area of dowels; push dowels firmly in place. If you like, set the blocks on the dowels at right angles to each other, as shown in the photo below.

Finish the weights with tung seal or mineral oil.

Design: Rick Morrall.

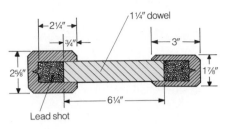

This cross-section *shows typical assembly, with optional holes for shot in the dowel ends.*

A set *of handsome cocobolo workout weights is a lasting gift for your favorite fitness enthusiast.*

Plant Trivets

Practical enough for outdoor use, handsome enough to put under a prized houseplant, these trivets are easy to make, provided you have a table or radial-arm saw with a dado head. Use rot-resistant redwood, cedar, or teak; for extra water resistance, seal the trivets with a clear water sealer.

Grid trivets

Dado blades let you make the cross-lap joints used to assemble intersecting boards into a grid.

One 4- to 6-foot-long piece of 1 by 6, 1 by 8, 2 by 6, or 2 by 8 provides wood for several grid trivets. For both 1-by and 2-by stock, begin by cutting ¾-inch-wide dadoes every 3 inches across the board. The depth of the cut should be exactly half the board's thickness.

Next, crosscut the dadoed board to the finished length for a square or rectangular trivet so that each length will have two or three dadoes. Now rip each piece into ¾-inch-wide pieces.

Assemble the strips into square or rectangular grids. To lock the parts together, countersink finishing nails into the bottom of a few of the joints; or use glue or glue and nails.

Round trivets

You'll need a saber, jig, or band saw to cut out the round trivets shown in the photograph. The smaller trivet, 4 inches in diameter, has round redwood-plug legs. The top is made from a square of 1 by 6; you can make the legs with a ½-inch plug cutter or use hardwood dowel.

The larger, 6-inch trivet has pie-wedge legs and takes shape from a block scored with dado blades. You start with a square of 2 by 8. Find the center, draw a 6-inch circle, and cut 2½-inch-wide, ¼-inch-deep grooves square to each other across the center. Clamp the block to your worktable and cut out the circle.

If you wish, you can add rubber-head tacks or stick-on squares to the feet to protect tabletops.

Design: Peter O. Whiteley.

This quartet of plant trivets is both good-looking and practical. The grids are made of interlocking 2 by 6's (left) or 1 by 6's (right). The large round trivet has pie-wedge legs; the small one has round legs.

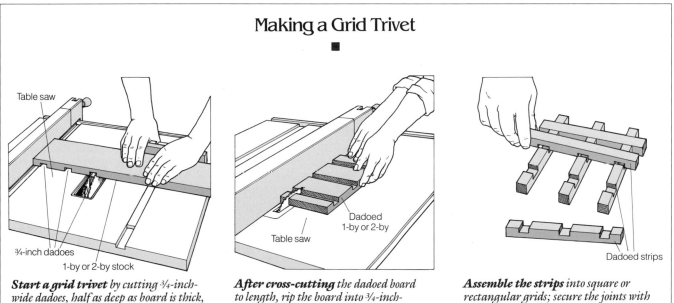

Making a Grid Trivet

■

Table saw

¾-inch dadoes
1-by or 2-by stock

Start a grid trivet by cutting ¾-inch-wide dadoes, half as deep as board is thick, every 3 inches across a 1-by or 2-by board.

Dadoed
1-by or 2-by
Table saw

After cross-cutting the dadoed board to length, rip the board into ¾-inch-wide strips.

Dadoed strips

Assemble the strips into square or rectangular grids; secure the joints with countersunk nails, glue, or both. Finish.

Plant Boxes

A tidy wooden plant box adds a special touch to a green and growing gift. You can make these boxes as permanent planters or simply as decorative "gift wraps" to dress up lowly nursery containers.

Two basic styles of boxes, designed for different sizes of nursery pots, are shown on these pages. The larger box has an inner sleeve; the smaller one, like those in the photograph, is just a jacket mounted on a base. The basic method of construction is the same for both types: they're butt-jointed and screwed or doweled together, with the screw holes capped with wooden plugs.

If you intend your box to be a permanent planter, drill drainage holes in the base and assemble the pieces with waterproof glue. Waterproof the box interior with a coat of silicone caulk, asphalt emulsion, or fiberglass; or line the box with a heavy plastic bag (punch holes in the bag to match the box drainage holes; staple bag in place). You might also add small feet to raise the box off floors or decks.

Make the boxes from whatever wood you prefer; we used Douglas fir and white oak, with walnut plugs for contrast. For these materials, a clear finish—oil or wax—looks best.

Note: Nursery pots and cans vary widely in size and configuration. You may have to adjust the dimensions we give on these pages to suit the pots you're working with.

Dress up a special gift plant *in its own handmade wooden planter box— one you can easily make yourself, in a variety of sizes.*

Big box for a 5-gallon can

The following instructions will make a box for a plant in a plastic pot a little over 12 inches tall, a little less than 11 inches in diameter, tapering to 9 inches at the base. Use a 2 by 12 to form the main jacket walls and the base; make the inner sleeve from a rough 1 by 6.

For the jacket, cut two pieces of 2 by 12 to 11 inches and two to about 15 inches (longer by twice the thickness of the 2 by 12). In the ends of the longer boards, drill three evenly spaced 1-inch holes ¾ inch deep and centered 1 inch in from the edge. Then drill pilot holes and drive 2-inch #12 flathead woodscrews through the 1-inch holes into the ends of the shorter 2 by 12s. Glue ¾-inch pieces of 1-inch dowel flush in the holes to cap the screws.

For the sleeve, cut two pieces of 1 by 6 to 11 inches and two to about 9 inches (shorter by twice the thickness of the rough 1 by 6, to produce an 11-inch square). Glue and nail these together, again setting the long sides over the ends of the shorter boards. Then set about a 9-inch-square base cut from a 2 by 12 flush to the bottom; nail it in place. Set nails and fill all holes.

Slide the jacket and sleeve assembly together, then set the can in place and raise the jacket until it covers the can as much as you wish. Mark the position, remove the can, then nail the pieces together from the inside.

If your plant comes in a metal can, chances are the can doesn't taper. In that case, size the base to match the can diameter; make the sleeve to fit the base, then the jacket to fit that. There will be a gap the thickness of the 1 by 6 sleeve around the can.

Smaller boxes for gallon cans & 4-inch pots

The construction sequence is the same for the smaller boxes, except the inner sleeve is replaced by just the base.

Gallon cans vary a great deal, too; here, we give instructions for enclosing a pot 7 inches tall and 6⅝ inches in diameter. Five pieces of 1 by 8 lumber—two cut to 6⅝ inches, one cut to 6⅝ inches square, and two cut to 8⅛ inches—form the box. Plug holes are ½ inch (you can buy plugs or use ½-inch dowel); the screws are 1¼-inch drywall screws. After cutting ¼-inch-deep plug holes in all side pieces, follow the steps pictured below to put this box together.

A 4-inch-square pot—really 3¾ inches tall and 4⅜ inches square—is wrapped in ½-inch stock, with a 1-inch-thick block serving as the base. The sides of this box may be joined with pairs of ¼-inch dowels glued into predrilled holes.
Design: William Crosby.

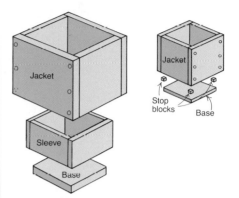

Two styles of planter boxes *cover different sizes of nursery pots. Adjust the jacket position of the larger (three-part) box for the pot or can height before you nail the pieces together.*

Putting Together a Small Box

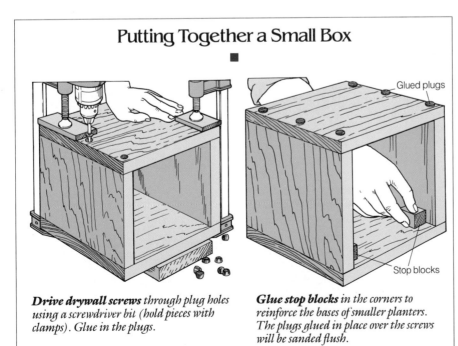

Drive drywall screws *through plug holes using a screwdriver bit (hold pieces with clamps). Glue in the plugs.*

Glue stop blocks *in the corners to reinforce the bases of smaller planters. The plugs glued in place over the screws will be sanded flush.*

Whirligigs

(Woodchopper also pictured on page 96)

Add whimsy to a friend's garden; give a folk-inspired whirligig that moves about with the wind. As the propeller rotates, so does the wire attached to it. The wire, in turn, activates the figure on the stand. On these pages, we feature two whirligig designs—a bucking bronco and an industrious woodchopper. You can decorate them any way you like—use the photographs at right as a guide, or develop your own designs. (If you wish to paint the figures, do so before assembly.)

Horse

Cut out all the pieces according to the dimensions in the drawings. (For enlarging and transferring instructions, see page 64.) Cut the propeller blades, horse pieces, and leg supports from ¼-inch hardboard. Glue the two horse pieces together with waterproof glue. Drill the holes in the horse and leg supports. Cut the propeller hub, the base, and the cap from clear pine or redwood (or other clear species).

Drill a ⅛-inch center hole in the propeller hub; also drill an offset hole for the ⅛-inch shaft wire about ¾ inch from the centered hole. In the hub edges, cut four equally spaced ¼-inch-wide, ¾-inch-deep grooves at 45° angles, as shown. Coat the ends of the blades with waterproof glue and insert them in the hub slots. Secure them with ¾-inch brass brads driven through the hub face.

Cut a ³⁄₁₆- by ³⁄₁₆-inch groove along the center of the base's top edge to hold the propeller shaft wire. Cut out the notch as shown.

Use an 18-inch length of ⅛-inch steel wire for the shaft. Bend one end into a "J" shape; when you slide the long leg through the center hole of the propeller hub, the short leg should enter the offset hole about ½ inch. Thread three ⅛-inch washers

Folk-art woodchopper *cheerfully chops away in perpetual motion on any brisk, windy day.*

on the shaft and set the shaft and propeller assembly in the groove. Mark the wire for the offset position; then remove it and bend it into shape, making four 90° bends (see facing page). Cut off the excess wire so the shaft fits in the groove.

Place the shaft and propeller assembly back into the groove, positioning the washers as shown. Apply grease in the groove to make sure the shaft rotates freely. Glue and nail the cap in place, using 1½-inch panel nails. Predrill if there's a danger of splitting. Secure the leg supports to the base using waterproof glue and ¾-inch brass brads. Attach the horse to the supports as shown, using a stove bolt, washers, and a locknut. Make sure the horse pivots freely.

Loop one end of a 9-inch length of piano wire around the offset in the shaft and twist it to close. Turn the offset in the shaft to the down position and position the horse's front hoof about ½ inch above the

This prancing pony *will add whimsical charm to your favorite gardener's plot. It's a good gift for the equestrian enthusiast on your Christmas list, too.*

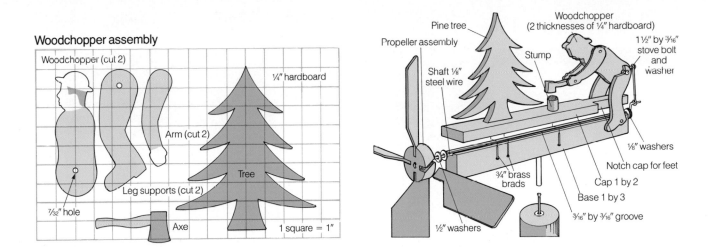

Woodchopper assembly

Woodchopper (cut 2)
¼" hardboard
Arm (cut 2)
Leg supports (cut 2)
⁷⁄₃₂" hole
Axe
Tree
1 square = 1"

Pine tree
Woodchopper (2 thicknesses of ¼" hardboard)
Propeller assembly
Stump
1½" by ³⁄₁₆" stove bolt and washer
Shaft ⅛" steel wire
¾" brass brads
⅛" washers
Notch cap for feet
Cap 1 by 2
Base 1 by 3
³⁄₁₆" by ³⁄₁₆" groove
½" washers

cap; then slip the other end of the wire through the ⅛-inch hole in the horse's front leg and twist it around itself, making a loose loop. Test the action by turning the propeller; adjust piano wire, if necessary. Cut off the excess wire.

Support the finished whirligig from underneath and locate the center of balance. Mark it, then drill a 1-inch-deep hole for the ⅜-inch copper tubing. Glue the tubing in place.

To mount the whirligig outdoors, drive a 16d (3½-inch) finishing nail into the top of a post, and place a ¼-inch washer over it. Mount the whirligig on the nail.

Woodchopper

This whirligig calls for many of the same components and building techniques as the horse. To begin, cut all hardboard pieces to size, as shown above. Glue the two body parts together with waterproof glue. Drill the holes in the body and leg supports. Cut the base and the cap from solid lumber as shown above; cut the propeller pieces as for the horse.

Build the propeller assembly as described for the horse, then cut the ³⁄₁₆- by ³⁄₁₆-inch groove in the base for the shaft. Using a 22-inch length of ⅛-inch steel wire, bend one end into a "J" shape; slide the long leg through the propeller hub, and insert the short leg into the offset hole. Bend the far end at two 90° angles as shown. Grease the groove to make sure the shaft moves freely, thread four ⅛-inch washers on the shaft,

and set the shaft and propeller assembly in the groove.

Assemble the woodchopper as shown, then secure his legs to the base. Notch the cap to fit around the legs, set the cap in place, and mark the best locations for both stump and pine tree; attach the stump and pine tree from below with glue and brads. Glue and nail the cap to the top of the base.

Next, twist one end of a 9-inch length of piano wire around the offset in the shaft, and turn the offset to the up position. Place the woodchopper's ax just above the stump, then attach the free end of the wire to the eyescrew on the woodchopper. Test the action, and adjust the wire if necessary. Cut off the excess wire.

Mount the whirligig on a post as described for the horse.

Horse assembly

¼" hardboard
³⁄₁₆" hole
⅛" hole
Horse (cut 2)
Leg support (cut 2)
1 square = 1"
⁷⁄₃₂" hole

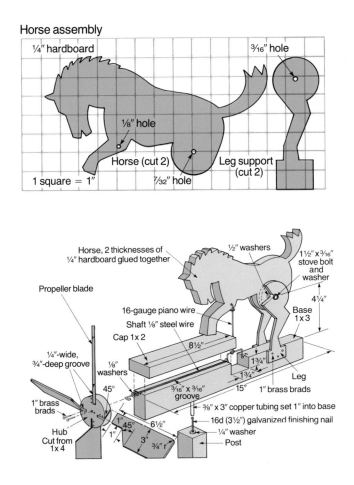

Horse, 2 thicknesses of ¼" hardboard glued together
½" washers
1½" x ³⁄₁₆" stove bolt and washer
Propeller blade
16-gauge piano wire
Shaft ⅛" steel wire
Cap 1 x 2
4¼"
Base 1 x 3
¼"-wide, ¾"-deep groove
⅛" washers
8½"
Leg
1¾"
1¾"
45°
15"
1" brass brads
³⁄₁₆" x ³⁄₁₆" groove
⅜" x 3" copper tubing set 1" into base
1" brass brads
Hub Cut from 1 x 4
45°
1"
1"
6½"
3"
¾" r
16d (3½") galvanized finishing nail
¼" washer
Post

Folding Easel

Young artists will be delighted with this versatile easel: its adjustable art boards provide generous space for creativity, and its large tray holds plenty of chalk, paint, and markers. Parents will appreciate its easy-to-build folding design: the easel is compact when folded and rigid when set up.

Materials. Here's what you'll need to complete the project.

32' of 1 by 2 clear fir or pine:4 @ 8'
1   4' by 4' sheet of ¼" tempered hardboard
3'   of ¼" quarter-round molding
3"   of ¼" hardwood dowel
10   brass flathead woodscrews, ¾" by #8, with finish washers
2   1½" butt hinges with screws
2   brass flathead woodscrews, 1½" by #8, with finish washers
*   2d, 4d, and 6d finishing nails*
2   mending plates, ¾" by 1½"
*   Wood glue*
*   Wood putty*
*   Chalkboard paint*
*   Gloss polyurethane finish*

1. Cut all 1 by 2 pieces to length: two 28-inch-long tray sides **A**, two 6¼-inch tray sides **B**, six 17½-inch tray crosspieces **C**, and four 48-inch legs **E**. Also divide the hardboard sheet into one 18½- by 26½-inch tray bottom **D**, two 18- by 24-inch art boards **F**, and two 1½- by 18-inch chalkboard spacers **G**.

2. Mark and drill holes for pivot screws in tray sides **A** and two legs **E**; mark and drill holes for locking dowels in remaining legs **E** (see Details 1 and 2). Drill holes in one crosspiece **C** as shown. Cut the dowel in half.

3. Join tray sides **A** and **B** with glue and 6d nails spaced 3 inches apart. Add crosspieces **C**, using glue and 4d nails. Set the nails and fill the holes. Cut the molding in half and glue in place where shown. Attach tray bottom **D** with glue and 2d nails, leaving a ¼-inch border all around.

4. Join legs **E** in pairs with hinges. Round over all wood edges, sand, and apply two coats of gloss polyurethane to all wood pieces, tray bottom, and one art board **F**. Paint the other board with chalkboard paint.

5. Attach the legs to tray sides **A** with 1½-inch screws and finish washers, leaving the screws just loose enough to permit easy movement. Glue the dowels in opposite legs (see Detail 1).

6. Stand the easel up and open the legs, resting the tray on the dowels. When the tray is level, mark the outline of each dowel on the tray underside. Cut away the tray within the outlines with a craft knife or chisel. Install the mending plates as shown in Detail 1 (they should pivot to lock and unlock the dowels in their notches). Using ¾-inch screws, attach art boards **F** and chalkboard spacers **G** to the legs as shown, setting their height as desired.

Design: Scott Fitzgerrell.

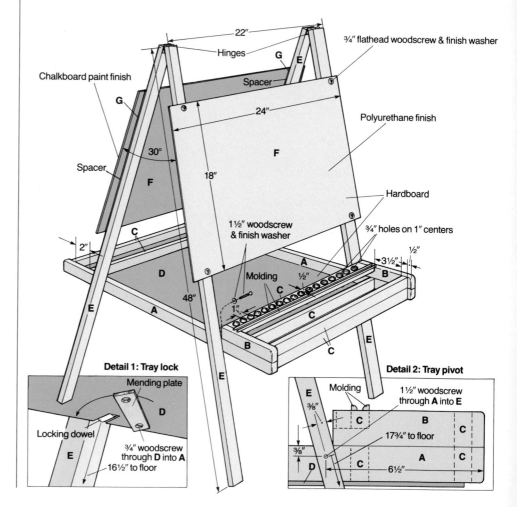

To paint a masterpiece, *every artist needs the right equipment. This sturdy, versatile easel fills the bill—and it's well suited for both chalk and marker work. As the inset photos show, the easel folds up compactly once the masterpiece is finished.*

Musical Instruments

(Xylophone also pictured on page 96)

Boom, rattle, and clack! Toddlers will love creating their own rhythm band with these simple musical instruments made from wood, leather, and bells. None of the instruments requires a sophisticated array of tools to make. The xylophone is the most challenging project; the hand bells, rasp, and drum are relatively simple.

Xylophone

To make this attractive xylophone, you'll need a drill with a ⅛-inch bit. You'll also need the following materials:

> *About 9' of ½"-thick, 1"-wide hardwood (for keys)*
>
> *2' of ½"-thick, 2½"-wide pine (for ends)*
>
> *3' of ½"-thick, 2"-wide pine (for sides)*
>
> *About 30" of self-adhesive foam weatherstripping*
>
> *2' of ⅛" hardwood dowel: 2 @ 12"*
>
> *About 26 ¼" wooden beads*
>
> *2 1" wooden beads*
>
> *Pearl or heavy crochet cotton (for stringing keys)*
>
> *Small nails*
>
> *Wood glue*

To make the keys, cut the hardwood into 11 pieces, in ½-inch increments from 12 to 7 inches; sand. Drill two holes horizontally through each key, drilling through center of wood

1 inch in from ends. (If you like, cut ends of keys at an angle as shown in the photograph. Mark and drill holes at the same angle.)

For the frame, cut two end pieces from 2½-inch-wide pine, one 7 and one 12 inches long. Drill one hole in each end of each piece, 1 inch in from the ends and ⅜ inch down from the top.

For the sides, cut two 14⅜-inch pieces from 2-inch-wide pine; angle your cuts so the sides will be flush with the ends. Glue and nail sides to ends about 1 inch in from edges. Sand and seal the wood.

Glue weatherstripping along the top of each side piece; position the keys on it. Thread a long piece of pearl cotton from one end of the frame through the drilled keys, adding ¼-inch beads between keys (and extras as needed between end keys and frame). Loop the cotton at the other end of the frame as shown below and thread it back through the other ends of the keys; pull tight and tie. To make mallets, insert dowels into the holes in 1-inch wooden beads; glue in place.

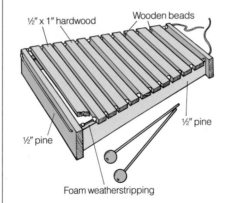

½" x 1" hardwood — Wooden beads — ½" pine — ½" pine — Foam weatherstripping

Hand bells

You'll need 12 inches of ⅞-inch dowel, three large bells, and three ¼-inch eyescrews.

Sand and round the ends of the dowel. Seal the wood; when dry, mark the desired location for the eyescrews (about two inches apart). Open each eyescrew slightly with pliers; screw into the wood. Put the bells into the screws; close the eyes with pliers.

For different sounds, you can make hand bells with 12-inch lengths of ½-inch dowel and 6 medium or 12 small bells and eyescrews.

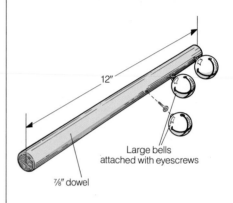

12" — Large bells attached with eyescrews — ⅞" dowel

Rasp

You'll need 16 inches *each* of ⅞-inch and ¼-inch dowel, as well as a handsaw.

Sand the dowels and round the ends slightly. Cut angled notches into the larger dowel; the sound will vary according to the amount of space between the notches. File and sand the notches; seal both dowels.

⅞" dowel — 16" — 16" — ¼" dowel

With a craft knife, cut two 9-inch leather octagons (9⅞ inches in diameter from point to point) for the drum's top and bottom. Pierce 16 evenly spaced holes around the edges of each octagon about ½ inch in from the edge as shown below. Also cut ³/₁₆-inch-wide strips for ties in lengths noted above. Soak the octagons and ties for about an hour in water. Center the leather top and bottom over the drum body so the sides of the leather octagons form flaps on all four sides. Run a 10-inch tie from top to bottom on all four corners first, pulling and knotting as tightly as you can. (You can use the needlenose pliers to pull the ties through the holes.) Then lace the sides as shown below, again pulling tightly and knotting. Cut off any excess leather above and below the knots, then let the leather dry completely.

Design: Andrea Shedletsky.

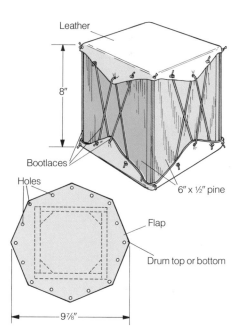

Sturdy handmade instruments—xylophone, drum, hand bells, and rasp—will keep junior musicians happily occupied and teach them rhythm skills along the way.

Hand drum

You'll need 3 feet of 6-inch-wide, ½-inch-thick pine and enough medium-weight leather to make two 9-inch octagons and 12 ties—eight ties about 14 inches long, four ties about 10 inches long. (Or use leather bootlaces, cut into ties.) You'll also need a saw, needlenose pliers, a sharp craft knife, and wood glue.

From pine, cut four 8-inch-tall sides for the drum, and four 1-inch squares to reinforce the corners. Cut the squares diagonally into triangles. Glue, then nail, two sides together at a time, using butt joints; repeat until all sides are joined. Glue the triangles into the corners; let dry overnight. Sand and seal the wood.

Play Kitchen & Doll House Cabinets

Watch your child's eyes light up on Christmas morning at the sight of a child-size play kitchen or a three-story doll house under the tree! Both projects start out as simple plywood boxes; that means they can do double duty as roomy storage cabinets.

Play kitchen

Our sleek kitchen set, pictured on the facing page, includes a range with a peekaboo door, a sink cabinet with a plastic sink, and a refrigerator with shelves.

Each piece is actually a cabinet. All three are constructed in the same way, except for the mounting of the doors. The cabinets are made from ½-inch birch plywood with ¼-inch hardboard backs.

Materials. Here's what you'll need to complete the project.

- 2 *4' by 8' sheets of ½" birch plywood (shop grade)*
- 1 *4' by 4' sheet of ¼" hardboard*
   3d finishing nails
- 2 *continuous hinges, one 1¹/₁₆" by 36" and one 1¹/₁₆" by 48", with ½" screws*
- 3 *magnetic catches*
- 1 *plastic sink tub, 5" by 12" by 14"*
- 3 *cabinet pulls*
   Wood glue
   Wood putty
   Nontoxic enamel

1. Cut all plywood pieces to size (see plywood cutting layout). Also divide the hardboard sheet into two 20- by 23½-inch backs **D** and one 20- by 36-inch back **E**.

2. Using a saber saw, make the cutout in one cabinet top **C** for the sink tub, making sure the hole is dimensioned to hold the tub securely. Also make the cutout in oven door **G** for the "window."

3. Assemble each cabinet with glue and nails, spacing nails 2 to 3 inches apart. Attach sides **A** or **B** to top **C**; attach bottom shelf **C** so its top surface is 2 inches up from the bottom of **A**. Add intermediate shelf **C** (two shelves for the refrigerator) and back **D** or **E**. Attach toekick **F**. Hang door **G** or **H** as shown in the large drawing, using a continuous hinge cut to fit (see Detail 1). Trim the range door slightly for a good fit.

4. Set the nails, fill the holes, and sand all surfaces. Apply a base coat of paint, then sand and dust well. Apply a top coat. When it's dry, paint circles on the rangetop with black enamel.

5. Screw on the door pulls and magnetic catches. Drop the tub in place.

Design: Don Vandervort.

(Continued on page 114)

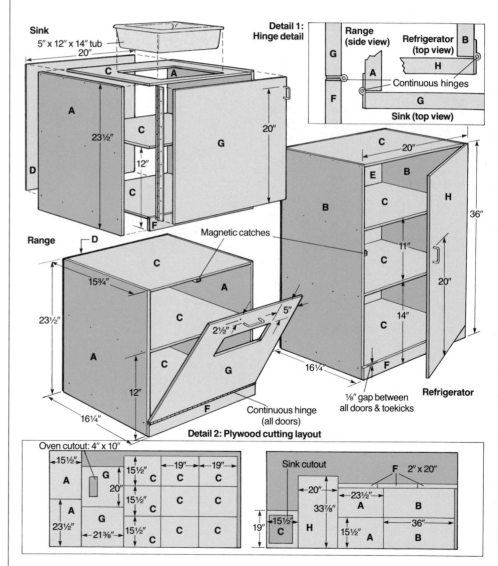

These charming doll house cabinets and the play kitchen components start from simple plywood boxes. The sink, range, and refrigerator, largely unadorned except for paint, can be built in a day. The town and country houses, dressed in 1/12-scale finery, are a bit more involved, yet each is an easy weekend project.

Doll house cabinets

Shown here and on page 113 are two versions of the same basic structure —one a charming country cottage, the other a sophisticated town house. Each is realistic without being time-consuming to build; construction is easy.

Both houses permit great freedom of decoration—let your imagination be your guide. Though each uses materials available at doll house specialty shops, you can fashion the decorative details from bits of standard molding or workshop scrap. Only basic tools are required, though a table saw is helpful for cutting the plywood.

Materials. Here's what you'll need to complete the project.

For one house:

1 4' by 8' sheet of ½" fir plywood (grade AB)

1 continuous hinge, 1¹⁄₁₆" by 30", with ½" screws

1 magnetic catch
   2d finishing nails
   Wood glue

Trim & finish for country house:

550 sq. in. fish-scale shingle strips

4' of 1" half-round molding for rakes
   Ready-made windows
   Ready-made door trim
   All-purpose patching compound

15' of ¼" by 1½" pine for half-timbering, door, chimney, and chimney pots
   Ivory and slate gray enamel
   Medium oak stain
   Scale brick paper

Trim & finish for town house:

8' of ¼" by 1½" pine for parapet, step, and curb

30" of scale dentil cornice molding
   Ready-made windows and door with classical trim

5' of scale decorative band molding

128" of scale dentil molding for quoins
   Navajo white spray enamel
   Scale brick paper

1. For either house, cut all pieces to size (see plywood cutting layout).

2. Glue and nail all joints, spacing the nails 2 to 3 inches apart. Assemble sides **A**, floors **B**, and back **C**; mount front **C** with a continuous hinge (for the country house, cut the hinge down to 21 inches). This completes the town house (except for walls **D**, added at the last— see step **3**).

To complete the country house, glue **E1** to **E2**, letting **E2** overlap; then glue and nail the pieces to the back. Nail through **E1** and **E2** into sides **A**; glue reinforcing pieces **F** in position as shown. Add four spacers **G**, trimming the hinge-side piece for door clearance.

3. To decorate the completed structure, take it to a doll house specialty shop or a hobby shop and experiment with the various items you'll find there: scale doors and windows, siding, shingles, fancy trim, and the like. Or decorate your house with pieces of standard molding.

Once you've chosen your materials, unscrew front **C**, and mark and cut openings for doors and windows. Size the openings to the manufacturer's specifications or, if you're building from scratch, size them to a scale of one inch per foot.

Prefinish the roof, walls, and trim; then glue the trim in place. To finish the country house as shown, whittle, finish, and attach half-timbering; then "plaster" the plywood with all-purpose patching compound, texturing by hand and with a whisk broom or stiff brush. Paint the shingles after attaching; paint the "plaster" when it's dry. Paint the interior, then glue walls **D** where desired. Reattach front **C**; add the catch.

Design: Scott Fitzgerrell.

Detail: Plywood cutting layout

Country house

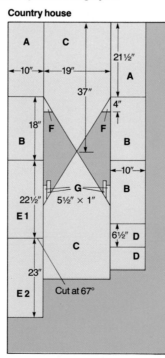

Town house

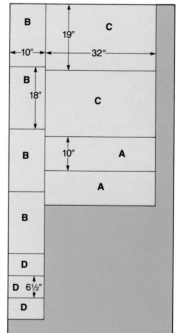

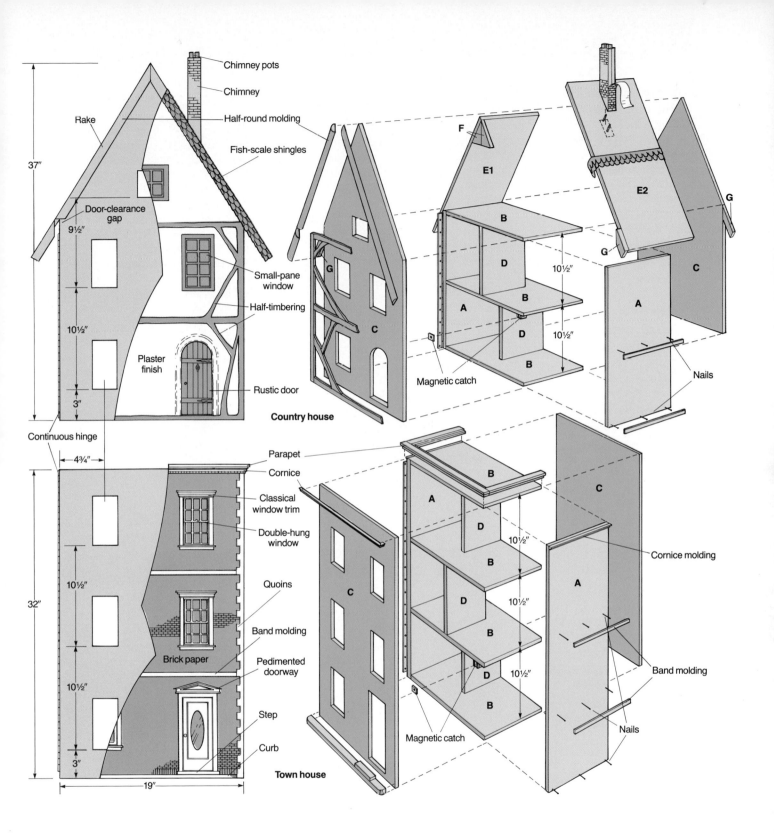

Country house

Chimney pots
Chimney
Half-round molding
Fish-scale shingles
Rake
37″
Door-clearance gap
9½″
Small-pane window
Half-timbering
10½″
Plaster finish
3″
Rustic door
Continuous hinge

F
E1
E2
G
G
B
C
D
A
B
10½″
A
D
10½″
B
Magnetic catch
Nails

Town house

Parapet
Cornice
Classical window trim
Double-hung window
4¾″
10½″
Quoins
Band molding
32″
Brick paper
10½″
Pedimented doorway
Step
3″
Curb
19″

B
A
C
D
10½″
B
D
10½″
B
D
10½″
B
Cornice molding
A
A
C
Band molding
Nails
Magnetic catch

Scooter Planes

(Also pictured on page 96)

Fantasy flights and the wild blue yonder will fill all youngsters' imaginations as they take off on these scooter planes. The old-fashioned "tail-dragger" biplane and the sleek jet both roll on three wheels; they're easily managed by pilots up to six years old.

Materials. Here's what you'll need to complete the project.

For the biplane:

3' of 2 by 10 (for fuselage)

6' of 1 by 6 (for wings, seat, back, and tail)

3' of 1 by 4 (for wheel top and sides and propeller)

13" of 1" hardwood dowel (for axle)

3' of 5/8" hardwood dowel (for wing struts and joystick)

1 round wooden drawer pull (for control knob)

1 3" caster and 2 5" rubber-tired wheels

3 lag screws, 3/8" by 4", each with 2 washers

    Glue

For the jet:

4' of 2 by 10 (for fuselage and control panel)

10" by 20" piece of 3/4" plywood (for wing)

2' of 1 by 4 (for wheel top and sides)

4' of 1½" closet pole (for engines)

6' of 1 by 6 (for seat)

13" of 1" hardwood dowel (for axle)

10" of 5/8" hardwood dowel: 2 @ 5" (for joysticks)

2 round wooden drawer pulls (for control knobs)

1 3" caster and 2 5" rubber-tired wheels

2 lag screws, 3/8" by 4", each with 2 washers

    Glue

Start either plane by enlarging all pattern pieces shown in the drawings on these pages (see page 64). Working from the patterns, cut out all the pieces. Make the wheel assemblies separately from the bodies; the axles are counterbored ¼ inch into the inside faces of the vertical side pieces. First glue (do not nail) the axle into position; then glue and nail the wheel sides to the wheel assembly tops, using countersunk finishing nails. Before mounting the wheel assembly to the wings, drill 3/16-inch pilot holes for lag screws, drilling through the sides and well into the dowel.

The biplane's wings should be assembled separately from the body. Cut five 7-inch pieces from the 5/8-inch dowel for the struts and joystick. Counterbore four holes for the strut dowels ¼ inch into the inside faces of the wings. Glue and nail together before mounting the wings to the body.

The tail of the biplane should slide snugly into the notch cut into the fuselage. The control panel for the jet has a similar joint, but the notch isn't as deep.

When the bodies and wings are together, screw on the wheel assemblies, glue and nail on the seats, and glue in the joysticks with knobs on top. Cut the closet pole for the jet engines, mitering one end of each piece, and glue and nail on.

Sand, seal, and paint the planes; then attach the wheels with 3/8- by 4-inch lag screws. (We left the biplane's propeller natural wood, then lag-screwed it to the front.) Paint your own insignia or buy large decals (available at some hobby shops).

When you're mounting the caster, you may find that the mounting plate is wider than the plane's body. In this case, add scrap blocks of wood to both sides of the plane to add width.

Design: Dr. Clois McClure (biplane); Peter O. Whiteley (jet).

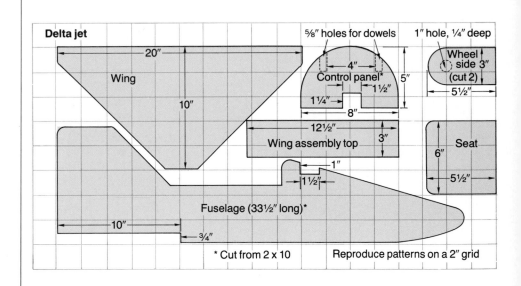

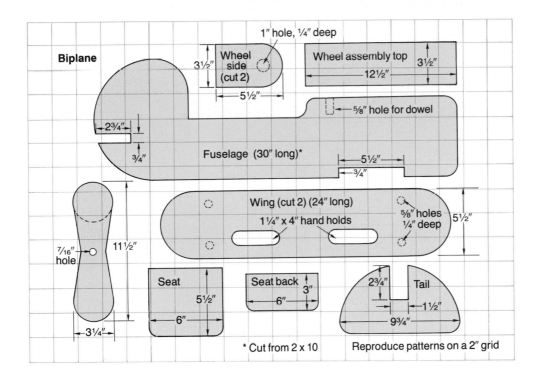

Biplane

1" hole, ¼" deep

Wheel side (cut 2)

3½"

5½"

Wheel assembly top

12½"

3½"

⅝" hole for dowel

2¾"

¾"

Fuselage (30" long)*

5½"

¾"

Wing (cut 2) (24" long)

1¼" x 4" hand holds

⅝" holes ¼" deep

5½"

7/16" hole

11½"

3¼"

Seat

5½"

6"

Seat back

6"

3"

2¾"

Tail

1½"

9¾"

* Cut from 2 x 10

Reproduce patterns on a 2" grid

Get your children's Christmas off the ground *with one of these cheerful wooden scooter planes. You can make a brightly colored old-time biplane or a streamlined jet—both roll on sturdy rubber wheels and will hold up through many hours of flight time.*

Custom Toybox Van & Wooden Wagon

Here's fun with a practical purpose. The bright, custom-designed van is a toybox; the classic oak wagon makes a rugged vehicle for toys, bears, and people.

Toybox van

You can make this van (shown on the facing page) to order for any child; its large, flat sides offer great opportunities for custom decoration. The van has an ample capacity, making it useful when the time comes to collect all those toys from around the Christmas tree.

Materials. Here's what you'll need to complete the project.

1   *4' by 4' sheet of ½" fir plywood (grade AB)*

3'   *of 2 by 2 clear fir or pine*

8'   *of ⅜" by 2¼" pine molding*

1   *continuous hinge, 1¹⁄₁₆" by 30", with ½" screws*

2   *friction lid supports*

8'   *of ⅜" vinyl weatherstripping*

4   *wheels, 1½" by 6" in diameter, with ½" hubs*

4   *lag screws, ½" by 3", with 2 washers each*
    3d finishing nails
    Wood glue
    Wood putty
    Nontoxic paint
    Striping tape and vinyl letters (optional)

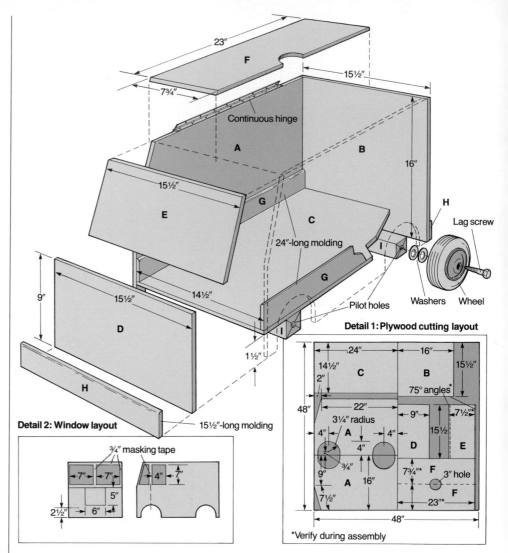

Detail 2: Window layout

Detail 1: Plywood cutting layout

*Verify during assembly

1. Lay out and cut plywood sides **A**, back **B**, bottom **C**, and front **D** (see Detail 1). Lay out windshield **E** and cut to length only. Cut the molding into two fillers **G** and two bumpers **H** as shown. Cut two 14½-inch-long axles **I** from 2 by 2 stock; mark center lines for them on **C**, 4 inches from each end.

2. Glue and nail the axles to the bottom, then add **A**, **B**, and **D**. Glue the fillers in place as shown.

3. Cut one long edge of windshield **E** at a 75° angle as shown. Hold it in position against **D**, mark its width, then cut the other long edge at a 75° angle. Glue and nail it in place.

4. Measure the top of the van and cut lid **F** in one piece. Cut the front edge at a 75° angle and cut the 3-inch hole as shown; then saw the piece in half. Cut the continuous hinge in half. Center it on each side and use it to attach the lids. Add weatherstripping where shown in the photo (this protects fingers from being pinched). Attach the friction lid supports (use the manufacturer's instructions and the photo as guides; the lids should open just past vertical).

5. Round over all edges, set the nails, and fill the holes; then paint. Paint the windows and grille, following the layout in Detail 2. Finish bumpers **H** and attach. Trim the van as desired. We used automotive striping tape and vinyl letters from a stationery store. *A word of caution:* These materials can be peeled off and possibly ingested. An alternative is to use nontoxic paint for the trim.

Finally, drill ⅜-inch pilot holes in the axles and add the wheels as shown.

Design: Bill Oetinger.

(Continued on page 120)

A capacious cargo hauler, *the bright, bold van toybox on the left is easy to build and can be decorated to suit your fancy. The wooden wagon on the right is an elegant, solid-oak heirloom designed to last for generations.*

Wooden wagon

To build our heirloom oak wagon, pictured on page 119, you'll need a moderate level of woodworking skill, a radial-arm or table saw with a dado blade, and components for the steamer (see Detail 1).

Materials. Here's what you'll need to complete the project.

9 board feet of 4/4 oak (grade to suit)
72' of 5/16" by 2" oak flooring: 6 @ 12'
6' of 2 by 6 Douglas fir (construction grade)
1 2' by 3' piece of 5/8" fir plywood (grade AD)
2' of 3/8" hardwood dowel
2 pieces of aluminum angle, each 3/4" by 3/4" by 10"
4 roller glides, 3/4" in diameter
2 galvanized steel rods, each 1/2" by 18"
8 1/2" washers
4 wheels, 10" in diameter, with 1/2" hubs
4 knock-on axle caps, 1/2" in diameter
96 brass flathead woodscrews, 1/2" by #6
10 flathead woodscrews, 3/4" by #6
28 drywall screws, 1 1/4" by #6
  Brads
4 carriage bolts, 1/4" by 1 1/2", with nuts and washers
1 machine bolt, 1/4" by 4", with locknut and 2 washers
1 machine screw, 5/16" by 3 1/2", with 2 locknuts and 2 washers
  Wood glue
  Wood putty
  Clear penetrating oil finish
  Black rubber mat, 34 3/8" by 16 3/8"

Cutting list

From 4/4 oak, cut:

2 Sides **A**: 13/16" by 5" by 36"
2 Ends **B**: 13/16" by 5" by 17 1/8"
2 Rear axle supports **L**: 13/16" by 5" by 12 1/8"
1 Rear support **K**: 13/16" by 5" by 12 3/8"
1 Rear crosspiece **J**: 13/16" by 5" by 12 3/8"
1 Front support **M**: 13/16" by 5" by 14"
1 Yoke top **N**: 13/16" by 5" by 14"
2 Front axle supports **O**: 13/16" by 5" by 7 1/2"
2 Yoke extensions **P**: 13/16" by 2" by 15"
1 Front crosspiece **Q**: 13/16" by 2 1/2" by 12 3/8"

From plywood, cut:

1 Bottom **C**: 5/8" by 17 1/8" by 35 1/8"

From oak flooring, cut:

8 Spacer blocks **D**: 5/16" by 2" by 1 15/16"
2 Spacer blocks **E**: 5/16" by 2" by 4 1/2"
2 Stake supports **F**: 5/16" by 2" by 36 5/8"
2 Stake supports **G**: 5/16" by 2" by 19 1/4"
24 Stakes **H**: 5/16" by 2" by 16"
12 Stake connectors **I**: 5/16" by 2" by 14"
3 Tongue pieces **S**: 5/16" by 1 3/4" by 29 1/2"
2 Handle pieces **T**: 5/16" by 1 3/4" by 8 1/4"
2 Handle pieces **U**: 5/16" by 1 3/4" by 3 1/4"

From Douglas fir, cut:

2 Bending form halves **R**: 1 1/2" by 5 1/2" by 36"

1. Cut all pieces to size (see cutting list). Rabbet sides **A** and dado sides **A** and ends **B**. Use Detail 3 to locate and mark half-lap joints between yoke top **N** and yoke extensions **P**; cut the joints to fit (see large drawing). Rabbet the ends of **N**. Cut profiles and drill axle holes in axle supports **L** and **O** (see Details 5 and 6). Shape the ends of yoke extensions **P** (see Detail 3); drill 1/4-inch bolt holes. Cut the dowel into twelve 1 1/2-inch pieces.

2. Glue and dowel sides **A** and one end **B** (use three dowels per joint). Slip in bottom **C**; add remaining end **B**. Using glue and brads, fasten spacer blocks **D** and **E** (see large drawing and Detail 3). Glue stake supports **F** and **G** to the blocks.

3. To make each stake section, glue and screw together four stakes **H** and two stake connectors **I** as shown; countersink the screws and slightly bevel the lower ends of the stakes.

4. Glue and screw crosspiece **J** to support **K**; add axle supports **L** (see large drawing and Detail 5). Glue

and screw support **M** to the underside of bottom **C** where shown in Detail 3 (**M** corresponds to the position of the front undercarriage). Center and drill a 1/8-inch hole through **M** and **C** and use as a guide to counterbore and drill **C** and **M** for the machine screw. Add the roller glides (see Detail 3).

Glue and screw yoke top **N** to axle supports **O** and yoke extensions **P**; add crosspiece **Q**. Drill a 5/16-inch hole in the center of **N**. Cut and screw an aluminum angle along each inside edge of **P** and trim flush at the ends.

5. Nail together and cut bending form halves **R** (see Detail 1). Make the steamer as shown, pour in about a quart of water, and bring to a boil. Add pieces **S**, cover, and steam for about 4 hours or until pliable (check water supply periodically). Put the pieces in the form as shown, making sure the long edges are flush. Tightly clamp and leave overnight. Release, apply glue to all mating surfaces, and reclamp; leave overnight.

6. Glue handle pieces **T** and **U** to the tongue (see Detail 2). Shape as shown. Trim and round over the

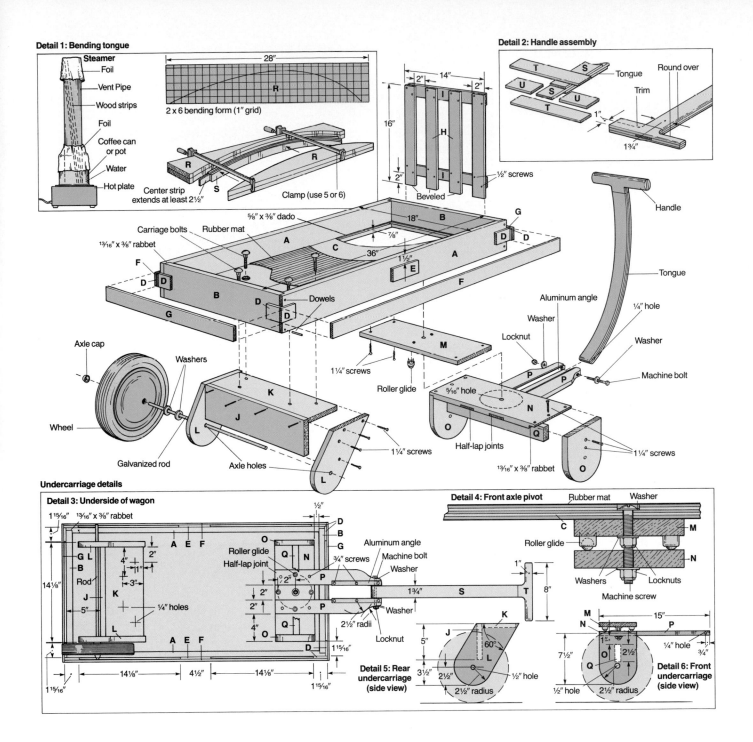

Detail 1: Bending tongue

Steamer
Foil
Vent Pipe
Wood strips
Foil
Coffee can or pot
Water
Hot plate

28″
2 x 6 bending form (1″ grid)
R

Center strip extends at least 2½″
R
S
R
Clamp (use 5 or 6)

2″ 14″ 2″
I
H
I
16″
2″
Beveled
½″ screws

Detail 2: Handle assembly

T S
U S U
T T
Tongue Round over
S
Trim
1″
1¾″

Handle

⅝″ x ⅜″ dado
18″ B G
Carriage bolts Rubber mat
7⁄8″
A 36″ D D
¹³⁄₁₆″ x ⅜″ rabbet
C
1½″
A
F E
D D B D Dowels
G F

Tongue

Aluminum angle
Washer
Locknut
¼″ hole
Washer
Machine bolt

Axle cap
Washers
M
1¼″ screws
Roller glide
P P
5⁄16″ hole
N
Wheel
Half-lap joints
O Q O
¹³⁄₁₆″ x ⅜″ rabbet
1¼″ screws
Galvanized rod
Axle holes
K J L
L L
1¼″ screws

Undercarriage details

Detail 3: Underside of wagon

1¹⁵⁄₁₆″ ¹³⁄₁₆″ x ⅜″ rabbet
½″
D B
G
A E F
14⅛″
G L
B
Rod
4″ 2″
1″
3″
J
5″ K
¼″ holes
L
O
Q N
Roller glide
Half-lap joint
2″
P
2″
2″
P
Q
4″ O
2½″ radii
A E F
D
1¹⁵⁄₁₆″
14⅛″ 4½″ 14⅛″
1¹⁵⁄₁₆″
¾″ screws
Aluminum angle
Machine bolt
Washer
1¾″ S
Washer
Locknut
1″ T 8″

Detail 4: Front axle pivot

Rubber mat Washer
C M
Roller glide
N
Washers Locknuts
Machine screw

Detail 5: Rear undercarriage (side view)

J K
60°
5″
L
3½″
2½″ ½″ hole
2½″ radius

Detail 6: Front undercarriage (side view)

M 15″
N P
1″
O 2½″
7½″
Q ¼″ hole ¾″
½″ hole 2½″ radius

---

other end of the tongue; drill the ¼-inch bolt hole. Plug all visible screws, round over sharp edges, sand, and apply two finish coats.

7. Drill four counterbore holes in bottom **C** for the carriage bolts (see Detail 3); attach the rear undercarriage. Attach the front undercarriage

(see Detail 4) and the tongue. Cut axles to length from the rods and install; mount the wheels as shown and attach the axle caps. Add the rubber mat and the stake sides.

Design: Don Vandervort.

Rocking Lion & Horse

Our mop-maned lion, a whimsical variation of the rocking horse theme, is sure to capture the imagination of any young child. The simple elegance of the fine hardwood rocking horse makes it an heirloom to cherish for a long time.

Rocking lion

This winning little lion is as quick to create as it is fun to look at; you can make it in a few hours once you have the materials.

Materials. Here's what you'll need to complete the project.

- 3' of 2 by 10 clear fir
- 22' of 1 by 2 clear fir: 1 @ 16', 1 @ 6'
- 8' of 2 by 6 clear fir
- 2' of 2 by 4 clear fir
- 8' of ⅜" hardwood dowel
- 2' of 1" braided rope
- 2 floor mop heads
  10d nails
- 2 wood cabinet pulls
  Wood glue
  Clear nontoxic finish
  Black felt-tip pen

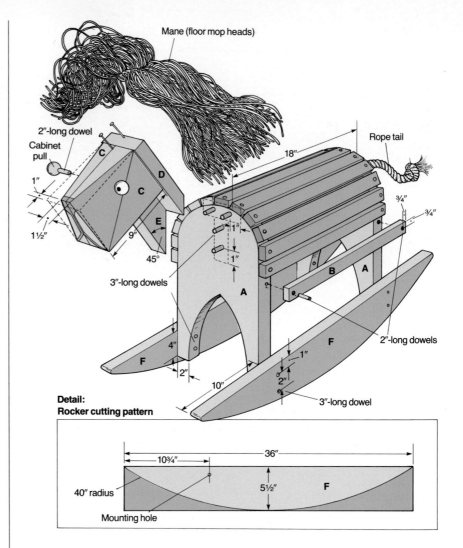

Detail:
Rocker cutting pattern

Cutting list

From 2 by 10 fir, cut:

2 Ends **A**: 1½" by 9¼" by 16"

From 1 by 2 fir, cut:

13 Body pieces **B**: ¾" by 1½" by 18" (cut 10 pieces from the 16-foot 1 by 2, 3 pieces from the 6-foot 1 by 2)

From 2 by 6 fir, cut:

2 Head pieces **C**: 1½" by 5½" by 9"
2 Rockers **F**: 1½" by 5½" by 36"

From 2 by 4 fir, cut:

1 Neck piece **D**: 1½" by 3½" by 9½"
1 Neck piece **E**: 1½" by 3½" by 7½"

1. Cut all pieces to size, following the cutting list. (Note: The lengths given for neck pieces **D** and **E**, which are cut at a 45° angle at one end, are for the longest sides.) Cut the tops of ends **A** to a 4⅝-inch radius and cut the arches between the legs as shown. Cut twenty-eight 2-inch and twelve 3-inch lengths of dowel. Mark and drill ⅜-inch holes in body pieces **B** as shown.

2. Starting at the top of ends **A**, attach pieces **B** with 2-inch dowels and glue. Use the holes in **B** as guides for drilling corresponding holes in **A**, keeping ends **A** parallel to each other and perpendicular to pieces **B**.

3. Rip the rounded edges from head pieces **C**, then join them by gluing and clamping. Cut the profiles in the head. Glue and nail pieces **D** and **E** to **C**.

These two spirited mounts *are off and running. The rocking lion is quick and easy to build; the rocking horse is a solid hardwood heirloom that requires more time and effort. Each is a sturdy design and will carry its rider many miles.*

4. Drill ⅜-inch head mounting holes in front end **A**. Hold the head in position and drill corresponding holes in **D** and **E**. Attach the head with glue and 3-inch dowels.

5. Cut rockers **F** as shown in the detail drawing; drill the top front mounting hole in each. Mark and drill a corresponding hole in each leg of front end **A** and temporarily assemble with dowels. Clamp the rear legs to the rockers and adjust the body until level. Drill the remaining mounting holes and fasten rockers **F** to legs **A** with glue and dowels.

6. Trim the dowels, round over all edges, and sand. Attach the pulls with glue and dowels. Finish; color the nose and eyes with a pen. Nail on the mane and attach the tail (pass it through a 1-inch hole drilled in back end **A**).

Design: Rick Morrall.

(Continued on next page)

Rocking horse

If you're a moderately experienced woodworker, you won't find it difficult to create this classic rocking horse, pictured on page 123. The beauty and durability of the completed project will repay your investment in time and materials many times over.

In addition to basic tools, you'll need a saber saw, a router, and a radial-arm or table saw to build the horse as shown; a band saw and belt sander are helpful. Both the level of difficulty and the tools needed are somewhat "adjustable," however; you could, for example, omit the inlaid bridle and girth—and the router they require.

Materials. Here's what you'll need to complete the project.

18   *board feet of ¾-inch ash, oak, or walnut (grade to suit)*
6'   *of ⅜" hardwood dowel*
2   *pieces of 1" hardwood dowel, each 3" long*
    24 sq. in. of leather
    Screw hole buttons: 20 @ ⅜", 2 @ ½"
4'   *of 1 by 6 pine or fir*
2   *round wooden picks*
4½"   *of ¼" threaded rod*
    Wood glue
    #12 flathead woodscrews: 24 @ 1½", 4 @ 1¾", 1 @ 2½", 3 @ 3"
    Finish

1. Using the grid-enlargement method described on page 64, transfer the cutting patterns (Details 1 and 3) to heavy paper and cut them out. Edge-join the boards by gluing and clamping to make "blanks" for body **A**, rockers **D**, and saddle halves **J** (see detail drawings); blind-dowel the body blank where shown in Detail 3 before gluing and clamping, using the 1½-inch-long dowel pegs. If you're not using a band saw, cut the saddle-half profiles before gluing; if you're using a band saw, cut the profiles after gluing. (Be sure the halves mirror each other.)

Pieces **K** and **L** and the optional bridle and girth inlays are ¼ inch thick. Rip these pieces from a dark hardwood (ours are walnut), or use ash or oak and stain it darker.

Trace the patterns for body **A**, legs **B** and **C** (made from single boards), supports **H**, and saddle halves **J**, then cut all pieces. Use a beam compass or, preferably, a saber saw to cut the rocker blank as shown in Detail 2; move the pivot point up 3¼ inches for each cut. Add reinforcing dowels to the feet and rockers where shown and shape the rocker ends.

Also cut two 2- by 14½-inch foot supports **E**, three 2- by 15½-inch footrests **F**, one 2- by 14-inch step **G**, and four ¾- by 2½-inch pieces **I**. Shape pieces **K** and **L** from the ¼-inch stock.

Mortise rocker ends ¼ inch deep where shown in Detail 3, tracing around the end of a foot support **E** to establish the size; be sure the centers of the mortises are 32 inches apart. Cut the four leg wedges from the 1 by 6 as shown in Detail 3.

To add the bridle and girth inlays, if desired, rout ³⁄₁₆-inch-deep by ¾-inch-wide grooves where shown in Detail 3; then glue ¼-inch by ¾-inch strips of hardwood in each groove. Sand flush when the glue is dry.

2. Unless otherwise indicated, assemble all the pieces with glue and the appropriate screws as shown in the exploded drawing. Drill counterbore holes and plug with screw hole buttons or dowels as indicated.

Be careful to drill adequate shank-clearance and pilot holes to avoid splitting the hardwood. Before assembling the horse, round over all exposed edges and sand.

Glue the leg wedges in place on legs **B** and **C**, aligning as shown in Detail 3. (Be sure to keep the left and right pairs of legs sorted as you work.) Place two legs on one side of the body, sanding their upper edges so they lie flat and positioning them by means of the alignment marks in Detail 3. Check that the centers of the hooves are 32 inches apart; then fasten the legs in place, observing the right- or left-side screw locations as shown. Add the two remaining legs to the other side in the same way.

3. Assemble rockers **D** and foot supports **E**. Add footrests **F**, gluing and doweling them in place as shown in Detail 3 and the exploded drawing. If your buckaroo needs a booster step, build it by gluing and doweling step **G** to supports **H**; use screws and two pieces **I** to lock the step assembly in place. Center the horse on the supports and screw the feet to the foot supports as shown.

4. Fasten one saddle half **J** to the body with 1½-inch screws, then add its mate, using 2½- and 3-inch screws (see exploded drawing and Detail 1). Glue and clamp the two remaining pieces **I** to the horse's head to act as mounts for the leather ears. Drill holes in mounts **I** where shown. Glue and clamp trim pieces **K** and **L** in position. Add ½-inch screw hole buttons for eyes. Round one end of each of the 1-inch dowel handles and drill the other end as shown. Drill holes in **A** and **K** (see Detail 3). Use the threaded rod to connect the handles and body.

5. Shape and sand the saddle, using the exploded drawing and the photo as guides. Do any final shaping, rounding, and finish sanding; then apply two or three coats of varnish or penetrating oil finish. Cut and roll the leather ears, insert them in ear mounts **I**, and secure them with wooden picks glued in ¹⁄₁₆-inch holes drilled through the mounts and ears.

Design: Louis Jewell.

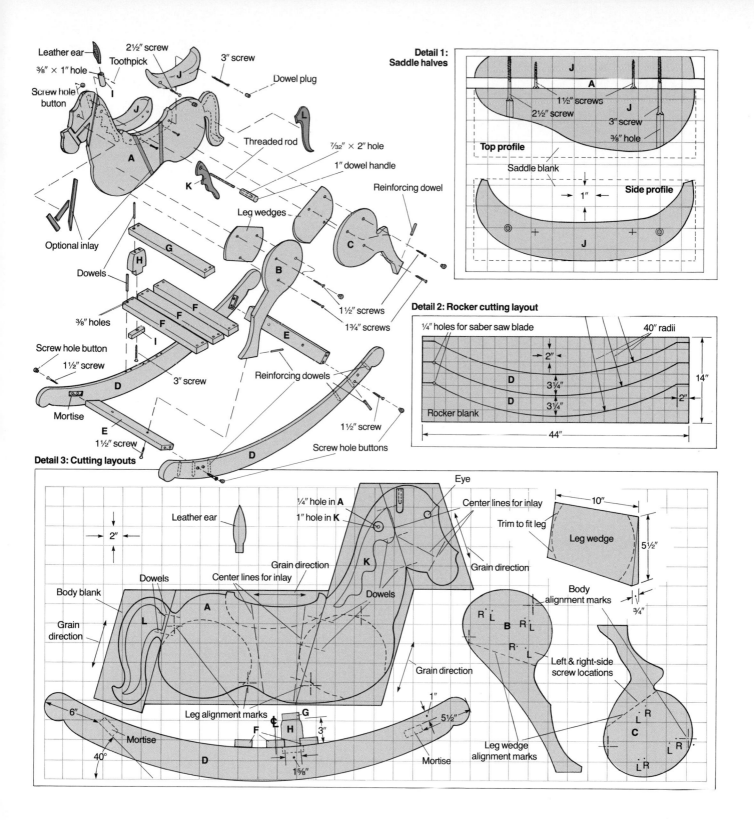

Playroom Furniture Set

If you're looking for a very special, one-of-a-kind gift for a child, this ingenious slot-together playroom set is the project for you. The simple charm of folk-style furniture is evoked in each piece, and each provides plenty of "blank canvas" for decorative painting. You can use the handpainted country patterns we show or develop your own motifs. The set is ideally suited for stencil work, découpage, or the like. Each piece also knocks down easily for storage or even for shipping, which raises the interesting possibility of building the set as a gift for someone far away.

You can mark, cut, and assemble the entire playroom set in a day. You'll need only a saber saw and basic tools, though a table saw will make short work of cutting the pieces and a router is helpful for rounding over edges. Refer to the drawings on pages 128 and 129 as you work.

Materials. Here's what you'll need to complete the project.

1	8' by 4' sheet of ½" Baltic birch plywood
8'	of 1 by 3 pine or fir
2'	of 1 by 4 pine or fir
29	drywall screws, 1¼" by #6
3	drywall screws, 2½" by #8
	2d finishing nails
	Wood glue
	Finish (see text)

Marking & cutting

1. Enlarge and transfer the patterns shown in Drawing 2 on page 129 to heavy paper (see page 64 for enlarging instructions). If you wish to decorate your set as shown, transfer the leaf and apple patterns to graph paper. Cut all patterns.

2. Trace the plywood patterns onto the plywood in the areas shown in the detail drawing, then cut all pieces to size. Make angled cuts at the top of all trestles: 82° for the table trestles, 77° for the others. Cut all slots and the pierced-work apples. Round the corners of the tabletop and bench-tops as shown in Drawing 1. Round over all edges, including the edges of the apple cutouts (if you have a router, use a ⅜-inch rounding-over bit set ¼ inch high). Don't round over the angled trestle tops or the slots in the trestles and chair seats.

Assembling the table & bench

1. Using stretchers **A** as patterns, mark and cut the angles at each end of 1 by 3 bench cleat **C** and the angles at the ends of table cleats **C**. Assemble stretcher **A**, trestles **B**, and cleats **C** with screws (see Drawing 1); use ³⁄₃₂-inch pilot holes and countersink the screws. For the second table cleat **C**, drill counterbore holes where shown and ⅛-inch pilot holes for the 2½-inch screws.

2. Invert tops **D** and the **ABC** assemblies; center and mark each **ABC** assembly on its top. Remove the **ABC** assemblies and apply glue to cleats **C** only; then fasten the **ABC** assemblies to the tops with five 2d nails through each cleat, driving the nails flush (do not set the heads).

Assembling the chair

1. For each chair, make cleat **C** by ripping the 1 by 4 as shown in Drawing 1 (side view). Using stretcher **A** as a pattern, mark and cut the angles at each end of the cleat. Assemble stretcher **A**, trestles **B**, and cleat **C** as shown, drilling countersink and ³⁄₃₂-inch pilot holes for the 1¼-inch screws.

2. With a file or rasp, cut back the front underside edge of the slot in chair seat **D** until chair back **E** can be angled at 77° (see Drawing 1). With all parts inverted and correctly positioned, mark the position of the **ABC** assembly on the underside of the seat; be sure chair back **E** fits snugly against cleat **C**. Remove the back and the **ABC** assembly, and apply glue to cleat **C** only; then fasten the **ABC** assembly to seat **D** with 2d nails through the cleat, driving the nails flush (do not set the heads). Using a 1¼-inch screw, fasten back **E** to cleat **C** as shown.

Finishing the set

To finish your set as shown, you'll need 2-inch alphabet stencils and ½-inch number stencils (both available at stationery stores); enamel undercoat and flat blue enamel; red, white, green, and brown artist's acrylics or oils; and matte varnish. Be sure all paints and the varnish are nontoxic.

1. Disassemble each piece. Apply undercoat and one or two coats of blue enamel to tops **D**, seats **D**, and backs **E**. When the paint is dry, apply a coat of matte varnish to all surfaces of each piece. Allow the varnish to dry thoroughly.

(Continued on page 128)

Baltic birch plywood *and interlocking construction make this playset strong, lightweight, and durable; country-style pierced and painted decorations make it delightful. You can build the set from a single sheet of plywood using only basic tools and a saber saw.*

2. Using the photo and Drawing 2 as guides, tape the leaf and apple patterns in position, then trace lightly around each pattern with a pencil. Remove the patterns and, using the photo for reference, paint in the red, white, and green portions of the designs. Let the paint dry; then use a little brown to create shadowing on the apples, and give each one a white highlight as well.

3. When all the paint is dry, tape the alphabet and number stencils in place and paint in each character with red. Paint all exposed plywood edges red as shown. Let the paint dry.

If you have a steady hand, box in the tabletop and benchtop apples with light, ruled pencil lines, then paint over your marks with red (see the photo for guidance).

4. After all the decorative painting is completely dry, apply two coats of matte varnish to protect your work. Follow the manufacturer's instructions, but omit sanding between coats.

Design: Pamela Silin Palmer & Karen Kariya of Faunus Designs.

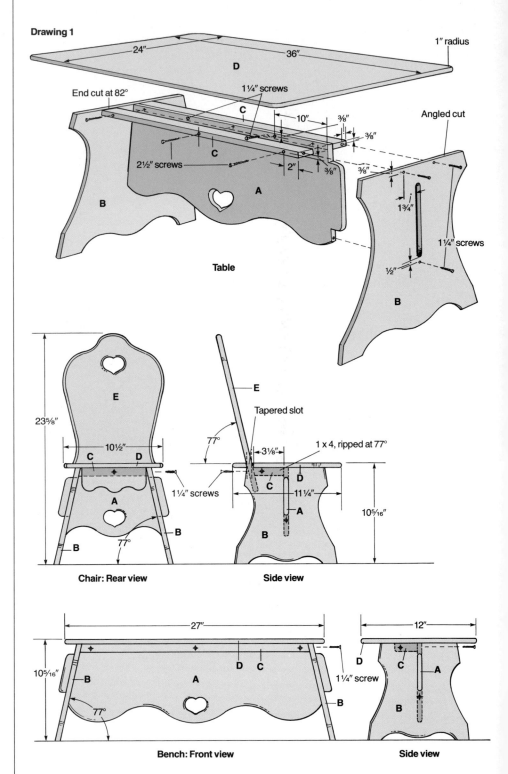

Drawing 1

Table

Chair: Rear view

Side view

Bench: Front view

Side view

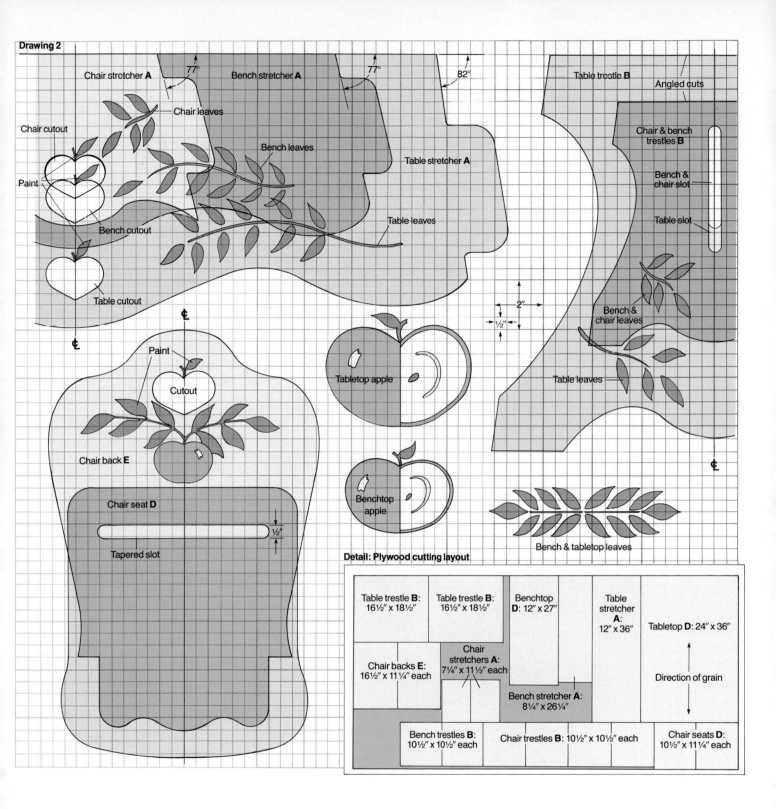

Drawing 2

Chair stretcher **A**   77°   Bench stretcher **A**   77°   82°   Table trestle **B**   Angled cuts

Chair leaves

Chair cutout

Bench leaves

Chair & bench trestles **B**

Paint

Table stretcher **A**

Bench & chair slot

Bench cutout

Table slot

Table leaves

Table cutout

2″

½″

Bench & chair leaves

Paint

Cutout

Tabletop apple

Table leaves

Chair back **E**

Chair seat **D**

½″

Tapered slot

Benchtop apple

Bench & tabletop leaves

Detail: Plywood cutting layout

Table trestle **B**: 16½″ x 18½″	Table trestle **B**: 16½″ x 18½″	Benchtop **D**: 12″ x 27″	Table stretcher **A**: 12″ x 36″	Tabletop **D**: 24″ x 36″
Chair backs **E**: 16½″ x 11¼″ each	Chair stretchers **A**: 7¼″ x 11½″ each			Direction of grain
		Bench stretcher **A**: 8¼″ x 26¼″		
Bench trestles **B**: 10½″ x 10½″ each	Chair trestles **B**: 10½″ x 10½″ each		Chair seats **D**: 10½″ x 11¼″ each

Making It Look A Lot Like Christmas

■

The fragrance of pine all through the house, the glittering tree, friends' greeting cards arranged on the mantle, the twinkle of lights —all these are a part of the special magic of Christmas. From the wreath on your front door to the handmade holiday cloth on your table, decorations convey an open-hearted welcome to family and friends. In the same way, gaily wrapped packages and special, handmade cards let your loved ones know how much you care.

On these pages, you'll find a wealth of ideas for decorating your home. Fruit-and-greenery wreaths, handmade Christmas stockings, glowing window stars, and whimsical ornaments are just a few of the decorations you'll learn how to create. In addition, you'll find inspiration in a charming selection of handmade gift wraps. These, along with a host of beautiful and original greeting cards, are sure to be treasured gifts in themselves. This year, use your special talents to make it look a lot like Christmas at your house.

One-of-a-kind Decorations

■

It's the very essence of Christmas: a house bedecked with twinkling lights, fragrant greenery, and well-loved ornaments. This season, make a special wreath, light up your windows, and create new ornaments to treasure—perhaps these whimsical cotton animals.

Living Christmas Trees

A living Christmas tree brings a happy sense of tradition to the holidays. It grows outside in the garden for most of the year, then comes indoors each Christmas to be transformed into a shining centerpiece for your holiday festivities.

Success with a live tree depends on three factors: careful selection of the tree at the nursery, vigilant care all year round, and tender treatment during the holiday season.

Selecting a tree

Living Christmas trees may be sold planted in containers or balled-and-burlapped. The latter are field-grown trees, dug up and wrapped before transport to the nursery. In the digging process, some (or even most) of the root system may be left behind in the soil, making the tree less likely to prosper. For this reason, a container-grown tree is usually your best bet, especially if it has spent a year or more—or even its entire life—in the container. Trees transferred from field to pot shortly before your purchase may not thrive, so be sure to ask when the tree you want was planted in its container.

Types of trees. Firs, spruces, and pines of many kinds are now available as living Christmas trees. The most popular firs are Douglas, Noble, Alpine (pictured at right), and white. Among spruces, Dwarf Alberta, Norway (pictured on page 134), and Colorado blue are good choices; suitable pines include Scotch, Japanese black, Monterey (pictured on page 135), and Aleppo. Norfolk Island pine (not really a true pine, despite the name) is another nice selection.

All these trees have different rates of growth. Pines, particularly Monterey and Aleppo, generally grow the fastest; firs and spruces may be considerably slower. Shape, height, and width also vary, so it's wise to get plenty of information before you buy. Ask at the nursery about the size and characteristics of different trees, and find out which type will grow best in your climate.

Caring for your tree

During the "off season," you'll need to find an appropriate outdoor spot for your tree. If it has spent a year or more in its container, you can keep it almost anywhere, from a full-sun location to a partly shaded area. But if your tree hasn't been in its pot for too long, you'll need to set it in partial shade, protected from winds.

Established trees often thrive without any fertilizer at all, but newly potted ones should probably receive one or two applications during their first year outside. If you decide to fertilize, do so during spring and summer, following the package label for timing and amounts. Just about any fertilizer will do; fish emulsion, organic fertilizers, and fast-acting or slow-release chemical fertilizers are all suitable choices.

Water all trees regularly; apply routine control for aphids and mites if necessary.

(Continued on next page)

This healthy Alpine fir has spent 10 years in its old-fashioned washtub; handles help the owners heft its 151-pound weight from garden to house.

Repotting your tree. When a tree still in a small or medium-size (3- to 10-gallon) container gets crowded roots, simply move it up to a container that's one size larger.

If you need to repot, you should do so in spring or summer. Begin by checking the rootball; if the roots are matted, score the outside of the rootball with a knife. Set the tree in its new container, then fill the space between the rootball and the bottom and sides of the container with potting soil.

Ultimately, of course, there will be no bigger size container to move up to (if you still want to be able to shift the tree indoors). When a tree in a big pot becomes rootbound, just remove it from its container, shave off several inches of roots and soil from the sides and bottom, and put the tree back in its pot with new soil beneath and beside the rootball.

Bringing your tree indoors

In cold parts of the country, living Christmas trees need a transitional period before coming into the house (see "Preliminary steps"); in milder regions, you can move your tree straight from garden to living room.

Preliminary steps. If you live in an area where the temperature dips below 20°F at night, it's best to take the tree through a transition stage before bringing it into the house. Suitable transition locations include windowed garages, porches, or basements—any unheated place that receives light during the day yet is protected from atmospheric cold. Leave the tree in its interim spot for several days.

The *day before* you plan to bring your tree inside, give it a thorough soaking. The soil will be less likely to dry out while the tree is inside, and if you give it a full day to drain, dripping from the pot will be minimized.

Moving the tree. Most large trees in containers weigh between 70 and 155 pounds, so handling them can be tricky. You may be able to put the tree in a container with handles, like that shown on page 133, and carry it by hand (with a helper) into the house or transitional location. Another option is to plant the tree in a permanent wood container with built-in casters. Alternatively, you can roll the tree in on a four- or five-wheel dolly—and leave it on the dolly throughout its indoor stay. If your tree must be carried up or down a flight of steps, you may need to rent a hand truck.

Protecting the floor. A tree in a fairly small container can simply be set in a terra cotta saucer (be sure to use the kind with a glazed interior). But you can really use anything that works, from a dishpan to an auto drip pan. It's often a good idea to put at least one thickness of plastic, or a sandwich of newspapers and plastic or foil, between pan and floor.

Indoor care. Most nursery instructions recommend an in-house stay of only 7 to 10 days, though a few go up to 14 days. Trees established in their containers for a year or more can get through their stint in the house with little or no water, but those recently transplanted from the field should be

This handsome Norway spruce *has enjoyed 22 Christmases in the house; its pleasing shape is perfect for decorating with cherished ornaments.*

watered every 2 or 3 days (set ice cubes on the soil for slow watering).

Dress-ups for containers. You may want to repot your tree into a handsome clay pot or a wood container (like that shown on facing page) that looks attractive both indoors and out. But trees in metal or plastic nursery cans will need to be dressed up for the holidays. If the container is too tall to be easily swathed in a sheet or quilt, try one of the three easy "wrap" ideas illustrated below.

Designs: Peter O. Whiteley.

Returning the tree outdoors

In cold climates, you'll need to reaccustom your tree to the outdoor temperature before setting it back outside. Move it to a transitional location—the same one you used before bringing it indoors (see "Preliminary steps")—and leave it there for 10 to 12 days (less if nightly lows are above 20°F). Then transfer it outdoors. Since it's possible for a container rootball to freeze outdoors, you may want to put a chicken wire cylinder around the container and fill it with hay or leaves—enough to surround and cover the container. Remove in the spring.

Planted only 3 years ago, this vigorous Monterey pine grew 2 feet in that time—now it reaches majestically to the ceiling.

Three Container "Wrapping" Ideas

■

Four plywood squares are covered with fabric and joined in pairs with cloth hinge to make a colorful "box."

Redwood lath, stapled to fiberglass screening, wraps around to become an attractive wood "container."

Pleated three-ply paper folded into 1-inch-wide bands makes an inexpensive wrap for a container of any size.

Fresh-cut Christmas Trees

You know it's really Christmas when the spicy fragrance of a freshly cut fir or pine tree fills your house. If you select your tree carefully and take a few precautions, a cut tree can stay fresh and green during its indoor holiday stay.

Choosing a fresh tree

The freshest Christmas tree is obviously one cut from a tree farm just a few days before December 25—but if you want your tree sooner than that (or don't want to trek to a tree farm), your best bet is to buy your tree as soon as possible after it arrives at your local tree lot. Though most trees come to the lots in good shape, they soon begin to dry out. Stop by and ask the lot owner when he or she expects a shipment; most lots get several during December. And don't be afraid to buy early; if properly cared for, the right tree will last for a month.

The most common trees on Christmas tree lots are Douglas firs, true firs (such as Noble and Grand firs), and Scotch pines. To find out if the trees are fresh, use this simple test: bend a needle with your fingers.

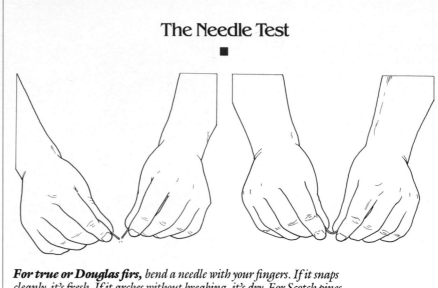

The Needle Test

For true or Douglas firs, bend a needle with your fingers. If it snaps cleanly, it's fresh. If it arches without breaking, it's dry. For Scotch pines, the opposite is true.

The needles of Douglas and true firs should snap cleanly; if the needles arch without breaking, find another tree. For pines, you want the opposite result. If Scotch pine needles *don't* snap, the trees are fresh; if they *do* snap, the trees are dry.

You can also test a tree simply by bouncing the trunk on the ground. A shower of needles is obvious proof that the tree is dry.

Once you find a fresh tree, protect it on the journey home. Before you tie it to the top of the car, tie it into a bundle with branches gathered around its trunk or wrap it in an old blanket.

Keeping the tree fresh

Moisture is the key to keeping your tree fresh and fire-safe. When you get the tree home, recut the trunk at least 1 inch above the end. This removes the air-filled tissue around the old cut and opens up the tree's vascular system, allowing moisture to be drawn up into the foliage. If you're not yet ready to put up the tree, stand it in a bucket of water outside, away from wind and direct sunlight.

For displaying the tree, it's best to use a stand that holds at least a gallon of water (this should do for all but the largest trees). Most commercial stands don't hold nearly that much, but there are exceptions; one type that's widely available at tree lots looks like a small plastic washtub with a spike coming through the bottom.

If you wish, add a commercial floral or tree preservative to the water.

Once the tree is in place, top off a large-capacity stand with water every day. If the water level in the stand falls below the base of the trunk, even overnight, the tree won't take up water through the cut end again and will dry out.

For additional safety, position the tree out of direct sunlight and well away from fireplaces or woodstoves. Make sure your Christmas lights are in good working order, and don't leave them on overnight or when you're away from home.

Finally, when the time comes to remove the tree, don't use it for firewood; it will burn at a furious rate, creating a fire too large for the fireplace. Instead, contact a Christmas tree pick-up service or cut the tree into small pieces and discard them in the trash.

The freshest, greenest tree *is the one you choose and cut for yourself at a tree farm.*
A bonus: the fresh-air outing's a great way to begin your holidays!

Four Types of Trees

■

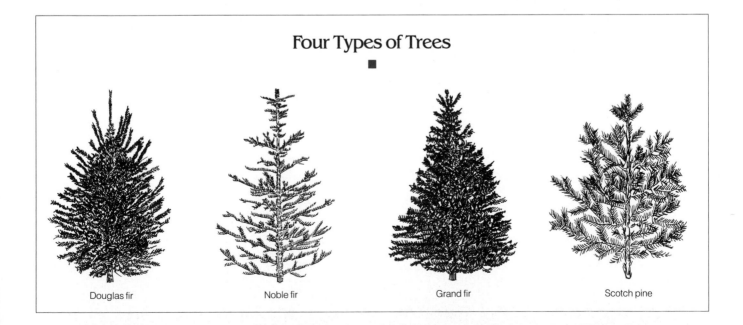

Douglas fir   Noble fir   Grand fir   Scotch pine

Live Ivy Wreaths

Green and growing ivy wreaths make a lively substitute for traditional cut greens. And even after the tinsel and the Christmas lights come down, these wreaths can be kept to enjoy in the new year.

It doesn't take months to grow our ivy wreaths. Once everything's at hand, you can make one in an hour. Here's the secret: each wreath contains three nursery-grown ivy plants, transplanted from their pots into a frame lined with moss and potting soil. You wrap and pin the vines in place to achieve the full-grown appearance, then decorate the basic wreath with whatever colorful fruits, pods, or cones you like—from kumquats to pine cones.

Besides three 4-inch pots of ivy, you'll need a ready-made wire frame, a bag of green sphagnum moss, 2 to 3 cups of potting soil, a spool of 22-gauge wire or heavyweight nylon monofilament line, and a pack of florist pins (sold at nurseries as plant pole pins).

Small-leafed English ivies work best. Choose young, well-branched plants with trailers a foot or so long. For different colors and textures, try variegated and ruffly-leafed kinds as well as the dark green needlepoint ivy shown here.

Follow the steps illustrated on this page. Don't worry if the foliage doesn't cover the moss completely; you can fill thin spots with decorations or a bow.

Ivy wreaths can hang outdoors or stay indoors for 2 to 3 weeks. Be sure to water regularly—daily, if necessary—to keep them moist. It's a good idea to water wreaths in the sink, where they can drain before rehanging. Well-drained wreaths shouldn't damage doors, but to help guard against staining, you can pin a circular sheet of plastic to the back of the frame.

If you move a wreath outdoors after the holidays, keep it in a shady spot, protected from scorching sun or frost. Remove decorations to let the foliage fill in. Once a month, apply a complete liquid fertilizer and pin or prune new growth to shape. Use the living wreath as a simple green centerpiece any time, or trim it with flowers and other fresh-cut material for special occasions.

Design: Connie Cumming.

Making the Wreath

1. Pack *soaked green sphagnum moss, wringing out a handful at a time, into a 12- to 14-inch frame to form a trough.*

2. Fill *trough with light-weight potting soil (as much as you can pack in lightly). Cover with a layer of wet moss.*

3. Wrap *moss-lined frame with 22-gauge wire or heavy nylon fishing line. Twist or tie off at back of frame.*

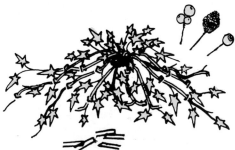

4. Make *three evenly spaced holes around ring by pulling moss apart. Unpot each plant, crumble soil, tuck trimmed rootball in hole, and press moss back in place.*

5. Wrap or zigzag *long vines to fit. Pin in place. Poke holes with a pencil to insert stemmed or wired fruits, nuts, berries, seed pods, cones, or flowers. Finish with a wired bow, if you like.*

A living wreath of dainty needlepoint ivy provides a welcoming touch on any front door.
Midwinter fruits (calamondin, kumquat, rose hips) add natural color, along with spiny cones
and two kinds of eucalyptus pods.

Wreaths on a Grand Scale

If there's a spot at your house that requires a big, bold splash of Christmas color, try filling it with one of these giant-size wreaths. Meant for outdoors, our big wreaths are easy to make if you have plenty of work space, power tools, and an ample supply of prunings. To speed and enliven the project, enlist the help of your friends; you might organize a party around the wreath-making, with guests bringing favorite greens, berries, and pods from their own gardens.

Making the frame

Each wreath is built on a doughnut-shaped piece of ½-inch plywood measuring 4 feet across. A standard 4- by 8-foot plywood sheet makes two wreaths. Use a nail, string, and a pencil to draw two 4-foot-diameter circles on the sheet; then draw a 2-foot circle inside each big circle.

Use an electric drill with a large bit to make a hole through the plywood, then insert the blade of a saber saw to cut the center circle. (Some saws allow you to stack the plywood and cut two forms at once—convenient if you're making two wreaths.) Finally, cut the outside circle.

To camouflage the wood, spray your wreath forms lightly with black or dark green paint.

A festive nontraditional wreath, this showstopper combines oranges, pyracantha, olive, magnolia, and sprigs of Chinese elm.

Choosing the greens

In selecting greens for your wreath, imagination is really the only limit. In addition to the traditional conifers—pine, fir, and the like—you might try other evergreens that can be pruned during the winter months.

If you use broad-leafed plants, bear in mind that thick, leathery foliage lasts longest. In the West, Strawberry tree (*Arbutus unedo*), silverberry (*Elaeagnus pungens*), eucalyptus, hollies, laurels (English and Portugal), *Ligustrum japonicum*, live oaks, *Magnolia grandiflora*, photinias, and raphiolepis are good choices. Berries, fruits, and pods add interest and color.

Assembling the wreath

Select and cut the greens you want; 6- to 9-inch lengths are easiest to manage. Then lay them around the form, experimenting with patterns. Choose sturdy greens for the backbone of the wreath, less long-lasting plants for accent (you can replace these later if necessary).

You can quickly secure foliage with a heavy-duty staple gun, though thick stems may require small fencing staples and a hammer. Encircle one edge of the frame with greens, overlapping the bottom end of one cut green with the top of the next.

Christmas-red ribbons brighten a background of green magnolia leaves; shiny apples, affixed with spikes, are accented with blue-gray dianthus foliage and seed pods of money plant (Lunaria annua).

High on the chimney goes a wreath with a bow, camellia, berried holly, choisya, skimmia, and magnolia. A masonry bit was used to drill the hole for the long supporting nail.

Encircle the remaining edge, then fill in the center.

As you work, step back to judge composition; tearing off greens that don't quite fit your image and replacing them is part of the fun. You may want to add bows or clusters of ornaments to the finished wreath. Check your results by holding the wreath upright so you can judge how the foliage hangs. Decide where you want the top of the wreath to be; put a large eyescrew through the back of the form at this point, halfway between the edges. Hang with strong wire.

The finished wreath will weigh 10 to 20 pounds. You can expect it to last for up to a month in cool, moist weather, a week or longer in warmer climates.

Putting the Wreaths Together

■

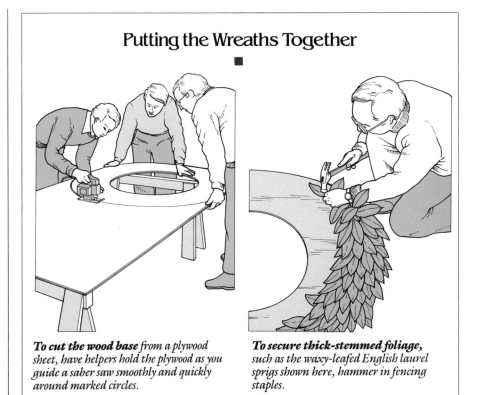

To cut the wood base from a plywood sheet, have helpers hold the plywood as you guide a saber saw smoothly and quickly around marked circles.

To secure thick-stemmed foliage, such as the waxy-leafed English laurel sprigs shown here, hammer in fencing staples.

Everlasting Wreaths

Gather together some garden prunings, a few pine cones, and dried grasses, add a handful of colorful dried or fresh leaves, flowers, berries, or fruits, and you have all you need to make a handsome everlasting wreath for yourself or special friends. The technique is simple and the cost minimal; you can even complete several wreaths in a day.

Our natural dried wreaths last from year to year; next holiday season, you can use your wreath again as is, if all the materials are dried, or strip off the trimmings and redecorate the base for a different effect.

Creating the base

To make a long-lasting wreath base, use any supple plant material you have in good supply. Each plant has its own special look and style. Birch, eucalyptus, and honeysuckle (shown on page 144) give you an even, rounded shape. Wisteria (shown at right) is nubby and twisted-looking; walnut clippings have a sculptural look. One of the most familiar materials—grapevines—has a rustic appearance. Bougainvillea (shown as a table decoration around a punch bowl, page 144) has a delicate, lacy quality, as do the twigs of the palm fruit stalk shown on facing page. Star jasmine or ivy (pictured in the kitchen wreath, page 145) can be wound into small, tightly woven wreaths.

To form the wreath, you'll need 2- to 5-foot strands of supple plant material with leaves removed—about 20 to 40 pieces, depending on the length and thickness of the branches and the wreath's size. Soak dried material in a solution of warm water and a little liquid dish soap until pliable (about 12 hours).

Extend a welcome *with twined wisteria prunings, pine cones, dried flowers, and fresh greens.*

If you're using fairly flimsy stems, such as palm flower branches, wrap them around a frame made from a wire hanger (as shown on facing page) to help them hold their shape. First, wrap a few strands around the hanger's hook; then wrap strands around the frame. Continue to add plant material, tucking in ends, until the wreath is slightly thicker than you ultimately want it to be (it will shrink as it dries).

Cuttings with pencil-thick stems, such as eucalyptus and grapevines, do not need extra support. Coil three 4-foot lengths into a 12- to 16-inch-diameter circle, allowing a few inches of overlap as shown on facing page; weave in the overlap. If necessary, wire the wreath in three or four places to secure the branches. Continue adding four or five strands at a time, tucking the ends into the existing form. Then wind the branches around—fairly loosely for an open wreath, much more tightly for a compact, smaller wreath.

(Continued on page 144)

Knobby twigs from a Washington palm fruit stalk are decorated with oak leaves, maple seeds, everlasting flowers, and teasels.

Grapevine wreath is trimmed with a holly sprig, pyracantha berries, and a branch tip (with seed pod) of Southern magnolia.

Forming the Wreath Base

■

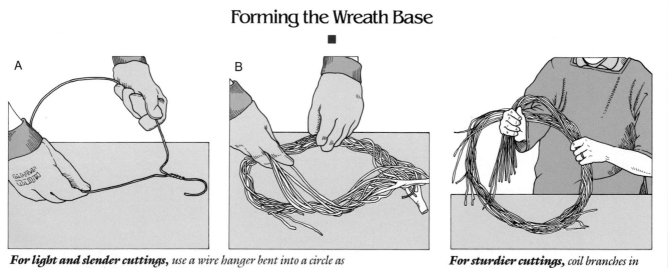

A B

For light and slender cuttings, use a wire hanger bent into a circle as a base; leave the hook for a hanger (A). Secure the stems around the hook, then wrap the rest around the frame (B).

For sturdier cuttings, coil branches in a 12- to 16-inch-diameter circle, weaving in overlap. Fill out the wreath with more branches, added a few at a time.

If you're using cuttings from fruit or nut trees, cut 6- to 12-inch-long branch ends. Wire these together to build the wreath shape, or wire them to a thin base of flexible material such as birch or willow.

Trimming the wreath

You can decorate your wreath base with fresh or dried materials (or both). In addition, you can wire on any sort of ornamentation you wish, as described below.

Dried decorations might include pine cones, seeds, pods, dried grasses, and dried flowers or herbs; check with your florist or floral supply store for dried plant material or other trim.

You can use wire to attach pine cones and most other large objects, though we used wooden skewers to

Add a festive touch to your holiday party with a garland of bougainvillea, pink straw flowers, and dried baby's breath around the punch bowl.

Delicate wreath with Renaissance air has a base of honeysuckle and bougainvillea. Dried flowers, lacy grasses, and plastic berries are the trim.

hold the garlic and lemons to the base of the kitchen wreath shown on the facing page. Bows can be wired on or tied directly to the wreath. Dried flowers or grasses can be tucked right into the branches.

If you like, you can also decorate your wreath with fresh materials. Some mild-climate possibilities are berries (nandina, pyracantha, California pepper), small fruits (dwarf pomegranate, calamondin, rose hips), and fresh foliage (eucalyptus or oak leaves). Other choices include hawthorn berries, sprigs of English holly or juniper, skimmia, salal, and *Daphne odora.*

Tuck stems of fresh leaves, berries, and flowers into the wreath. Most of the choices listed above will dry and discolor in about a week, so replace them as needed. Use raffia or wire to tie on stems of longer-lasting plant material such as dwarf pomegranates and pepper berries.

Special trimmings like small toys, wooden or straw animals, and kitchen utensils can personalize a wreath as a gift. Wreaths can also be decorated with traditional Christmas ornaments.

Designs: Françoise Kirkman, Kathy Brenzel, Eva Shaw, Rose Wagner.

Palm flower branchlets make an airy wreath for Christmas giving; eucalyptus pods, buds, and leaves are the finishing touches.

Garlic and lemons, set off by sprigs of rosemary and bay, stud this ivy kitchen wreath. A wooden fork and spoon and a cheerful red bow complete a colorful gift for your favorite cook.

Fresh Fruits & Greenery

In colonial days, fresh fruits—especially those from the tropics—symbolized bounty and welcome. Our updated versions of fruit-and-greenery decorations convey the same generous feeling—and add a delicious fragrance to your home.

These decorations can take a variety of forms, from swags to wreaths to table centerpieces. For the greenery base, use any evergreens that you have handy; pine boughs, cedar, holly, ivy, boxwood, and magnolia leaves are just a few among many options. Choose the fruit according to your color preferences. The bright citrus hues of tangerines, oranges, and lemons make a lively display; for subtler but equally rich color, use Christmas-red apples, pine cones, and evergreens. You may want to experiment with other food combinations—pomegranates, pears, limes, nuts, and even artichokes all add interesting variety.

These decorations will usually stay fresh-looking for 2 to 3 weeks if they're kept cool. Birds, squirrels, and changes of temperature take their toll, though, so outdoor decorations, particularly fruit, should be refreshed as needed.

Making a wreath or cluster

To form the frame for a wreath, you can use chicken wire, a ready-made form of straw or styrene foam, or wire about the thickness of a coat hanger. To make a wire frame, bend the wire into a hoop of the desired diameter. Tie three or four 6- to 8-inch lengths of greens at a time onto the hoop with florist's wire, overlapping them around the circumference.

To attach apples or other stemmed fruit to the wreath, simply wire them in place by the stem end. For citrus, pomegranates, and other stemless fruit, put 1-inch eyescrews into one end of the fruit (pierce only the rind), then run wire through the eyescrew and attach it to the greens. You may need to put in another eyescrew from the back and wire it to the frame. You can also use wire to attach pine cones and any bows or ribbons you wish.

To form a cluster, start with a chicken wire frame (see instructions on page 150), then add greens, fruits, berries, and pine cones, securing them with wire.

Making a swag

For a swag like that shown on the facing page, begin with 3 feet of fairly strong chain suspended at a convenient height for working; then secure the fruit to the chain with fine wire. To attach stemmed fruit, twist the wire around each stem and thread it through the chain links. For fruit without stems (such as oranges and lemons), use 1-inch eyescrews in place of stems. Insert each screw carefully, trying to pierce only the rind; if not punctured beyond the rind, fresh fruit should remain edible for several days and will look fresh for a week or two if kept outdoors or in a cool room.

After attaching the fruit to the chain, simply tuck pine cones and sprigs of evergreen between the fruit. The weight of the fruit should hold the cones and greenery in place, but you can use wire if necessary. Tie a satin ribbon to the top of the chain, and the swag is complete.

Other decorations

Fresh fruits and greens can also dress up your holiday table or hang as garlands indoors or out. To make a garland, see pages 148 and 149. Table centerpieces may be long garlands of fruits and greenery, or a circle of pine boughs, leaves, and apples centered around a pineapple—the colonial symbol of hospitality. To make your table decorations last longer, anchor the greens in a shallow, water-filled container with florist's sponge material.

An evergreen garland, framing a bright, pomegranate-studded wreath, makes a graceful display for a balcony.

A fresh fruit swag fills the air with the inviting fragrance of lemons and oranges. Apples, pine cones, and evergreen sprigs provide color and texture accents.

Holiday Garlands

A centuries-old tradition for "decking the halls," garlands of fresh greens are still among the most adaptable of holiday decorations, as well suited to kitchens or hallways as to mantelpieces or front doors. There's almost no limit to the kinds of greens and decorations you can use in a garland. And with our quick and easy assembly method, you'll find it a snap to make several—some for indoors, some for outside.

Selecting the greens

If you wish, you can make the garlands from traditional holly, ivy, and bay. But many other evergreens are also suitable. In the West, you can use redwood, cedar, and Douglas fir (shown on facing page); all three scent the air as they dry. Hollyleaf cherry (also shown on facing page) and toyon are excellent substitutes for holly. Evergreens found in the East include pine, spruce, hemlock, red cedar, fir, yew, and juniper. Such broadleaf evergreens as American holly, winter creeper, and English ivy also make attractive greens for garlands. Evergreen magnolia, Oregon grape, and English laurel, available in many areas, are other alternatives.

Making the frame

The frames for our garlands are made from aluminum screening (the sort used to cover rain gutters). It's sold in 6-inch-wide, 4-foot-long strips; though strong, it's easily cut with kitchen shears.

The drawings on the facing page show how to cut and bend the aluminum to hold greens and decorations. First, put on work gloves to protect your hands. Then cut three-fourths of the way across the strips with scis-

The fragrance of oranges and lemons mingles with that of fresh bay and rosemary in this all-natural garland. Dwarf live oak and manzanita provide additional greenery.

sors; bend back every other strip (you'll stuff greenery through the mesh). For extra strength, weave an additional piece of wire along the uncut top of the screening before decorating it.

Adding the greens & decorations

Once the frame is cut and hung in place, it's the work of a few minutes to stuff in the greens. Keep the pieces of greenery small, so they won't pull loose from their own weight. For the bottom row, wrap each strip around a bunch of greenery to create a firm base; then tuck more greenery through the mesh from the front. For the top row, push the ends of the twigs through the aluminum from the front and weave the stems back through to secure.

When the greens are in place, add the decorations. Many of these can simply sit right on top of the garland or nest among the leaves, but fine wire is useful for hanging objects or bows, and for anchoring items that won't stay in place.

Your decorations can be as simple or as elaborate as you wish. Certain decorations—Christmas ornaments, bows, and candy canes, for example —are always appropriate (see photo on facing page). But keep in mind that sparing decoration can make a very dramatic garland; for example, a plain green swag strung with twinkling lights is both simple and dramatic.

For a lavish holiday display, put together a fresh garland of Douglas fir and hollyleaf cherry; the greenery makes a pleasing background for shining ornaments, candies, ribbons and bows, as shown in the close-up, above.

For an "all-natural" garland, you could start with a base of greenery and fresh herbs, as shown on the facing page, then add fruit for a colorful and fragrant decoration (attach the fruit to the garland as directed on page 146). If you use bay and rosemary and add citrus fruit, as we did, you can even use parts of the garland in your holiday cooking.

For a really special touch, hang a garland on the mantel or near the Christmas tree in place of a child's Christmas stocking. Put small wrapped gifts on the garland when you make it, labeling or color-coding them so each child knows which present is his. On Christmas Eve, you can add a small doll, truck, or other unwrapped gift.

Design: Myriam Kirkman.

Making the Frame

■

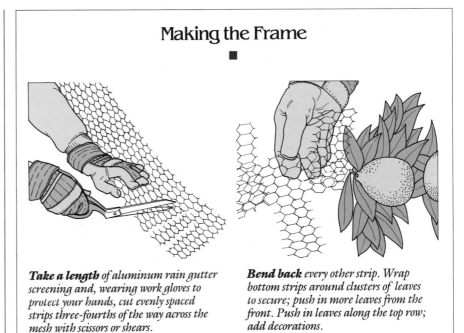

Take a length of aluminum rain gutter screening and, wearing work gloves to protect your hands, cut evenly spaced strips three-fourths of the way across the mesh with scissors or shears.

Bend back every other strip. Wrap bottom strips around clusters of leaves to secure; push in more leaves from the front. Push in leaves along the top row; add decorations.

Greenery Clusters

Here's a quick, easy way to turn extra snippets of greenery into a handsome decoration for a door or wall.

You'll need a wire hanger and a 12- by 18-inch rectangle of chicken wire or ½-inch hardware cloth. Stiff hardware cloth makes a sturdier frame, but chicken wire is more flexible and a bit easier to work with.

First, pull the hanger into a diamond shape as shown below. Then, wearing work gloves to protect your hands, fold the hardware cloth or chicken wire onto the hanger. Now tuck your greens into the frame, working from the bottom up. Cedar, fir, spruce, and pine are all good candidates; you might also use holly or pyracantha. Finish off the cluster with ribbons, ornaments, fresh fruit, or other decorations.

Hang the cluster with the hanger hook, or trim off the hook and push foliage and frame onto a nail.

These clusters will stay fairly fresh outdoors if the air is chilly; in non-freezing weather, a light misting will help preserve the greenery.

A cheerful holiday cluster *is easy to make with a little chicken wire and any bits of greenery you have handy.*

Making the Frame

■

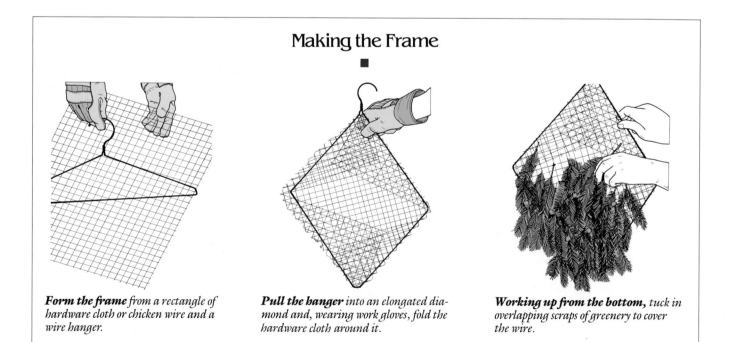

Form the frame *from a rectangle of hardware cloth or chicken wire and a wire hanger.*

Pull the hanger *into an elongated diamond and, wearing work gloves, fold the hardware cloth around it.*

Working up from the bottom, *tuck in overlapping scraps of greenery to cover the wire.*

Kissing Bough

A traditional decoration in England and colonial America, a sphere of greenery, especially one containing winter-fruiting mistletoe, holly, or ivy, symbolizes rebirth in the midst of winter. Any kind or combination of greens and decorations makes a fresh-looking kissing bough to hang in your house for the holidays.

Almost any type of evergreen will do; choices include pine, fir, spruce, magnolia leaves, and eucalyptus as well as the traditional holly, ivy, and mistletoe. Experiment with different clippings from your garden, and check the seasonal offerings at produce markets and florist's shops.

The frame is made from two hemispherical wire baskets of the type used for sphagnum moss planters. Buy the baskets (they're often painted green) from your local garden center; if necessary, cut and remove some of the wire struts or intermediate hoops (as shown below) to open up the structure of the finished frame. Wire the baskets together, then wrap the seam in several places with green florist's tape to keep the two halves from shifting. Secure the greens to the frame with fine wire. If you wish, you can wire on ornaments, fruits such as apples, or any other decorations you choose.

To complete, add a bow and a ribbon at the top to act as a decorative hanger. Suspend mistletoe from the bottom, then hang up the decoration in a likely spot for warm and loving holiday greetings.

Design: Françoise Kirkman.

Mistletoe dangles from a handsome kissing bough of fragrant spruce, inviting affectionate holiday greetings.

Making the Bough

To make the frame, join a pair of planter baskets with wire after snipping off any unwanted struts with wire cutters; wrap joint with florist's tape.

Attach greens to the frame with fine wire; wire on any decorations. Finish off with mistletoe on the bottom and a ribbon on top for hanging.

Accordion-folded Ornaments

Paper folding is an art in the Orient, where it's usually associated with holidays and gift giving. The easy-to-make ornaments pictured here —a flower, butterflies, and a dove —all involve pleating paper into accordion-like folds.

Quality construction papers, available in art stores in a variety of colors, are most durable, but you can also use medium-weight gold or silver foil papers that will shimmer near Christmas tree lights.

Making the ornaments

The flower and butterfly ornaments start with 4- by 9-inch paper rectangles (one sheet for the flower, two sheets for each butterfly). For the dove, you'll need to make a pattern; see page 64 for instructions on enlarging and transferring.

You'll also need colored silk cord, yarn, or string; glue; a ruler; a hole punch or needle; and pipe cleaners for the butterfly antennae.

To make the ornaments, follow the directions at right. To finish each flower, punch a hole at the top with a hole punch or needle; attach yarn or string for hanging. On the dove, poke two holes about 1 inch apart on body fold between wings; add string. Attach string to center ties on butterflies.

Design: Dennis Leong.

How to Make the Ornaments

■

Flower

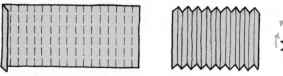

Starting at one end, accordion-fold into ½-inch-wide strips. Press folds together at center; tie with string, yarn, or silk cord. Fan out each half; glue ends.

Butterfly

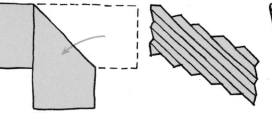

Fold right side back so protruding ends are of equal length. Starting ½ inch from diagonal fold, accordion-fold side A into ½-inch-wide strips. Then turn over and repeat on side B. Compress folds; tie below center. Repeat with a second sheet of paper. Tie wings together with a pipe cleaner; bend wings out.

Variation. Fold and tie one piece of paper as above for wings. Fold and tie second piece as for flower (top). Tie both together; fan out folds.

Dove

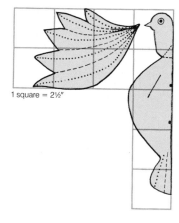

1 square = 2½"

Scale up pattern to desired size (we used 2½-inch squares). Place on paper with center of body along fold; cut out. Unfold; score along fold lines. Crease across neck, fold head back, and refold dove along center line. Accordion-fold tail and wings: outward on dotted lines, inward on broken lines. Cut a 1-inch slot in each side of body. Slip wings into slots; tape on inside to secure.

Light and shadow *play over the accordion folds of paper dove, flower, and butterflies as they float through the boughs of a Christmas tree.*

Dazzler Ornaments

Using shimmering polyester film and foil paper, you can create a galaxy of twinkling ornaments for this year's Christmas tree. Our fanciful stars, moon, chrysanthemum, fish, and spiral are faceted for extra sparkle; the spiky starburst has a dramatic three-dimensional effect.

Polyester film ornaments

Use mirrored .003 or .005 polyester film (available in art supply stores) to create these quick and easy ornaments. You'll also need a fine-tipped felt pen, a ruler, a pointed instrument for scoring, scissors or a craft knife, glue, and thread for hanging.

Using the patterns shown below as guides, draw the outlines to whatever size you wish. (Wash your hands before handling the film, and have a damp, soft towel to wipe off ink lines and fingerprint smudges.) Then cut out the ornaments with scissors or a craft knife. Within the outlines, cut along gray lines or score and fold along green dotted lines to create the light-reflecting facets.

To make each small star, you cut two shapes, then slit each one so the two pieces can be put together. The moon and its companion star are simply scored and folded. The chrysanthemum, fish, and spiral are cut as marked in the center areas; the cut pieces are then bent outward to catch the light.

To hang the ornaments, punch a tiny hole at the top and attach a length of thread.

Starburst ornament

Though time-consuming to make, this shining starburst is so dramatic it's worth the effort. The starburst is assembled from twelve 5-inch circles of shiny foil or colored paper. To speed cutting the circles, fold the paper to make many layers. Draw the circle pattern on the top layer with a compass or by running a pencil around the rim of a glass. Then cut all the layers at once.

After cutting the circles, fold the top one in half three times, matching edges. (The fold lines will mark the circle into eighths.) Unfold. Set a quarter in the center of the circle; outline the quarter with a pencil. With all circles stacked, cut through them along the fold lines to the boundary of the small center circle.

Form spikes by wrapping the cut portions of each circle around a pencil point; glue the corners down as shown on the facing page. When all the spikes are made, stack the 12 segments together, right sides up.

To put the pieces together, use buttons and thread. Take a stitch with a needle and thread through all layers from top to bottom, then pass the thread through a small button and go back up through the layers to the top. Attach a button on top, pull both buttons tight, and knot the thread, making a loop on top for hanging.

Designs: Peter O. Whiteley and Dennis Leong.

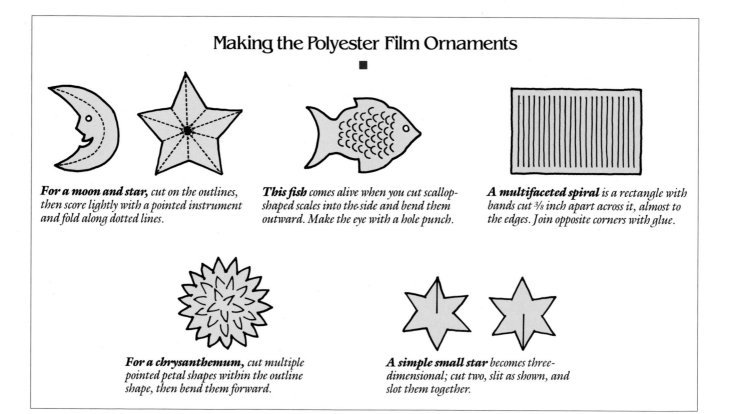

Making the Polyester Film Ornaments

For a moon and star, cut on the outlines, then score lightly with a pointed instrument and fold along dotted lines.

This fish comes alive when you cut scallop-shaped scales into the side and bend them outward. Make the eye with a hole punch.

A multifaceted spiral is a rectangle with bands cut ⅜ inch apart across it, almost to the edges. Join opposite corners with glue.

For a chrysanthemum, cut multiple pointed petal shapes within the outline shape, then bend them forward.

A simple small star becomes three-dimensional; cut two, slit as shown, and slot them together.

This spectacular golden starburst *is made from sheets of foil; give it a place of honor on your tree.*

Add sparkle to your Christmas tree with easy-to-make polyester film ornaments— a chrysanthemum, man-in-the-moon, fish, spiral, and two kinds of stars.

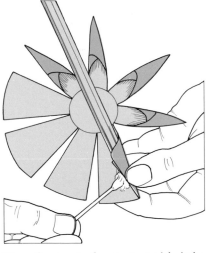

To make our starburst, *start with circles of foil. On each circle, form points around a pencil tip; stick with glue.*

Little Box Ornaments

Shiny little boxes made from coated paper and filled with inexpensive gifts can decorate your Christmas tree until they're given as favors to holiday guests. Or use the boxes on an exciting "Advent tree" for children: attach stick-on numbers to the boxes and hang them on your tree, then open one each day until Christmas.

Look for coated paper (a lightweight tag board with color or foil on one side) in art supply stores. From a 20- by 26-inch sheet you can make four boxes, each about 2 inches on a side. You'll also need a pencil, ruler, hole punch, compass, art knife, scissors, and gold string or cord for hanging boxes on branch tips.

To make the boxes, rule a grid of 2-inch squares on the back side of a sheet of coated paper. Draw the boxes on the grid following the pattern below and using a compass to draw the rounded tabs. Cut out the boxes with an art knife or scissors. Lightly score the fold lines (dotted lines on the pattern) with a sharp point. Punch holes in the tabs as shown below; cut 1-inch slits for the tabs where indicated in the pattern. Fold the sides inward to form the box.

To decorate the boxes, use gummed or adhesive stickers (gold stars, numbers, or animal shapes) from a stationery store. Or cut your own designs from adhesive plastic.

After you've filled the boxes with little gifts or candies, simply fold the top pieces closed so that the tabs protrude; then add a string for hanging.

Design: Françoise Kirkman.

Making the Boxes

■

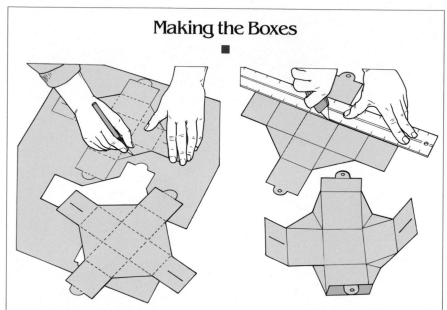

On the reverse side of a sheet of coated paper, rule a grid of 2-inch squares. Then draw the boxes (use a compass to outline the tabs) and cut them out.

Lightly score the dotted fold lines using a ruler and a sharp point. Punch holes in the tabs, cut slits to fit the tabs through, and fold to form a box.

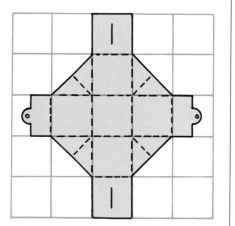

A collection of bright little gold boxes on the tree holds little gifts and candies, ready for giving.

Origami Ornaments

Ornaments inspired by *origami*, the traditional Japanese paper-folding craft, are colorful, inexpensive, and easy to make. You need only a few materials—a box of the slightly shiny, lightweight origami paper, string, white glue, and scraps of colored tag board or paper.

To make the Santa, we used an 8-inch square of paper and folded it as shown in the drawing below. Complete the Santa by adding a beard, trim, and hanger. You can secure the arms in place with glue, if necessary.

For the tree, use a 5-inch square and fold as for the Santa; stop when you have the triangle in the fourth step. Take two horizontal tucks to give a tiered effect. Glue on a tag board star, a hanger, and tiny ornaments made of contrasting origami paper.

To make the reindeer, start with a 6-inch square of paper and follow the folding instructions. Cut antlers from tag board and glue on.

Make the bell by folding a 7-inch square according to the drawing. Finish the bell by separating the points at the top and folding them down on each side of the bell; secure with glue. Invert the figure and glue a clapper into the opening and a handle at the top.

***Cheerful origami ornaments** are cleverly folded, then decorated with your individual touches.*

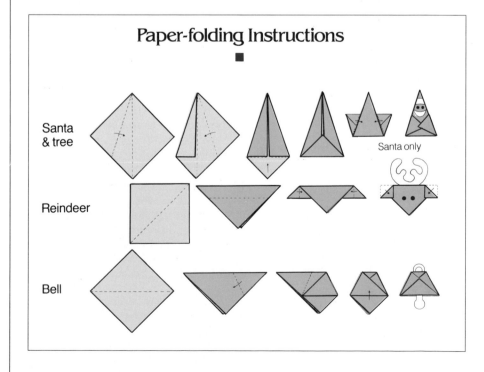

Paper-folding Instructions

Santa & tree

Santa only

Reindeer

Bell

Folk Art Ornaments

Christmas tree ornaments often express the folk art traditions and symbols of a country or people. In the United States, with its many ethnic communities, the handmade treasures that some of us bring out of the closet each year may go back generations—to the "Old Country" of our grandparents or great-grandparents. Or they may be updated versions of centuries-old crafts.

The ornaments shown on this and the following two pages are just a sampling of the diverse designs created in many of the world's countries. Some, like the Polish eggshell ornaments shown at right, are strictly traditional; others, like the Latvian mittens shown on the facing page, are adapted to new materials.

Polish eggshell ornaments

Decorating blown eggs with paper is a Polish craft tradition; the swan and the festive pitcher are done in often-used folk art motifs. Blow the eggs first: use a sharp point such as a large needle or compass point to make a small hole at both ends of an egg, being sure to break the yolk. Work over a bowl, holding the egg carefully to avoid crushing it. Blow hard through one end until all the raw egg is out. Rinse well and set aside to dry. Using the patterns, cut out the pitcher or swan pieces from heavy art paper.

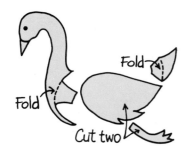

Fold

Fold

Cut two

Eggshell *ornaments are patterned on swan and pitcher motifs from Polish folk art tradition.*

To assemble the swan, fold back tabs and use to attach pieces to shell, putting head at egg's largest end. Glue wings and feet to both sides; use gold thread to hang from tree.

To assemble the pitcher (shown at right), roll top piece and base into cylinders around a pencil and glue together. For pitcher top, fit cylinder over one end of shell; glue strips down over sides of shell. Fold spout as indicated; glue to top by tabs. Attach base and handle with glue. To finish, draw geometric or floral designs on egg with felt-tip pens.

Design: Laura Ferguson.

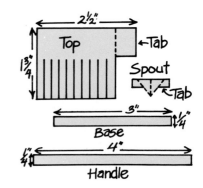

Make cuts on solid lines. Fold on dotted lines.

Latvian mittens

The idea of hanging mittens (and socks) on a tree comes from Latvia. Before Christmas, hostesses decorated their trees with gaily patterned hand-knit mittens. At the party's end, each guest would take a pair to warm his or her hands on the homeward journey across the snow. We have adapted this idea to create purely decorative mittens cut from colored felt.

You'll need pencil, scissors, felt, glue, and ribbon or braid. Trace a mitten shape around a hand on a double thickness of felt. Cut out four pieces (a pair of mittens). For designs, cut out hearts, flowers, or other motifs from contrasting felt and attach them with a little glue. Make mittens by machine-stitching close to edge, leaving wrist edge open. Join each pair with a length of patterned ribbon. If you have children, you can start a family tradition by making (and dating) a new pair of mittens, sized to the child's hand, each year.

Design: Laura Ferguson.

Colorful mittens *made of felt are a Latvian Christmas tradition. In times past, actual gloves were hung on the tree so guests could warm their hands on the homeward trip.*

Rollicking *horse, pig, and cat of felt are decorated with scraps of fabric. They're adapted from traditional Estonian ornaments.*

Estonian animals & paper chains

Fabric ornaments in the shape of animals are traditional in Estonia, on the northern shores of the Baltic. The authentic ornaments are made from printed fabrics or from plain-colored fabrics embroidered on one side with peasant motifs—but to make our simpler version, you just embellish felt animals with printed fabric cutouts. Use cookie cutters or your own designs to make a rooster, pig, horse, or cat. You'll need felt, fabric scraps, thin satin ribbon for hanging, bells, pinking shears, polyester stuffing, and glue.

For each animal, use pinking shears to cut two pieces of felt, one slightly bigger than the other, in contrasting colors. Pin pieces, wrong sides together, with a little stuffing between the two halves; machine-stitch around the shape close to the edge. To decorate the animals, glue on flowers and hearts cut from fabric scraps. Use bells for eyes; stitch a ribbon loop to the back of each ornament for easy hanging.

The paper chains shown above are also traditional Estonian tree decorations. Fold a 2-inch-wide, 2-foot-long piece of colored tissue paper in half lengthwise. With a craft knife, make cuts as shown in the diagram below. Open out carefully and pull apart gently.

Design: Laura Ferguson.

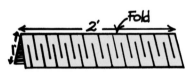

Make cuts on solid lines

Japanese lanterns

The pyramid-shaped ornaments pictured on page 160, their shapes inspired by Japanese lanterns, employ an adaptation of a contemporary Japanese wrap-and-weave technique used to make colorful decorative spheres. The authentic decorations are made with thin strands of embroidery floss or string, but for our simpler version, you can use narrow satin ribbon or three-ply needlepoint yarn.

(Continued on next page)

You will also need firm cardboard, a craft knife, tape, scissors, and glue. Each lantern also requires 3 yards *each* of three colors of ⅛-inch-wide satin ribbon (or 3 yards total of wider ribbon or silk cords), scraps of fringe for tassels, and about 1½ feet of silk cord.

To make a lantern, cut out the form from the pattern shown below; then assemble as shown in the drawings, also below.

Design: Kathy Avanzino Barone

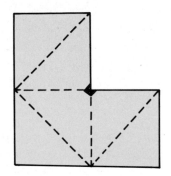

Measure *and double the size of this pattern (or scale it up to make a larger lantern). Hanging loop goes in center notch; bottom tassel goes just inside bottom right-hand corner.*

Stone and paper lanterns *found in Japanese gardens inspired these ribbon-bound and tasseled ornaments.*

How to Make the Ornaments

■

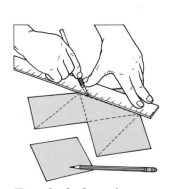

To make the form, *draw the pattern on cardboard. Cut out with a craft knife; score on dotted lines, then fold.*

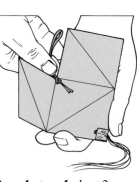

To make tassels, *knot 2 strands of fringe in the middle. Tape in bottom tassel (see pattern). For hanger, cut a 14-inch length of silk cord, loop, and knot. Place knot in notch.*

Tape the form *together. Tape tassels in corners. Place ribbons side by side and tape ends to the starting point. Wrap as shown, keeping ribbons taut.*

Continue wrapping, *keeping rows of ribbons side by side. When form is covered, trim the ribbons; glue down the ends.*

Lamé Ornaments

Light up your tree with a glittering galaxy. These golden stars and moons are easy to make and can be assembled quite rapidly. For 10 to 15 ornaments, you'll need ½ yard of gold or silver lamé with white polyester backing, cotton and metallic threads, and a small bag of polyester stuffing.

Making the ornaments

Begin by drawing simple star and moon patterns on paper. You can use one pattern or vary the sizes of the ornaments as we've done with our moons. (Our star is 5 inches across; the large moon measures 5 inches from tip to tip; the small one, 3 inches.)

Fold the fabric in half with right sides together; pin on the patterns, trace their outlines with a pencil, and cut through both layers, adding a ¼-inch seam allowance. Baste along the penciled outline, allowing a 1½-inch hole for stuffing; then machine-stitch, using ¼-inch seams. Clip seams at angles of star arms and at ¼-inch intervals on concave curve of crescent moon.

Turn shapes right side out; fill firmly with polyester stuffing. Hand-stitch opening closed. To make a loop for hanging, run metallic thread through tip of star or moon.

Design: Francoise Kirkman.

The moon and stars shimmer and shine from the branches of your Christmas tree when you stitch these quick-and-easy ornaments from gold or silver lamé. You can make a whole treeful in a day.

Fragrant Stitched Ornaments

Satin or cotton ornaments filled with herbs and spices make especially festive Christmas decorations. They're fragrant on the tree, and the scents may last for several seasons.

To make them, you'll need scraps of thin satin or printed cotton, sharp scissors, pinking shears, lace and ribbons for trim, and metallic thread for hangers. For stuffing, use store-bought potpourri or kitchen spices such as cloves, anise, cinnamon, or coriander.

Satin ornaments

Copy the shapes from the photograph at right and enlarge them on graph paper to the size you want (see page 64); add ½ inch all around for seam allowance. If you want to sketch your own design, keep it simple—satin can be tricky to turn. Cut two pieces of each motif. With right sides together, stitch around shape with a ½-inch seam, leaving a 2-inch opening at the top. For cloud and star, pin 5-inch-long pieces of ribbon into seam allowance, long ends toward the center, before stitching. For heart, stitch a piece of lace to right side of front before stitching the two pieces together.

Clip curves and corners, turn shape right side out, and stuff tightly with potpourri. Hand-stitch opening closed, stitching a hanging loop of metallic thread into place as you sew. For angel, hand-stitch around wings through all thicknesses of material. Hand-stitch bird's wing to body; sew on a bell for the eye.

Tree sachets

The flowered sachet bags shown on the facing page were inspired by potpourri bags from the Provence region of France.

For the bags, start with two rectangular pieces of fabric, each about 3½ by 4 inches; for the pouch, cut a 5-inch-diameter circle. To make the heart, cut two pieces of fabric with pinking shears in the shape of a heart.

Sachet bag. Place fabric rectangles with right sides together and sew around three sides close to the edge, leaving top open. Turn right side out, press, and pink top edge. Fill half full with herbs or spices; fasten with a ribbon loop stitched in place with a scrap of lace. To hang, slip a length of metallic thread under the ribbon, loop it, and tie closed.

Pouch. Place pinked fabric circle wrong side up, put a spoonful of potpourri in the center, gather up to form a bag, and tie tightly with a ribbon bow. Stitch a loop of metallic thread into the center of the opening to hang.

Heart. With wrong sides of fabric together, machine-stitch around heart close to pinked edge, slipping a tablespoon of filling in when half sewn. Attach a ribbon loop to the top to hang heart on the tree.

Design: Laura Ferguson.

Shimmering and scented, these bright satin ornaments are fun to stitch and stuff with sweetly fragrant potpourri.

Delicate sachets *are easily made from charming print fabric scraps, ribbons, and lace; stuff them with potpourri or aromatic kitchen spices for a delicious holiday fragrance.*

Barnyard Animal Ornaments

(Also pictured on page 132)

With a needle and thread, white cotton, and colorful acrylic paints, you can create an animal farm to adorn a Christmas tree, decorate a wreath, or even use as a table decoration. Wherever they're displayed, these fanciful creatures are sure to delight.

Materials

For 10 to 12 ornaments:

½ yard tightly woven cotton (such as pima), 45 inches wide

1 small bag polyester stuffing

White cotton thread

Waxed or unwaxed white dental floss

Acrylic paints

Tracing paper

Carbon paper

Darning needle

Small paintbrush

Making the animals

Enlarge and transfer the patterns at right, following the instructions on page 64. With carbon paper, transfer outlines to single-thickness fabric pieces.

To assemble each ornament, pin marked fabric piece to an unmarked one. Baste along penciled outline, leaving a 1½-inch stuffing hole on animal back or chicken stomach and a ½-inch opening on ram's horns and dog's ears. Machine-stitch along outline as shown on the facing page, or hand-sew details if you prefer. Cut out pattern, allowing a ¼-inch seam; clip fabric at angles and curves. Remove pins.

Turn animal right side out. Starting with small features like legs or beak, pack taut with stuffing. Hand-stitch hole closed. Stuff ram's horns loosely; dog's ears should not be stuffed.

Lightly pencil in quilting lines (visible in photo at right), then hand-sew with a running stitch, using a darning needle and dental floss.

Pencil designs lightly on animals and paint with acrylics. After the paint dries, hand-stitch the ram's horns and dog's ears in place. For the cow's tail, twist two pieces of string together and sew on at two points.

Design: Françoise Kirkman.

1 square = 1″

Packed with personality and charm, these little animals will perk up any Christmas tree or green decoration. Stitch up a whole barnful!

Stitching the Animals

■

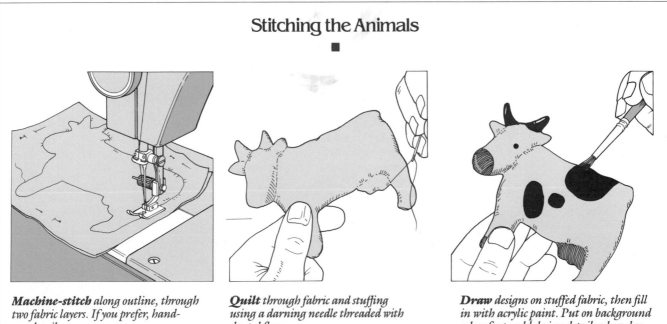

Machine-stitch along outline, through two fabric layers. If you prefer, hand-sew details.

Quilt through fabric and stuffing using a darning needle threaded with dental floss.

Draw designs on stuffed fabric, then fill in with acrylic paint. Put on background colors first; add design details when dry.

Hand-molded Ornaments

Your whole family can get into the act when you make hand-molded ornaments from specially formulated dough or clay. Ornaments can be as simple or sophisticated as you wish—just set out materials and turn your sculptors loose. On these pages, we show you how to make ornaments from cornstarch dough, colored synthetic clay, and "bread" dough.

Cornstarch dough ornaments

These simple little ornaments are made with a cornstarch–baking soda mixture, then air-dried. You can shape them by hand or, for quicker, easier shaping, use a cookie cutter.

To make the dough, you'll need:

> 1   cup cornstarch
> 2   cups baking soda
> 1⅓ cups water

Blend cornstarch and baking soda in a pan; stir in water until smooth. Bring mixture to a boil over medium-high heat, stirring constantly; boil for about 4 minutes. Remove from heat and keep stirring for about 2 more minutes. The dough should have the consistency of stiff mashed potatoes. If you want a stiffer dough (for rolling into coils), simply work it a bit longer. Cover the dough with a piece of plastic wrap and set aside to cool for about 30 minutes.

On wax paper, roll out the dough to about ¼ inch thick—no thicker, or the ornaments will crack severely when dry. Cut dough into shapes, using cookie cutters, if you like. Insert a wire loop in the top of each ornament for a hanger.

Let ornaments dry in a cool, dry place for a day or two, turning often to prevent warping. Decorate with acrylic paints. When paint is dry, coat with a glossy spray-on glaze. To hang, string lengths of yarn or cord through wire loops.

Bread dough ornaments

To make these ornaments, first mix up the dough; then mold, bake, and paint your designs.

Here's our basic recipe for bread dough:

> 1   cup salt
> 4   cups all-purpose flour
>   Up to 2 cups water

Mix salt and flour; add 1 cup water, then gradually add more water until dough is moist enough to knead. Knead dough until smooth and pliable. Wrap in plastic wrap and refrigerate for up to several days.

To make the ornaments, mold figures as desired. You can pinch off tiny pieces to make noses or other small shapes; a garlic press is a good tool for making curlicues (see our wreath, shown on facing page). To keep the ornaments from being too heavy and to prevent cracking, keep the thickness to ½ inch or less. Insert a loop (made of wire or half a paper clip) in the top for hanging.

Bake the ornaments on a baking sheet in a 275° oven until dry, hard, and very, very light brown (about 1 hour, depending on the size of the ornaments).

When cool, paint with acrylic paint and spray with a glossy spray-on glaze. Add any ribbons or other finishing touches.

Clay ornaments

For these ornaments, you use a claylike modeling material specially formulated for molding and baking in a home oven. The "clay" comes in a rainbow of colors; look for it in craft and toy stores.

To make the ornaments, knead the clay to soften it, then mold as desired, using the same techniques as for bread dough ornaments. Arrange on a baking sheet; bake in a 275° oven for the time stated on the package.

When the ornaments have cooled, mount them on a background such as the painted wooden or bread dough hearts shown in the photograph on the facing page. Wooden hearts can be purchased at craft shops and painted; glue on a ribbon loop for hanging. Make bread dough hearts as directed at left, making sure to insert a wire hanging loop before baking.

Finish the ornaments by coating with a glossy spray-on glaze.

Design: JoAnn Bowen.

Cookie cutters, cornstarch, baking soda, and a little paint are all you need to create these cheerful little ornaments.

Miniature angels hover on charming heart backgrounds; the angels and crèche are created from modeling material and baked in the oven.

Bread dough Christmas wreath, Santa, and lollipop, painted with acrylic paint or simply glazed, add a touch of whimsy to your tree.

Slot-together Animal Ornaments

These bright and fanciful critters are fashioned out of foam-core board and slotted together. After their stint on the Christmas tree, you can store them flat in a box until the next holiday season.

To make the animals, you'll need 3/16-inch-thick foam-core board, acrylic paints, acrylic varnish (optional), a craft knife, and paper and other materials such as cotton, twigs, and wood veneer or balsa for decorating the basic animal shapes.

Slots cut in the body parts of the animals allow the pieces to slip together without glue. Each slot is 3/16 inch wide (the thickness of the board).

Begin by enlarging and transferring the patterns shown on the grid, below right, onto a grid of 1/2-inch squares, following the instructions on page 64.

You can mark a 1/2-inch grid directly onto the foam-core board using a soft lead pencil (draw lightly so marks are easy to erase), then transfer the patterns to the board. Or, if you'll be making more than one of each animal, transfer the pattern to lightweight cardboard and cut it out.

Cut out the foam-core shapes with a sharp craft knife, keeping the blade as vertical as possible as you cut. Paint, varnish if desired, then decorate as you like. You could use twigs for the reindeer's antlers, cotton balls for the lamb's wool, and wood veneer or balsa cut into shapes for the bird's tail, crest, and claws.

To complete, slot the pieces together, pierce a hole in each ornament, and attach thread for hanging.

Design: Françoise Kirkman and Lukie Graef.

Cheerful animal faces *peek out from among the branches of your Christmas tree when you put together these whimsical slotted critters. Bird, reindeer, lamb, rabbit, and cat all come apart for easy storage.*

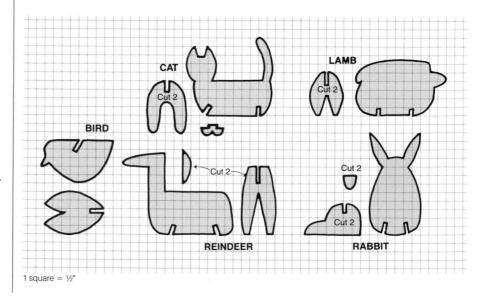

CAT — Cut 2

LAMB — Cut 2

BIRD

REINDEER — Cut 2

RABBIT — Cut 2

1 square = 1/2"

Luminarias

Candles glowing through brown paper lunch bags filled with sand may not sound exotic. But when masses of them twinkle like earthbound stars, outlining streets, sidewalks, windows, and roofs, the effect is quite magical.

Welcoming Christmas with such candlelit paper lanterns—*luminarias*—is one of the oldest Southwestern holiday traditions. On Christmas Eve, you can see luminarias shining in every neighborhood and town, even atop the rangeland fence posts of isolated ranches.

It's hard to verify the origins of the luminaria tradition. One folklorist traces the custom back to pagan Spain, where it was believed that the fires kept lightning away and the ashes gave fertility to the soil. But it's certain that setting out lanterns to light the way for the Holy Family at Christmas goes back as far as 1534. In that year, Franciscan Padre Motolinía described an Indian village in New Spain "decorated" with small bonfires so numerous they "resemble the starry skies."

Today, Southwesterners light luminarias at any time of year to welcome guests to their homes; placed along a driveway or at a house entry (as in our photograph), their hospitable glow creates a warm and festive greeting.

It's easy to create luminarias to light up your own home for a special Christmas evening.

To make a luminaria, you need a lunch bag with top turned down 2 inches for extra stability, sand (about half of a 1-pound coffee can per bag is plenty), and a 10- or 15-hour unscented votive candle.

Nothing extends a more festive welcome *to a holiday house party than a pathway lighted with twinkling luminarias. They're so easy and inexpensive to make that you'll have no trouble putting together a dramatic display.*

A few notes from Southwestern experts: For best effect, set luminarias an equal distance (20 to 30 inches) apart, bag seams to the back, candles straight. Luminarias can survive winds of up to 10 mph. If a bag does catch on fire, it will burn no lower than the sand line. Luminarias can be used safely on tile or adobe roofs. Add more sand—a full pound—when you make them for a roof.

Lighted Wood Stars

In Scandinavia, where the winter night comes early, lighted stars glow in almost every window at holiday time to welcome guests and cheer passersby. The stars may be made with a variety of materials, from foil to straw; most popular, though, are natural wood and thin wood strips.

Our four stars are made from balsa wood or wood veneer. Balsa is both inexpensive and easy to work with; veneer, sold in strips and sheet rolls at lumberyards, is more costly but has an interesting grain. Both balsa and veneer are thin enough to cut with scissors, though mat knives are better for cutting the star points.

The top and bottom stars shown on the facing page are made of 3- by 36-inch balsa strips, 1/32 inch thick—two strips for the top (four-pointed) star, three for the bottom one (the starburst). The six-pointed star shown at center of the facing page is made from wood veneer; the woven star (photo inset) uses wood veneer or strips planed from 18-inch pine boards.

All four stars have two identical sides, sandwiched together with glue and dowels. You just glue 2½-inch pieces of ¼-inch dowel (or balsa posts) between the two sides, then weight the stars while the glue dries.

The stars are lighted by 6-watt night bulbs anchored between two posts glued to the inside top of the star. When purchasing the electrical socket, bulb, and cord, be certain to have the dealer explain its proper assembly to you.

Design: Kathy Brenzel.

How to Make Four Stars

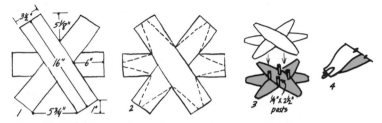

Four-pointed star. *Cross and glue two pieces of balsa. Trim points. Repeat. Join two completed sides together by gluing dowel posts between.*

Six-pointed star. *Cut three pieces of wood veneer and lay flat in star shape. Mark and glue. Trim points. Repeat. Join stars; glue and clip points.*

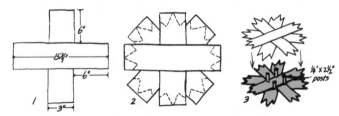

Starburst. *Cross and glue two balsa pieces together, then two more. Glue together into an eight-sided star. Trim points. Repeat. Join two stars with posts.*

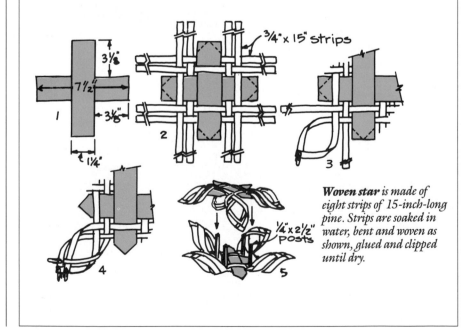

Woven star *is made of eight strips of 15-inch-long pine. Strips are soaked in water, bent and woven as shown, glued and clipped until dry.*

Stars aglow *in your window extend a warm welcome to family and holiday guests. The four-pointed star (top) and starburst (bottom) are balsa wood; the six-pointed star (middle) and woven star (inset) are wood veneer.*

"Stained Glass" Windows

Vibrant, glowing colors from these tissue-paper panels can turn a window into a cheery focal point this holiday season. The window-size panels are easy and fun to make. You start with a piece of clear plastic, then use polyurethane to attach pieces of precisely cut or loosely torn tissue paper.

Materials

You'll need enough 54-inch-wide, .004 to .010 clear plastic (sometimes called clear vinyl) to more than cover the window or door you want to decorate. In addition, buy plenty of tissue paper in assorted colors. You'll also need a yardstick, a roll of newsprint or brown wrapping paper, a pencil, a black felt-tip marker, masking tape, newspapers, 1 pint of satin-finish polyurethane, a 2- or 3-inch paintbrush, scissors or a craft knife, and a roll of double-sided tape.

Design & assembly

Start by measuring the glass area in the window or door. To make your pattern, reproduce it at same size on newsprint or brown paper sized at least 1 foot larger than the glass on all sides. Lightly sketch the outline of your design with a pencil; when you're satisfied, go over it with the felt marker. For multipane windows, you can plan one big design and later cut it to fit panes.

Use the clear plastic straight off the roll, so it appears clear and relatively free of distortion, or wad it up and leave it overnight before using to make it look like antique glass. (Flatten out the plastic before starting to work; if wrinkles are too deep, it will be difficult to attach the tissue.)

A four-part design, cut from one big panel, installs in windows with double-sided tape across top and bottom of each panel.

Lay the plastic over the paper pattern and cut it to extend about 1½ inches beyond the window's outline. Tape plastic to the pattern so it won't slide around.

Polyurethane is the "glue" that attaches the tissue scraps. Before you open the polyurethane, be sure to provide adequate ventilation where you're working. Follow the precautions stated on the can, and work in old clothes—polyurethane can't be removed from fabric. Protect the surrounding floor with newspapers.

Cut or tear tissue before you start "gluing," so you can work fast and avoid getting your hands too sticky. As you apply the tissue, you'll find that overlapping colors produce a wealth of secondary colors and new shapes. To get the most from overlapping effects, don't make pieces too small. And don't worry about exactly following the pattern—enjoy the random surprises. You'll probably have to do some later cutting or tearing to fill in design details.

To make the tissue pieces stick to the plastic, paint on a thin coat of the polyurethane, starting in the center of the design. Cover about a square yard at a time, less if your design is complicated. Position the tissue pieces and press them lightly in place with your fingertips.

Backlit Christmas tree glows cheerily on glass-paneled door.

This whimsical quilt-patterned panel has rectangles, hearts, and triangles cut with scissors. Its geometric design has charm but doesn't require great artistic ability.

You can add the black lines of traditional stained glass with black tissue paper, ¼-inch-wide illustrator's tape, or marking pens. The latter two can be applied only after the polyurethane has dried.

After the first layer of tissue is down, add a second coat of polyurethane, then more paper. Some of our examples have four or five layers. You probably won't need to add another complete coat of polyurethane after the second application, though you may have to add small touch-up coats between thick layers of tissue.

Complete layering the tissue so that it extends beyond the outline of the window, then add a final coat of polyurethane. Leave the panel flat on the ground until dry. Following the outline of the window on the pattern, cut the panel to size with scissors or a craft knife.

Before mounting the panel on the window or door, clean the glass and remove any condensation that could keep the tape from sticking. Face the tissue side toward the living space; run the tape along the top and bottom edges of the plastic backing. Panels may need extra tape on the sides to hold them in place, and you may have to add more tape after a few weeks. After the holidays, you can remove tape from glass with a single-edge razor blade. To store panels, fold in half, plastic sides together, and roll up.

The sparkling colors of your creation may be ephemeral. If it's in direct sun for much of the day, the tissue paper will slowly fade over a few weeks' time. But in indirect light, the colors may stay vibrant for several years.

Design: Whitney Miller, Suki Diamond, and Peter O. Whiteley.

Inspired by a greeting card, cityscape uses cut shapes, mostly in one layer. Pieces were arranged, then polyurethane was applied.

Christmas Log Cabin Tablecloth

Symbolic of the warmth and hospitality of early American family life, the log cabin design is a particularly appropriate pattern for a festive holiday tablecloth. It combines compatible prints in reds and greens for spiraling blocks. Arrange the completed blocks on point, as shown, or play with other possibilities for your own setting variation.

Materials

For 60-inch-square tablecloth
(all fabric is 45 inches wide):

1	*yard dark green print fabric (A)*
³/₄	*yard medium green print fabric (B)*
¹/₂	*yard light green print fabric (C)*
⁷/₈	*yard dark red print fabric (F)*
¹/₂	*yard medium red print fabric (E)*
¹/₄	*yard light red print fabric (D)*
⁵/₈	*yard white print fabric (G)*
7¹/₄	*yards 5-inch-wide border print trim or 1¹/₄ yards print fabric for border*
3¹/₂	*yards white fabric for lining*
	Thread
1	*sheet acetate*
	Craft knife
	Metal ruler
	Graph paper

Piecing the patchwork

Note: Preshrink and press fabrics.

1. Measure, mark, and cut all print fabrics (except border print and white print **G**) into 2-inch-wide strips along the crosswise grain of the fabric. Cut 13 strips from fabric **A**, nine strips from **B**, four strips from **C**, two strips from **D**, six strips from **E**, and 12 strips from **F**. Cut light red strips **(D)** into 25 center squares, each 2 inches.

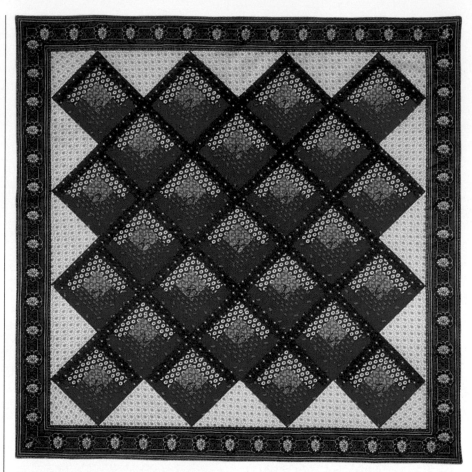

Overall design *of our tablecloth features log cabin blocks on point; dark print block edges form a crisscross pattern.*

Set your holiday table *with cozy, old-fashioned charm—stitch up a log cabin patterned tablecloth in warm reds and greens.*

Close-up detail *shows one way to mix and match prints, colors, and a handsome border print.*

2. To machine-piece 25 log cabin blocks speedily, use the railroading method shown below. Lay the first log strip, right side up, on a flat work surface. Lay all your center squares, right sides down, along this strip, aligning the raw edges as shown and making sure to leave cutting space between squares. Pin and sew in one long seam.

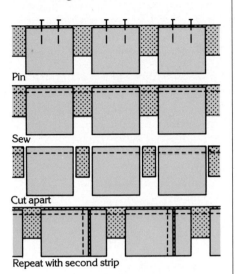

Pin

Sew

Cut apart

Repeat with second strip

Cut the center pieces apart, using the edges of the pieces as your guide. Press seam allowances toward each strip. With right sides facing and raw edges aligned, lay these units along a strip of the same fabric to make a second seam. Pin, stitch, trim, and press as you did before. For the next two seams, use your second color fabric.

For each block, begin with center square **(D)** and light green logs **(C)**; following diagram below, stitch subsequent logs in counterclockwise direction. Finished block should measure 9½ inches square.

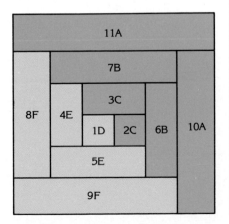

3. To make patterns for large (edge) and small (corner) triangles, draw a 9-inch square on graph paper and divide it as shown below. *Add ¼-inch seam allowance to all edges.* Cut cardboard or acetate templates from your patterns.

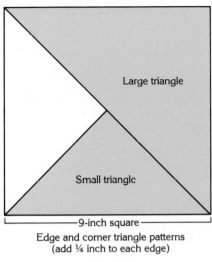

Large triangle

Small triangle

9-inch square

Edge and corner triangle patterns
(add ¼ inch to each edge)

4. On white print **(G)**, measure and mark four small triangles and 12 large triangles. Cut pieces.

5. Begin piecing at top corner. With right sides facing and raw edges aligned, pin and stitch small triangle to top edge of block, as shown below. Press seam, and all seams that follow, toward edge. Stitch large triangles to side edges of block in same manner to make first row.

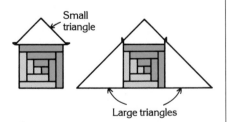

Small triangle

Large triangles

For second row, stitch together three blocks, following patchwork diagram below; attach large triangles to side edges of first and third blocks to complete row. Continue stitching blocks and triangles together for subsequent rows; stitch rows together to complete patchwork.

6. On border trim, measure and mark four strips, each 65 inches long. Cut strips. (If not using border print trim, cut and piece 5-inch-wide strips of print border fabric to make four strips, each 65 inches long.) Stitch the borders to the tablecloth top, mitering corners. Press tablecloth carefully.

Lining the tablecloth

1. Cut lining fabric into two lengths, each 1¾ yards. With right sides facing, sew pieces together along selvage edges, using *⅝-inch seam allowance.* Cut off selvages and press seam open.

2. Lay lining, right side up, on floor or large work surface; smooth out wrinkles. Lay tablecloth, right side down, over lining and pin together at edges. Stitch around edge, using ¼-inch seam allowance and leaving 12 inches open on one edge. Turn right side out and press.

3. Pin opening; hand-stitch closed. Topstitch 1 inch from edges.

Design: Nancy Shelby.

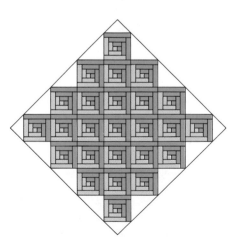

Christmas Stockings

What family's Christmas would be complete without stockings hung by the fire, awaiting a cargo of Christmas treats? Our giant-size versions will hold large and important presents as well as an assortment of trinkets and goodies. The stockings pictured are made from bright patterned and gingham fabric; you can choose any colors and patterns that suit your fancy. Embellishing the stockings with bows, beads, buttons, and tiny trinkets is where the fun comes in—you can personalize each one to reflect the interests and personality of the child (or adult) for whom it's intended.

Materials

For one stocking:

1 yard prequilted cotton fabric, 45 inches wide

1 yard cotton or polyester fabric for lining, 45 inches wide

1 yard ruffled lace or 1 package rickrack or bias cording (for cuff trim)

Small amounts of contrasting fabric for decorations

Buttons, ribbons, beads, bells, miniature trinkets, etc. (optional)

Embroidery floss (optional)

Making the stocking

1. Enlarge and transfer the patterns below, following the instructions on page 64.

2. Pin the patterns to quilted fabric and cut out; repeat for lining fabric.

3. If you want to add a name to the front cuff, cut out and machine-appliqué letters in a contrasting fabric; or hand-embroider the name, using a satin stitch. If you wish, you may also appliqué or embroider numbers on the toe of the stocking front to represent the year the stocking is being given.

4. Decorate the front of the stocking as desired. To add a Christmas tree as shown in the photograph on the facing page, cut out a tree shape from green fabric and a slightly smaller piece of polyester quilt batting. Machine-appliqué or hand-stitch to the stocking front. Decorate with bows, beads, and buttons sewn on by hand. Sew on any other trinkets or decorations you wish—perhaps as tiny presents under the appliquéd tree.

5. To make the cuff, machine-stitch cuff front to back, right sides together, along one side seam. Position ruffled lace, rickrack, or bias cording trim upside down and stitch to right side of long edge. Stitch cuff front and back lining pieces together as for cuff pieces, then stitch lining to cuff, right sides together, along bottom edges. Sew together remaining side seams of cuff and cuff lining. (The top edges of the cuff will still be open.) Turn and press.

6. To make a loop for hanging the stocking, cut a strip of the quilted fabric 4 inches long by 1½ inches wide. Fold in half lengthwise, right sides together, and sew the raw edges with a ¼-inch seam allowance; turn and press.

7. If you plan to add bias cording or rickrack to the stocking edges, baste it in place on the stocking front, with decorative edge facing toward center of stocking. Then sew stocking front to stocking back with right sides together, using a ¼-inch seam allowance; clip curves and turn.

8. Stitch front stocking lining to back stocking lining with right sides together; do not turn.

9. To complete the stocking, insert lining into stocking. Position cuff inside stocking, with raw edges of cuff top and stocking top aligned; right side of cuff will be against right side (inside) of lining. Pin. Also pin stocking loop in place at back corner of stocking top. Keeping cuff lining out of the way, stitch cuff top edge to both stocking and stocking lining top; be sure to catch loop ends in stitching. Turn cuff to outside of stocking; fold cuff lining back underneath cuff, between cuff and stocking front. Turn under lining's raw edge and hand-stitch lining under cuff to cover the stocking-cuff seam. Finally, hand-stitch little bells to cuff edge, if desired.

Design: JoAnn Bowen.

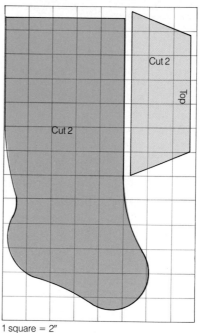

1 square = 2"
¼" seam allowances included

One, two, three in a row... *special stockings stitched for each child's first Christmas are enlivened with bells, stitchery, and whimsical appliqués.*

Favorite teddy *bear and furry dog are appliquéd and embroidered; this stocking has bias cording trim all around.*

Appliquéd Christmas tree *is decorated with buttons and bows; beneath it are trinkets signifying the child's special interests.*

Handmade Gift Wraps & Cards

■

Beautifully wrapped packages and one-of-a-kind greeting cards are joys to receive. When the cards and wrappings are handmade, they add a special dimension to your gift-giving; many of those you'll find in this chapter are delightful gifts in themselves!

Surprise Gift Cones

(Also pictured on facing page)

Delight children and grown-ups alike with holiday surprises in brightly colored gift cones. Made of cardboard and wrapping paper, the cones hold small treats wrapped in colorful tissue paper. You can make a handful of cones in just a few minutes, then fill them with inexpensive party favors, small cookies, or candies. (A single cone also makes an unusual wrapping for a special gift placed under the tree.)

For a pretty and festive display, arrange the filled cones in a basket, ready to offer to holiday guests.

You'll need thin cardboard or two-ply (medium-weight) bristol paper, several colors of wrapping paper, some ribbon, and some large adhesive stickers (about 1¼ inches in diameter). Also have at hand transparent tape, scissors, and—if needed—tissue paper for an inner wrap.

Cut the cardboard into 5-inch or larger squares; the cones in the photograph were made from 11½-inch squares. Cut the wrapping paper into a square 1 inch larger on each side than the cardboard, then follow the directions below.

Design: Françoise Kirkman.

Create a cornucopia of bright paper gift cones, pack them with small presents or goodies—and you're ready with gifts for drop-in holiday guests.

Assembling the Cones

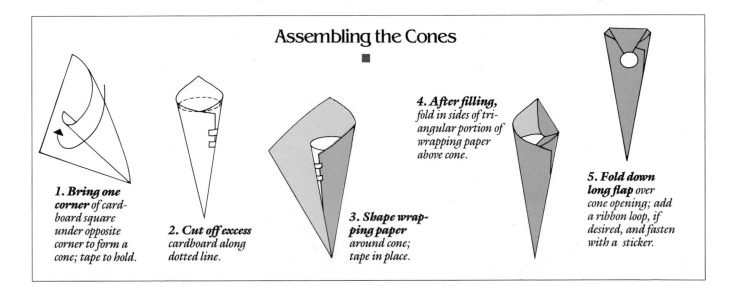

1. Bring one corner of cardboard square under opposite corner to form a cone; tape to hold.

2. Cut off excess cardboard along dotted line.

3. Shape wrapping paper around cone; tape in place.

4. After filling, fold in sides of triangular portion of wrapping paper above cone.

5. Fold down long flap over cone opening; add a ribbon loop, if desired, and fasten with a sticker.

Christmas Village Boxes

Here's a selection of whimsical boxes you can use and enjoy both during and after the Christmas season. Beneath the tree, these charming little "houses" join ranks to form a holiday village, keeping special gifts under wraps until Christmas morning. After New Year's Day, they're handy storage boxes; depending on the size and shape, you can use them to hold letters, recipe cards, or toys.

Choosing the materials

Before you buy the materials, determine the size of the gift you want to enclose and what future use the box will have. Both will dictate the box's dimensions. Then buy heavy gray mounting board, chip board, or double-weight illustration board and single-weight colored mat board (available from art supply stores), cotton or cotton-polyester fabric in different colors or patterns, white glue, and spray adhesive. You'll also need a heavy-duty craft knife or mat cutter, scissors, a ruler, rubber bands, masking tape, and a pencil.

Assembling a box

For the house walls, measure and draw four rectangles of identical height on the heavy cardboard or double-weight illustration board; draw matching triangular peaks on top of two of the rectangles for gable walls, then cut out all four pieces with a craft knife or mat cutter. Also cut two roof sections; each should be ¾ inch wider than the rectangular house sides and ¾ inch longer than the gable slope.

For the cloth covering, cut four pieces of fabric 1 inch larger on all sides than the boards. To cut fabric for the roof, position the pair of roof boards ³⁄₁₆ inch apart on the fabric, then cut fabric with a 1-inch border all around. Erase any pencil marks to make sure they don't show through light-colored fabric.

To attach fabric to box pieces, lightly coat board and the back side of fabric with spray adhesive (be careful not to saturate), then press glued sides of fabric and board together. Lightly spray a 1-inch border on back of board and wait until glue is tacky (just a few seconds), then fold in corners and sides of fabric, pulling to smooth out any wrinkles. Glue roof pieces centered on fabric, leaving a ³⁄₁₆-inch gap between.

For the lining, cut pieces of single-weight mat board ³⁄₁₆ inch shorter on each side than the double-weight board pieces. Apply white glue to back of each piece and center mat board on back of fabric-covered sections. Weight each with a few books. When the glue is dry (1 to 2 hours), glue together the edges of the four walls, assemble with masking tape, and secure with rubber bands (remove rubber bands and masking tape after an hour or two to avoid leaving marks on box). Be sure corners are square while drying.

After the side seams are dry, glue one side of the roof to the house; leave the other side loose to allow access into the finished box. Weight with an open book and let glue dry. Then cut a plain piece of the heavy cardboard to fit snugly inside the bottom of the box and glue it in place so it adheres to the box sides; it should touch the bottom edge of the mat board wall lining and the sides of the heavy cardboard.

Design: Mike Frederickson.

Putting the Boxes Together

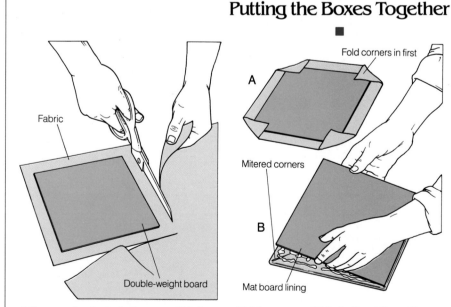

After cutting board pieces, cut fabric with scissors so there will be 1-inch borders on all sides.

Fabric
Double-weight board

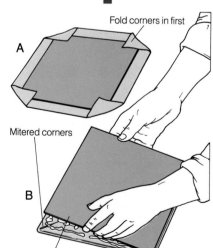

Fold corners in first
A
Mitered corners
B
Mat board lining

Fold corners of fabric first (A) to allow mitered folding of sides. Press on glue-spread lining to hold fabric in place (B).

Masking tape
Rubber bands

Secure glued walls with masking tape and rubber bands. When dry, glue one side of roof in place; weight with an open book.

Wrap up your Christmas *with a whole village of these cheerful cardboard and fabric boxes.*
Lettering on the door or a face in the window can serve as gift "tags." The bright containers can
be put to a number of uses after the holidays are over.

Box-Bags

Folded into geometric baglike boxes, then decorated with markers, cutouts, and ribbon, shiny colored papers are easily transformed into elegant or whimsical gift packages. Because you can make them any length or width, they're especially handy for odd-shaped gifts—you can design them to fit anything from swim fins to a folding umbrella!

We made our box-bags with heavy glazed paper, colored and shiny on one side; you can also use two-ply (medium-weight) bristol paper. For cutting and assembling, you'll need a ruler, scissors, a sharp knife, and a glue stick.

To make each box, follow the directions at right, using the gift itself as a guide for the box dimensions. Decorate the finished boxes to suit your fancy, with precut stencil letters, felt-tip markers, colored stickers, or anything you choose.

Design: Françoise Kirkman.

Making the Box-Bags

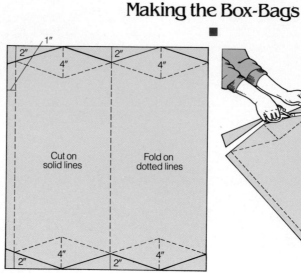

Cut on solid lines   Fold on dotted lines

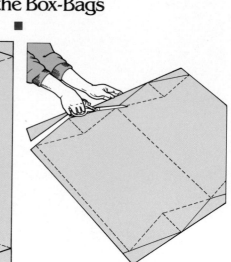

Measure and mark lines on wrong side of paper. End dimensions are for all box sizes; height and width depend on gift size.

Cut out box outline with scissors if using glazed paper, or a sharp knife if you're using heavier bristol paper.

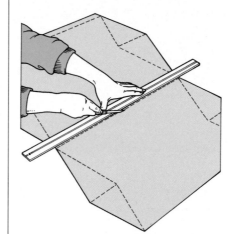

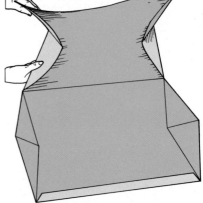

With the back of a knife blade, lightly score wrong side of paper along all dotted fold lines.

Fold in top and bottom edges; pinch to crease along fold lines. Also fold under side flap.

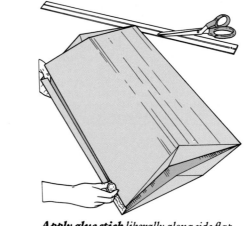

Apply glue stick liberally along side flap. Reach inside box; press flap to inside of box front.

Give your imagination free rein *when you create these fanciful box-bags. Make them in any size; decorate them any way you please—with ribbon, stickers, paper cutouts, even a sprig of pine.*

Covered Boxes to Keep

Bright coverings transform ordinary boxes into handsome containers to keep and use long after the holidays have passed. Our rectangular boxes sport coats of charming printed fabrics or colored paper; foil, paper, and even swaths of ribbon dress up cylindrical cartons.

Start collecting boxes and containers several months before Christmas. Use cottage cheese cartons, oatmeal containers, or shoe boxes; or purchase sturdy, inexpensive cardboard boxes with lids from variety or stationery stores. Then cover them as described below.

Fabric-covered boxes

Measure the height of the box you plan to cover. Then cut a piece of fabric 2 inches wider than the box is tall and long enough to wrap around all four sides with a 1-inch overlap.

Place the box on its side on the wrong side of the fabric, positioning it so fabric extends 1 inch beyond box at top and bottom. Coat box and fabric (except for extending borders) with spray adhesive. Starting at one corner, wrap fabric around box. Overlap fabric at starting corner; glue down flat.

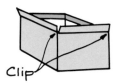

Box Bottom

Clip corner edges of fabric at both top and bottom of box; spray and fold edges to inside of box top and around outside of bottom.

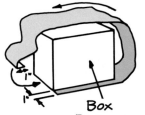

Clip

Cut a piece of fabric about ⅛ inch smaller all around than bottom of box; spray and glue onto bottom.

Cut a piece of contrasting fabric large enough to cover box lid and wrap around inside lid edges. Trace box top onto back side of fabric; spray and glue, matching top to traced lines. Clip from edge of fabric toward center at corners.

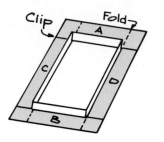

Clip   Fold
A
C
D
B

Spray and glue flaps A and B: fold flaps up and fold sides around corners, then fold edges inside lid. Glue flaps C and D around sides of lid and inside.

C   D

Paper-covered boxes

Use brightly colored art or construction paper and either rubber cement or white glue. Draw shapes freehand or trace from a book; add details with felt-tip pens.

Circus cage. Glue paper onto top and bottom of a large, deep box. Draw, then cut out, one or more circus animals; draw in faces, then glue animals onto box. Glue thin paper strips for bars around sides of box and some cut-out shapes for a design on top of box. Cut wheels from lightweight cardboard, cover with colored paper, and draw in spokes; glue wheels to sides of box so box is raised up 1 to 2 inches.

Dog. Glue paper around sides and on bottom of an oatmeal carton. Then cover lid separately, using the same paper or a contrasting color. Draw, then cut out, head and tail shapes from lightweight cardboard, adding tabs where pieces will attach to carton. Cover both sides of head with paper; cover tail with felt. Cut slots in top and bottom of carton. Insert tab of head into slot in carton top; insert tail tab into bottom slot. Fold tabs and secure with tape on inside. Cut out felt ears, eyes, nose, and spots; glue in place. Cut out four strips of paper about 8 inches long and 2 inches wide. Roll up each strip and secure with tape; glue rolls onto carton for legs.

Carousel. Remove lid and cut down the sides of an oatmeal carton so it measures 6 inches high; glue colored paper around sides. Draw, then cut, horses and poles out of contrasting paper and glue onto sides. Make a cone shape large enough to overlap edges of carton lid and glue onto lid. Decorate cone with strips of colored paper. Cut a smaller cone to fit on top of first cone; poke hole in top, cover with paper, and glue in place. Finish off with a small dowel wrapped with a paper flag.

Flower pot. Cover a 1-quart cottage cheese container with copper-colored foil paper and glue in place. Trim container cover to remove rim; glue on copper-colored foil. Tape a multicolored tissue paper flower and green tissue paper leaves onto a thin dowel about 8 inches long and poke dowel into center of top.

Barber pole. Glue white paper onto a cardboard mailing tube. Secure a wide red ribbon at the top of the tube with tape, then wind ribbon diagonally around tube; tape ribbon at bottom. Tie a 1-inch-wide gold ribbon into a bow around top of tube. Finish off with a styrene foam ball covered with blue tissue paper. Be sure to leave a tail of tissue paper at the bottom of the ball; the paper acts as a stopper for the tube and prevents the ball from tumbling off the top.

Colorful gift boxes *covered with bright fabrics serve double duty; after the holidays, they store scarves or jewelry.*

Gaily decorated containers *are also toys to delight young recipients; the covers lift off easily to receive treasures.*

Imaginative wraps *hold sweet gifts of candy or dried fruits. Fill them later with potpourri or soaps.*

How to Pack the Gifts You Mail

■

It's an easy matter to distribute Christmas gifts to family and friends who live nearby. But when you want to send that handmade wine rack long-distance to Uncle Ralph, or a treasured perfume to Mom back home, you'll have to deal with wrapping your gifts for mailing.

Of course, many stores will mail gifts that you buy from them. But if you're sending a cartonful of gifts purchased in various places, or something you've made yourself, packing will probably be your responsibility.

How do you ensure that your gifts will arrive in mint condition? The best insurance on Christmas gifts sent through the mails is a good job of wrapping and packing. Below, we outline some of the basic essentials to keep in mind when you're preparing your packages.

Selecting a container

Choosing the right container is essential. Folding boxes of lightweight cardboard, like the boxes stores use to package clothing purchases, are not suitable for gifts that are mailed. And while reinforced bags, paperboard boxes, heavy mailing tubes, and wooden crates are acceptable in some cases, the preferred container for most shipping is a corrugated fiberboard box.

You can find used fiberboard boxes at small stores (large stores usually crush their boxes) or buy them from packaging or moving companies; check the Yellow Pages under Boxes. Look on the bottom of a corrugated box for a small round imprint indicating its strength. The bottom number indicates the maximum weight it can hold. If you choose a used corrugated carton for packaging, check it carefully for flaws. A crushed corner or torn edge is a weak spot that's quickly and easily damaged.

Select a container large enough to allow for adequate cushioning, but not so large that its contents will be joggled. If you can't find the right size, cut down a larger box as shown on facing page.

Liquids should be mailed in leakproof containers with enough absorbent cushioning to soak up the entire contents. Effective absorbent materials include cotton padding, pulverized paper (not to be confused with shredded paper), and blotting paper. Remember that it's illegal to send alcoholic beverages by U.S. mail or to ship them across state lines by private carrier.

Cushioning the contents

Generous padding diffuses vibrations from rough handling and gives contents extra protection. Cushioning materials can be anything from wadded or shredded newspaper to corrugated cardboard to popcorn. More sophisticated stuffings include bubble plastic (with large or small bubbles), polystyrene pellets, and polyethylene foam. These are not only effective, they're lightweight, helping to minimize postage costs. Consider these materials if your gift is particularly fragile. If you use newspaper, remember that the ink is apt to leave smudges on clean surfaces. It's a good idea to protect decorative wrapping paper or other surfaces with a sheet of clean tissue paper before you pack them.

When you pack, protect breakables by using professional packing procedures. First, pad the bottom of a box with 3 or 4 inches of popcorn, polystyrene pellets, or densely packed shredded newspaper. Wrap each item with bubble wrap, foam, or corrugated cardboard, put everything in a snug-fitting inner box, and finally, put that container into the first box with at least 2 more inches of cushioning between the two at sides and top.

After the top padding is in, put your package to the test. Pick up the box and shake it front to back and side to side. If there's any jostling or shifting, repack the contents with more cushioning.

Before you seal the box, slip in an extra address label; this will help the mail service get your package to its destination even if something happens to the outer label.

Closing the package

The brown paper and twine that were once synonymous with a well-packed gift are now obsolete. Twine can catch in postal machinery, and paper can tear, sometimes defacing the address. You're better off taping the unwrapped box shut.

Use wide reinforced kraft paper tape, carton sealing tape, or pressure-sensitive (no lick) filament (strapping) tape, available at hardware and stationery stores. Masking and transparent tapes can break or come loose in cold weather.

Addressing & labeling the package

Stick a clearly printed address label on the top of the package, being sure to include the zip code. (If the mailing service has to check for you, the package will be set aside, usually causing a delay.) Cover the label with transparent tape so that rain can't smear the ink. Notations such as "Fragile" and "Perishable" may go unnoticed, but they're worth a try.

Insurance

What most people don't realize about package insurance is that, to collect on a claim, you must be able to prove the contents' value with sales slips. (Insuring a handmade afghan for $500 is pointless; the mail company will repay you only for the yarn.) So save shopping receipts, keep records of gifts sent, and don't mail anything irreplaceable.

Choosing a shipping method

You may choose to use either the U.S. post office or a private mailing service. The post office offers several options; the fastest delivery is via *express mail*, airport to airport. You take the package to the post office at a major airport; the recipient picks it up at his or her closest major airport the same or next day. (Post office–to–post office and post office–to–addressee services are also available.) These services aren't offered everywhere and they're expensive, but in a pinch they might be worth it.

Other post office options are *parcel post* and *priority mail* (essentially air parcel post). Parcel post is the least expensive and the slowest; priority mail is faster but more costly.

Private mail companies offer a variety of services at a range of prices. The fastest and most expensive option is same-day or overnight service via air freight; other options may be delivery by truck or rail.

In comparing prices and options, be sure to ask about box size and weight limits, insurance rates, and deadline dates for guaranteed delivery by Christmas.

Creating a Tailor-made Carton

■

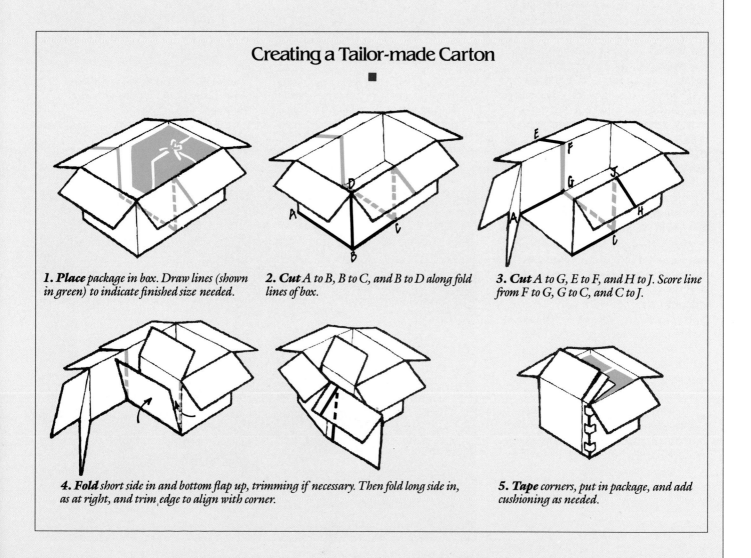

1. Place *package in box. Draw lines (shown in green) to indicate finished size needed.*

2. Cut *A to B, B to C, and B to D along fold lines of box.*

3. Cut *A to G, E to F, and H to J. Score line from F to G, G to C, and C to J.*

4. Fold *short side in and bottom flap up, trimming if necessary. Then fold long side in, as at right, and trim edge to align with corner.*

5. Tape *corners, put in package, and add cushioning as needed.*

Nursery-rhyme Boxes

Beloved nursery-rhyme characters come to life atop these fanciful gift boxes, providing entertainment long after the gift has been opened.

Making Jack jump over the candlestick or replaying Humpty Dumpty's great fall is easier than you might think. You just attach a cardboard wheel to the gift box with a roundhead brass brad, then glue part of your nursery-rhyme figure or scene—the part that will move—to the wheel. The rest of the figure stays stationary, glued directly to the box.

For example, glue holds our goose's body and wing to the box at points beneath the head and wingtip; the golden egg is glued to a blue cardboard wheel that rotates beneath the goose's body. Jack-be-Nimble's candle is stationary—but Jack himself "jumps" on a golden wheel, and the candle flame flickers on a separate yellow wheel. Humpty Dumpty's wall stands still, while his figure tumbles on a wheel; Jack Horner's head, arm, and torso rotate to dip a thumb into a Christmas pie. The mouse runs up the clock while a black and gold pendulum swings; only the clock face is fixed in place.

The wheels and figures are both cut from lightweight colored cardboard, available at stationery or art supply stores. To give the figures a greater variety of color and pattern, you can cut the pieces from plain white bristol board and cover them with wrapping paper. Cut the paper using the cardboard pieces as a guide, then use a glue stick to glue the two together.

Before assembling your nursery-rhyme scene, cover the box tops and bottoms separately with plain glossy wrap. To make the wheel, use a compass to draw a circle, then cut it out with pinking shears to give it a decorative edge.

To make the figures, enlarge and transfer our patterns (see page 190), following general instructions on page 64. You'll first need to scale the figure size to the wheel; use tracing paper to work out the scale, as shown below.

Design: Françoise Kirkman and Myriam Kirkman.

(Continued on page 190)

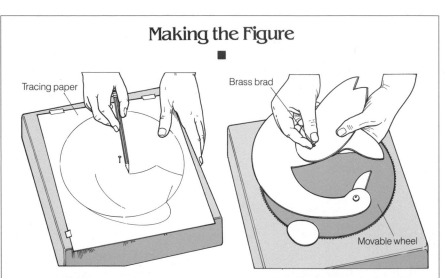

Making the Figure

Draw a circle *on tracing paper, using a compass; scale your figure to the circle. Transfer design to cardboard; cut out.*

Secure circle and figure *to box with brad. Glue egg on wheel, wingtips and head onto box.*

Jack Horner's *head, arm, and torso are mounted on a movable wheel that lets him dip his thumb in a Christmas pie—and pull out a plum.*

Young eyes will shine *at the sight of favorite nursery rhymes come to life. Movable parts atop these bright packages help Jack-be-Nimble vault over his candlestick and Jack Horner pull out a plum from his pie. On other boxes, Humpty Dumpty tumbles, the mouse runs up the clock, and the goose lays her golden egg.*

To determine finished size, see page 189

Piñata Boxes

This jolly collection of gift boxes is inspired by Mexico's traditional piñatas—paper-wrapped pottery jars or hollow papier-mâché forms filled with candies, fruits, and small gifts. Our gift boxes, decorated in the piñata style, add color and fun to a mantelpiece display or a collection of presents under the tree.

Inexpensive and easy to assemble, the wraps shown in the photograph each take under an hour to make. If you wrap and decorate the lids separately (as with the reindeer box), the boxes can be saved and reused.

Any plain box makes a fine piñata box; odd-shaped containers work well, too (our colorful bird starts with a large cottage cheese carton). You may not even need a container at all—our Christmas tree, for example, is simply a large cone of lightweight cardboard, open at the bottom (you might use it to cover a pretty gift plant).

Materials you'll need are a glue stick, scissors, transparent tape, felt-tip pens, lightweight cardboard, and several packs of solid-color tissue paper.

First, cover the box (or the box and lid separately) with one or two colors of plain tissue paper; tape in place. Then decorate the package.

Create a south-of-the-border spirit *under your Christmas tree with an assortment of colorful boxes wrapped piñata-style. Our Spanish mission, Christmas tree, reindeer, friendly skunk, and Aztec bird are just a few of the ideas you might try.*

Below, we show how to cut the decorative fringes from packs of tissue paper and how to apply them to the boxes. You can draw on features with felt-tip pens; make antlers, noses, and tails from separate cardboard shapes.

Design: Françoise Kirkman and Myriam Kirkman.

Making the Fringes

■

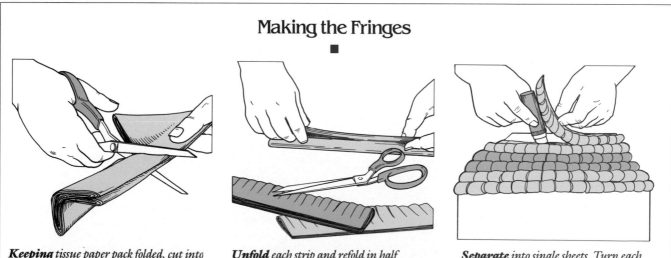

Keeping *tissue paper pack folded, cut into even strips 3 to 7 inches wide. Most fringe shown above is cut from 3-inch strips.*

Unfold *each strip and refold in half lengthwise. Make cuts every ½ inch through folded edge, three-quarters of the way across.*

Separate *into single sheets. Turn each inside out (so fringe puffs out). Glue to package, one at a time, overlapping rows.*

Traditional Japanese Gift Wraps

Artisans of old Japan developed an art called *tsutsumu*—wrapping gifts in simple but elegant ways. They felt that a beautiful package was as gratifying as the present itself.

The gift wraps on this and the following two pages, borrowed from this delightful tradition, lend a unique touch to your Christmas giving. Using pieces of fabric or paper with other materials you may already have around the house, you can create dazzling wraps that are both elegant and inexpensive.

Most of the wraps pictured here were originally designed for a specific use. The kimono bags (page 194), for example, were made as a wrap for *sembei* (rice crackers); the origami envelopes on page 194 for *shiruko*, a sweet drink powder; and the tissue paper flowers (facing page) for packaging small amounts of money. The *furoshiki* (cloth square) was used in Japan to carry everything from groceries to porcelain.

For the packages pictured on these pages, we used shiny art paper, colored tissue and printed rice paper, lightweight cotton and silk scraps, and silk cording. For ties, you can also use jute, twine, rope, or raffia. (Look for rice paper in Japanese specialty shops or stationery stores.)

***Snip, fold, and tie** a square of brilliant-hued fabric to create* furoshiki—*a simple, elegant approach to gift wrapping.*

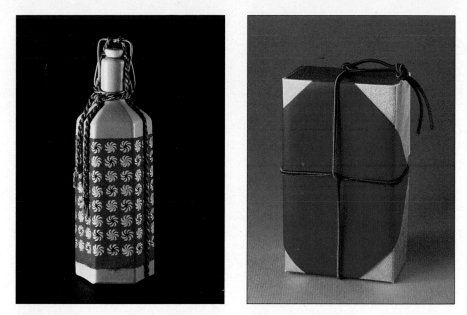

Dress up a gift box or bottle with a simple swath of paper. Position a bright paper square on a box, a patterned strip around a bottle, then tie it all up with a silken cord.

Fashion a garden of tissue flowers to hold tiny gifts; just a twist of gaily colored papers makes the package.

Box and bottle dress-ups. You can add an individual touch to a plain gold, silver, or colored gift box simply by cutting out a square of contrasting paper, setting it at an angle across the top of the box (see photo above), and tying it with a silk cord. To dress up a wine bottle (or any other bottle), cut a piece of colored tissue, wrapping paper, or rice paper wide enough to cover the front and back labels and long enough to fit around the bottle with a little overlap. Secure it with a 36-inch-long cord tied around the bottle base and neck as shown in the photo.

Tissue flowers. To make these colorful wraps for small gifts, cut two square pieces of paper: one square of colored tissue, another, slightly larger square of patterned rice paper. Stack the two squares, tissue on top. Center the gift on the double paper, gather up the corners, and simply twist to close.

Furoshiki. These wraps are made of fabric. The examples on the facing page are 3-foot squares, but you can cut your fabric to any suitable size. Hem or pink the edges. To wrap a rectangular box, place the box in the center of the square as shown in the diagram below.

Tuck one fabric corner under the box, then roll until the box is covered on all four sides. Pull the pointed ends of the fabric up, then pull tightly to the center; tie in a double knot. To wrap a square box like the green one in the photograph, place the box in the center of the fabric square and tie all four corners in a knot in the center.

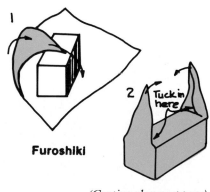

Furoshiki

(Continued on next page)

Origami envelopes. These little paper envelopes are perfect for flat gifts and small stocking stuffers. Their front pouches can hold miniature greeting cards or tags. Make them any size (the ones pictured below are 5-inch squares). To fold, follow the diagrams below. Make fold A, bringing the bottom edge to C, two-thirds of the way up; make fold B to turn the top edge under. Fold at C to bring the top down over the bottom. Turn over, then make a point at one end and make fold D; make fold E and slip the pointed end into the opening to complete.

Bright little kimono bags can be folded in a jiffy to hold small gifts; finish the tops with stickers, ties, even pretty favors or ornaments.

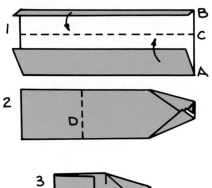

Kimono bags. Inspired by the shape of a kimono, these festive little bags hold small gifts. Begin each bag by cutting paper to twice the size of the object you wish to wrap. Then fold into a bag shape, following the diagram at right. For best results, fold the bottom flaps around a small box or block of wood; remove before taping the flaps.

Tape the bottom flaps together, then finish the tops in any way you wish—by tying, stapling, or using a foil seal. Tags and miniature objects attached to the tops add an extra decorative touch.

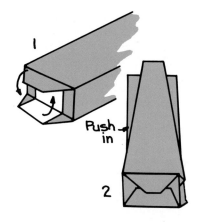

Cleverly folded origami envelopes hold very small or flat gifts; tuck a message or a gift tag into the built-in pocket.

Tailor-made Quick Wraps

Have an odd-shaped present to wrap? You can do it in no time using this quick-and-easy wrapping idea. Amusing and whimsical, our tailor-made wraps can hold anything from a gold necklace to a pair of athletic socks. If you wish, you can let the package design hint at what's inside —a small stuffed animal concealed inside a brown paper teddy bear, for example. To hold an array of small related gifts, you can even assemble a colorful train complete with engine and caboose.

Directions are simple—just cut two pieces of colored bristol board or heavy paper into a simple shape, making sure the package is large enough to hold the gift that will go inside. You can invent your own patterns or use ours (shown below), enlarging them to the size that fits your gift. (To enlarge patterns, see page 64.) If you want to add extra color and pattern to your wraps, you can cut them out of plain white bristol board, then cut identical shapes out of bright wrapping paper and attach them with a glue stick. Add as many decorative touches as your fancy dictates, using contrasting paper, adhesive stickers, even ribbon. Stack the two pieces atop each other, decorated sides facing out. Staple neatly around the perimeter, leaving an opening for the gift. Insert the gift, then staple shut.

Design: Mike Frederickson and Myriam Kirkman.

Golden comet, cheerful train, and friendly Teddy hold odd-size gifts handily; you just cut them to size, then decorate to your heart's content.

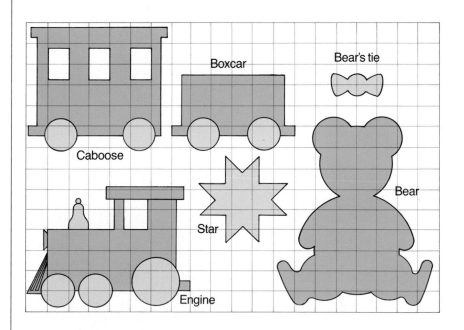

Hand-printed Gift Wraps

(Also pictured on front cover and page 178)

The bold graphic quality of these delightful hand-printed papers belies their humble origins. To create the large repeated motif, you use sheets of corrugated cardboard; a plain old potato makes the smaller graphic designs and monograms.

Potato graphics

To make these sprightly designs, start with a raw potato, turnip, or rutabaga. Letters or a graphic motif, carved into the vegetable's surface, can be inked and stamped onto cards or stationery as well as on gift wraps.

First, slice off the end of the vegetable to provide a smooth printing surface. Next, sketch the letter or motif on the cut surface with a felt-tip pen, keeping in mind that your stamp will print the reverse of the design as it appears on the vegetable. Using a sharp craft knife, cut away around the letter or motif to a depth of about ¼ inch.

Round and oval vegetables provide natural curves for letters such as O, C, and D. You can carve out the centers with an apple corer.

Ink the design on a stamp pad, then stamp it onto your wrapping paper. You can use plain glazed or unglazed wrapping paper or even tags.

If you plan to save the vegetable for a second printing session in a few days, wrap and refrigerate it.

Design: Myriam Kirkman.

To make gift wrap *that really is one of a kind, why not print it yourself? Personalize a package with potato-printed lettering, or create an all-over motif with background stripes using—surprise—corrugated cardboard.*

Corrugated cardboard prints

To print this wrapping paper, you use corrugated cardboard as you would a wood or linoleum block. Draw a design on the smooth outer surface and cut around it, then peel the flat top layer off the background. The exposed ridges create a stylized, linear design.

Materials you'll need are cardboard from a large, fairly lightweight box, a sharp craft knife, metal ruler, rimmed baking sheet or other flat tray, plastic sheeting, linoleum printing ink, brayer, and sheets of lightweight colored or brown paper large enough for wrapping packages.

Cut the cardboard into a square or rectangle, then sketch your design on one side. Cut through the top layer with the craft knife; use a straightedge as a guide for straight lines. Peel off the top layer of the background to expose the corrugation. You can also peel some areas inside the design if you wish.

Pour ink onto the baking sheet and work with the brayer until the ink is slightly tacky. Allow it to soak in briefly.

For printing, lay wrapping paper on plastic sheeting placed over a soft surface such as a rug. Roll ink onto cardboard, covering all surfaces. Turn cardboard inked side down onto paper; press firmly all over with the palm of your hand to transfer your design.

Repeat process until paper is covered. Let paper dry flat overnight.

Design: Andrea Shedletsky.

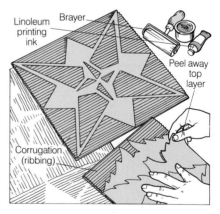

Linoleum printing ink · Brayer · Peel away top layer · Corrugation (ribbing)

Peel away *the top layer of cardboard to expose the ribbing. Cutout shapes print solid; ribbing prints as background.*

Stenciled Gift Wrap

(Also pictured on page 178)

With one simple holly stencil design applied in several ways, you can create a variety of delightful packages in no time. The design options are almost limitless; below are a few suggestions.

Materials

Paper of your choice
.005 clear or frosted polyester film
Glass backed with white paper
Large, flat piece of noncorrugated cardboard or heavy paper
Styrofoam meat trays or egg cartons
Red acrylic artist's paint
Green acrylic artist's paint
Craft knife with #11 blade
Stencil brushes
Masking tape
Ultra-fine-line permanent pen
Red fine-line felt or roller-tipped pen
Ruler

Stenciling the paper

For complete stenciling instructions, turn to pages 66 and 67. Below, we outline the general steps to follow in making designs with our holly motif.

First, trace our full-size pattern onto the polyester film, using an ultra-fine-line permanent pen. To cut stencils, place film on a piece of glass backed with white paper. Then, using a craft knife with a #11 blade, cut two stencils—one for the red berries, one for the green leaves.

To stencil, lay the paper to be stenciled on a piece of heavy cardboard. Tape the stencil on top of the paper. Pour some paint into a styrofoam meat tray "palette," pick it up with the end of a flat-bottomed stencil brush, and dab it onto the paper.

To make our design variations, see below.

Holly on grid design. Select a sheet of brown or wrapping paper; using a ruler and red fine-line pen, draw parallel lines 2 inches apart along the paper's entire length. Then draw another line ¼ inch from each original line, forming a double line as shown in the photograph below. Rotate the paper and repeat the process to form a grid. Keep your lines as straight as possible so the lines meet at exact right angles. Finally, stencil a holly motif in the center of each square of the grid.

Holly outlines. You can use a series of holly motifs to form square, oblong, or round designs on top of a box as shown in the photograph. Stencil the holly with all sets of leaves facing in the same direction, or reverse the direction of every other set of leaves to create a crisscross effect. If you use the second approach, stencil just one set of berries in the center of each cluster.

To tailor the design to the particular box you want to use, lay the box lid on your wrapping paper and lightly trace its outline with a pencil. Plot out your design so it will be evenly and pleasingly placed on the box top; you can pencil in a light line to help you align the centers of the holly motifs. Stencil in the holly. When the paint is dry, erase the pencil lines.

Design: Gayle Bryan.

This stencil pattern *can be traced full-size onto polyester film.*

One simple holly motif *does it all—you can stencil wrapping paper with a grid-and-holly motif as shown on the two boxes at top, or stencil holly in rows or circles on the box tops. For a slightly different effect, double up the motif in a crisscross pattern as shown on the box at front.*

Glitter Gift Wraps

Dust your packages with sparkling glitter for a truly dazzling display under the Christmas tree. Decorating packages with glitter is inexpensive, easy, and works on any paper. Here, we show you several special ways to use glitter on gifts you wrap.

To make our sparkling wraps, you'll need wrapping paper, cardboard or heavy paper, craft glue (which dries quickly and minimizes buckling), and glitter. A 1¾-ounce jar of glitter is sufficient for 8 to 20 packages, depending on size and coverage.

Glittery letters

This simple approach to applying glitter is great for mailed gifts, since the decorations can't get crushed.

To make letters and shapes like the stars shown on facing page, bottom, you can cut out your own cardboard templates or buy ready-made stencils. Wrap the package in glazed or foil paper in the color of your choice. Keep the paper as tight as possible to prevent it from buckling when the glue is applied.

Position the stencil patterns on top of the box and apply glue evenly over the cut-out areas. (If you are using more than one color of glitter, as we did, do all the stencils for one color first, apply glitter, then follow with other colors in sequence.) Shake glitter onto glue and press it in gently with your fingers. Work over newspaper or a large box lid so unstuck glitter can be collected and reused. Shake off excess glitter; allow to dry thoroughly.
Design: Françoise Kirkman.

Picture packages

A more elaborate approach to using glitter, our picture packages feature a treasure trove of miniature trinkets and decorations applied to a basic glitter-covered shape. You can have fun collecting tiny toys, small bells, wreaths, and other items—stickers, seashells, and feathers—throughout the year. Nearer to the holidays, you can make or buy small cookies or candies to attach to your packages.

To create these boxes, first wrap them in glazed or foil paper, keeping the wrap as tight as possible to minimize buckling. (Since these wraps are so special, you may want to wrap the box lid and bottom separately, so recipients can keep them after the holidays.)

Draw a simple design to fit your box (such as our sleigh, Christmas stocking, or tree) on cardboard or heavy paper and cut out. Carefully trace the outline with a ballpoint pen on top of the box. If there are contrasting areas within the design (such as the sleigh runners and the stocking toe, heel, and cuff), draw these in, too.

To apply glitter, outline your designs first with one color; after that's done, go back and fill in solid areas with other colors (unless you want an outline only, as for our Christmas tree design). Work with one color at a time. Outline the design in the first color with craft glue. Shake glitter onto the paper and press gently to set; shake off excess to reuse. Next, apply glue to the small areas, such as the stocking toe and heel, where you want the second color of glitter. Apply glitter and shake off excess. Now fill in the large solid areas with glitter.

Allow the package to dry completely. Then select the trinkets you want to add and arrange them on the box top. When you've settled on their placement, glue them in place.

If you wish, you can glue on a gift tag and outline that with glitter, too. Lay the package flat for several hours or until it's completely dry. Finally, shake off excess glitter one last time and add ribbon and a bow as desired.
Design: Winnie Willcox.

Applying Glittery Letters

■

Hold stencil letters against wrapped package and apply craft glue through the letters.

Shake out glitter onto glued areas and press gently; shake box to remove excess glitter.

All that glitters *needn't be gold—these beautiful packages get plenty of glitz from a dusting of inexpensive glitter. The fun comes in adding tiny trinkets and treasures to dress up each sparkling design.*

Holiday greetings sparkle *atop a package hand-decorated with glitter, applied using stencil letters and designs.*

Photo Gift Tags

Nameless nametags—the term almost contradicts itself. But these easy-to-make tags not only provide an under-the-tree picture album of family and friends, they personalize your gifts. Children who cannot read will know who the packages are from, or which ones are for them. These friendly tags can also remind the receiver what a distant relative or friend looks like.

To create tags, photocopy any black-and-white or color photograph. For color photos, use a color photocopier, if available; you may have to adjust a black-and-white photocopy machine to get a good image from a color picture.

Trim the photocopy, if necessary, to make the most pleasing composition. Then draw a tag shape on a piece of heavy construction paper or tag board and cut it out, keeping in mind the size of your photograph. Next, center the photo on the tag and glue the photo to the tag, using spray adhesive. (If you wish, you can mount the untrimmed photocopy on a tag, then trim the edges of the photo even with the edges of the tag.) Punch a hole at the top, string with yarn or silk cord, and attach to the gift.

Design: Mike Frederickson.

A picture says it all*: With these photo gift tags, gift givers can send faraway friends and loved ones a special personalized greeting along with a package.*

Embossed Cards & Tags

Shimmering on tree, card, or package, these embossed ornaments bring a touch of elegance to the holidays. To create them, you trace pictures onto sheet metal and rub gently to raise surfaces, then cut out.

Your designs—bows, stars, reindeer—go atop paper-thin sheets of copper, brass, or aluminum. To find the metal, check with auto parts stores or machine shop suppliers for "shim stock," or buy sheet metal or foil at well-stocked art or hobby stores. The material should be about .005 inch thick. If you can't find the metals, you can use smooth parts of heavy-duty disposable aluminum pans, such as pie pans.

You'll also need a thick magazine or pad of newspaper, a ballpoint pen, an ice cream stick, utility scissors, tape, and a nail and hammer to poke holes.

To create an embossed tag or card, draw, trace, or photocopy a simple design on a piece of paper. (One easy design idea is to trace around a favorite cookie cutter, as we did for our reindeer and star.) Tape the paper to a sheet of the metal, then place the metal on the magazine or newspapers. Outline the main features of the image using a ballpoint pen; be sure to press hard. To give added depth, turn the metal over and, following the raised lines, press parallel lines using the pen's point. To create large raised areas, rub the back of the metal sheet with an ice cream stick. Finally, cut out the image with a sturdy pair of utility scissors.

To attach an embossed image to a greeting card, use double-stick tape on the back of the metal. To attach an embossed tag to a gift or hang a Christmas ornament on the tree, use a nail and hammer to punch a small hole near the top, then run a ribbon or a silk cord through the hole.

Design: Françoise Kirkman and Phyllis Dunstan.

Add an elegant touch of gold or silver to greeting cards and packages with designs hand-embossed on paper-thin metal sheets. Copy a favorite design or picture, or create your own.

Embossing the Image

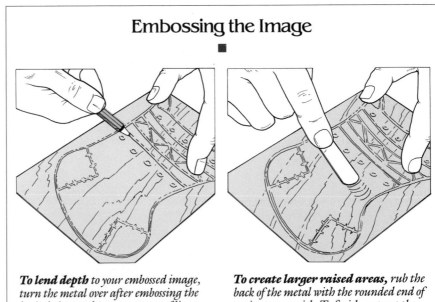

To lend depth to your embossed image, turn the metal over after embossing the basic design and press a new set of lines parallel to the original ones.

To create larger raised areas, rub the back of the metal with the rounded end of an ice cream stick. To finish, cut out the image with utility scissors.

Punched Paper Cards

With a sheet of tracing paper, a needle, and a little imagination, you can transform plain white or colored paper or note cards into your own unique custom-embossed Christmas cards. The technique is so simple you'll probably be tempted to create a whole line of designs for Christmas mailing.

Start with high-quality paper—use bristol or heavy writing paper with matching envelopes from an art supply or stationery store. You'll also need a 40-inch square of ⅛-inch-thick polyester quilt batting, available at fabric stores. To punch the holes, use a hole-punch (sold at art supply stores) or a large darning needle with a cork pushed on the threading end to make it easy to hold. Use tracing paper and a soft pencil to draw your design.

The design can be anything that strikes your fancy, but be sure to pick something with bold, simple lines. You can trace simple patterns from art books or draw your own on the tracing paper. Put the tracing on one side of the card. Fold the batting to make four layers, then place the opened card on top and poke holes through tracing and card front, following your pattern. The indentations will appear as raised dots on the flip side of the card.

To get a double-embossed effect, turn the card over and poke more holes from the other side. Don't make the holes too close together or the paper may tear.

To create an interesting edge, cut around the outside of your design, as shown for the pine trees and Santa below. You can also line the card with colored paper cut to the same size and glued along the crease, as we did for the pine trees.

Depending on the paper thickness, you can make up to five cards at the same time by stacking them. For best results, the needle should go through the paper layers without too much effort.

Design: Françoise Kirkman.

Punching the Card

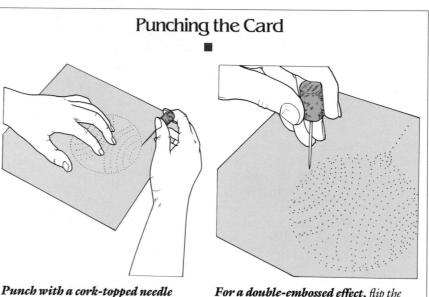

Punch with a cork-topped needle *through the line drawing on tracing paper to the card underneath, using folded batting for cushioning.*

For a double-embossed effect, *flip the punched card over and punch again from the underside, taking care not to make the holes too close together.*

Delicate traceries *of tiny holes make one-of-a-kind greeting cards; use our simple needle-punch technique and invent your own designs.*

Needlepoint Cards

(Also pictured on page 178)

Jewel-like colors and a soft, silky texture make these cards extra special. You embroider a design on needlepoint paper, then frame it in a precut mat. Your greeting goes on white or light-colored paper on the back.

You'll need sturdy, perforated needlepoint paper, available at needlecraft shops. (This paper allows 16 stitches to the inch.) Also buy 5- by 7-inch precut mats and envelopes to fit them (or make your own envelopes as described on page 205). In addition, you'll need paper, pencil, permanent felt-tip markers or acrylic paints (optional), colored or white paper for backing, glue, scissors, six-ply cotton embroidery floss, and a needle with a long eye.

To determine the size of your design, measure the inside dimensions of the mat. Cut needlepoint paper to size with a ½-inch allowance on all sides.

Use our patterns, create your own design, or borrow from designs in art books. (To enlarge and transfer, see page 64.) Once the design is on paper, outline it with a felt-tip pen and place the needlepoint paper over it. Then trace the design with a pencil. If you wish, color in the background with markers or paints. Start stitching at the top right-hand corner of the design; use a half-cross-stitch and slant all stitches upward to the right as shown below.

Glue your finished work to the mat; cut out paper backing in a coordinating color. Glue a second, slightly smaller, piece of white or light-colored paper onto the backing and inscribe it with your message.

Design: Andrea Shedletsky and Joan Melim.

Pretty enough to frame, *these needlepoint cards make delightful little Christmas gifts all by themselves.*

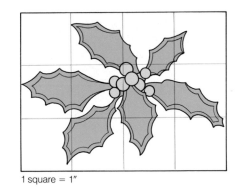

1 square = 1″

3-D Cards

Three-dimensional Christmas greetings are quick to make and good fun to receive. And they have their own identities. Hanging or standing up, they won't get lost in the crowd of holiday cards. Some of our cards are simply folded shapes; others are made of interlocking shapes that stand upright but can fold flat for storage and mailing. Some make unique place cards for your holiday table, as well as highly individual greeting cards.

Make your 3-D cards from medium-weight paper—metallic or colored—or bristol board. You'll also need scissors, pencil, pen, and thread for hanging.

Dove

Simplest of our 3-D cards, the dove is easily produced in quantity for mailing or for tree decorations. Draw the dove outline on a folded piece of colored or metallic paper as shown at right. If you wish, you can experiment with the design; variations in the curves will produce marked differences in the birds that emerge. If you'll be mailing the dove card, be sure to make it the correct size for the envelope you want to use. (To make your own envelopes, see facing page.)

Cut out the dove along the solid lines; fold on the dotted lines. Then fold along the paper fold line to make the dove's wings extend as shown in the photo.

Peaceful doves *and a gold-topped Christmas tree were originally sent flattened, in envelopes, as Christmas cards. Unfolded at their destination, they become pretty three-dimensional greetings.*

If you wish, you can add eyes made of sequins or adhesive colored paper. Write your message along the lower curve of the dove's body (you can write on each side) and punch a hole with a needle for threading a string.

Design: Bill Cheney.

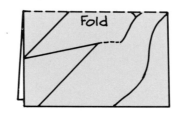

Christmas tree

Our Christmas tree card goes 3-D the minute it slides out of the envelope. Copy the pattern here, or cut your own. To make the pattern, fold a piece of ordinary paper in half. Draw a three-branched half-tree centered on the fold; make the bottom two branches almost equal in size. Cut out and unfold. Place the unfolded pattern on a folded piece of green paper (paper should be colored on both sides) so that the tips of the two lower branches just reach over

the edge of the fold as shown below. Trace around the pattern with a pencil. Cut the two trees together, leaving them attached at the two branch tips along the fold. Bend back each tree in half along a line from tip to bottom, and glue the two inner halves together just inside the center folds. Flatten out to write your message. For sparkle, add three small gold legal seals to the top; stick each one to the other two, edges matching. Attach yarn for hanging, or let the card stand on its own.

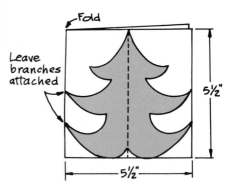

A fanciful folding tree or star can become a place card at your holiday table (above) or, folded flat for mailing, can be sent as a unique greeting card or invitation (right).

Tree & star

To create several of these cards, start by making templates. Choose either the star or the tree. For the tree, use the tinted shape; for the star, use the black lines. For either, transfer the two shapes from the drawings onto pattern paper or a predrawn 1-inch grid (see page 64). Cut out the templates and trace them onto heavy paper or bristol board. Cut out one of each piece, in contrasting colors if you like. Cut slots in both pieces and fold along the dotted lines as shown in the drawings. Write your message on the inside of the card; or, if you plan to use it as a place card, inscribe it with your guest's name.

Then fold both pieces part way and insert the slots of the smaller piece into those of the larger piece.

To "texture" the trees as shown above, cut thin triangular wedges in the branches at about ½-inch intervals.

Design: Françoise Kirkman.

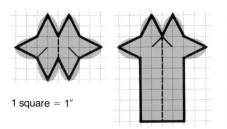

1 square = 1"

Envelopes

To make your own custom-sized envelope, measure a piece of heavy colored paper to a size slightly larger than the card. Cut and fold as shown below; seal sides and one end with a glue stick. Insert your card and glue down the top envelope flap.

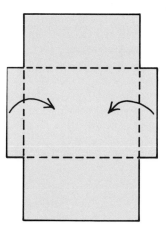

Cut-and-fold Cards

(Also pictured on page 178)

These greeting cards are a joint effort: the sender provides a two-dimensional paper card, and the recipient cuts and folds it to make a three-dimensional holiday ornament. Using one of our simple patterns, you can create a stack of inexpensive paper cards that fold to become self-mailing.

With the help of a printer, you can have fifty to a hundred 8½- by 11-inch cards printed photo-direct in black ink on one side of white or colored bristol board (the same weight as index cards). In general, you should allow 1 to 5 days for printing, though some "instant" printers require only a few hours.

Once the basic black-line elements are printed on the cards, you add color by hand, write in any personal messages, and fold and seal the cards for mailing.

The grids and designs on this page will help you create your cards. Design A can be varied to produce two different shapes. Cut out around all eight points for the double-pointed ornament shown in the photo, second from left; for the bird or the tall cards, cut out around the points at the top and the large solid outline at the bottom. (For the bird, you'll need to add extra lines to indicate cutout wings and tail.) Design B makes the small house shape or circus wagon.

Begin by enlarging and transferring the pattern of your choice (see page 64 for help).

Use blue grid paper, or draw your grid on white illustration board using a light blue pencil (offset printing won't pick up the blue). The squares on our grid equal ½ inch, making a design that fits onto an 8½- by 11-inch card. As you draw, be sure to align tabs with slots.

After blue-penciling the shape you choose, draw the final image you want to print using a fine-tipped black marker. Add your Christmas greeting, simple numbered instructions for assembly, and any decorative elements you want to be printed in black on all your cards. If you wish, you can use purchased press-on letters and borders, available at art supply stores.

Once the cards are back from the printer, you can add color with paint, adhesive-backed paper, decorative stickers, stamps, or photographs. Personal messages can be added and the cards folded in half or thirds (as indicated by the X's on our diagrams) for addressing and mailing. Use stickers to seal the folded cards.

When your friends receive your creations, they can cut and fold them into ornaments following your written instructions and hang them using bright yarn or thread.

Design: Françoise Kirkman and Phyllis Dunstan.

A

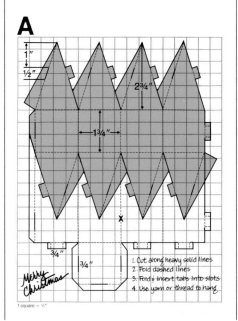

1. Cut along heavy solid lines
2. Fold dashed lines
3. Fold & insert tabs into slots
4. Use yarn or thread to hang

Merry Christmas

1 square = ½"

B

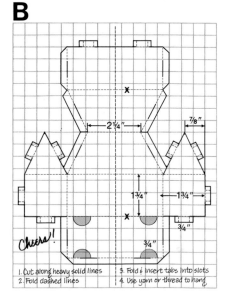

Cheers!

1. Cut along heavy solid lines
2. Fold dashed lines
3. Fold & insert tabs into slots
4. Use yarn or thread to hang

Both sender and recipient *get into the act to create these cleverly designed three-dimensional cards. You make a flat, fully-colored card for mailing; when your friends receive the card, they fold it to make a fanciful ornament that bears your greetings.*

Quilt Cards

(Also pictured on page 178)

Reminiscent of traditional geometric quilt designs, these cheerful fabric-covered cards are surprisingly easy to make. You simply use fusible web to bond scraps of fabric to a heavy paper card. Our simple yet versatile pattern allows you to cut out three different shapes and mix and match them to your heart's content.

Materials are few: scraps of lightweight fabrics, some fusible web (sold at fabric stores by the yard or prepackaged), and plain cards and envelopes available at art or stationery stores.

Trace our full-size pattern pieces onto lightweight cardboard and cut them out. Place them on the wrong side of your fabric and trace the outlines; also trace onto fusible web. Cut out shapes from both fabric and web. Arrange shapes, fabric over web, on your card; cover with a pressing cloth. Using a steam iron set at "wool," press for 10 seconds without moving the iron. Turn the card over and press the reverse side.

Design: Carla Hoff and Florence Goguely.

Bright fabric scraps *from your sewing basket are easily transformed into charming greeting cards—with the help of fusible web and a steam iron.*

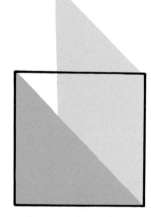

You can trace *and cut out these three geometric shapes; use them as guides for making cardboard patterns.*

Applying the Fabric

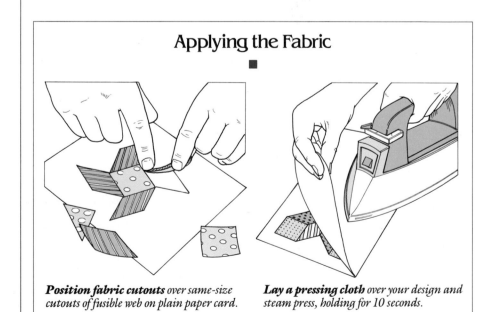

Position fabric cutouts *over same-size cutouts of fusible web on plain paper card.*

Lay a pressing cloth *over your design and steam press, holding for 10 seconds.*

Cutout Photo Cards

A portrait—especially the round, smiling face of a child—tucked inside a Christmas card is a pleasure to make as well as to receive. To give recipients a peek at what's inside, our handmade photo cards have front-page cutouts in a variety of shapes.

Purchase white or colorful paper and matching or coordinating envelopes. For standard 3½- by 5-inch photos, you'll want at least 6- by 9-inch paper.

You can either draw your own cutout shape or trace around a favorite cookie cutter. If you draw your own, place a piece of tracing paper over the photo and lightly pencil in the outline to frame the subject nicely. Fold the card paper in half and transfer your design to the front of the card.

To use a cookie cutter, fold the card paper in half and position the photo temporarily on top. Place the cookie cutter over the part of the photo you want to show through and carefully pull the photo out from under. Trace around the cutter onto the front of the card.

For either method, neatly cut out the shape with embroidery or fingernail scissors or a craft knife. Add extra decorations such as foil stars or cutouts, or color in a drawing (like our snowman) around the cutout. Finally, glue the photograph in place with a glue stick and inscribe the card.

Design: Florence Goguely.

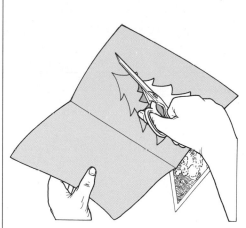

Use small scissors or a craft knife to cut out your design on the front of the card.

Photo cards are always fun to receive, especially when you've dressed them up with cleverly shaped cut-out windows like these.

Festive Holiday Fare

■

From a candlelit buffet table laden with luscious cakes, candies, and fruits to a cozy kitchen nook set for a one-dish family supper on Christmas Eve, offerings of good food and drink express the open, generous yuletide spirit. Around the holidays, almost any gathering can become a celebration—and each occasion calls for a special menu that will both reflect the festive holiday mood and be easy to organize smoothly.

In this section, we take you on a culinary tour through the holiday season, starting with a tree-cutting picnic and progressing right through to Christmas Day dinner. In between, there's a warming soup supper for a caroling get-together, a tempting array of sandwiches and goodies for a children's party, a sumptuous all-dessert buffet—even an easy-on-the-cook Scandinavian smörgåsbord you can create entirely from the deli. And for Christmas dinner, you can choose amongst a mouth-watering array of centerpiece roasts, from a golden goose to a succulent beef roast, with all the trimmings. All the recipes and instructions you'll need to create wonderful holiday meals are here—to cook, to serve, to enjoy.

Yuletide Celebrations

■

Good food and drink, high spirits and merriment abound during the holiday season. From the elegance of the Holiday Open House party (see page 216) shown below to the cozy intimacy of a special Christmas Morning Breakfast, the menus and recipes in this chapter provide a wealth of ideas for all your holiday entertaining.

Tree-cutters' Tailgate Picnic

When the weather is crackling-crisp and the yuletide season is drawing near, it's time for a trip to your local Christmas tree farm. To make the occasion extra festive and satisfy fresh-air appetites, put together this easy-traveling picnic lunch for your tree-cutting crew. The centerpiece is roasted chicken; you can buy it already cooked or roast it at home. Purple eggs and a bright corn-and-red-pepper salad add colorful and piquant accents; homemade biscuits round out a satisfying meal for four.

> **MENU**
> *Roasted Chicken*
> *Corn & Red Pepper Relish Salad*
> *Pickled Beets & Purple Eggs*
> *Poppy Seed–Herb Drop Biscuits*
> *Butter*
> *Carrot & Celery Sticks*
> *Crisp Molasses Cookies*
> *Milk or Sparkling Apple Juice*

For the fastest start, pick up cooked chicken at the supermarket or a delicatessen; for four servings, you'll need two chickens, each about 1½ pounds (cut them in half to serve). If you want to cook your own chicken, buy a 3½- to 4-pound bird and roast it at 375°, allowing 20–25 minutes per pound, until a meat thermometer inserted in the thickest part of the thigh (not touching bone) registers 185°. When cool enough to handle, quarter the chicken for serving.

To make the meal, start the chicken if you are cooking your own, then start the eggs; they need to marinate for at least an hour, but will keep for up to 1 week.

While the biscuits bake, make the corn salad and cut up carrots and celery. Transport cold foods and beverage in one insulated chest; if the chicken and biscuits are hot, pack them in another chest. Buy thin crisp molasses cookies, or raid your supply of pre-Christmas baking.

Corn & Red Pepper Relish Salad

⅔ cup distilled white vinegar

¼ cup sugar

¼ teaspoon **each** celery seeds and mustard seeds

¼ cup minced onion

1 package (10 oz.) frozen corn kernels, thawed and drained

½ cup canned red peppers or canned pimentos, drained and thinly sliced

Salt and pepper

In a 2- to 3-quart pan, bring vinegar, sugar, celery seeds, mustard seeds, and onion to a boil over high heat. Reduce heat to medium and simmer, uncovered, for 5 minutes. Remove from heat and stir in corn and red peppers; season to taste with salt and pepper. Let cool completely.

Serve, or cover and refrigerate for up to 1 week. Drain before serving, or lift from dish with a slotted spoon. Makes 2½ cups (4 servings).

Pickled Beets & Purple Eggs

1 can (1 lb.) whole pickled beets

4 hard-cooked large eggs, shelled

Pour beet liquid into a small deep bowl and add eggs, turning to coat well. Top with beets, cover, and refrigerate for at least 1 hour or up to 1 week. Turn eggs occasionally during first hour, then once every day or so to ensure a uniformly deep color.

To serve, lift eggs and beets from liquid with a slotted spoon. Makes 4 servings.

Poppy Seed–Herb Drop Biscuits

1½ cups all-purpose flour

1 tablespoon **each** baking powder and poppy seeds

½ teaspoon **each** salt and dry thyme leaves

⅓ cup butter or margarine, cut into chunks

¾ cup milk

Butter or margarine

In a large bowl, stir together flour, baking powder, poppy seeds, salt, and thyme leaves. With a pastry blender, 2 knives, or your fingers, cut (or rub) in the ⅓ cup butter until mixture resembles coarse cornmeal. Pour in milk; stir until dough is evenly moistened.

Drop dough in ¼-cup portions about 1 inch apart in a greased 9-inch round baking pan. Bake in a 450° oven until tops of biscuits are well browned (15 to 18 minutes). Serve hot or cold, with butter. Makes 8 large biscuits (4 to 8 servings).

Tree-trimmers' Buffet Supper

Gather family and friends together to deck the halls and adorn your Christmas tree, then reward their artistic efforts with this elegant and festive buffet for eight. The handsome cheese-stuffed pork roast is made ahead, so the filling can cool until firm and easy to cut. You can also make the wild rice salad, mulled cranberries, and tempting raspberry tart a day or two before the party. Even the artichokes can be boiled or steamed in advance, leaving you free to join in the decorating from start to finish. (You'll need about 16 small artichokes—two for each guest.)

MENU

Pork Loin Stuffed with
Two Cheeses
Mulled Cranberries
Small Boiled or Steamed
Artichokes
Wild Rice Salad
French Bread
Raspberry Jam Tart
Gewürztraminer   Apple Juice

Pork Loin Stuffed with Two Cheeses

- 4   ounces cream cheese, at room temperature
- 4   ounces ripened or unripened goat cheese (such as Montrachet or Bûcheron)
- 1   teaspoon ground sage
- ½   teaspoon dry thyme leaves
- 1   boned pork loin end roast (about 3 lbs.)
- 12   to 15 large canned grape leaves, drained

    Thyme sprigs (optional)

In a bowl, thoroughly blend cream cheese, goat cheese, ½ teaspoon of the sage, and ¼ teaspoon of the thyme leaves; set aside.

Open roast and lay flat, fat side down. Cover with plastic wrap and pound with a flat mallet to make a 9- by 11-inch rectangle. Fill roast so you can reroll it to original shape. First, line meat down center with a double layer of grape leaves, extending leaves 3 to 4 inches beyond roast at each end. Then spoon cheese mixture down center of leaves and fold ends over filling, making sure there are no holes or thin pieces at roast ends where filling could seep out as meat cooks. Lap leaves over sides, forming a neat roll. Roll meat around filling to enclose closely but not tightly; tie.

Place roast, fat side up, in a 9- by 13-inch baking pan. Rub remaining ½ teaspoon sage and remaining ¼ teaspoon thyme leaves on roast. Insert a meat thermometer into thickest part of meat (not into filling). Roast, uncovered, in a 375° oven until thermometer registers 160°F (about 1¼ hours). Let cool; let stand until serving time (no longer than 4 hours). Serve at room temperature. (If you do not plan to serve meat within 4 hours, cover and refrigerate cooled meat; bring to room temperature before serving.) To serve, cut meat into ¾- to 1-inch-thick slices; garnish with thyme sprigs, if desired. Makes 8 servings.

Mulled Cranberries

In a 3-quart pan, combine 3 cups **fresh or frozen cranberries**, 1⅓ cups **sugar**, 6 tablespoons **orange-flavored liqueur**, and 2 **cinnamon sticks**, *each* about 2½ inches long. Cover and cook over low heat until berries are translucent (about 15 minutes), stirring gently until sugar is dissolved. If made ahead, cover and refrigerate for up to 2 days; serve cold or at room temperature. Makes 8 to 12 servings.

Wild Rice Salad

- 1½   cups wild rice
- 3   cups regular-strength chicken broth
- ⅓   cup salad oil
- 2   tablespoons raspberry or wine vinegar
- 2   tablespoons minced shallot or onion
- 2   teaspoons Dijon mustard
- ¼   teaspoon pepper

Rinse rice with water and drain. In a 2- to 3-quart pan, bring rice and broth to a boil. Reduce heat so liquid is just simmering; cover and cook, stirring occasionally, until rice is tender to bite and almost all liquid is absorbed (about 50 minutes). Let cool.

In a small bowl, mix oil, vinegar, shallot, mustard, and pepper. Stir into cooled rice. Serve, or hold at room temperature for up to 4 hours. If made ahead, cover and refrigerate for up to 2 days; bring to room temperature to serve. Makes 8 servings.

An elegant cheese-filled pork roast *is the centerpiece for our festive Tree-trimmers' Buffet Supper. The roast, accompaniments, and dessert can be made ahead and will wait on your buffet table until the last bauble has been hung.*

Raspberry Jam Tart

1   cup plus 2 tablespoons
     all-purpose flour

¼   cup sugar

⅓   cup firm butter or
     margarine, cut into
     chunks

1   large egg yolk

½   cup plus 1 tablespoon
     raspberry jam

⅓   cup (about 4 oz.)
     almond paste

3   large eggs, separated

¼   teaspoon baking powder

⅛   teaspoon almond extract

1   to 2 tablespoons sliced
     almonds

In a food processor or a bowl, combine 1 cup of the flour, 2 tablespoons of the sugar, and butter. Whirl (or rub with your fingers) until fine crumbs form. Add 1 egg yolk; whirl or stir with a fork until dough holds together, then press into a smooth ball.

Evenly press dough over bottom and sides of a 10- to 11-inch tart pan with a removable bottom. Bake in a 350° oven until crust is light gold (about 12 minutes). Spread ½ cup of the jam over bottom of crust.

In a bowl, beat almond paste, 3 egg yolks, remaining 2 tablespoons flour, remaining 2 tablespoons sugar, baking powder, and almond extract until smooth.

In another bowl, beat egg whites until they hold soft peaks. Beat about half the whites into almond batter, then fold in remaining whites. Pour batter over jam in crust. Spoon remaining 1 tablespoon jam onto center of mixture; scatter almonds over top of tart.

Bake in a 350° oven until tart is well browned (about 25 minutes). Let cool completely. If made ahead, cover and let stand overnight. To serve, remove pan sides; cut tart into wedges. Makes 8 servings.

Holiday Open House

(Pictured on page 212)

Christmas is the season to welcome good friends into your home for a warm and spirited get-together. Make this year's open house one to remember with a colorful, varied all-appetizer buffet for 24.

From plump Shrimp with Green Goddess Dip to savory little fila finger snacks, this menu offers something for everyone.

Our selection of crudités (for dipping along with the shrimp) features radishes, cherry tomatoes, snow peas, cucumbers, baby carrots, and red bell peppers, but you can serve any vegetable that's available and appealing. To serve Meat-wrapped Fruits, simply wrap peeled melon wedges in thin slices of prosciutto; wrap unpeeled apple and pear wedges, drizzled with lime juice, in thinly sliced mild coppa. (You'll need about ¼ pound of each meat for 1 melon and 2 apples or pears.)

As for beverages, you'll usually please everyone if you offer champagne, sparkling cider, club soda, and a selection of fruit juices and soft drinks.

MENU

Shrimp with Green Goddess Dip
Italian Eggplant Relish
Layered Cheese Torta
Thinly Sliced Baguettes
Basket of Crudités
Savory Fila Appetizer Pastries
Cheese-Mushroom Fingers
Meat-wrapped Fruits
Champagne   Sparkling Cider

Shrimp with Green Goddess Dip

2½ to 3 pounds cooked, shelled, deveined medium-size shrimp (30 to 36 per lb.)
      Green Goddess Dip (recipe follows)
      Whole chives

Arrange shrimp in a large bowl or on a platter; cover and refrigerate until serving time or for up to 4 hours. To serve, spoon Green Goddess Dip into a serving bowl and garnish with chives. Offer shrimp with dip. Makes 24 servings.

Green Goddess Dip. In a blender or food processor, combine 2 cloves **garlic**, minced or pressed; ½ cup *each* coarsely chopped **parsley**, **green onions** (including tops), and **watercress**; 1 teaspoon **onion salt**; 2 teaspoons *each* **dry tarragon** and **anchovy paste**; and 4 teaspoons **lemon juice**. Whirl until smooth. Stir in 1 cup *each* **mayonnaise** and **sour cream** until well combined. Makes about 3 cups.

Italian Eggplant Relish

1   *large eggplant (about 1½ lbs.)*
2   *large red bell peppers*
½   *cup olive oil*
1   *large onion, finely chopped*
1½ *cups thinly sliced celery*
3   *cloves garlic, minced or pressed*
¼   *cup tomato paste*
1   *cup water*
¼   *cup red wine vinegar*
1   *tablespoon **each** sugar and drained capers*
2   *tablespoons coarsely chopped fresh basil or 1 teaspoon dry basil*
1   *cup sliced ripe olives*
¼   *cup pine nuts*
      Butter lettuce leaves (optional)

Cut unpeeled eggplant into ½-inch cubes. Seed and dice bell peppers; set aside. Heat oil in a 12- to 14-inch frying pan over medium heat. Add eggplant; cover and cook, stirring occasionally, until eggplant begins to soften (about 5 minutes). Uncover and continue to cook, stirring often, until eggplant begins to brown (about 10 more minutes).

Mix in bell peppers, onion, celery, and garlic; cook, stirring often, until onion is soft (6 to 8 minutes). Add tomato paste, water, vinegar, sugar, capers, basil, and olives. Cook, stirring often, until mixture is very thick (about 10 more minutes). If made ahead, let cool, then cover and refrigerate for up to 1 week.

Pour pine nuts into a small frying pan. Cook over medium heat, stirring often, until lightly browned (about 5 minutes). Sprinkle over relish. Garnish relish with lettuce leaves, if desired; serve cold or at room temperature. Makes 6 cups.

Layered Cheese Torta
(Make 2 for the party)

2   *large packages (8 oz. **each**) cream cheese, at room temperature*
2   *cups (1 lb.) unsalted butter, at room temperature*
      Sun-dried Tomato Topping & Filling (recipe follows)

In large bowl of an electric mixer, beat cream cheese and butter until very smoothly blended; scrape mixture from bowl sides as needed.

Cut two 18-inch squares of cheesecloth; moisten with water, wring dry, and lay out flat, one on top of the other. Smoothly line a 5- to 6-cup straight-sided plain mold, such as a loaf pan, terrine, charlotte mold, or clean flowerpot, with the cheesecloth; drape excess over rim of mold.

Set two sun-dried tomato sections in mold bottom. With your fingers or a rubber spatula, make an even layer of ⅙ of the cheese mixture. Cover with ⅕ of the Sun-dried Tomato Filling, extending it evenly to sides of mold. Repeat until mold is filled, finishing with cheese.

Fold ends of cheesecloth over torta and press down lightly with your hands to compact. Refrigerate until torta feels firm when pressed (about 1 hour). Then invert onto a serving dish and gently pull off cloth (if allowed to stand, cloth will act as a wick and cause filling color to bleed onto cheese).

If made ahead, wrap airtight in plastic wrap and refrigerate for up to 5 days. Makes 14 to 16 servings.

Sun-dried Tomato Topping & Filling. Drain 1 jar (10½ oz.) **sun-dried tomatoes in olive oil**, reserving 2 tablespoons of the oil. Center 2 tomato sections in mold bottom for topping. Whirl remaining tomatoes with reserved oil in a blender or food processor until finely chopped.

Savory Fila Appetizer Pastries

1 package (1-lb. size) fila (thawed if frozen)
⅔ cup (⅓ lb.) butter or margarine, melted
   Spicy Lamb Filling (recipe follows)
   Feta Cheese Filling (recipe follows)

Unroll fila and lay flat; cut sheets in half crosswise and cover with plastic wrap to prevent drying.

Use half the fila for each filling. Work with a half sheet of fila at a time; lightly brush with butter before filling.

Fill and shape pastries as directed below, then place shaped pastries about 1½ inches apart on greased baking sheets. Brush tops with butter and cover with plastic wrap while shaping remaining pastries.

To shape lamb logs, fold buttered half-sheet of fila in half crosswise. Brush again with butter. Place 1½ tablespoons of the Spicy Lamb Filling along short end of each piece; fold in sides, then roll up dough jelly roll style.

To shape cheese triangles, cut buttered fila half-sheet lengthwise into thirds. Place 1 tablespoon of the Feta Cheese Filling in upper corner of each strip and fold corner down over filling to make a triangle. Fold triangle over onto itself. Then continue folding triangle from side to side all down length of strip, as if you were folding a flag.

(After shaping pastries, you may freeze them for up to 1 month. To freeze, place shaped pastries in freezer until firm; then carefully stack in a rigid container, placing foil between each layer of pastries. Do not thaw before baking.)

Bake pastries in a 375° oven until well browned and crisp (10 to 15 minutes; 20 to 35 minutes if frozen). Serve hot; or let cool to room temperature, then serve. Makes about 32 lamb logs, about 48 cheese triangles.

Spicy Lamb Filling. Place a wide frying pan over medium heat; crumble in 2½ pounds **lean ground lamb**. Add 2 large **onions** (chopped) and 4 cloves **garlic** (minced or pressed). Cook, stirring often, until onion is soft and meat is browned. Spoon off and discard any excess fat. Add ⅔ cup *each* **catsup** and chopped **parsley**; 1 cup **dry red wine**; 1 can (1 lb.) **stewed tomatoes**; and 1 teaspoon *each* **pepper** and **ground nutmeg**.

Cook, stirring occasionally, for 10 minutes. Increase heat to high and continue to cook, stirring constantly, until almost all liquid has evaporated. Remove pan from heat and let filling cool for about 10 minutes.

If made ahead, cover and refrigerate for up to 2 days; bring to room temperature before using.

Feta Cheese Filling. In large bowl of an electric mixer, combine 8 ounces **ricotta cheese**; 8 ounces **feta cheese**, crumbled (about 2 cups); 1 small package (3 oz.) **cream cheese** (at room temperature); 2 tablespoons **all-purpose flour**; 2 large

eggs; ½ teaspoon **ground nutmeg**; ¼ teaspoon **white pepper**; and ½ cup finely chopped **parsley**. Beat until mixture is well blended.

If made ahead, cover and refrigerate for up to 2 days; bring to room temperature before using.

Cheese-Mushroom Fingers

½ cup (¼ lb.) butter or margarine
1 pound mushrooms, thinly sliced
1 large onion, finely chopped
2 cloves garlic, minced or pressed
1 large red bell pepper, seeded and chopped
10 large eggs
2 cups small curd cottage cheese
4 cups (1 lb.) shredded jack cheese
½ cup all-purpose flour
1 teaspoon baking powder
¾ teaspoon **each** ground nutmeg, dry basil, and salt

Melt butter in a wide frying pan over medium-high heat. Add mushrooms, onion, and garlic and cook, stirring often, until onion and mushrooms are soft. Add bell pepper and cook, stirring, for 1 more minute.

In a large bowl, beat eggs lightly. Beat in cottage cheese, jack cheese, flour, baking powder, nutmeg, basil, and salt until blended; stir in mushroom mixture. Spread in a well-greased rimmed 10- by 15-inch baking pan. Bake in a 350° oven until firm (about 35 minutes).

Let cool for 15 minutes; cut into ¾- by 2-inch strips. Serve warm or at room temperature. If made ahead, cover and refrigerate for up to 2 days; reheat in a 350° oven until hot (about 15 minutes). Makes about 6 dozen.

Expandable Buffet Party

Is this the year you've decided to throw a really big holiday bash? If so, our expandable holiday buffet may be just the thing you need to make your party a roaring success.

Our basic menu serves 25 people but can be adjusted to accommodate multiples of that number; about 125 guests is the maximum. The chart below right shows how much food and drink you'll need for every 25 guests.

MENU

Cold Sliced Turkey, Ham, Mortadella & Roast Beef

Cheese Tray

Mayonnaise, Mustard, Whole Berry Cranberry Sauce

Three-Bean Salad

Marinated Mushrooms

Carrot & Raisin Salad

Fresh Fruit Salad

Pasta Salad

French Bread   Butter

Dry White & Red Jug Wines

Sparkling Water   Apple Cider

Double Cheese Bread

Pumpkin Bread

Spice Cake with Caramel Icing

Pork Sausage Cake

Seed Cake

Coffee   Tea

The party's simple framework allows you to do as much or as little cooking as you wish. We suggest you buy cold meats, cheeses, salads, loaves of French or other plain bread, and condiments to go with the assortment of delectable quick breads and cakes featured here. If you like to bake, you can make all our cakes and breads yourself; if you don't (or if you're short on time), you can purchase similar items from a bakery. Likewise, favorite homemade salads of your choice could certainly take the place of purchased salads.

Present a well-filled buffet table and plenty of small plates. Let guests help themselves, going back frequently to sample various combinations. Present the food in the following varieties and amounts.

Cold sliced meats. Fill trays generously with three or four kinds of meat and plan to replenish them for each 50 servings. Garnish with watercress, parsley, or lettuce leaves.

Cheeses. Choose three or four cheeses, such as Jarlsberg, Edam, Gouda, and jack. Serve cheeses whole or in large chunks. (Chunks of cheese stay fresh longer than slices or cubes.) As the party grows in size, buy bigger chunks rather than more variety. Place them all on the buffet at the beginning of the party, with knives for guests to cut the cheeses themselves.

Condiments. Limit the mustard selection to Dijon, which goes with everything. You can buy cranberry sauce or make it yourself.

Salads. Equal quantities of four or five kinds are appropriate. Choose a variety of purchased or homemade salads, all made with ingredients that won't wilt or darken on standing. Good choices include fresh fruit, pasta, potato, marinated vegetable, mixed bean, shredded carrot, cucumber, cabbage, and celery root salads. Plan to bring out refills for every 50 servings.

Butter. Soften sticks of butter, then pack into one or more crocks, smoothing tops so filled crocks look attractive.

Breads. Buy French bread or other local specialties, such as dark rye or whole wheat breads. Put out a complete selection and hold duplicates in reserve. Cut a few slices of each loaf to get guests started, then let them cut their own so breads stay fresher.

Desserts. Both of our sweet quick breads and all three fine-grained, boldly flavored cakes can be made weeks ahead, then stored in the freezer until party time. They take only about an hour to thaw. Decorate or ice the cakes shortly before serving; slice cakes and quick breads immediately before the party, keeping the slices together for an attractive presentation and to preserve freshness.

Quantities required for buffet supper party

Number of guests	25	50	75	100	125
Cold sliced cooked meats (pounds)	8	16	24	32	40
Chunks of cheese (pounds)	7	14	21	28	35
Mayonnaise, as a condiment (cups)	1½	3	4½	6	7½
Dijon mustard (cups)	½	1	1½	2	2½
Whole berry cranberry sauce (cups)	3	6	9	12	15
Salads (gallons)	3	6	9	12	15
Breads (5- by 9-inch loaves)	2–3	3–4	4–5	5–6	6–7
Butter (pounds)	½	1	1½	2	2½
Cakes (10- to 12-cup size or 9-inch-diameter two-layer cakes)	2–3	4–5	6–7	8–9	10–11
Wine (cases)	1	2	3	4	5
Mineral water (quarts or liters)	6	12	18	24	30
Coffee (cups ground; use 1 cup per 2½ quarts of water)	3½	7	10½	14	17½

Meats, cheeses, and salads galore *make an abundant buffet offering without a lot of fuss. Just pay a visit to your favorite deli or supermarket and select a pleasing combination of flavors, colors, and textures.*

Beverages. For convenience, have beverages at a separate self-serve station, along with cups, glasses, and spoons. Pre-chill bottles in large plastic garbage cans or bags filled with ice. To serve, place the bottles in ice-filled tubs. Borrow or rent electric coffee makers; remember that it takes 45 minutes to 1 hour for large machines to brew coffee. If you want to serve hot tea, have a coffee maker or large thermos filled with hot water and provide a selection of tea bags.

Double Cheese Bread

⅔ cup (⅓ lb.) butter or
    margarine, at room
    temperature
1⅓ cups sugar
 4 large eggs
 3 cups all-purpose flour
 1 cup whole-wheat flour
 4 teaspoons baking powder
½ teaspoon baking soda
 1 teaspoon salt
1½ cups chopped walnuts
⅔ cup **each** milk and white
    wine (or use all milk)
1½ cups (6 oz.) shredded
    sharp Cheddar cheese
 1 cup (4 oz.) crumbled
    blue-veined cheese
 1 tablespoon **each** poppy
    seeds and sesame seeds

In large bowl of an electric mixer, beat butter and sugar until fluffy. Add eggs, 1 at a time, beating well after each addition.

Stir together flours, baking powder, baking soda, salt, and walnuts. Add dry ingredients to butter mixture alternately with milk and wine. Divide batter in half; stir Cheddar cheese into 1 portion, blue cheese into other portion.

(Continued on next page)

Grease and flour-dust two 5- by 9-inch loaf pans. Spoon half the Cheddar cheese batter into each pan, distributing down 1 long side; then spoon half the blue cheese batter alongside. Sprinkle poppy seeds over Cheddar cheese batter and sesame seeds over blue cheese batter.

Bake in a 350° oven until a wooden pick inserted in center of bread comes out clean (about 1 hour). Let loaves cool in pans for 10 minutes, then turn out onto racks to cool completely. If made ahead, wrap airtight and freeze; let thaw unwrapped.

To serve, carefully cut bread into ¾-inch-thick slices; it has a tendency to crumble. If you like, cut slices in half lengthwise. Makes 2 loaves (25 servings).

Note: If you prefer, you can make 1 Cheddar loaf and 1 blue cheese loaf; just put all the Cheddar batter in 1 pan, all the blue cheese batter in another pan. Bake as directed.

Pumpkin Bread

⅔ cup (⅓ lb.) butter or margarine, at room temperature

2½ cups sugar

1 can (1 lb.) pumpkin

3⅓ cups all-purpose flour

1 teaspoon **each** baking powder, baking soda, and salt

4 teaspoons ground cinnamon

2 teaspoons ground allspice

1 cup raisins

1 cup broken walnuts or pecans

In large bowl of an electric mixer, beat butter and sugar until fluffy. Blend in pumpkin.

Stir together flour, baking powder, baking soda, salt, cinnamon, and allspice. Thoroughly blend dry ingredients into pumpkin mixture, then stir in raisins and walnuts. Spoon batter evenly into a greased, flour-dusted 10-inch tube pan or 12-cup fluted tube pan.

Bake in a 350° oven just until bread begins to pull away from pan sides and a wooden pick inserted in bread comes out clean (about 55 minutes). Let bread cool in pan for 10 minutes, then turn out onto a rack to cool completely. If made ahead, wrap airtight and freeze; let thaw unwrapped. To serve, cut into about ½-inch-thick slices. Makes about 25 servings.

Everybody's favorite part of the buffet is the table of baked goodies. Here, the tempting offerings include (clockwise from top) Double Cheese Bread, Seed Cake, Pork Sausage Cake, and sliced Pumpkin Bread served with cranberry sauce.

Spice Cake with Caramel Icing

1   cup (½ lb.) butter or margarine, at room temperature
2¼ cups sugar
5   large eggs
3   cups all-purpose flour
1   tablespoon **each** ground cloves and ground cinnamon
1   teaspoon baking powder
½   teaspoon baking soda
1   cup sour cream
1   cup raisins
    Caramel Icing (recipe follows)
    Blanched almonds

In large bowl of an electric mixer, beat butter and sugar until fluffy; add eggs, 1 at a time, beating well after each addition. Sift together flour, cloves, cinnamon, baking powder, and baking soda.

Add flour mixture to butter mixture alternately with sour cream, blending in 2 or 3 additions. Stir in raisins.

Pour batter into a greased, flour-dusted 10-inch tube pan. Bake in a 350° oven just until cake begins to pull from pan sides and a wooden pick inserted in center comes out clean (about 1 hour). Let cool in pan for 10 minutes, then turn out of pan onto a rack to cool completely. If made ahead, wrap airtight and freeze; let thaw unwrapped.

Up to a day before serving, spread all the icing very thickly over top of cake; some will flow irregularly down sides. Decorate with almonds. To serve, cut into thin slices. Makes 12 to 16 servings.

Caramel Icing. Melt ½ cup (¼ lb.) **butter** or margarine in a 2- to 3-quart pan. Add 1 cup firmly packed **brown sugar** and ⅓ cup **half-and-half** or whipping cream. Quickly bring to a full boil; boil, stirring, for 1 minute. Remove from heat and let cool to lukewarm. Add 2 cups **powdered sugar** and beat until smooth.

Pork Sausage Cake

1   pound uncooked bulk pork sausage
1   cup raisins
1   cup chopped walnuts or pecans
1½   cups **each** granulated sugar and firmly packed brown sugar
2   large eggs
3   cups all-purpose flour
2   teaspoons pumpkin pie spice
1½   teaspoons ground ginger
1   teaspoon baking powder
1   cup water
2   teaspoons instant coffee granules or powder
1   teaspoon baking soda
     Pecan halves and candied cherries (optional)

In a large bowl, mix sausage, raisins, walnuts, sugars, and eggs. Mix flour, pumpkin pie spice, ginger, and baking powder. Stir together water, instant coffee, and baking soda. Add flour mixture and liquid alternately to sausage mixture. Pour into a greased, flour-dusted 10-inch tube pan or 12-cup fluted tube pan.

Bake in 350° oven until a wooden pick inserted in center comes out clean (about 1 hour and 25 minutes; lightly cover cake with foil if it begins to brown excessively). Let cool in pan for 10 minutes, then turn out onto a rack to cool completely. If made ahead, wrap airtight and freeze; let thaw unwrapped.

To serve, decorate with pecans and cherries, if desired. Cut into very thin slices. Makes 12 to 16 servings.

Seed Cake

¾   cup (⅜ lb.) butter or margarine, at room temperature
2   cups granulated sugar
4   large eggs
4   teaspoons grated lemon peel
3   cups all-purpose flour
2½ teaspoons baking powder
½   teaspoon ground nutmeg
1   cup milk
1   tablespoon **each** caraway seeds, poppy seeds, and anise seeds
    Powdered sugar

In large bowl of an electric mixer, beat butter and granulated sugar until fluffy. Add eggs, 1 at a time, beating well after each addition. Stir in lemon peel.

Stir together flour, baking powder, and nutmeg. Add dry ingredients to butter mixture alternately with milk; blend well.

Spoon about ¼ of the batter into a greased, flour-dusted 10-inch tube pan or 12-cup fluted-tube cake pan. Scatter caraway seeds on top. Cover with ⅓ of the remaining batter and sprinkle with poppy seeds. Top with half the remaining batter and sprinkle with anise seeds; spoon in remaining batter and smooth top.

Bake in a 350° oven until a wooden pick inserted in center comes out clean (about 1 hour). Let cool in pan for 10 minutes, then turn out onto a rack to cool completely. If made ahead, wrap airtight and freeze; let thaw unwrapped.

To serve, dust with powdered sugar and cut into thin slices. Makes 12 to 16 servings.

Easy-going Holiday Suppers

Casual good cheer reigns when you put on one of these easy-going holiday finger feasts for your friends or family. One supper features fresh cracked crab and artichokes to dunk in melted butter; the other is a hearty beef rib feast that ends with a rich, spicy, zabaglione-topped pudding. Both meals are easy on the cook; many of the foods can be prepared ahead or even purchased already cooked.

So all guests can reach the food easily, seat no more than six per table; duplicate the setup for more people. To get everybody into the spirit, hand out large napkins or bibs and provide finger bowls with small damp towels.

MENU #1
*Cracked Crab with
Melted Butter
Cooked Artichoke Halves
French or Sourdough Bread
Butter
Sauvignon Blanc or
Pinot Chardonnay
Mincemeat Tarts
Rum Eggnog*

Buy the crab cracked, cook the artichokes the day before, and buy the tarts and eggnog. Instead of crab, you could serve large boiled shrimp in the shell.

Cracked Crab with Melted Butter

Allow about 1½ pounds (or 1 small) **cooked Dungeness crab** in the shell for each serving. Have crabs cleaned and cracked at the market.

At home, rinse crab under cool running water to remove loose bits of shell. Pile crab into a wide serving bowl; if desired, rinse crab backs and lay on top as garnish. Serve, or cover and refrigerate for up to 6 hours.

Melt about ⅓ cup **butter** or margarine for each serving. As you shell crab to eat, dip meat into warm melted butter.

Cooked Artichoke Halves

Select 4 to 6 very large **artichokes**. Break off small outer leaves (bracts), then cut off thorny tips of artichokes with a knife. Use scissors to snip thorns from remaining outer leaves. Peel stem and trim off the end. Cut each artichoke in half lengthwise and cut out the fuzzy "choke." At once, drop artichokes in acid water to cover (2 tablespoons **vinegar** for each 4 cups **water**).

When all artichokes are trimmed, place them in a 5- to 6-quart pan. Add 8 cups **water**, 3 tablespoons **olive oil**, 2 tablespoons **vinegar**, ½ teaspoon *each* **dry thyme leaves** and **dry rosemary**, 1 teaspoon **mustard seeds**, 2 **bay leaves**, ½ teaspoon **whole black peppercorns**, 8 **whole allspice**, and 6 **whole cloves**. Cover and bring to a boil, then reduce heat and simmer until artichoke bottoms are just tender when pierced (30 to 40 minutes).

Lift from water; serve hot or at room temperature. Or let cool, then cover and refrigerate; bring to room temperature to serve. To eat, dip leaves and bottom into the melted butter served with the crab. Makes 4 to 6 servings.

MENU #2
*Roast Ribs
Roasted Potato Balls
Edible-pod Peas
Black Bread   Butter
Cabernet Sauvignon or Barbera
Steamed Pudding with
Zabaglione Sauce
Brandy   Nuts in Shells*

Cutting the potatoes is the most time-consuming chore, but you can do it the day before. Make the steamed pudding at least a day ahead, or buy it.

Because the beef ribs tend to smoke when cooking, be sure your kitchen venting system is working.

For a showy presentation, whip up the zabaglione at the table over an alcohol flame, then pour it over the warm pudding.

Roast Ribs

Have your butcher prepare 9 to 10 pounds **beef ribs** in large sections (6 to 7 ribs per piece). Mix together 2 teaspoons *each* **dry rosemary**, **dry thyme leaves**, and **rubbed sage**. Rub herbs over all surfaces of ribs. Sprinkle lightly with **salt** and **pepper**.

Arrange ribs in a single layer on racks in roasting pans (you need 2 pans, each at least 12 by 15 inches); ribs may have to overlap slightly. Roast in a 500° oven until meat between ribs is done to your liking (cut to test); allow 25 minutes for rare, 35 minutes for well done. Fat from meat smokes as ribs cook, so have venting system on high. Cut between ribs to serve. Makes 6 servings.

Roasted Potato Balls

Peel 12 pounds large **thin-skinned potatoes**. Cut into ¾- to 1-inch balls with a melon baller, or cut into ¾- to 1-inch cubes with a knife; save scraps for soup or to pan-fry. To prevent darkening, immerse potatoes in water as you cut them. (At this point, you may cover and refrigerate until next day.)

Pour ¾ cup (⅜ lb.) melted **butter** or extra-virgin olive oil into 2 rimmed 10- by 15-inch baking pans. Drain potatoes, add to pans, and stir to coat with fat. To each pan, add a 6- to 8-inch sprig of **fresh rosemary** or 1 teaspoon dry rosemary. Bake in a 500° oven until potatoes are golden brown and tender when pierced (about 1 hour). Shake pans occasionally to turn potatoes, or turn them gently with a wide spatula (stirring breaks off the brown surface). If made ahead, keep warm for up to 45 minutes. Turn into warmed serving dishes and season to taste with **salt**. Makes 6 servings.

Edible-pod Peas

Remove ends and strings from 1½ pounds **edible-pod peas** (use Chinese pea pods, also called snow or sugar peas; or use sugar-snap peas). Rinse peas. Bring to a boil enough **water** to cover peas; add peas to water and cook, uncovered, just until bright green and tender-crisp to bite (1 to 2 minutes). Drain at once and immerse in **cold water**, mixing gently to cool peas. Drain and serve. If made ahead, cover and refrigerate until next day. Makes 6 servings.

Steamed Pudding with Zabaglione Sauce

Prepare **steamed pudding** for 6 from your favorite recipe or from the Persimmon Pudding recipe on page 243, or purchase it. Heat to serve.

To make the sauce, put 4 large **egg yolks**, ¼ cup **dry white wine**, 3 tablespoons **sugar**, and 1 tablespoon **brandy** in a round-bottomed pan (or a metal bowl that can be set over direct heat—hold it steady with a potholder). Using a wire whisk, beat ingredients over direct heat (medium on a stove or an alcohol flame) until sauce is about tripled in volume and holds an impression when whisk is lifted (3 to 4 minutes). Pour warm sauce over pudding. Makes 6 servings.

*A **high-spirited evening's in store** when you put together an easy-on-the-cook feast like this one, which features fresh cracked crab and artichokes to dunk in butter.*

Holiday Potluck Supper

■

One easy way to gather friends together for a dinner party is to stage a potluck. Our menu provides a hearty and balanced supper for 12 to 15. As the host or hostess, you make the main course—a roast turkey with savory stuffing. Ask each guest to select one of the accompaniments; you supply the recipe. For the salad, simply ask someone to bring mixed greens with a favorite vinaigrette dressing. All dishes are easy to make ahead and transport, and all can be completed or reheated at your house with very little fuss.

MENU

Shrimp Cheese Stack
Turkey with Stuffing
on the Outside
Brown Giblet Gravy
Mashed Potato Casserole
Savory Green Beans & Tomatoes
Mixed Greens with Vinaigrette
Spicy Frozen Pumpkin Squares
Chilled Dry White Wine
Coffee

Shrimp Cheese Stack

2 *large packages (8 oz.*
   each*) cream cheese, at*
   room temperature

2 *tablespoons*
   Worcestershire

¼ *teaspoon grated*
   lemon peel

1 *tablespoon lemon juice*

½ *cup thinly sliced green*
   onions (including tops)

⅛ *teaspoon liquid hot*
   pepper seasoning

1 *bottle (12 oz.) tomato-*
   based chili sauce

1 *tablespoon prepared*
   horseradish

¾ *pound small cooked*
   shrimp
   Assorted crackers

In a bowl, beat cream cheese, Worcestershire, lemon peel, lemon juice, onions, and hot pepper seasoning until smooth. Spread on a 10- to 12-inch rimmed serving plate. (At this point, you may cover and refrigerate until next day.)

Just before serving, stir together chili sauce and horseradish; spread over cheese layer. Top with shrimp and serve with crackers. Makes 12 to 15 servings.

Turkey with Stuffing on the Outside

1 *turkey (14 to 24 lbs.),*
   thawed if frozen
   Salt and pepper
   About ¼ cup (⅛ lb.)
   butter or margarine,
   at room temperature
   Homemade Bread
   Stuffing (recipe follows)
   Brown Giblet Gravy
   (recipe follows)

Remove turkey neck and giblets; reserve for gravy. Rinse turkey inside and out; pat dry. Sprinkle cavities of bird with salt and pepper. Place untrussed bird, breast down, on a V-shaped rack in a roasting pan (at least 11 by 15 inches). Skewer neck skin against back. Rub all over with some of the butter.

Roast in a 325° oven, uncovered; allow 15 minutes per pound for turkeys weighing up to 16 pounds, 12 minutes per pound for birds 16 pounds and over. Baste turkey several times with butter during roasting. When bird is done, a meat thermometer inserted in thickest part of thigh

(not touching bone) should register 185°F; internal temperature of breast should be 165°F.

About 1½ hours before turkey is due to be done, remove from oven. Tilt rack, draining all juices from bird, then lift bird and rack to another pan. Scrape all drippings from roasting pan and reserve.

Lift turkey from rack and place, breast up, directly in roasting pan. Rub breast with more butter. Return to oven; meanwhile, prepare broth for Brown Giblet Gravy (recipe follows). Continue to roast turkey; spoon Homemade Bread Stuffing around bird 45 minutes to 1 hour before it's done (when turkey is done, stuffing should be heated through and crusty on top).

Skim and discard all fat from reserved pan juices and use juices in Brown Giblet Gravy. Before carving, let turkey and stuffing stand for about 20 minutes, draped with foil. (It can stand longer if necessary.) To serve, lift turkey to a large platter and place stuffing alongside. Serve with hot gravy. Makes 12 to 15 servings.

Homemade Bread Stuffing. Melt ¼ cup (⅛ lb.) **butter** or margarine in a wide frying pan over medium heat. Add 3 large **onions**, chopped; cook, stirring, until soft. Then add ½ cup (¼ lb.) **butter** or margarine, 1½ teaspoons **dry marjoram leaves**, and ¾ teaspoon *each* **dry rubbed sage**, **dry thyme leaves**, and **pepper**. Set aside.

In a 5-quart container, combine 3 quarts day-old **whole wheat or white bread cubes**, 2 cups chopped **celery**, and ½ cup chopped **parsley**. Add onion mixture; toss to coat bread. Season with **salt**. Makes about 3 quarts.

Brown Giblet Gravy. Melt ¼ cup (⅛ lb.) **butter** or margarine in a 3-quart pan; add **turkey liver** and cook, turning as needed, just until firm. Remove from pan and chop.

Thinly slice **turkey heart and gizzard**; add to pan along with 2 **carrots**, finely chopped; 1 **onion**, finely chopped; and ½ cup finely chopped **parsley**. Cook over high heat, stirring, until mixture is very well browned. Pour in ¼ cup **dry sherry** or dry vermouth; boil until liquid has evaporated.

Add **turkey neck** and 6 cups **regular-strength chicken broth**. Bring to a boil; then reduce heat, cover, and simmer for 1½ hours.

Pour broth mixture through a wire strainer set over a bowl; discard residue and return liquid to pan. Pour in reserved **juices from roast turkey** (skimmed of fat). Bring to a full boil. Meanwhile, stir together 4 to 6 tablespoons **cornstarch** and 6 tablespoons **water**. When broth mixture comes to a boil, stir in as much of the cornstarch mixture as needed to make a medium-thick gravy. When gravy is thickened, stir in chopped turkey liver. Makes about 6 cups.

Mashed Potato Casserole

4½ to 5 pounds russet
      potatoes (about 8 large
      potatoes)
1   large package (8 oz.)
      cream cheese, at room
      temperature
1   cup sour cream
2   teaspoons garlic salt
½   teaspoon pepper
¼   cup (⅛ lb.) butter or
      margarine
      Paprika

Peel potatoes. In a 5-quart pan, bring about 2 inches water to a boil; add potatoes, cover, and boil until tender throughout when pierced (about 40 minutes). Drain, then mash well.

In small bowl of an electric mixer, beat cream cheese and sour cream until smooth; gradually add to potatoes, beating until smoothly blended. Beat in garlic salt and pepper. Turn mixture into a buttered shallow 3- to 4-quart casserole. Dot with ¼ cup butter; sprinkle lightly with paprika. Cover with lid or foil. (At this point, you may refrigerate for up to 3 days; bring to room temperature before baking.)

Bake, covered, in a 400° oven until heated through (50 to 60 minutes). Makes 12 to 15 servings.

Savory Green Beans & Tomatoes

2½   pounds green or wax
      beans, cut into 2-inch
      pieces
4   large tomatoes
10   tablespoons (¼ lb. plus 2
      tablespoons) butter or
      margarine
1   large onion, chopped
½   pound mushrooms, sliced
3   cloves garlic, minced or
      pressed
1   teaspoon salt
1½   teaspoons **each** dry basil
      and dry oregano leaves
1½   cups soft bread crumbs
⅓   cup grated Parmesan
      cheese

Arrange beans on a steaming rack over 1 inch of boiling water; cover and steam until tender when pierced (8 to 10 minutes). Rinse in cold water, drain, and set aside. Cut tomatoes into thin wedges; set aside.

Melt ¼ cup of the butter in a wide frying pan over medium-high heat. Add onion, mushrooms, and ⅔ of the garlic. Cook, stirring, until onion is soft and all liquid has evaporated. Stir in salt and 1 teaspoon *each* of the basil and oregano. Combine mushroom mixture with beans and tomatoes; transfer to a shallow 3-quart baking dish.

Melt remaining 6 tablespoons butter in a small pan. Stir in remaining garlic, bread crumbs, cheese, and remaining ½ teaspoon basil and oregano. Cover with lid or foil. (At this point, you may refrigerate beans and topping separately for up to 2 days.)

Sprinkle crumb mixture over beans. Bake, covered, in a 400° oven for 20 minutes (30 minutes if refrigerated); uncover and bake until heated through (about 5 more minutes). Makes 12 to 15 servings.

Spicy Frozen Pumpkin Squares

2½   cups gingersnap cookie
      crumbs (about 45
      2¼-inch cookies)
½   cup (¼ lb.) butter or
      margarine, melted
2   quarts vanilla ice cream,
      softened
1   can (1 lb.) pumpkin
⅔   cup firmly packed brown
      sugar
½   teaspoon salt
1   teaspoon **each** ground
      cinnamon, ginger, and
      cloves
½   cup chopped nuts

In a 9- by 13-inch baking pan, stir together cookie crumbs and butter. Press evenly over bottom and 1 inch up sides.

In a 4- to 5-quart bowl, combine ice cream, pumpkin, sugar, salt, cinnamon, ginger, and cloves; beat until well blended. Pour mixture into crust; sprinkle with nuts. Cover tightly with foil and freeze for at least 8 hours or up to 1 week. To serve, let stand at room temperature for 20 minutes; then cut into squares. Makes 12 to 15 servings.

Children's Christmas Party

A friendly caterpillar, a drift of fluffy white snowflakes, and sugarplum visions are the imaginative elements in this lively Christmas party for 10 children. The sinuous caterpillar sandwich contains your choice of two simple fillings; both can be made a day ahead. Bite-size balls of rich hazelnut or almond paste dipped in dark chocolate make the sugarplums; the hot milk drink is spiced with cinnamon and orange peel (offer a fruit punch, too, if you like). Make popcorn to fill the role of snowflakes; purchase cellophane-wrapped candy canes. Alongside the sweets, offer a basket of your young guests' favorite fruits—perhaps bananas, apples, pears, and easy-to-peel tangerines.

MENU
Caterpillar Sandwich with Ham
or Tuna Filling
Chocolate-dipped Sugarplums
Popcorn Snowflakes
Candy Canes
Spiced Milk   Fruit Punch
Fruit Basket

Caterpillar Sandwich

10	small soft dinner rolls, **each** about 3 inches in diameter
	Ham Salad or Tuna-Carrot Salad (recipes follow)
21	pitted ripe olives or seedless grapes
2	small celery sticks

Split each roll in half horizontally; fill rolls with your choice of ham or tuna salad. Arrange filled rolls in an "S" shape on a serving tray. Spear olives on wooden picks; push 2 olives into either side of each roll for legs (or simply set olives alongside rolls). Push remaining olive, cut in halves, into front roll for eyes. For antennae, push celery sticks into front roll. You may assemble the sandwich up to 1 hour ahead, then cover it with a damp cloth and hold at room temperature until serving time. Makes 10 servings.

Ham Salad. In a bowl, blend 2 cups **ground cooked ham**, ½ cup **mayonnaise**, ⅓ cup **sweet pickle relish**, and 1 teaspoon *each* **prepared mustard** and **Worcestershire**. If made ahead, cover and refrigerate until next day. Makes 2 cups.

Tuna-Carrot Salad. In a bowl, combine 1 can (9¼ oz.) **solid-pack tuna**, drained and flaked; ½ cup *each* chopped **sweet pickles** and **mayonnaise**; and ¾ cup coarsely shredded peeled **carrot**. Stir gently to blend. If made ahead, cover and refrigerate until next day. Makes 2 cups.

Chocolate-dipped Sugarplums

1	pound (3½ cups) hazelnuts, whole or in large pieces; or 3 cups whole blanched almonds
2	cups powdered sugar
5	to 6 tablespoons egg whites (whites of about 3 large eggs)
	About 6 ounces semisweet chocolate chips

Spread hazelnuts in a shallow baking pan. Toast in a 350° oven until pale golden beneath skins (10 to 15 minutes), shaking pan occasionally. (If using almonds, toast for 8 to 10 minutes.) Let nuts cool slightly, then pour into a dishcloth and fold cloth to enclose. Rub briskly to remove as much of skins as possible (omit this step if using almonds). Lift nuts from cloth and let cool.

Coarsely chop nuts. Then, in a food processor or blender, grind nuts, about ⅓ at a time, until mealy.

Return all nuts to food processor and add sugar and 5 tablespoons egg whites. Process until a paste forms, adding more egg whites as needed. (Or mix ground nuts with egg whites and sugar with a heavy-duty mixer on low speed; or knead by hand until mixture sticks together.) If mixture is too soft to shape, wrap in plastic wrap and refrigerate for about 1 hour.

Roll nut paste into 1-inch balls; set 1 inch apart on wax paper–lined rimmed baking pans, pressing balls down to flatten bottoms slightly.

In the top of a double boiler over simmering water or in a small pan over lowest possible heat, stir chocolate chips just until melted. Dip each ball (by hand) into chocolate to cover top half; return to paper-lined pan, chocolate side up. Refrigerate, uncovered, until chocolate is set (about 30 minutes). If made ahead, cover and refrigerate for up to 1 week; let stand at room temperature for about 15 minutes before serving. Makes 3 to 4 dozen.

Spiced Milk

10	cups milk
3	thin strips orange peel (orange part only), **each** about 4 inches long
2	cinnamon sticks, **each** 3 to 4 inches long

In a 3- to 4-quart pan, combine milk, orange peel and cinnamon sticks. Heat over low heat, uncovered, stirring occasionally, until warm (do not boil). Makes 10 servings.

From the land of "let's pretend" comes this high-spirited Christmas party just for children. A quirky caterpillar sandwich is surrounded by candy canes, popcorn "snowflakes," and plump, chocolaty sugarplums. Add festive cups of warm spiced milk, and watch your group of hungry youngsters eat it all up!

No-cook Holiday Smörgåsbord

■

In Sweden, the smörgåsbord (which translates loosely as "sandwich table") is a lavish feast of regional delicacies; weeks of cooking might go into its preparation. Here, though, we offer a streamlined version for the busy holiday season. The secret to its ease of preparation lies in the shopping. If you take advantage of the selection of ready-to-eat Scandinavian foods in supermarkets, delicatessens, and gourmet stores, the result is an elegant and practically effortless holiday smörgåsbord.

Our buffet suits many occasions, from brunch to dinner or late supper; the amounts we suggest will serve 24 guests for dinner.

Serving buffet style is customary, though you may certainly set up tables for sit-down dining. You may want to offer the coffee and dessert from a sideboard. In Sweden, a different plate is used for each course; we suggest a smörgåsbord sampler with everything on one plate.

MENU

Fish
Herring in Spices
Herring in Sour Cream
Danish Sprats
Smoked Salmon with
Egg & Chives
Fresh Shrimp

Meats
Meatballs and/or
Assorted Cold Cuts
Baked Ham with Crab Apples

Salads
Pickled Fresh Cucumbers
Coleslaw with Apple

Cheeses
Norwegian Gjetost
Jarlsberg
Danish Blue

Breads
Thin Crispbread
Lefse

Condiments
Lingonberries or Whole Berry
Cranberry Sauce
Whole or Sliced Pickled Beets
Mustards

Dessert
Coffee
Cookies   Apples

Fish. Buy 2 jars (about 12 oz. *each*) herring in spices, 2 jars (about 12 oz. *each*) herring in sour cream, and 2 tins (about 16 oz. *total*) Danish sprats, also called Danish smoked sardines. You'll also need about 1 pound thinly sliced smoked salmon (lox). Next to it, arrange mounds of finely chopped onion and sieved hard-cooked egg yolks and whites. Guests pile the onion and egg on a salmon slice and then roll it up to eat out of hand.

Buy 2 pounds medium-size shrimp, cooked, shelled, and deveined. Skewer shrimp with wooden picks and mound in a glass bowl over cracked ice.

Meats. Buy 5 to 6 pounds Swedish-style meatballs at a delicatessen; heat meatballs in their own gravy. Lift out meatballs with a slotted spoon and transfer them to a chafing dish or serving bowl on an electric warming tray. Blend 1 cup sour cream into the gravy; heat (do not boil), then spoon over meatballs. Serve warm, garnished with finely snipped chives; offer wooden picks for spearing.

Assorted cold cuts can be served in addition to (or in place of) the meatballs; include at least 24 slices Danish salami, 12 slices head cheese, and 24 slices smoked beef. If you're offering cold cuts instead of meatballs, you will need to double or triple these amounts.

Buy a 5-pound or larger canned ham or a fully cooked whole or half butt or shank ham. Bake as the package directs (a day in advance if you wish). Serve warm or cold, garnished with spiced crab apples.

Salads. Buy 1 quart pickled fresh cucumbers and 2 quarts coleslaw; at serving time, garnish coleslaw with sliced red-skinned apple, coated with lemon juice to prevent darkening.

Cheeses. Purchase 2 pounds *each* of Danish blue and Jarlsberg, and 1 pound of Norwegian gjetost.

Breads. Buy 2 packages (7 to 8 oz. *each*) thin crispbread and 2 packages (13 oz. *each*) lefse (or substitute an equivalent amount of Armenian cracker bread).

Condiments. Buy 1 or 2 jars (14½ oz. *each*) lingonberries, or 1 or 2 cans (1 lb. *each*) whole berry cranberry sauce. You'll need 2 cans (1 lb. *each*) whole or sliced pickled beets. For mustards, serve a selection of your favorites—perhaps a coarse mustard, a spicy brown variety, and a sweet-and-hot mustard.

Dessert. You need about 1½ pounds Danish butter cookies and a basket filled with about 24 apples.

Christmas Carolers' Soup Supper

After a jolly round of door-to-door caroling, warm up red cheeks and cold fingers with a simple, delicious supper of hearty vegetable-sausage soup and buttered dark bread. Up to 16 hungry singers can make a satisfying meal from our menu; for a smaller group, just cut the soup recipe in half and store one of the sturdy pumpernickel loaves in the freezer.

With a little advance planning, you can have this supper on the table within minutes after you step in from outside. Both soup and bread can be completed well ahead of time; the simple accompaniments—fruit, cheese, and raw vegetables to nibble—require almost no preparation.

MENU

Green Bean & Sausage Soup
Radishes & Cucumber Spears
Molasses Pumpernickel Bread
Butter
Jarlsberg Cheese
Grapes & Crisp Apples
Cider or Beer

Green Bean & Sausage Soup

8   slices bacon, cut into ½-inch pieces

4   medium-size onions, chopped

3   quarts regular-strength chicken broth

8   medium-size thin-skinned potatoes (about 3 lbs. **total**), peeled and cut into ½-inch cubes

4   medium-size carrots, thinly sliced

½   cup chopped parsley

2   teaspoons dry dill weed

1   teaspoon dry marjoram leaves

½   teaspoon white pepper

2   pounds green beans, cut into 1-inch lengths

2   pounds smoked bratwurst or kielbasa (Polish sausage), thinly sliced

In a 10- to 12-quart pan, cook bacon over medium heat until crisp. Lift out, drain, and set aside; discard all but 1 tablespoon of the drippings.

Add onions to drippings in pan and cook, stirring occasionally, until soft (about 10 minutes). Stir in broth, potatoes, carrots, parsley, dill weed, marjoram, and white pepper. Bring to a boil over high heat; reduce heat, cover, and simmer until potatoes mash easily (about 30 minutes).

With a slotted spoon, lift out half the vegetables; transfer to a food processor or blender. Whirl until smooth, then return to pan. (At this point, you may let cool, then cover and refrigerate until next day. Reheat to simmering to continue.)

Add green beans and bratwurst to soup. Bring to a boil; reduce heat and simmer, uncovered, stirring occasionally, until beans are tender (about 15 minutes). Skim and discard fat. Makes 16 servings.

Molasses Pumpernickel Bread

2   tablespoons butter or margarine

2   cups milk

1½   teaspoons salt

½   cup dark molasses

2   packages active dry yeast

⅓   cup firmly packed dark brown sugar

½   cup warm water (about 110°F)

1½   cups whole bran cereal

3   cups rye flour
     About 4½ cups all-purpose flour

1   large egg yolk beaten with 1 tablespoon water

Melt butter in a small pan over medium heat; stir in milk, salt, and molasses. Set aside.

In a large bowl, sprinkle yeast and sugar over water; let stand until bubbly (5 to 15 minutes). Add milk mixture, bran cereal, rye flour, and 2 cups of the all-purpose flour; beat until well blended.

With a heavy spoon, stir in about 1½ cups more all-purpose flour to make a stiff dough. Turn out onto a floured board and knead until smooth and satiny (10 to 15 minutes), adding more all-purpose flour as needed to prevent sticking.

Place dough in a greased bowl; turn over to grease top. Cover and let rise in a warm place until doubled (about 1½ hours).

Punch dough down, divide into 2 equal portions, and knead each briefly to release air. Then shape each into a smooth ball; flatten slightly. Place each loaf on a greased baking sheet, at least 10 by 15 inches. Cover and let rise in a warm place until almost doubled (about 40 minutes).

With a razor blade or sharp floured knife, make ½-inch-deep slashes on tops of loaves, forming a tick-tack-toe design. Brush tops and sides with egg yolk mixture.

Bake in a 350° oven until bread is richly browned and sounds hollow when tapped (30 to 35 minutes). Transfer to racks and let cool. Makes 2 loaves.

Festive Dessert Buffet

Dazzle your holiday guests with a sweet-lover's dream: a sumptuous buffet that's *all* desserts.

The star of the show is Bûche de Noël—the traditional French Yule log, a rolled chocolate sponge cake filled and frosted with mocha buttercream. Offer two other cakes as well: a date and apricot fruitcake and a walnut torte layered with jam and whipped cream. Add our simple Chocolate Truffles and an array of pretty party cookies, and you have a selection that's sure to tempt any sweet tooth.

Our menu easily serves up to 24 guests. You can bake and freeze all the cookies well ahead of time. Make the fruitcake at least a few days or up to 2 months ahead; its flavor mellows as it ages. The Bûche de Noël can be completed a day in advance; for a party of 24, you'll need to make two bûches (each serves about 12).

Sparkling cranberry cocktail and good hot coffee help balance the sweetness of the desserts—but if you want to go all out for richness, try our Praline Eggnog (or keep it in mind for another holiday get-together).

MENU
Bûche de Noël
Western Fruitcake
Walnut-Rum Torte
Red & Green Apples
Finnish Ribbon Cakes
(page 11)
Spritz (page 10)
Swedish Ginger Thins (page 21)
Almond Crescents (page 7)
Chocolate Truffles
Sparkling Cranberry
Blush Cocktail
Coffee   Praline Eggnog

Bûche de Noël
(Make 2 for the party)

6   large eggs, separated
¾   cup sugar
6   ounces semisweet chocolate, melted and cooled
    Basic Cooked Buttercream (recipe follows)
1½ teaspoons instant coffee granules or powder
¼   cup unsweetened cocoa or ⅓ cup ground sweet chocolate
¼   cup boiling water
    Holly leaves
    Red candied cherries

Butter a rimmed 10- by 15-inch baking pan, line with wax paper, and butter paper. Set aside.

In large bowl of an electric mixer, beat egg yolks and sugar until thick and lemon-colored. Blend in melted chocolate. Using clean, dry beaters, beat egg whites until they hold moist, distinct peaks; gently fold into chocolate mixture.

Pour batter into prepared pan; spread evenly. Bake in a 350° oven until surface of cake looks dry (12 to 14 minutes). Let cool in pan for 5 minutes, then turn out onto a large dishtowel. Peel off wax paper; trim off edges of cake. Place towel and cake on a large rack; let cool.

To fill and frost roll, set aside ½ cup of the buttercream. In a small bowl, stir together coffee, cocoa, and boiling water until smooth. Blend coffee mixture into remaining buttercream.

Spread cake with about half this mocha buttercream. Lift edge of cloth on a short end of cake, then gently guide cake into a smooth, tight roll. Refrigerate, wrapped in cloth, until chilled. Then unwrap and place on a serving tray, seam side down.

Neatly spread ends of log with reserved plain buttercream. Frost log with remaining mocha buttercream; lightly stroke icing the length of the log with the tines of a fork or tip of a knife to create a barklike pattern, swirling here and there to make "knots." Draw a tree-ring pattern on the ends of the log with a wooden pick dipped in a little of the mocha buttercream.

Decorate with a cluster of holly leaves and candied cherries. Refrigerate for at least 3 hours before serving. Makes about 12 servings.

Basic Cooked Buttercream. In small bowl of an electric mixer, beat 5 large **egg yolks** until thick and lemon-colored. Set aside. In a pan, blend ¾ cup **sugar** and ¼ cup **water**. Bring to a boil over high heat; then boil until syrup registers 232°F on a candy thermometer (syrup will spin a thread). Pour hot syrup into egg yolks in a thin, steady stream, beating constantly. Add 1 cup (½ lb.) **butter** (at room temperature); continue to beat until mixture is cool and fluffy. Cover and refrigerate until thick enough to spread well or for up to 3 weeks; stir well before using. Makes about 2½ cups.

Western Fruitcake
(Make 1 or 2 for the party)

1   package (8 oz.) pitted dates, quartered
2   cups quartered dried apricots
1   cup golden raisins
1   cup **each** whole blanched almonds and walnut pieces

1   cup green or red candied
    cherries
¾   cup **each** all-purpose
    flour and sugar
½   teaspoon baking powder
3   large eggs
1   teaspoon vanilla
    Rum or brandy
    (optional)

Butter a 5- by 9-inch loaf pan; line
with baking parchment or wax paper,
then butter paper. Set pan aside.

In a large bowl, combine dates,
apricots, raisins, almonds, walnuts,
and cherries. In another bowl, stir
together flour, sugar, and baking
powder; add to fruit mixture and
mix evenly.

Beat together eggs and vanilla.
Stir thoroughly into fruit mixture.
Spoon batter into prepared pan and
spread evenly; press batter into
corners of pan.

Bake in a 300° oven until golden
brown (about 1½ hours). Let cool in
pan on a rack for 10 minutes, then
turn out of pan. Peel off paper and let
cake cool on rack.

Wrap in foil; refrigerate for at least
2 days or up to 2 months before serving. If desired, sprinkle top of cake
with 1 tablespoon rum or brandy
once a week. Makes 1 loaf.

Walnut-Rum Torte
(Make 1 or 2 for the party)

2   cups walnut pieces or
     whole blanched almonds
⅓   cup all-purpose flour
1   teaspoon baking powder
¼   teaspoon salt
12   large eggs, separated
1⅓   cups sugar
1½   cups whipping cream
     About ½ cup rum
     (optional)
     About 1 cup raspberry
     jam
     About ½ cup chopped
     walnuts or almonds

In a blender or food processor,
whirl the 2 cups walnuts until finely
ground, using on-off pulses; be care-

(Continued on page 232)

This luscious array of sweets *is as pretty as it is delicious. Shown
(clockwise from top) are Walnut-Rum Torte, traditional Bûche de Noël,
chocolate-dipped Spritz cookies, Western Fruitcake, Almond Crescents
and Finnish Ribbon Cakes, additional Spritz cookies and Swedish Ginger
Thins, and glorious Chocolate Truffles.*

ful not to overgrind. Mix ground nuts with flour, baking powder, and salt; set aside.

In large bowl of an electric mixer, beat egg whites on high speed until foamy. Gradually add ¼ cup of the sugar and beat just until whites hold moist peaks (about 2 minutes).

In another large bowl, beat egg yolks on high speed until thick and lemon-colored. Gradually add ¾ cup of the sugar, beating until mixture holds soft peaks (about 8 minutes). Sprinkle nut mixture over beaten yolks and fold to blend; then gently fold in beaten whites.

Divide batter equally between 2 buttered, flour-dusted 9-inch cheesecake pans (at least 3 inches deep) with removable bottoms. Bake in a 350° oven until cakes spring back when gently pressed in center and begin to pull slightly from pan sides (about 35 minutes). Remove from oven and let cool thoroughly in pans on racks.

Run a knife around pan sides; then carefully remove sides. With a sharp serrated knife, trim off uneven and rough edges. Cut layers in half horizontally. In a bowl, beat cream with remaining ⅓ cup sugar until it holds stiff peaks; set aside.

Cut a 9-inch cardboard circle and cover it with foil. Place 1 of the layers, cut side up, on foil-covered circle. Spoon about 2 tablespoons of rum (if used) evenly over cake layer; spread about ⅓ cup of raspberry jam over layer, then spread ¼ of whipped cream over jam.

Place a second layer of cake on top of whipped cream. Repeat layering with rum, jam, and whipped cream. Top with another layer of cake. Continue until all layers are stacked; place top cake layer cut side down.

Spread top of cake with remaining whipped cream; sprinkle with chopped walnuts. Cut into wedges to serve. Makes 12 to 16 servings.

Chocolate Truffles

12 ounces semisweet chocolate, coarsely chopped

6 tablespoons whipping cream
   About 6 tablespoons unsweetened cocoa or ground sweet chocolate

Place chocolate and cream in a 2- to 3-quart pan over lowest possible heat. (If heat is too high, chocolate will separate.) Stir constantly until chocolate is melted and well blended with cream. Cover and refrigerate just until mixture is firm enough to hold its shape (about 40 minutes).

Spread cocoa on a small plate or a piece of wax paper. Using your fingers or 2 spoons, quickly shape about 1 teaspoon of the chocolate mixture at a time into a ball; then roll in cocoa until completely coated. Arrange in a single layer in a container. Cover and refrigerate until firm or for up to 2 weeks; serve at room temperature. Makes 2 to 2½ dozen.

Praline Eggnog

1¼ cups sugar

6 cups milk

3 cinnamon sticks, **each** about 3 inches long

1 vanilla bean (about 7 inches long), split in half lengthwise

2 cups whipping cream

12 large eggs
   Ground nutmeg

In a 3- to 4-quart pan, melt half the sugar over high heat, stirring constantly until it is a golden liquid; lumps will melt as you stir. Do not let syrup scorch. Remove from heat; at

once add milk, cinnamon sticks, and vanilla bean (mixture will sputter).

Return pan to medium heat and stir until caramelized sugar is dissolved. Cover and refrigerate until cold (at least 3 hours) or until next day. Remove spices. Rinse vanilla bean; reserve for other uses.

Beat cream until it holds soft peaks; set aside. Beat eggs with remaining sugar until about tripled in volume. Using a wire whisk, blend eggs and half the cream into caramelized milk. Pour into a 4- to 5-quart punch bowl, top with remaining cream, and sprinkle with nutmeg. Serve cold. Makes 24 servings, about ⅔ cup each.

Sparkling Cranberry Blush Cocktail

About 1⅓ cups thawed frozen cranberry juice concentrate

4 bottles (about 25 oz. **each**) or 3 quarts sparkling apple juice or cider, chilled

12 thin lemon slices, halved

Pour cranberry concentrate and apple juice into a punch bowl or several pitchers. Ladle into punch cups or pour into champagne glasses; garnish each serving with a lemon. Makes 24 servings, ½ cup each.

Christmas Eve Family Supper

A cozy and comforting oven-baked meal reflects the spirit of a close-knit family Christmas Eve. The aroma of baking polenta and sausage fills the kitchen while you put together a simple green salad. For an extra-special dessert, make Chestnut Clouds—meringues topped with chestnut cream, served atop orange-scented custard. Or, if you prefer a simpler finale, offer a refreshing lemon sorbet and your favorite purchased or homemade cookies.

MENU

*Oven Polenta & Baked Sausage
with Sweet Red Peppers
& Mushrooms*
Sicilian Green Salad
Chestnut Clouds
Chianti or Gewürztraminer
Sparkling Water with Lemon

Oven Polenta & Baked Sausage with Sweet Red Peppers & Mushrooms

- 5 *large red bell peppers, stemmed, seeded, and cut into large slices*
- 3/4 *pound mushrooms, thickly sliced*
- 1 1/2 *to 2 pounds mild or hot Italian sausages*
- 5 *cups regular-strength chicken broth*
- 1 1/2 *cups polenta (Italian-style cornmeal) or yellow cornmeal*
- 1 *small onion, chopped*
- 1/4 *cup (1/8 lb.) butter or margarine, cut into small pieces*
- 2 *cups (8 oz.) shredded jack cheese*

Spread bell peppers and mushrooms in an even layer in a shallow 9- by 13-inch oval or rectangular baking dish. Lay sausages on vegetables. Bake in a 350° oven until sausages are lightly browned and no longer pink in center (cut to test), about 50 to 60 minutes; after 10 to 15 minutes, stir vegetables to moisten with pan drippings.

Meanwhile, in another shallow 9- by 13-inch rectangular or oval baking dish, stir together broth, polenta, onion, and butter. Place in oven alongside sausage mixture. Bake, uncovered, until liquid is absorbed (45 to 50 minutes). Remove polenta from oven and sprinkle with cheese.

Serve polenta, sausages, and vegetables from baking dishes; or, if desired, transfer to a large platter. Makes 4 to 6 servings.

Sicilian Green Salad

- 1 *head romaine, rinsed and patted dry*
- 2 *oranges, peeled, white membranes removed*
- 1 *can (2 1/4 oz.) sliced ripe olives, drained well*
- 1/4 *cup orange juice*
- 2 *teaspoons red wine vinegar*
- 1/2 *teaspoon salt*
- 1/4 *teaspoon paprika*
- 1/4 *cup olive oil or salad oil*

Tear romaine into bite-size pieces and place in a large bowl. Thinly slice oranges crosswise; place oranges and olives atop romaine. In a jar, combine orange juice, vinegar, salt, paprika, and oil; shake to blend well. Pour over salad and toss lightly to coat. Makes 6 servings.

Chestnut Clouds

- 4 *large eggs, separated*
- 2/3 *cup sugar*
- 1 *teaspoon vanilla*
- 2 *cups milk*
- 2 *tablespoons orange-flavored liqueur*
- 1/2 *teaspoon grated orange peel*
- 1/4 *teaspoon cream of tartar*
- 1/2 *cup whipping cream*
- 1 *small can (about 8 3/4 oz., or 3/4 cup) chestnut spread*
- *Thin strands of orange peel*

Place egg yolks in top of a double boiler with 1/3 cup of the sugar and vanilla; mix thoroughly. In a 1- to 2-quart pan, bring milk to scalding over medium-high heat; gradually stir into egg mixture. Place double boiler over simmering water and cook, stirring constantly, until custard coats a metal spoon in a smooth, velvety layer (10 to 15 minutes). Stir over ice water to cool. Stir in liqueur and grated orange peel. If made ahead, cover and refrigerate for up to 1 day.

In large bowl of an electric mixer, combine egg whites and cream of tartar; beat until foamy. Gradually add remaining 1/3 cup sugar and beat until mixture holds stiff, moist peaks. Bring about 1 inch of water just to simmering in a 10- to 12-inch frying pan over medium heat. Reduce heat so bubbles do not break the surface. With a large spoon and spatula, shape meringue into 5 or 6 large oval mounds and slide as many as will fit into pan of water. Cook, turning once, until meringues feel set when lightly touched (about 4 minutes). With a slotted spoon, lift out and drain on a rack. Blot off excess moisture with a paper towel. Repeat to cook remaining meringues. If made ahead, cover lightly and refrigerate for up to 1 day.

Shortly before serving, beat cream until it holds stiff peaks. Fold in chestnut spread. Pour equal portions of custard sauce into 5 or 6 rimmed dessert plates. Set a meringue on top of each; mound chestnut cream over meringues. Garnish with thin strands of orange peel. Makes 5 or 6 servings.

Christmas Morning Breakfast

On Christmas morning, wake up to a satisfying traditional breakfast that's as festive as it is easy to put together. Start the meal with chilled orange juice and champagne; then offer scrambled eggs, sautéed sliced ham, and warm Christmas bread filled with nuts and candied cherries. Alongside, provide a basket or pretty plate of juicy winter pears, apples, oranges, or other fruit in season. Freshly brewed coffee is always welcome, of course—but to make the breakfast as special as the occasion, serve mugs of our cinnamon-spiced New Mexican Hot Chocolate as well.

Only the sweet yeast bread requires advance preparation. You can bake it up to a month ahead and freeze, then reheat it.

MENU
Orange Juice   Champagne
Cherry-Almond
Christmas Wreath
Butter
Sautéed Ham Slices
Scrambled Eggs
Fresh Fruit in Season
New Mexican Hot Chocolate
Coffee

Cherry-Almond Christmas Wreath

1   *package active dry yeast*
¼   *cup warm water (about 110°F)*
½   *cup warm milk (about 110°F)*
3   *tablespoons sugar*
¼   *cup (⅛ lb.) butter or margarine, at room temperature*

1½ *teaspoons salt*
½   *teaspoon ground cardamom*
2   *large eggs*
1   *teaspoon grated lemon peel*
     About 3½ cups all-purpose flour
     Cherry-Almond Filling (recipe follows)
     Sugar Glaze (recipe follows)

In large bowl of an electric mixer, sprinkle yeast over water and let stand for about 5 minutes to soften. Stir in milk, sugar, butter, salt, cardamom, eggs, and lemon peel. Beat in 2 cups of the flour, a cup at a time. Then beat on medium speed for 3 minutes, scraping bowl frequently.

If using a dough hook, beat in enough of the remaining flour (about 1¼ cups) to make a soft dough. *If mixing by hand,* stir in about 1¼ cups flour with a heavy spoon, mixing to make a soft dough.

Scrape dough out onto a floured board and knead until smooth (5 to 10 minutes), adding more flour as needed to prevent sticking. Place dough in a greased bowl; turn over to grease top. Cover and let rise in a warm place until doubled (about 1½ hours).

Punch dough down and knead briefly on a floured board to release air. Then roll into a 9- by 30-inch rectangle. Crumble Cherry-Almond Filling and scatter it over dough to within 1 inch of edges. Starting with a long side, roll up dough tightly, jelly roll fashion. Moisten edge with water; pinch to seal.

Using a floured sharp knife, cut roll in half lengthwise; carefully turn cut sides up. Loosely twist half-rolls around each other, keeping cut sides up. Carefully transfer to a greased and flour-dusted 12- by 15-inch baking sheet and shape into a 10-inch circle; pinch ends together firmly to seal. Let rise, uncovered, in a warm place until puffy (45 to 60 minutes).

Bake in a 375° oven until lightly browned (about 20 minutes). Run wide spatulas under wreath to loosen; then transfer to a rack. Drizzle glaze over wreath while still warm.

If made ahead, do not glaze; let cool on a rack, then wrap airtight and hold at room temperature for up to 24 hours or freeze for up to 1 month (thaw unwrapped). To reheat, wrap in foil; place in a 350° oven until heated through (about 15 minutes). Makes 1 large wreath.

Cherry-Almond Filling. In large bowl of an electric mixer, beat ¼ cup (⅛ lb.) **butter** or margarine (at room temperature), ¼ cup **all-purpose flour**, and 2 tablespoons **sugar** until smooth. Stir in ⅔ cup finely chopped **blanched almonds**, ¼ cup *each* chopped **red and green candied cherries**, ½ teaspoon grated **lemon peel**, and ¾ teaspoon **almond extract**. Cover and refrigerate.

Sugar Glaze. In a small bowl, blend ⅔ cup **powdered sugar**, 1½ teaspoons **lemon juice**, and 1 tablespoon **water** until smooth.

New Mexican Hot Chocolate

4   *cups milk*
3   *cinnamon sticks, **each** about 3 inches long*
6   *ounces bittersweet or semisweet chocolate, broken into pieces*
⅓   *cup slivered almonds*
2   *tablespoons sugar*

In a 2-quart pan, combine milk and cinnamon sticks. Warm over low heat, stirring occasionally. Meanwhile, combine chocolate, almonds, and sugar in a blender. Whirl until a coarse powder forms.

Increase heat under milk to high; stir milk until it's just at the boiling point. Lift out cinnamon sticks and set aside. Pour half the milk into blender; cover (hold on lid with a thick towel) and whirl to combine. Pour in remaining milk and whirl until blended. Split cinnamon sticks lengthwise into halves; put a section in each of 6 mugs and fill with hot, foamy chocolate. Makes 6 servings.

Celebrate Christmas morning *with a festive breakfast that features a luscious sweet bread wreath, tender scrambled eggs, fresh fruit and juicy ham slices. To drink, offer hot spiced chocolate and "a bit of bubbly," too.*

Christmas Day Feasts

■

Christmas Day is finally here, and it's time to bring family and guests together around a festive holiday table. Create a feast worthy of the occasion—like this lavish Roast Pork Dinner (see page 244)—from any of the sumptuous menus in this chapter.

Roast Turkey Dinner

(Pictured on page 239)

"Turkey with all the trimmings" is deliciously updated in this impressive Christmas Day dinner for 10 guests. An elegant radicchio-shrimp salad leads up to the star attraction— a whole boned turkey filled with savory rice-sausage stuffing. Spicy plum sauce, butter-steamed peas, and an unusual carrot-parsnip tart complement the golden turkey; wine-poached pears with a tangy Stilton custard finish the feast in grand style.

Ask your butcher to bone the turkey for you—or do it yourself, following our simple instructions.

MENU

Radicchio, Shrimp & Dill Salad
Boned Turkey with Rice & Sausage Stuffing
Chinese Plum Sauce
Carrot-Parsnip Tart
Peas with Lettuce
Port-poached Pears with Stilton Custard

Radicchio, Shrimp & Dill Salad

2   heads radicchio, **each** 4 to 4½ inches in diameter

2   to 3 tablespoons slivered prosciutto, Black Forest or Westphalian ham, or dry salami

½   cup olive oil or salad oil

1   pound cooked, shelled, deveined medium-size shrimp (30 to 36 per lb.)

3   tablespoons red wine vinegar

2   to 3 tablespoons chopped fresh dill
    Salt and white pepper
    Dill sprigs

Cut core from each head of radicchio. Run cold water through cored center; remove 10 of the largest leaves (save remaining leaves for another salad). Wrap leaves in paper towels and enclose in a plastic bag, then refrigerate to crisp (at least 2 hours) or for up to 3 days.

In a 1- to 2-quart pan, combine ham and oil. Warm over low heat, uncovered, until oil picks up ham flavor (about 10 minutes). Let cool.

In a bowl, mix oil-ham mixture, shrimp, vinegar, and chopped dill. Season to taste with salt and white pepper. (At this point, you may cover and refrigerate for up to 1 day.)

To serve, place 1 radicchio leaf on each of 10 salad plates. Mound shrimp mixture equally in leaves; garnish with dill sprigs. Makes 10 servings.

Boned Turkey with Rice & Sausage Stuffing

1   turkey (10 to 12 lbs.), thawed if frozen
    Rice & Sausage Stuffing (recipe follows)
    Salad oil
    Salt and pepper

Begin by boning turkey. First, remove giblets and neck; reserve for your favorite giblet gravy. Release legs if trussed (held with skin or wire). Rinse bird, drain, and pat dry.

Turn turkey breast down. With a small, sharp knife, cut through to backbone from neck to tail. Holding tip of knife parallel to bone, cut and scrape meat from carcass, pulling flesh and skin back as you cut; take care not to pierce skin.

For each side, first follow contours of back, working toward breast. Slide knife tip along ribs to wing socket. Carefully cut tendons around joint. When joint is well exposed, press back on wing to snap loose. Guide knife along shoulder blade and wishbone to cut free.

Next, follow contours of back to hip socket. Cut hip socket free in the same way as for wings. Cut down toward breastbone around the ribs to cartilage and keel. Then, gently pulling and cutting, separate keel and cartilage from breast. Lift out carcass (use to make broth, if desired). Pull off and discard lumps of fat. Cover bird and refrigerate until ready to stuff or until next day.

When ready to roast turkey, lay bird out flat, skin side down. Mound dressing onto center of bird, shaping dressing to resemble the missing carcass. Lift edges of back over rice, overlapping skin slightly; secure with small skewers. Pull neck skin over back; skewer. Fold wingtips over back.

Gently turn turkey over, rub lightly with oil, and carefully place on a V-shaped rack in a 12- by 14-inch roasting pan.

Roast, uncovered, in a 350° oven until a meat thermometer inserted in thickest part of thigh on inside of leg registers 175°F—2 to 2½ hours. (Since optimum temperatures for breast at center and thigh are 170°F and 185°F, respectively, and both cook at the same rate, we suggest 175°F as the best compromise.)

Remove turkey from oven and let rest on rack for at least 30 minutes. Carefully transfer bird to a large carving board. To serve, cut bird in half lengthwise with a very sharp knife. Remove skewers, then lay each half cut side down. Slice off wings; then, using leg to anchor bird, slice breast halves diagonally to include some dressing with each serving. Cut off thighs and separate drumsticks, then slice meat from thighs. Season to taste with salt and pepper. Makes 10 to 12 servings.

Rice & Sausage Stuffing. In a 3- to 4-quart pan, combine 2½ cups **pearl rice**, 3 cups **regular-strength chicken broth**, 1 teaspoon *each* **rubbed sage** and **dry thyme leaves**, and ½ teaspoon **dry rosemary**. Cover and bring to a boil over high heat. Reduce heat to low; cook without stirring until liquid is absorbed (about 15 minutes).

Remove casings from 1½ pounds **mild Italian sausages** and crumble meat into a 10- to 12-inch frying pan. Cook over medium-high heat, stirring occasionally to break up big chunks, until meat is lightly

(Continued on next page)

browned and no longer pink in center (cut to test). Add ½ cup **raisins**; stir often until raisins puff. With a slotted spoon, lift out meat and raisins and add to rice; let cool.

Rinse and drain ¾ pound **mustard greens**. Cut off coarse stems; discard. Chop greens; add to sausage drippings. Cook over medium-high heat, stirring often, until leaves are wilted, bright green, and beginning to brown (about 8 minutes). Add greens, drippings, and 1 cup (about 5 oz.) grated **Parmesan cheese** to rice; mix. If made ahead, cover and refrigerate until next day.

Chinese Plum Sauce

    2   cans (1 lb. **each**) plums
        in heavy syrup
    ¾   cup water
    1   tablespoon salad oil
        Spice Mixture
        (recipe follows)
    ½   cup tomato sauce
    1   medium-size onion,
        chopped
    1   tablespoon **each**
        soy sauce and
        Worcestershire
    ¼   teaspoon liquid hot
        pepper seasoning
    1   tablespoon rice vinegar
        or wine vinegar

Drain plums, reserving 1¼ cups syrup (discard remaining syrup). Remove pits from plums; then whirl plums, water, and reserved 1¼ cups syrup in a blender until puréed. Set aside.

Heat oil in a 3- to 4-quart pan over medium-high heat; stir Spice Mixture into hot oil. Add plum purée, tomato sauce, onion, soy, Worcestershire, and hot pepper seasoning. Boil, uncovered, stirring often, until reduced to 3 cups (about 25 minutes). Stir in vinegar. Serve

warm, or cover and refrigerate for up to 3 weeks. Makes 3 cups.

Spice Mixture. Blend 1 teaspoon **Chinese five-spice** (or ¼ teaspoon *each* ground cinnamon, cloves, ginger, and anise seeds); ½ teaspoon *each* **ground cinnamon**, **ground cumin**, and **dry mustard**; and ¼ teaspoon **pepper**.

Carrot-Parsnip Tart

        Press-in Pastry
        (recipe follows)
    2   cups **each** shredded
        peeled carrots and
        parsnips
    ½   cup water
    3   large eggs
    1½ teaspoons grated
        orange peel
    1   teaspoon grated
        lemon peel
    2   tablespoons all-purpose
        flour
    ⅔   cup sugar
    1   cup lemon-flavored
        yogurt
    ½   cup pecan halves

Evenly press pastry over bottom and sides of a 9-inch tart pan with a removable bottom. Bake in a 325° oven until pale gold (15 to 20 minutes). Remove from oven.

While crust is baking, place carrots, parsnips, and water in a 10- to 12-inch frying pan. Bring to a boil over high heat; then reduce heat to low, cover, and simmer, stirring occasionally, until vegetables are very soft to bite and liquid has evaporated (about 12 minutes). Remove from heat and let cool.

In a bowl, whisk eggs, orange peel, lemon peel, flour, sugar, and yogurt until blended. Stir in carrots and parsnips. Pour mixture into tart shell. Evenly arrange pecans on top in a double row around rim. Bake in a 325° oven until tart no longer jiggles in center when pan is gently shaken (40 to 45 minutes).

Let cool on a rack for at least 10 minutes; or let cool completely, then cover and refrigerate until next day. Run a knife between crust and pan

rim before serving, then remove rim. Makes 10 servings.

Press-in Pastry. In a food processor or a bowl, combine 1 cup **all-purpose flour** and 3 tablespoons **sugar**. Add ⅓ cup firm **butter** or margarine, cut into small pieces; whirl or rub with your fingers until fine crumbs form. Add 1 large **egg yolk**; process or stir with a fork until dough holds together when pressed.

Peas with Lettuce

    6   tablespoons butter or
        margarine
    4   cups shredded iceberg
        lettuce
    2   packages (1 lb. **each**)
        frozen tiny peas, thawed,
        drained well
    6   tablespoons lightly
        packed minced parsley
    ¾   teaspoon sugar
    ¼   teaspoon ground
        nutmeg
        Salt

Melt butter in a 12-inch frying pan over high heat. Add lettuce and cook, stirring, until wilted (2 to 3 minutes). Immediately stir in peas, parsley, sugar, and nutmeg. Cook until peas are heated through and juices are boiling. Season to taste with salt. Makes 10 servings.

Port-poached Pears with Stilton Custard

    4½ cups port
    1   cup plus 6 tablespoons
        sugar
    10 firm-ripe pears
        (stems left on), peeled
    3   large egg yolks
    1   cup milk
    ⅔   cup crumbled Stilton
        cheese, at room
        temperature
    ½   teaspoon vanilla
        Shredded orange or
        lemon peel (optional)

Holiday turkey—*boned and shaped around a rice stuffing*—*takes on an elegant new look in our savory Roast Turkey Dinner. Equally original accompaniments include a radicchio-shrimp salad, a tasty carrot-parsnip tart, tiny peas, and spoonfuls of spicy plum sauce. Richly sauced poached pears provide the finishing touch.*

In an 8-quart pan or a 12-inch frying pan with a domed lid, bring port and 1 cup of the sugar to a boil over high heat. Lay pears on their sides in pan. Then reduce heat, cover, and simmer until pears are tender when pierced (10 to 15 minutes); gently turn pears over halfway through cooking. Lift pears from syrup and transfer to a large bowl.

Boil syrup over high heat, uncovered, until reduced to 1¼ cups (20 to 25 minutes). Pour over pears and let cool. Cover and refrigerate until cold (at least 2 hours) or until next day; turn pears over in syrup after 1 hour.

In a bowl, lightly whisk together egg yolks and remaining 6 tablespoons sugar. Pour milk into top of a double boiler; place directly over medium heat and bring milk to scalding, stirring often. Gradually whisk milk into yolks and sugar. Return mixture to top of double boiler.

Set top of double boiler in place over simmering water. Cook, stirring constantly, until custard is thick enough to coat the back of a metal spoon (about 10 minutes). Immediately add cheese; stir just until cheese is melted. Remove from heat and stir in vanilla. Let cool, then cover and refrigerate until cold (at least 4 hours) or until next day.

To serve, turn pears over in syrup, then lift from syrup and set aside. Carefully spoon syrup on 1 side of each of 10 rimmed dessert plates, dividing equally. Then spoon cheese custard equally on other side of plates. Lay 1 pear atop syrup and custard on each plate; garnish with orange peel, if desired. Makes 10 servings.

Roast Goose Dinner

(Pictured on page 242)

Bring the spirit of Dickensian England to your holiday table with this Christmas feast for eight. The meal centers around a golden, crisp-skinned roast goose, served with port wine sauce and tender poached apples and prunes. And for dessert, there's a traditional steamed pudding —flamed with brandy, garnished with holly, and crowned with a fluffy, vanilla-scented whipped cream sauce.

To offset the richness of meat and pudding, we've selected a trio of lighter accompaniments. The first course is simply cooked, chilled leek halves, topped with tiny shrimp and a tangy mustard-lemon sauce. Citrus flavors stand out in the yam casserole, too—it's a combination of yam, orange, and onion slices, accented with honey and almonds. Bright, savory spinach-stuffed tomatoes add Christmas color as well as fresh flavor to the meal.

Though this menu is lavish and varied, it doesn't require you to spend all Christmas Day in the kitchen. The leeks and yam casserole can be prepared a day ahead; you can wash the spinach for the stuffed tomatoes the day before, too. The pudding can be steamed up to 2 weeks before Christmas and stored in the freezer. The day of the feast, you can devote your attention to roasting the goose.

A final note: Though you may be able to buy fresh geese during the holiday season, they're usually sold frozen. Fresh or frozen, these birds are often a special-order item. Unless you live near a supplier carrying frozen geese in stock all year round, be sure to order well in advance.

MENU
Chilled Leeks & Shrimp
Roast Goose with
Giblet Wine Sauce
Port-poached Fruit
Layered Yam Casserole
Spinach-stuffed Tomatoes
Persimmon Pudding

Chilled Leeks & Shrimp

8   leeks, **each** about 1 inch in diameter
½   cup whipping cream
¾   cup mayonnaise
1½ tablespoons lemon juice
3   tablespoons Dijon mustard
    Salt and pepper
8   romaine leaves
¾   to 1 pound small cooked shrimp

Trim and discard leek roots and all but about 1½ inches of dark green leaves. Discard tough outer leaves. Cut leeks in half lengthwise; rinse each half under cold running water, separating layers to wash out dirt.

Place leek halves in a single layer in a wide frying pan; add water to cover. (If pan won't hold all the leeks at once, cook in 2 batches.) Bring water to a boil over high heat; reduce heat, cover, and simmer until stem ends are tender when pierced (5 to 7 minutes). Lift out leeks; let cool, then cover and refrigerate until next day.

In a small bowl, beat cream until it holds soft peaks. Combine mayonnaise, lemon juice, and mustard; fold in cream. Season to taste with salt and pepper. (At this point, you may cover and refrigerate for up to 6 hours.)

Just before serving, arrange romaine leaves on 8 individual plates or on a serving platter. Place 2 leek halves on each leaf and distribute shrimp evenly over leeks. Pass dressing at the table. Makes 8 servings.

Roast Goose with Giblet Wine Sauce

1   goose (11 to 13 lbs.), thawed if frozen
    Giblet Wine Sauce (recipe follows)
    Parsley springs (optional)
    Shredded orange peel (optional)

Remove goose giblets and reserve for sauce. Pull out and discard lumps of fat in neck and body cavities. Rinse bird with cold water, drain, and pat dry. With a fork, prick skin at ½-inch intervals in thigh and lower breast areas. Turn bird breast down and fasten neck skin to back with a skewer. Tie drumsticks together or tuck them into the loose skin at bottom of cavity.

Place goose, breast down, on a rack in a large roasting pan (at least 11 by 17 inches). Roast, uncovered, in a 400° oven for 1 hour. Every 30 minutes, ladle out fat accumulating in roasting pan (or siphon out with a bulb baster); reserve 2 tablespoons for sauce. Discard remaining fat or save for other cooking uses. Meanwhile, prepare stock for Giblet Wine Sauce (recipe follows).

After goose has roasted for 1 hour, reduce oven temperature to 325°. Protecting your hands, turn goose breast up on rack and insert a meat thermometer into thickest part of breast (not touching bone). Continue to roast, siphoning fat from pan every 30 minutes, until thermometer registers 175°F—about 1½ more hours for an 11-pound bird, about 2 more hours for a 13-pounder.

Lift goose from roasting pan, remove skewers and string (if used), and place bird breast up on a platter. Keep warm while you prepare Giblet Wine Sauce and Port-poached Fruit.

Surround goose with poached fruit; garnish with parsley and orange peel, if desired. Present at the table.

To carve, cut off tips and first joints of wings. Holding remaining wing section with fingers, sever from body by forcing knife through side of breast into joint while twisting wing.

To carve legs, turn goose breast side down and cut through back skin to expose joints next to center back. Anchor a fork firmly in thigh and press drumstick down to board; then cut between leg and body at joint. Repeat for other leg. Separate thighs and drumsticks at joints, then cut along bone to divide each into 2 pieces.

Remove each side of breast by sliding a knife between meat and keel bone. Cut down to breastbone along wishbone and around to wing joint. Cut meat free in 1 piece; thinly slice each breast crosswise. Trim off any clinging pieces of meat from the carcass.

Serve sliced goose with Giblet Wine Sauce and Port-poached Fruit. Makes 8 to 10 servings.

Giblet Wine Sauce. Reserve goose liver for other uses. Chop remaining **goose giblets** and set aside. Pour 2 tablespoons **reserved goose fat** into a 2- to 3-quart pan and set over medium-high heat. Add giblets; cook, stirring, until well browned. Add 1 small **onion**, chopped; cook, stirring, until golden. Add 2 cups **water**; 1 **chicken bouillon cube**; 1 stalk **celery**, cut into pieces; 1 **bay leaf**; and ¼ teaspoon **dry thyme leaves**. Bring to a boil; then reduce heat, cover, and simmer for 1½ to 2 hours while goose roasts.

To **browned particles in roasting pan,** add hot giblet-vegetable mixture; scrape browned bits free. Pour mixture through a wire strainer into a 1- to 2-quart pan; discard residue. Boil liquid rapidly to reduce to 1¼ cups. Add ½ cup **port**; return to a boil. Season to taste with **salt** and **pepper**. Serve as is; or, if desired, thicken juices by stirring in 1½ tablespoons **cornstarch** mixed with 1½ tablespoons **water**. Stir until sauce boils and thickens (about 1 minute).

Port-poached Fruit

In a pan, heat 1½ cups **port** just until hot. Remove from heat, add 2 cups (one 12-oz. package) **pitted prunes**, and let stand for 10 minutes; then drain off port and reserve. Meanwhile, peel, core, and quarter 4 or 5 **Golden Delicious apples**.

In a wide frying pan, melt 2 tablespoons **butter** or margarine. Add apples and 2 tablespoons **lemon juice**; turn fruit to coat. Add port; cover and simmer over medium-low heat until apples begin to soften (about 4 minutes). Uncover; increase heat to high, add prunes, and cook, turning fruit frequently, until apples are translucent and sauce clings to fruit (about 2 minutes). Makes 8 to 10 servings.

Layered Yam Casserole

3½ to 4 pounds yams, scrubbed
¼ cup sliced almonds
1 large onion, thinly sliced
3 oranges
½ cup (¼ lb.) butter or margarine, melted
2 tablespoons honey
Salt and pepper

In a 5- to 6-quart pan, bring 2 inches of water to a boil. Add yams; when water returns to a boil, reduce heat, cover pan, and cook until yams are tender when pierced (20 to 30 minutes). Drain and let cool; then peel and cut diagonally into ¼-inch-thick slices.

Spread almonds in a shallow baking pan and toast in a 350° oven until golden (about 8 minutes), shaking pan occasionally. Set aside. Arrange ⅓ of the yams in an even layer in a shallow 3-quart baking dish. Top with half the onion; then arrange half the remaining yams atop onion. Top with remaining onion and yams.

Remove and discard peel and all white membrane from 2 of the oranges; then slice oranges and arrange on top of yams. Squeeze juice from remaining orange and combine with butter and honey; pour evenly over yam mixture. Sprinkle lightly with salt and pepper. Cover with lid or foil. (At this point, you may refrigerate until next day.)

Sprinkle almonds over top of casserole and bake, covered, in a 325° oven for 45 minutes (55 minutes if refrigerated). Uncover; continue to bake until almonds are slightly crisped and casserole is heated through (about 5 more minutes). Makes 8 servings.

(Continued on next page)

In the tradition of a Victorian Christmas, *present a succulent golden roast goose with wine-poached fruit. The accompaniments—a chilled shrimp-and-leek starter, savory stuffed tomatoes, and an orange-scented yam casserole—add a light, fresh touch to the menu.*

Spinach-stuffed Tomatoes

8 medium-size tomatoes
1 tablespoon butter or margarine
1 tablespoon salad oil
1 medium-size onion, chopped
¾ pound spinach, rinsed well, coarsely chopped
1¼ cups (about 6¼ oz.) shredded Parmesan cheese
2 tablespoons fine dry bread crumbs
⅛ teaspoon ground nutmeg

Cut off the top fourth of each tomato; reserve for other uses, if desired. With a small spoon, scoop out pulp to make hollow shells. Chop pulp and place in a colander to drain.

Melt butter in oil in a wide frying pan over medium-high heat. Add onion and cook, stirring, until soft. Stir in drained tomato pulp and spinach and cook, stirring, until spinach is wilted (3 to 4 minutes). Stir in 1 cup of the cheese, bread crumbs, and nutmeg.

Fill tomatoes with spinach mixture and arrange in an ungreased baking pan; sprinkle evenly with remaining ¼ cup cheese. Broil 4 inches below heat until cheese is lightly browned (3 to 4 minutes). Makes 8 servings.

Persimmon Pudding

1½ cups **each** sugar and all-purpose flour
1½ teaspoons ground cinnamon
½ teaspoon ground nutmeg
1 tablespoon baking soda
3 tablespoons hot water
1½ cups ripe persimmon pulp
2 large eggs
1½ cups chopped pitted prunes
1 cup coarsely chopped almonds, walnuts, hazelnuts, or pistachio nuts
½ to ¾ cup brandy
2 teaspoons vanilla
1½ teaspoons lemon juice
¾ cup (⅜ lb.) butter or margarine, melted and cooled to lukewarm
Holly sprigs (optional)
Soft Sauce (recipe follows)

In a bowl, mix sugar, flour, cinnamon, and nutmeg. In a large bowl, stir together baking soda and hot water, then mix in persimmon pulp and eggs. Beat until blended. Add sugar mixture, prunes, almonds, ⅓ cup of the brandy, vanilla, lemon juice, and butter. Stir until evenly mixed.

Scrape batter into a buttered 9- to 10-cup pudding mold (either plain or tube-shaped) with lid or a deep 9- to 10-cup metal bowl. Cover tightly with lid or foil. Place on a rack in a deep 5- to 6-quart (or larger) pan. Add 1 inch of water, cover pan, and steam over medium heat until pudding is firm when lightly pressed in center (about 2¼ hours for tube mold, 2½ hours for plain mold). Add boiling water as needed to keep about 1 inch in pan.

Uncover pudding and let stand on a rack until slightly cooled (about 15 minutes). Invert onto a dish; lift off mold.

If made ahead, let cool completely. If desired, wrap pudding in a single layer of cheesecloth and moisten evenly with 3 to 4 tablespoons of the brandy. Wrap airtight in foil and refrigerate for up to 2 weeks; freeze for longer storage (thaw wrapped). To reheat, discard cheesecloth, wrap pudding in foil, and steam on a rack over 1 inch of boiling water in a covered 5- to 6-quart pan until hot (about 45 minutes).

Garnish pudding with holly, if desired. To flame pudding, warm 3 to 4 tablespoons brandy in a 2- to 4-cup pan until bubbly. Carefully ignite (not beneath a vent, fan, or flammable items) and pour over pudding. Slice and serve with Soft Sauce. Makes 8 servings.

Soft Sauce. Separate 2 large **eggs**. In a bowl, beat whites until they hold soft peaks; gradually beat in ½ cup **powdered sugar** until whites hold stiff peaks. In another bowl, using the same beaters, beat egg yolks with ½ cup **powdered sugar** and ½ teaspoon **vanilla** until very thick. Fold whites and yolks together. Serve; or cover and hold at room temperature for up to 2 hours (stir before serving). Makes about 2¼ cups.

Roast Pork Dinner

(Pictured on page 236)

As impressive as it is delicious, this roast pork dinner for 12 to 14 people features a succession of varied and mouthwatering courses, from a rich, creamy pistachio soup to a refreshing salad of fennel and watercress to the final triumph—a dessert trifle made with fresh oranges and chocolate. A zesty cranberry-pepper sauce gives the succulent pork roast an extra-special touch.

MENU

Cream of Pistachio Soup
Roast Pork
with Cranberry-Pepper Sauce
Mashed Potatoes & Broccoli
Minted Carrots
Fennel & Watercress Salad
Fresh Orange & Chocolate Trifle

Cream of Pistachio Soup

    3   cups shelled (6 cups
        or 1½ lbs. in shell)
        natural, roasted, or
        roasted salted pistachio
        nuts
    ½   cup (¼ lb.) butter or
        margarine
    1   large onion, finely
        chopped
    1   cup chopped celery
    2   cloves garlic, minced
        or pressed
    ⅓   cup dry sherry
    2   large cans (49½ oz.
        each) regular-strength
        chicken broth
    ¾   cup long-grain white
        rice
    4   parsley sprigs
    1   bay leaf
    2   cups whipping cream
        Whole chives

Rub off as much of the pistachio skins as possible, then set nuts aside. Melt butter in an 8-quart pan over medium heat; add onion, celery, and garlic. Cook, stirring, until onion is very soft but not browned (about 15 minutes); stir often.

Add sherry, 1½ cups of the pistachios, broth, rice, parsley, and bay leaf. Bring to a boil; then reduce heat, cover, and simmer until rice is tender to bite (about 30 minutes). Discard bay leaf.

Whirl soup in a food processor or blender, a portion at a time, until very smooth. Pour through a wire strainer and discard residue. Return soup to pan.

Add cream to soup and stir over medium-low heat until steaming (5 to 7 minutes). Pour into a tureen or individual bowls; garnish with whole chives and sprinkle with remaining 1½ cups pistachios. Makes 3½ quarts.

Roast Pork with Cranberry-Pepper Sauce

    1   can (1 lb.) whole berry
        cranberry sauce
    ¼   cup lemon juice
    1   boned, rolled, and tied
        half leg of pork
        (5 to 7 lbs.)
        Salt and pepper
    3   tablespoons canned
        green peppercorns,
        drained
    ½   teaspoon cracked black
        pepper

To make cranberry-lemon baste, pour cranberry sauce into a wire strainer set over a bowl; let drain. Measure out ¼ cup of the cranberry liquid and combine with lemon juice. Stir any remaining cranberry liquid back into cranberry sauce; set sauce and baste aside.

Place pork, fat side up, on a rack in a roasting pan. Sprinkle lightly with salt and pepper. Roast, uncovered, in a 400° oven for 20 minutes, then reduce oven temperature to 325° and continue to roast until a meat thermometer inserted in the thickest part of roast registers 170°F—about 2 more hours for a 5-pound roast, about 2¾ more hours for a 7-pound roast (allow 24 to 28 minutes *total* per pound).

About halfway through cooking time, pour cranberry-lemon baste over meat, then baste meat with pan juices every 30 minutes until done.

When meat is done, transfer to a platter or board; keep warm. Skim and discard fat from pan juices and pour juices into a sauce boat. In a serving bowl, combine peppercorns, cranberry sauce, and cracked pepper. Serve meat with juices and cranberry sauce. Makes 12 to 14 servings.

Mashed Potatoes & Broccoli

    5   pounds russet potatoes
    2   pounds broccoli
    6   tablespoons butter or
        margarine
    ½   cup milk
        Salt and pepper

Peel potatoes and cut into ½-inch cubes. Set aside. Cut off broccoli flowerets; peel stalks. Finely chop tender parts of stalks and all but a few flowerets; discard tough parts of stalks.

In an 8-quart pan, bring 4 quarts of water to a boil. Add potatoes, cover, and cook until tender when pierced (about 15 minutes). Add all broccoli and cook just until tender to bite (about 3 minutes). Don't overcook or broccoli will lose its bright color. Drain well, discarding water.

Remove whole flowerets from drained vegetables in pan. Add butter and milk to vegetables; stir over low heat until butter is melted. With a potato masher, mash vegetables smoothly. Season to taste with salt and pepper. Spoon vegetables into a warmed bowl; garnish with reserved whole broccoli flowerets. Makes 12 to 14 servings.

Minted Carrots

3 pounds carrots, peeled
¼ cup (⅛ lb.) butter or margarine
1 cup golden raisins
1 cup regular-strength chicken broth
½ cup firmly packed fresh mint sprigs
4 teaspoons firmly packed brown sugar
Salt and pepper

Cut carrots into matchstick pieces about ¼ inch wide, ¼ inch thick, and 3 to 4 inches long.

Melt butter in a 12-inch frying pan over medium heat. Add carrots, raisins, broth, ¼ cup of the mint sprigs, and sugar. Bring to a boil; then reduce heat, cover, and simmer until carrots are tender-crisp to bite (about 10 minutes). Uncover and boil over high heat until liquid has evaporated (5 to 10 more minutes), shaking pan often and gently lifting and turning carrots with a spatula.

Meanwhile, strip leaves from all but 3 or 4 of remaining ¼ cup mint sprigs. Finely sliver leaves.

Discard cooked mint sprigs from carrot mixture; season carrots to taste with salt and pepper. Turn onto a warmed platter and sprinkle with slivered mint; garnish with mint sprigs. Makes 12 to 14 servings.

Fennel & Watercress Salad

1 pound watercress
4 large carrots, peeled and cut in half lengthwise
6 medium-size heads fennel (3 to 3½ lbs. **total**), ends trimmed to within 1 inch of bulb
6 ounces Parmesan cheese
1 cup olive oil or salad oil
½ cup white wine vinegar
1 tablespoon Dijon mustard
Salt and pepper

Pluck off tender watercress sprigs to make 12 cups; rinse well, then wrap in paper towels and enclose in plastic bags. Refrigerate to crisp (about 30 minutes) or until next day.

With a vegetable peeler, evenly pare 50 to 60 long, thick, wide strips down length of carrots; reserve remaining parts of carrots for another use. Tightly curl carrot strips and place in ice water, wedging curls against ice cubes to preserve the curl; refrigerate for at least 15 minutes or up to 1 hour.

Trim any bruises from fennel, then cut heads into quarters lengthwise; remove and discard core and leaves. Thinly slice sections crosswise to make about 9 cups.

Cut cheese into very thin shavings with a cheese slicer or knife. Set aside.

Drain carrot curls on paper towels. In a large bowl, mix oil, vinegar, and mustard. Add carrots, fennel, and watercress; mix well. Arrange on a platter or 12 to 14 salad plates. Offer cheese, salt, and pepper to add to taste. Makes 12 to 14 servings.

Fresh Orange & Chocolate Trifle

1 cup sugar
½ cup water
1 vanilla bean (about 6 inches long), split lengthwise; or ½ teaspoon vanilla
3 unpeeled thin-skinned oranges (3 to 4 inches in diameter), cut crosswise into ⅛-inch-thick slices and seeded
⅓ cup orange-flavored liqueur
3 ounces (½ cup) chopped semisweet or milk chocolate
1 cup whipping cream, whipped
Pastry Cream (recipe follows)
1 purchased 9-inch sponge cake layer, torn into bite-size chunks
Semisweet or milk chocolate curls

In a 10- to 12-inch frying pan, bring sugar, water, and vanilla bean to a boil (if using vanilla extract, add later, as directed). Add oranges; reduce heat and simmer, uncovered, stirring occasionally, until peel looks translucent (about 20 minutes). Lift out oranges and vanilla bean (reserve for Pastry Cream). Set aside.

Measure syrup in pan, adding any liquid that has accumulated with oranges. Boil to reduce to ⅔ cup, or add water to make ⅔ cup. Stir in liqueur, then vanilla (if used). Set aside.

Set aside 5 of the best-looking orange slices. Coarsely chop enough of the remaining slices to make ⅔ cup; set aside. Arrange all remaining slices, overlapping as needed, in bottom and slightly up sides of a wide 2- to 2½-quart glass bowl.

Gently fold the ⅔ cup chopped oranges, chopped chocolate, and whipped cream into Pastry Cream.

Ladle about ¼ of the cream mixture into orange-lined bowl and spread gently to cover oranges. Scatter about half the sponge cake pieces over cream. Slowly spoon half the reserved syrup over cake, letting it soak in. Repeat to make a second layer, using about ⅓ of the remaining cream mixture and all the remaining cake pieces and syrup. Spoon in remaining cream mixture, being sure to cover cake. Garnish with reserved orange slices and chocolate curls. Cover and refrigerate for at least 3 hours or until next day. To serve, spoon into dessert bowls. Makes 12 to 14 servings.

Pastry Cream. In a 2- to 3-quart pan, stir together ½ cup *each* **sugar** and **all-purpose flour**. Blend in 2 cups **milk** and add 1 **vanilla bean** (use the one the oranges cooked with, or add vanilla extract later, as directed). Bring to a boil over medium-high heat, stirring.

In a bowl, beat 4 large **egg yolks** to blend. Stir ½ cup of the hot milk mixture into yolks, then stir all back into pan. Stir over low heat for 5 minutes. Lift out vanilla bean, rinse, and let dry, then reserve to use again. (If not using bean, add ½ teaspoon vanilla.) Let cool, then cover and refrigerate for at least 3 hours or up to 2 days.

Roast Beef Dinner

This elegant dinner for 8 to 10 guests features a substantial beef roast. As a starter, offer paper-thin prosciutto slices (you'll need ½ to ⅓ lb.) with cracked pepper and a touch of olive oil. Serve up the roast with a corn "risotto" and rolls of Swiss chard; then offer a mid-meal refresher of Cabernet Sauvignon Ice. Follow with ripe Brie, toasted baguette slices, and chilled watercress tossed with your favorite light dressing. (Buy 1 to 1¼ lbs. Brie, one or two baguettes, and two or three large bunches of watercress.) For dessert, present luscious White Chocolate Baskets.

MENU
Prosciutto with Pepper & Oil
Beef Rib Roast
with Tangerine Glaze
Corn Risotto
Swiss Chard, Florentine Style
Cabernet Sauvignon Ice
Brie with Toasted Baguettes
& Watercress
White Chocolate Baskets

Beef Rib Roast with Tangerine Glaze

4   cups tangerine or orange juice

1   beef rib roast (7 to 10 lbs.)

1   pound small whole onions (about 1 inch in diameter), peeled

2   jars (8 oz. **each**) vacuum-packed whole chestnuts; or 2 cans (15½ oz. **each**) whole chestnuts in water, drained

    Tangerine wedges and rosemary sprigs

3   tablespoons orange-flavored liqueur

In an 8- to 10-inch frying pan, boil tangerine juice, uncovered, over high heat until reduced to about ⅔ cup; stir to prevent scorching. Set glaze aside.

Set beef, fat side up, directly in a roasting pan (at least 12 by 15 inches). Roast, uncovered, in a 325° oven until a meat thermometer inserted in thickest part (not touching bone) registers at least 130°F for rare—about 2 hours and 20 minutes for a 7-pound roast, about 3 hours and 20 minutes for a 10-pound roast (allow 20 minutes *total* per pound).

About 2 hours before roast is done, put onions in pan; 1 hour later, add chestnuts. About 10 minutes before roast is done, brush half the tangerine glaze over both meat and onions.

Transfer roast, onions, and chestnuts to a platter; let stand for about 20 minutes before carving (keep warm). Garnish with tangerine wedges and rosemary.

Skim and discard fat from pan juices, then add remaining tangerine glaze to pan juices. Bring to a boil over medium-high heat, scraping pan to loosen crusty bits. Add liqueur; pour into a serving dish. Carve meat, then spoon sauce over individual portions. Makes 8 to 10 servings.

Corn Risotto

Melt 6 tablespoons **butter** or margarine in a 10- to 12-inch frying pan over high heat. Add 1 large **onion**, finely chopped. Cook, stirring often, until onion is slightly browned.

Add 4 cups fresh or frozen **corn kernels** (you'll need 6 ears of corn or two 10-oz. packages frozen corn kernels). Then stir in 1 cup **whipping cream**. Stir over high heat until almost all liquid has boiled away; remove from heat.

Finely sliver 1 small fresh or canned **black or white truffle** (at least ½ oz.). Stir ¼ of the slivers (and liquid from canned truffle) into corn mixture; set aside remaining slivers.

Pour corn into a shallow 1½-quart baking dish. Scatter 2 cups (8 oz.) shredded **fontina cheese** over corn. Bake, uncovered, in a 400° oven until cheese is melted and slightly browned (about 10 minutes). Sprinkle remaining truffle slivers over cheese. Makes 8 to 10 servings.

Swiss Chard, Florentine Style

2   pounds green Swiss chard

1   tablespoon lemon juice

3   tablespoons olive oil
    Salt and freshly ground pepper
    Lemon wedges

Wash chard leaves well. Cut off discolored stem bases and discard, then cut off stems at base of leaves. Set stems and leaves aside separately.

In a 5- to 6-quart pan, bring 3 quarts of water to a boil. Push stems down into water. Cook, uncovered, until limp (about 4 minutes). Lift out.

At once, push leaves gently down into boiling water and cook until limp (1 to 2 minutes). Lift out carefully and drain. To preserve the best green color, immerse at once in ice water. When cool, drain.

Select 8 to 10 of the largest, most perfect leaves and set aside. Chop remaining leaves and stems together. Mix with lemon juice and 2 tablespoons of the oil. Season to taste with salt and pepper.

Lay out reserved leaves; mound an equal amount of chopped chard on each. Fold each leaf to enclose filling; set seam side down on a serving dish. If made ahead, cover and refrigerate for up to 24 hours.

To serve, drizzle with remaining oil and accompany with lemon wedges to squeeze on individual servings. Makes 8 to 10 servings.

Cabernet Sauvignon Ice

¾ cup sugar
1 cup water
1½ cups Cabernet
    Sauvignon
1½ cups white grape juice
¾ cup lemon juice
    Mint sprigs (optional)
    Red grapes (optional)

In a 1- to 1½-quart pan, combine sugar, water, and wine. Bring to a boil, then reduce heat and simmer gently for 5 minutes. Remove from heat; let cool. Stir in grape juice and lemon juice; cover and refrigerate until cold (at least 1 hour).

Pour mixture into 2 or 3 divided ice cube trays or a shallow 9-inch square metal pan. Freeze until solid (about 4 hours).

If ice is frozen in a pan, let it stand at room temperature until you can break it into chunks with a spoon. Then place ice cubes or chunks, ⅓ to ½ at a time, in a food processor; use on-off bursts to break up ice, then process continuously until ice is a velvety slush. Or beat all the ice with an electric mixer, gradually increasing speed from low to high as ice softens.

Spoon into a container; cover and freeze until solid (or for up to 1 month). Garnish servings with mint and grapes, if desired. Makes about 5 cups (8 to 10 mid-meal servings).

White Chocolate Baskets

8 ounces white chocolate
    White Chocolate Mousse
    (recipe follows)
    Poached Cranberries
    (recipe follows)
    Thin strands of
    orange peel

Place chocolate in the top of a double boiler over simmering water. Stir

An elegant succession of courses leads diners from the smoky flavor of prosciutto to the sweetness of white chocolate in this imaginative menu. Beef rib roast with Swiss chard and corn risotto is followed by a frosty wine-flavored sorbet, then a Brie-and-salad combination. Delicate white chocolate baskets of fluffy mousse are the grand finale.

chocolate occasionally just until melted. Remove from hot water.

While chocolate is melting, grease 8 to 10 muffin cups (2½-inch diameter) with solid vegetable shortening. Line each cup with a 5-inch square of plastic wrap (shortening helps hold wrap in place). Do not trim off excess plastic. Place about 1 tablespoon melted chocolate in bottom of each cup. With a small brush, paint chocolate up pan sides. Refrigerate until firm (about 1 hour) or for up to 1 week. Lift chocolate cups from pans and carefully peel off plastic; avoid touching chocolate.

Fill each chocolate basket with an equal amount of cold White Chocolate Mousse and top with a few Poached Cranberries (and some of the cranberry poaching liquid, if desired). Garnish with orange peel. To eat, scoop out mousse with a spoon, then crack chocolate basket into bite-size pieces. Makes 8 to 10 servings.

White Chocolate Mousse. Place 6 ounces **white chocolate** in the top of a double boiler over simmering water; stir occasionally until melted. In a small bowl, beat 3 large **egg whites** until foamy. Gradually beat in 1 tablespoon **sugar**, beating until stiff. Fold in hot melted chocolate until blended. In another small bowl, beat ½ cup **whipping cream** until stiff. Add cream to egg white mixture; fold to blend. Cover and refrigerate until cold (at least 1 hour) or until next day.

Poached Cranberries. In a 1- to 1½-quart pan, combine ½ teaspoon grated **orange peel**, ¼ cup **orange juice**, 2 tablespoons **sugar**, and ¾ cup **fresh or frozen cranberries**. Simmer, uncovered, until cranberries pop (about 5 minutes). Let cool, then cover and refrigerate until cold.

Make-ahead Christmas Dinner

If Christmas Day is too hectic for lots of cooking, or if you've had your traditional holiday dinner on Christmas Eve, this make-ahead menu may be just the thing you're looking for. It's a delicious dinner for six, starring a creamy, delicate seafood lasagna that can be assembled the day before serving. You can also make the spicy, crisp-fried legumes well in advance (or just buy salted nuts). The colorful vegetable salad and rich, chocolate-crusted eggnog pie *must* be made ahead—to give the pie filling time to set and allow the salad's flavors to blend. Put together the quick and easy bacon-wrapped date appetizer the day of the party, purchase beverages and rolls—then relax and enjoy your own party!

MENU

Bacon-wrapped Dates
Legume Crisps or Salted Nuts
Apéritif of your choice
Festive Salad Bowl
Scallop Lasagna
Warm Dinner Rolls   Butter
Chocolate Swirl Eggnog Pie

Bacon-wrapped Dates

12   *slices bacon*
24   *pitted dates*

Cut each bacon slice in half crosswise. Place half-slices on a rimmed baking sheet and broil 6 inches below heat until partially cooked but still soft (about 2½ minutes). Transfer to paper towels and let drain; discard excess fat from pan.

Preheat oven to 400°. Place 1 date at end of each bacon piece and roll up; place seam side down on baking sheet. Bake until bacon is crisp and dates are heated through (about 7 minutes). Serve warm. Makes 2 dozen.

Legume Crisps

1   *cup dried garbanzo beans, brown or red (decorticated, sometimes called Persian) lentils, or green or yellow split peas*
3   *tablespoons salad oil*
    Cumin Salt, Curry Salt, Red Spices Salt (recipes follow), or coarse salt (optional)

Sort legumes and remove any debris. In a 2- to 3-quart pan, bring 4 cups water and any one of the legumes (except red lentils) to a boil over high heat. Cover and remove from heat; let stand until grains are just tender enough to chew. Allow about 15 minutes for garbanzo beans or brown lentils, about 10 minutes for green or yellow split peas.

To prepare red lentils, put in a bowl and cover with about 4 cups hottest tap water; let stand until lentils are just tender to bite (about 10 minutes).

For each legume, line a rimmed 10- by 15-inch baking pan with several layers of paper towels. Spread drained legumes out in pan and let dry for about 1 hour; blot occasionally with more paper towels.

In a 10- to 12-inch frying pan, stir legumes and oil over medium-high heat until legumes smell toasted and become dry and crisp to bite (5 to 10 minutes). Spread out on paper towels to drain; blot off excess oil with more towels.

Pour legumes into a serving bowl. Flavor with seasoned salt or coarse salt, if desired; serve immediately or store airtight for up to 2 weeks. Makes about 1½ cups.

Cumin Salt. Combine ½ teaspoon **coarse salt**, ¼ teaspoon *each* **ground cumin** and **celery salt**, and ⅛ teaspoon *each* **ground red pepper** (cayenne) and **garlic powder**.

Curry Salt. Combine 1 teaspoon **coarse salt**, ¾ teaspoon **curry powder**, and ½ teaspoon **dry mustard**.

Red Spices Salt. Combine ¾ teaspoon **coarse salt**, ½ teaspoon *each* **chili powder** and **paprika**, and ½ teaspoon **ground red pepper** (cayenne).

Festive Salad Bowl

1   *pound green beans, cut diagonally into 2-inch pieces*
1   *can (6 to 8 oz.) water chestnuts, drained and sliced*
½   *pound mushrooms, sliced*
1   *can (8 oz.) pitted ripe olives, drained*
16 *to 18 cherry tomatoes, halved*
2   *jars (6 oz. **each**) marinated artichoke hearts*
½   *teaspoon dry basil*
¼   *teaspoon **each** dry oregano leaves and grated lemon peel*
2   *teaspoons lemon juice*
    Garlic salt and pepper

In a 3-quart pan, bring about 1 inch of water to a boil over high heat. Add beans. When water returns to a boil, reduce heat, cover, and cook until beans are tender-crisp to bite (4 to 7 minutes). Drain and plunge immediately into cold water; when cool, drain again. Place beans in a salad bowl.

Add water chestnuts, mushrooms, olives, and tomatoes to beans. Drain artichokes, reserving marinade; add artichokes (halved, if large) to bean mixture.

In a small bowl, combine reserved marinade, basil, oregano, lemon peel, and lemon juice; stir into vegetables. Season to taste with garlic salt and pepper. Cover and refrigerate for at least 4 hours or until next day. Makes 6 to 8 servings.

Scallop Lasagna

- 2 *pounds bay or regular scallops*
- 1/3 *cup butter or margarine*
- 1 *cup chopped green onions (including tops)*
- 1 *clove garlic, minced or pressed*
- 1/2 *teaspoon fresh or 1/4 teaspoon dry thyme leaves*
- 1/3 *cup all-purpose flour*
- 1 *cup **each** regular-strength chicken broth and whipping cream*
- 1/2 *cup dry vermouth or dry white wine*
- 1 *package (8 oz.) dry lasagna noodles*
- 2 *cups (8 oz.) shredded Swiss cheese*

Rinse scallops well and drain; if using regular scallops, cut into 1/2-inch pieces. Set aside.

Melt 1 tablespoon of the butter in a 12- to 14-inch frying pan over medium-high heat. Add onions, garlic, and thyme; cook, stirring, for 1 minute. Add scallops and cook,

stirring often, until opaque in center; cut to test (2 to 3 minutes). Remove from heat and pour scallop mixture into a large strainer set over a bowl; let drain for 20 to 30 minutes.

Meanwhile, melt remaining butter in frying pan over medium heat. Add flour and stir until it turns a light golden color. Remove from heat and smoothly mix in broth, cream, and vermouth. Return to high heat and bring to a boil, stirring; then set aside.

Fill a 4- to 5-quart pan 3/4 full with water and bring to a boil over high heat. Add lasagna and return to a boil; boil, uncovered, until tender to bite (about 10 minutes). Drain. Rinse lasagna with cold water until cool; drain again and set aside.

Pour liquid drained from scallop mixture into a 1- to 1 1/2-quart pan. Bring to a boil over high heat; boil, uncovered, until reduced to about 2 tablespoons. As liquid cooks down, stir frequently to prevent scorching. Mix liquid into cream sauce.

Line bottom of a buttered 9- by 12-inch baking pan or dish with 1/3 of the lasagna noodles. Spread noodles with 1/3 of the sauce; top with 1/3 of the scallop mixture, then with 1/3 of the cheese. Repeat layers twice more, ending with cheese. Cover pan with lid or foil. (At this point, you may refrigerate until next day; bring to room temperature before baking.)

Bake lasagna, covered, in a 350° oven for 20 minutes. Uncover and continue to bake until cheese is golden (about 20 more minutes). Let stand for 15 minutes to firm before cutting; lift out portions with a wide spatula. Makes 6 servings.

Chocolate Swirl Eggnog Pie

- 1/4 *cup cold water*
- 1 *envelope unflavored gelatin*
- 2 *tablespoons cornstarch*
- 1/2 *cup sugar*
- 2 *cups commercial eggnog*
- 1 1/2 *ounces semisweet chocolate, melted*
- 1 *cup whipping cream*
- 6 *tablespoons rum or 3/4 teaspoon rum flavoring*
  Chocolate Crust (recipe follows)
  Semisweet chocolate curls

Pour water into a small bowl and sprinkle with gelatin; set aside. In a pan, stir together cornstarch, sugar, and eggnog; cook over medium heat, stirring, until thickened. Stir in softened gelatin. Divide mixture in half and stir melted chocolate into 1 portion. Refrigerate both portions until thick but not set.

In a bowl, beat cream until it holds soft peaks; fold whipped cream and rum into plain portion of filling, then spoon into cooled Chocolate Crust. Spoon chocolate portion over top. With a knife, gently swirl chocolate layer through rum layer. Refrigerate until well chilled. Sprinkle with chocolate curls before serving. Makes 8 servings.

Chocolate Crust. In a large bowl, combine 1 cup **all-purpose flour**, 1/4 cup firmly packed **brown sugar**, 3/4 cup finely chopped **nuts**, and 1 ounce **semisweet chocolate**, grated. Stir in 1/3 cup **butter** or margarine, melted; press mixture over bottom and sides of a 9-inch pie pan. Bake in a 375° oven for 15 minutes. Let cool.

New Year's Day Brunch

■

The enticing aromas of ham, baked apples, sizzling potatoes, and an egg-rich "Dutch baby" pancake welcome your guests to this delightful brunch party—an unbeatable way to kick off the new year. The meal presented here serves six, but it can easily be scaled up to handle more people if you have (or have access to) more than one oven.

Ham, apples, potatoes, and even the batter for the Dutch baby can be prepared from 4 hours to a full day in advance. Purchase or make your favorite bran muffins ahead, too, then reheat them at brunch time. The foamy milk punch must be served right from the blender—but whipping it up is a matter of seconds.

MENU
Milk Punch
Bran Muffins   *Butter*
Herb-crusted Ham
Tender Dutch Baby
Oven-crisp Potato Cake
Crunch-top Baked Apples
Champagne

Milk Punch

> 4   *cups milk*
>   *Ice cubes*
> ¼   *cup powdered sugar*
> 2   *teaspoons vanilla or ½ to ¾ cup bourbon whiskey*
>   *Ground nutmeg*

Pour 2 cups of the milk into a 4-cup glass measure; add enough ice cubes to make 3 cups. Add 2 tablespoons of the sugar and pour into a blender. Holding on lid, whirl mixture on high speed until it's a smooth slush. Add 1 teaspoon of the vanilla (or half the bourbon) and whirl to blend. At once, pour punch into three 8-ounce glasses; sprinkle each serving with nutmeg. Repeat with remaining ingredients to make 3 more servings. Makes 6 servings.

Herb-crusted Ham

> 1   *shank-end picnic ham (5½ to 6½ lbs.)*
> ¼   *teaspoon **each** fennel seeds, whole black peppercorns, dry thyme leaves, and dry rubbed sage*
> ¼   *cup fine dry bread crumbs*

Rinse ham and pat dry. Set on a rack (with thickest layer of fat under skin on top) in a 12- by 15-inch roasting

Wake up to the new year in style *with this satisfying brunch. A tempting medley of flavors—ham, buttery potatoes, egg-rich Dutch baby, and sweet bran muffins—is accented with a peppery watercress garnish.*

pan. Bake, uncovered, in a 350° oven until a meat thermometer inserted in thickest part of ham (not touching bone) registers 140°F (about 2 hours).

Meanwhile, whirl fennel seeds, peppercorns, thyme, sage, and bread crumbs in a blender until spices are coarsely ground. (Or crush spices with a mortar and pestle or a rolling pin and mix with crumbs.) Set aside.

When meat thermometer registers 140°F, remove ham from oven and let cool for about 30 minutes; it will still be quite warm, but you should be able to touch it. With scissors and a sharp knife, cut hard skin on top of ham from fat; break skin into pieces to eat while warm, if desired.

Pat seasoned crumb mixture evenly over fat on ham. Return to oven and continue to bake until meat thermometer registers 160°F (about 45 more minutes). If crumbs begin to darken more than you like, lay a piece of foil over dark area. Let ham stand for 15 to 30 minutes, then carve and serve hot; or let stand for up to 4 hours and serve at room temperature. If you do not plan to serve ham within 4 hours, cover and refrigerate cooled ham; bring to room temperature before serving. Makes 6 servings (with leftovers).

Tender Dutch Baby

3   *large eggs*
6   *tablespoons all-purpose flour*
1   *tablespoon granulated sugar*
6   *tablespoons milk*
3   *tablespoons butter or margarine*
   Powdered sugar
1   *lemon, cut into wedges*

In a blender or food processor, whirl eggs with flour, granulated sugar, and milk until batter is smooth, scraping down sides of container several times. (At this point, you may cover and refrigerate until next day; stir well before baking.)

Put butter in an ovenproof 10- to 12-inch frying pan. Set pan in a 425° oven on a rack placed slightly above center until butter is melted (about 4 minutes). Tilt pan to coat bottom with butter, then quickly pour in batter. Bake until pancake puffs at edges (it may also puff irregularly in the center) and is golden brown (about 15 minutes).

Working quickly, cut pancake into 6 wedges and transfer to dinner plates, using a wide spatula; pancake may deflate somewhat after cutting. Sprinkle pancake liberally with powdered sugar; offer lemon wedges to squeeze onto pancake to taste. Makes 6 servings.

Oven-crisp Potato Cake

3   *large russet potatoes (about 1½ lbs.* **total***)*
¼   *cup clarified butter or melted margarine; or use 2 tablespoons* **each** *melted butter and salad oil, stirred together*
   Salt and pepper

Peel potatoes and carefully cut into slices about ⅛ inch thick, using a sharp knife or a food processor. Coat bottom and sides of a 10- to 12-inch ovenproof nonstick frying pan with some of the butter. Neatly overlap potato slices in an even layer in pan. Evenly drizzle remaining butter over potatoes; brush lightly with your fingertips to coat slices without disturbing them.

Bake on lowest rack of a 425° oven until potatoes on bottom are well browned (about 45 minutes; lift with a spatula to check). Remove from oven. Invert a rimmed pan that's larger than the frying pan (such as a 12- to 14-inch pizza pan) over frying pan. Using potholders to protect your hands, quickly flip potatoes onto rimmed pan; be careful not to drip hot fat on yourself. With a spatula, push cake back in shape, if necessary. (At this point, you may cover potatoes and let stand for up to 4 hours.)

Return potatoes to oven and continue to bake until cake is browned on the bottom (about 20 more minutes).

Invert potato cake onto a small platter. Use a spoon to break cake into portions, or cut into wedges with a knife. Season to taste with salt and pepper. Makes 6 servings.

Crunch-top Baked Apples

6   *Golden Delicious, Winesap, or McIntosh apples,* **each** *about 3 inches in diameter*
1   *cup granola-style cereal (break up any large lumps before measuring)*
¼   *cup (⅛ lb.) butter or margarine, at room temperature*
3   *tablespoons firmly packed brown sugar*
½   *cup apple juice*
   Whipping cream, half-and-half, or light cream (optional)

Core apples with an apple corer. Mix cereal with butter and sugar, then press ⅙ of the mixture into center of each apple, mounding any extra on top. Set apples slightly apart in a 9- by 13-inch rectangular or shallow 10- by 14-inch oval baking dish. Pour apple juice around apples in dish.

Bake, uncovered, in a 350° oven until fruit is tender when pierced (about 30 minutes). If made ahead, cover and let stand at room temperature until next day. Serve warm or at room temperature, spooning fruit into individual bowls with some of the baking juices. Offer cream to pour over apples, if desired. Makes 6 servings.

Index